# SOLIPSISM
by
Terry Oakes

intercept studios

To
Paul.
Best Wishes
Terry Oakes

Book design, formatting, and layout by Andrew Oakes, for Intercept Studios
© 2020 Intercept Studios

Cover design by Andrew Oakes, for Intercept Studios

First edition. Published 2020

ISBN: 8561152061
EAN: 979-8561152061

Published by Intercept Studios

intercept studios

www.interceptstudios.com

# ACKNOWLEDGEMENTS

This book would not have been possible without the skill and patience of the following:

Andrew Oakes,
Jonathan Oakes,
Cheryl Hudgell,
Joy Rillera,
and especially, my wife Irene.

Dreams are real while they last, and do we not live in dreams?
*(Alfred Lord Tennyson: The Higher Pantheism)*


The artist, like the God of creation, remains within or behind or beyond
or above his handiwork, invisible, refined out of existence...
*(James Joyce – possibly quoting Flaubert)*


So, I came face to face with the biggest terror a writer faces, a blank piece
of paper...
*(Hubert Selby Jr.)*


... (this God may have) 'brought it about that there is no earth, no sky, no
extended thing, no shape, no size, no place, while at the same time ensur-
ing that all these things appear to me to exist just as they do now'.
*(Rene Descartes: 1596 – 1650)*


*(Chambers Twentieth Century Dictionary)*
VERONICA – true image.
DOMINO – a long cloak of black silk with a hood.

Where am...I – say *'I'*? Who am...I – say *'I'*? If I am...*'I'* – am *I* young? Am *I* old? Am *I* yet to be born? Am *I* dead? The lumber of the world? When is this? Is this...*then?* Is it...*now?* Is it...*when?* Has Time's winged chariot been misdirected or grounded?

What if none of the answers to the above questions are applicable? What if there is no past? What if there is no future? What if there is only the infinitesimal present moment? Inside the human mind, within its memory, within its anticipation of things to come – even within its dreams – there is no such thing as chronology. So...

...it begins – or re-begins. Starts – or re-starts. Solipsism. Confrontation, conflict, construction. An encounter with the void. A struggle against nothingness. The chasm of emptiness invaded and pervaded by thought, by creation and a perceived existence – which, in a particular way, condemns nihility to its own kind of confrontation, conflict and construction. But first there is only...

WHITENESS
WHITE-NESS
WHITE
WHITE SPACE
before...

You are dreaming of the sea. As undulant and black as melted lead, as restless as a serpent, it convolves and reforms, replicating endless armies of waves. Ferreting and probing, its surges test the defences of its eternal enemy – the land. But it is an enemy that resists. One that opposes reclamation. One that combats both the attrition and the erosion of its plenitudinous mass. Ceaseless attacks of white horse warriors are steadfastly repelled, disabled and reconstituted as dappled blankets of foam along numberless, nameless beaches. Casualties of war. A war that directs and prostrates them along the small stretch of terra firma on which you presently stand – naked, alone, bare feet set among multitudinous pebbles. Wind tugs at your hair. Cold spray sprinkles your face. A covetous body of water confronts you. Seemingly only moments ago it nibbled at that dark peninsula. Now it covers it, devours it, swallows it like proffered carrion. Looking down you watch as vanguard froth swirls about your ankles with the rapacity of an over solicitous poulp, while further allied elements above you gain ever increasing momentum. It is an exercise in moon madness – but one that fails to disturb you. Unable to move or retreat you experience no trepidation – even as an unfettered gale drives ragged black nimbi from an obscured horizon, threatening to unbalance you, to topple you into a torrent that is suddenly knee high. An uncoiling swell, as monstrous as a primeval dragon, rears up before you. Smashing down in an explosion of argent fury, it engulfs you to your chest. Yet your only reaction is to raise a hand from the water's briny clutches, to wipe spattered froth from your face. There is a compelling need to observe the final moments. Cumuli skim madly across the heavens, racing on the wings of a hurricane, ululating elegiac symphonies to the end of the world. But it is an end that means little to you, for it is an end in which your own demise incorporates the end of the all. Dissolution of the individual subsumes the existence of the whole. Lightning splashes the sky with silver and rain cascades onto your upturned face. Complete immersion is but moments away. Reason commands that you should be terror-struck, but the crazy logic of dreams holds sway. Yet another mighty surge approaches and you stare defiantly up through its tubular corridor at the moon, a glowering eye in the rack. Descending, the wall of water engulfs you and you are submerged, drifting weightlessly, free of earth's cloying embrace. Darkness abides. A darkness commensurate with indifference, illustrating the inevitable state and ultimate truth, delivering a knowledge that both comforts and confirms. Stoically you recapitulate a life of temporal existence, of progressive Pythagorean moments leading idly to the now. And now nothingness rules, without exception, without deviation. Illusion of substance grants but flickering, self-deluding pictures in the isolation, totally devaluating and invalidating the physicality of life. Even birth, the opposite alpha, is conceived by extraneous dispensation, leaving death the only truly independent absolute. A singular definite fact on an otherwise indefinite journey, its destination the one and only reality – and arrival is imminent. Reassured by its encroaching inevitability you detachedly contemplate the fact that your lungs will not immediately fill with water when you die, but that a contractile nerve will activate and seal off a main ventricle. You will, in fact, asphyxiate. Consideration of this is clinical and impartial, the condition somehow having ceased to hold subjective significance. Penetration of atavistic fear exposes the release of self-awareness. Expiration of the physical creates recognition of the subliminal. Responsibility abandoned, obligation relinquished, there remains only an acceptance of destiny. Liberation. A kind of freedom. Peace…

He…I…(who?) – let us say 'I', awake/s with a jolt. (back to the symbolic counterpoint) His…my – let us say 'my', eyes pierce the darkness of the room. A pulse pounds in my temples and my heartbeat accelerates to staccato. Gazing down the length of my torso, above the thrown back bedsheet, my flesh looks almost blue amidst the eerily gathered moonbeams fingering through the large skylight. Sweat glistens on my chest and, as I raise my head, I can feel its sticky wetness in the folds of my throat. A nervous wipe of skin dampens a palm before I drop my head back onto the crumpled pillow, staring up through the glass at the sky, which is calm – unlike the dream – and peppered with pinpoint stars. In the distance I can hear the swish and sigh of the sea: normal, tranquil, its rhythm like a lullaby in the night.

Nevertheless, in spite of the calm hiatus, the images of the nightmare continue to slice through my dazed brain like a scythe. My attitude within its jurisdiction was disturbing, my indifferent welcome of its created fate disquieting. In spite of everything I cannot believe I still hate myself and my own existence that much. Once, perhaps…But now it alarms me to think that I would have given in so willingly, submitted without a struggle, allowed myself to be extinguished without attempting some kind of escape. Dichotomously, I feel panic-stricken that I felt no panic; only a morbid resolve. If the dream is not representative of my present state of mind – and with ambitions of the past accounted for – could my impassive response be a form of subconscious prognostication? A prescient glimpse, even? Could it mean – when the time comes – that my outlook will still be so? Only a momentous calamity – one greater than the last – would cause such acquiescence, make me behave in a manner Domino's death could not. An encounter with the Gorgon's head did not turn me to stone. Mental circumnavigation of guilt and avoidance of a somewhat tempting prospect of self-mortification allowed me to press on regardless. Of course, this was achieved by a certain lack of conviction, suffused with a pusillanimous restraint; deep down, I always knew the consideration to be lacking. It was more a matter of going through the motions, and in doing so, learning just how selfish and self-obsessed a human being can be. Wrapping about me a muffler of false sentiment and creating an expiation worthy of remorse, I deluded myself and proceeded to wade through the stream of a fraudulent life with impunity. Knowing that the other thing was there, at my shoulder, was enough. It became a self-created solace – under control, manipulated, carried about like a home-made time bomb. A lady poet once proposed that death was a servant who would come when beckoned. Such an exquisite casuistry was tailormade to my situation, and I accepted it freely, exercising it as a spiritual leitmotiv whenever I found myself confronted by conscience. With this weapon I nipped the *felo de se* flower in the bud, so to speak, and filled the emptiness with something that could be – rather than with something that was. And it had seen me through…until now.

Although recently troubled more and more by dreams of an unsettling nature, this is the first time I have dreamed of my own imminent death, and memory of it now touches my spine like an ice-cold finger. Even trapped within their own parameters the images seemed to possess a certain substance of reality, fanning me with the wings of that said servant: *'And I looked, and behold a pale horse: and his name that sat on him was death, and Hell followed with him.'*

A shake of the head fails to abate the doom-laden thoughts, which have become intrusive, as though relayed to me by some external force. I remember someone once describing the effect of hypnotic suggestion, of the awareness of reality, alongside an inability to cling to it; the will involuntarily yielding to the directives. I feel as though I am experiencing such a condition now, as images and visions appear to be projected into my mind. Rubbing my face with protesting hands, and kneading white knuckles into eye sockets that feel full of sand, alleviates nothing. Perhaps I am still asleep. Can I still be dreaming? After squeezing my eyes so tightly shut that they hurt, I open them again, expecting…what? I am still in my room; moonbeams continue to probe through the skylight glass; while a survey of a plebeian surround exhibits a small table, two battered chairs and an untidy bed as ostensibly firm and palpable. To anticipate anything different would be stretching the boundaries of probability; but a small doubt remains – either because of an intellect's vulnerability at such an hour, or because of a recurrence of events.

On times, in the past, I have awakened from dreams of a similar intensity to find myself existing, for a while, in a non-apperceptive state, captively observing images as they parade before my eyes like a procession of ethereal, dancing marionettes. Once again, I stare, transfixed, as they flit by: light, bright, weird, fickle in reality, out of reach, my senses unable to catch them or hold them for analysis. Even though they remain hazy and difficult to discern, I think I see faces. I think I see *her* face – but that is not unusual; being constantly aware of her trenchant absence – if that's not a contradiction in terms – my guilty eye glimpses her accusing apparition in every darkened corner. These current phenomena, though – if that is what they are – seem different, more wrapped up in other events: with portents of doom and destruction on a vast scale; with terror and mortal plight; with suffering and with torment. I think I see the pale, deathly features of Veronica – but blurred in some way; corpses, both human and animal, floating on a sea of blood; burning buildings; murderous mobs, roaming the desolation; incongruous robed figures, dressed in white; cities bathed in unearthly glows. And amidst the farrago, a pulsating vision of a face: malformed, ape-like and evil, possessing an odd familiarity that is difficult to reconcile.

But they pass so quickly I doubt they were there at all. A conclusion that recognises the work of an agitated imagination, suffusing the scenes into a montage, out of which it tries to construct a composition, attempts to decipher the surrealistic creations into something comprehensible.

Not always so ominous, this personal, flickering peepshow has been, on occasions, maieutic, from which some of my more imaginative paintings have materialised. Momentarily freezing into definition, they become accessible enough for capture. Like some psychic automatic camera of the inner eye, the images remain framed, allowing me time to arise from a state of pseudo slumber, to scribble down notes, or execute rough sketches, before the projections waver and lose identity, before becoming buried in the storage vault of the subconscious, smothered in cerebral dust, lost forever.

However, I feel no urgency to incorporate these present visualizations into oils or acrylics as they seem charged with vibratory adumbrations – signposts, pointing to a real and terrible future. Definitely not creative inspirations or compositional enigmas of art, they spring forth as variable possibilities – arbitrary jigsaw pieces of some universal puzzle.

Such an ambiguous milieu disturbs my sensorial balance; I feel alternately hot and chilled. Massaging the muscles of my arms – which suddenly seem to be quite numb – I posit the reason being my recumbent position. Could it be something more? The reaction of my body is lethargic, its response to my brain's demands indolent. A constriction clutches at my heart. Is it pathological? Maybe I'm sickening for something. Veronica, in her worldly wisdom, would, no doubt, diagnose a psychosomatic cause: a physical consequence of a dispirited mind. Looking down at my body, I impulsively dig a thumbnail into my left pectoral – wincing with gratitude at the pain and smiling into the night at my infantile consolation of reality. Alongside the pain, comes an apparent coldness of reason, which commands me to rise from the bed. I obey and pad naked to the bathroom, where I splash my face and upper body with icy water. Rubbing vigorously with a towel, I stare into the mirror. My face – a hazy vignette in the darkness – unfurls as a gaunt, drawn mask, as though lacking some integral life source. The flesh is etiolated, unvitalised, stretched tightly over bone, not quite real, like latex. Becoming more accustomed to the gloom, my eyes continue the perusal – there being no immediate desire on my part to return to the dubious dreamland of the bed – and a nagging doubt about the authenticity of now persists. Intuitively, I still feel a lack of conviction concerning my senses of sight and touch. In spite of the manifest tangibility of water, towel, mirror, walls and other miscellanea, a residual smack of imagination – or illusion – remains. I would not be totally surprised to awaken and find myself somewhere else.

Cupping my hands again and again under the softly flowing liquid, I treat myself to more and more sudden splashes of water, until it seems I must rid myself altogether of the face's external shell. Beneath my eyelids the dream sea continues to dance: its cold, soothing embrace enduring, penetrating my mind through the very pores of my skin. I relish the extreme fantasy of following its penetration with sharp – claw like? – fingernails, of digging and tearing the integument, laying bare the subcutaneous material of pure skull bone. From there it would require only a nominal attack by those – claws? – to expose the fibrillation of living brain matter and to permeate it with sober, cleansing air. To wrench the physicality of the brain from the spirituality of the mind, to separate extension from attribute, to create a living sculpture of the Cartesian duality – that would endow the *cogito* with new life; bequeath monadology with fresh meaning. But contemplation of such fantastical abstractions denies the most probable activity – that of tissue and fibre running down electrochemical impulses like a well-worn battery.

The haunted visage before me tells me nothing. It is just a face, larval, concealing the turmoil behind it. Once more it is my reaction to its blandness that opens up the can of worms, my guilt transforming it into an accusing, condemning nemesis. Trapping the thing under trembling fingers does not appease; the neurosis survives.

*(There's no art to find the mind's construction in the face.)*

Removing my hands, I peer down into the handbasin as the water slides away, its diffused reflections forming a microcosmic sidereal order in the gloom – the mouth of the outlet pipe becoming a swirling black hole at its centre. Optically magnetic, speciously acceptable, it fleetingly immerses me in its feasibility. Only the coldness of my flesh and the consciousness of the surround robs me of the little scene's cathartic qualities. I close my eyes against it before opening them again. Nothing has changed. The eidolon is still there – but different.

Although the ghostly outlines of my jaw and cheekbones remain, my other features – nose, eyes, mouth – have all apparently disappeared.

With a small explosion the mirror shatters.

Splinters into tiny spiderweb cracks.


"Some dedicated artist you turned out to be."

I heave open eyelids that have been welded together, as heavy as tungsten steel. Managing to blink once or twice, I try to clear away blurred vision, but white daylight stings like salt and tears form in the optic corners. My head aches beneath a king-sized hangover and I raise a sausage fingered hand to my throbbing forehead.

"I suppose you realise the time – it's gone eleven."

Summoning Herculean strength, I succeed in opening my eyes sufficiently to squint in the direction of the disapprobative voice.

Veronica stands at the side of the bed, hands on hips, legs apart; but there is a smile on her face. Sunlight reflects off her hair like a halo. "Come on, come on," she chides. "Are you going to stay there all day? My God; can you sleep or what?" Without waiting for an answer, she turns on her heel and saunters off in the direction of the diminutive kitchen. Her blue denims look as though they have been sprayed on and I watch the callipygous retreat with a more appreciative awareness.

"It's my favourite pastime, "I manage. "Got to keep practicing for the big one, huh?"

"Oh, very funny, I'm sure," she calls back over her shoulder.

But sudden recollection of the nightmare brings a chill so cold that icy sweat dampens the palms of my hands. Raising them up to probe, I sigh with relief as the natural undulations of my facial features become apparent. Having never really existed, of course, the anomaly lingers only as a blur of paramnesia. I had lucidly dreamed an awakening – even though it felt more like I had stepped into a painting by Giorgio de Chirico or Paul Delvaux. It has happened before – although, it must be said, not so vividly. My imagination, even in repose, is a cogent force, but I never thought it could become so volant, reach such a high plane of conviction. Residual fear should be squashed by common sense, conciliated by the cold light of day; and yet the pseudo realism of the *Machinino* simulacrum hangs in the air like a mist, granting more of a spurious than veritable acceptance of a pragmatic diagnosis.

Veronica returns carrying a tray with two steaming mugs of coffee and a plate of crumbling biscuits. Sitting on the edge of bed she balances the load gingerly on her knees. I reach out and relieve her of one of the mugs.

"This is all I could find," she complains. "It's like mother Hubbard's out there."

The first mouthful feels good, rejuvenating, attacking the dryness in my throat and subduing that awful aftertaste of sleep. Taking another sip, I look up. Veronica is watching me intently, a concerned look in her eye.

"You've had another one of those dreams," she states, flatly. It is not a question.

Peeking over the rim of my mug I observe her once again. Her loose, tousled shock of fair hair hangs about her shoulders like some luxurious exotic plant; while her heart shaped face – even with somewhat less than flawless skin, and a jaw that could be considered a little too strong – harbours the most striking pair of eyes I have ever seen. Clear blue pools of emotive sparkle, so open and penetrative they emit a stare that is sometimes challenging, and occasionally intimidating. A smallish nose, faintly retroussé, rests above a soft lipped mouth, moulded into a pouting, almost petulant expression. She sits and watches me like a cat, awaiting some confirmation of her observation. At a loss for a pithy or defensive answer, I admit, bluntly:

"Yeah, okay – another one."

After a momentary hesitation, as if in doubt, she reaches forward to gently touch my cheek with her fingertips. "Does it still –?"

"What?"

She withdraws her hand. "Never mind."

Knowing what she is referring to, I mumble something about the dreams being unconnected with the absence of Domino, but my response is obviously unconvincing.

"Then what do you make of them?" she enquires. "What do you think they mean?"

I shrug. "Who knows? More than likely just the after effects of too much booze and not enough food. Maybe they're indicative of the D.T.'s."

"Don't be flippant," she snaps.

"I'm not being flippant," I protest. "It's just that I don't know how else to react to them. I'm no psychanalyst; you can't expect me to expound doctrinaire interpretations about something of which I know so little." To compensate, I take her hand and press it to my lips – a gesture of infantile gallantry.

"Doesn't it bother you," she persists, "that they're getting worse? It's starting to show, you know – in your appearance, I mean." Frowning slightly, she shakes her head. "I only wish I could help in some way."

"But you do," I attempt to persuade her, earnestly.

"I do? How?"

"By simply...*being.* Your presence here is the most therapeutic treatment I can think of."

Swiftly withdrawing her hand, she scowls at me. "There, see what I mean? You're at it again. You really should learn to take your health more seriously. Besides," she adds, "you had your chance."

Quickly digesting her rebuke, I continue with the topic of my wellbeing. "I'm okay," I insist, at the same time catching her look of disapproval. "Honestly; you worry too much."

"Well, I can't help that, can I? I mean, *someone* has to – since you're obviously irresponsible. You could, at least, *try* to do something for yourself. This obsessive, *maudit* trip of yours is starting to become a little –" It is my turn to cast a disapproving glance. "Oh, shit." She winces. "Look, I don't mean to sound heartless, but it has been...quite a while now."

"How long is...'quite a while'?" I ask, with more than a hint of acerbity.

"I suppose it's as long as you intend to make it," she retorts, somewhat frustratedly.

"Thank you, doctor. I feel much better now."

"Being sarcastic won't help."

"Neither will empty rhetoric, sweetie."

"Oh, God, here we go again. Why must we always end up quarrelling?"

"Is that what we're doing?"

"Look, I'm sure you're not going to believe me, but I think I know what you've been going through these last few..." As I raise my eyebrows, she sighs, dejectedly. "Okay, okay. I can see this is doing no good. It never does. I should have known better. Let's face it, you don't need my help. You don't need anyone's help."

I ruminate on this as she lowers her gaze. Staring into her mug, she sips at the contents like a mouse, before replacing it back on the tray. It is such ordinary, everyday actions that draw us together, that make us human; so, I relent. "Sorry, love. Didn't mean to sound so offhanded. It's just that I'm…I'm resentful of outside advice, that's all. I find it…intrusive. Can't really explain why."

"But that's exactly my point. All this damned introversion. How do you expect to come to terms with…with…this thing, if you persist in keeping everything locked away in that little artistic box of yours?" To emphasise her point, in a seemingly light-hearted manner, she taps the side of my forehead with her finger; but her eyes continue to betray a more earnest intention.

"Just part of my nature, I suppose," I tell her. "Never did have much of a gregarious inclination, you know that."

"Don't I, though? Nevertheless, there's a big difference between being simply non-gregarious and being downright bloody reclusive. Tell me, when was the last time you went out? I mean – *out* – and actually conversed with someone – other than yours truly?"

"Oh, I go out. I have to – in order to exist. I have to shop for supplies: food and –"

"Booze?" she finishes for me. "Mustn't forget the booze, must we? Which means it's alright to ignore even the most basic lunchtime or prandial provisions – just as long as your alcoholic trips into temporary oblivion are provided for."

"You're browbeating again, love."

"So, what – since you completely ignore cajoling or pleading? At least I can provoke a reaction – of sorts – by bullying – albeit hostile."

"Ah! Ah!"

She glares at me, ferociously. "What the hell is that supposed to mean?"

"Amateur psychology. Goad the subject into retaliatory responsiveness, break down the isolation barrier, and then, by a process of discourse and elaboration, tempt forth a self-expurgation. Next patient, please."

"God! But you can be infuriating on times. Why are you always so sceptical of people's intentions – even your friend's?"

"I have no friends."

"Well, thank *you!*"

"Present company excepted, of course."

"Bull-*shit!*" She is angry now. "Why do I get the feeling I'm wasting my life here? Again!" Snatching away my mug, she stands up.

"Hey!" I protest. "I haven't finished with that yet."

"Oh! I'm sure you'd much prefer the contents of one of those bottles over there. Go ahead. Don't mind me."

"Christ! Veronica, will you stop this already? I don't want an alcoholic drink; I want that damned coffee."

Taking a deep breath, and with great effort she attempts to subdue her sense of irritation. After a few moments and several suspirations, she hands the beverage back to me – but not without ostentatious contempt.

"Thank you," I say, meekly, endeavouring to propitiate.

She stands and glares at me, moving her weight from one foot to the other and back again; crossing and uncrossing her arms. Taking a sustained and purposeful swallow, I hope the lull will mitigate the situation. It seems to do the trick; she softens.

"Look, love," she says. "I'm only trying to help – you do know that, right? I'm concerned for you. You accuse me of worrying too much, and maybe I do. I worry about your physical health, and I worry about your mental health – living out here, like some kind of indigent *des Esseintes*, in this…this…" she waves a hand about in frustration, searching for some adequate, demeaning adjectives "…battered, dilapidated sea-shanty – where you exist on nutritiously inferior diets, too much liver eroding liquor, and reside in some kind of unwholesome, autistic fantasy of your very own."

"Some artists do live in a kind of an autistic state – especially the more imaginative types. It can actually be a prerequisite of the job."

"So, you've expounded before; but you know my views on that. It's unnatural and it's unhealthy to take it to such an extreme. You're alone too much and for too long; losing contact with reality. There again, that's really what you want, isn't it?"

She is right, of course. Slowly but surely, I have been creating an isolated retreat for myself. Even though I've managed to ward off the creeping despair that resided within me – and, to a great extent, supressed it – I am still immured, unready or unable to meet outside commitments head-on. As it is, this current piece of work – commissioned by an acquaintance of Veronica's, a fan of vintage science fantasy covers from way back – must be classed as some kind of breakthrough; a few weeks ago, I would not even have considered taking it on. Only Veronica's perseverance and constantly applied pressure forced a gradual capitulation and final consent. 'All he wants is a figure,' she had said. 'A fantasy figure – a nude – like the ones you used to deliver before the bloody computers decimated your livelihood. I'll even bloody-well pose for you again, if need be. You could do it standing on your head.' The girl is indefatigable, refusing to give up on me. These days my most constant companion – which means little as far as overall human contact is concerned; recent alternative companionship having been confined to the more aloof, unsavoury confreres of the demon drink – she remains my only true friend; although, before Domino, she was much more. Nostalgically, now, I remember our time together with lamenting affection. We were content – in an uncomplicated way – and innocent. Not to the peaks and troughs of a sexual relationship, but to the cruel changeability and impermanence of the world. We thought – as all universal romantics do – that things would stay as they were – not forever, of course, but for a foreseeable future that was too far away to be bothered about. But any attempt to ignore the small, ephemeral whimsies – which inevitably broadened into more troublesome events – turned out to be pure sophistry; or, as one of my more 'intellectual' drinking buddies proclaimed – after I had sobbed my story onto a slouched shoulder in the early hours of an extended binge – 'naïve, impershipient exshtravagansh.'

The rending of this undefiled probity was not entirely Domino's doing, but her dark beauty and ambient mystery certainly did not help. As in most situations of this kind, at first it developed slowly, almost unperceptively – the alienation of Veronica running concurrently with my attraction to Domino – quietly gaining momentum like a runaway train. Until the unavoidable melee exploded, that was – casting Veronica as its number one victim, who emerged from the emotional onslaught confused and badly hurt. By this time, though, I was so captivated by the enigmatically vivacious Domino that I – to my eternal shame – barely noticed. The new temptress became my obsession, my life, my interest over and love above all else – including my work. Even though any notion of it was rejected by me at the time, with hindsight it is easy to recognise the deterioration. Indeed, that torrid, myopic period almost caused its complete creative demise. Something that must have further exacerbated Veronica's deprivation, as she had been my principle source of encouragement and inspiration – my muse. Throughout our relationship she had been my living model, posing – on various occasions almost to the point of petrifaction – while I sketched and painted her from every conceivable angle: standing,, sitting, reclining, stretching; dressed, undressed, partly dressed; once – for a Gothic horror theme – Ophelia-like, lying in a coffin, half-filled with dyed liquid to resemble blood. Within this period her identity oscillated like an emotional pendulum in my head. Sometimes, after a prolonged session of transferring flesh to paint, she became little more than an abstraction of light and shade – a living chiaroscuro; while, on other occasions, she came to represent the ultimate in humanity: a gorgeous, naked soul in corporal form. Such an amour should not be unenduring, should not be left to wither and die; and obviously it has not been. Much to my disgrace, though, the influence – at least until recently – has resided almost exclusively within the beating heart of

Veronica. How else can her return be accounted for? Why does she continue to put up with my moods, my malice, my querulous temperament and my – to her – irritating, retreatment? Why does she relentlessly bully and badger her art loving friends and acquaintances into contemplating my thinner and thinner output of work? I dread to think of the verbal abuse inflicted on the tenuity of said friendship, or even camaraderie, she has – or had – with them whenever there's been a failure by me to deliver the expected artwork. Since every single 'commission' has been brought about by her persuasive efforts, it was she who suffered the backlash and caught the flack – while I merely sulked like an over indulged brat in the wings. And yet her self-assurance remains – overtly – unimpaired, as she ascends again and again to meet each new challenge; defending my reputation like a guard dog. And her diligence appears to be – slowly but progressively – perficient; I have almost completed her latest object of inducement: a depiction of an 'alien' female warrior standing against an extra-terrestrial backdrop: a science-fantasy image, popular years ago when adorning book jackets of novels written by the likes of Edgar Rice Burroughs, Jack Vance, Robert E. Howard, etc. The extra blandishment of Veronica's nude body illuminated before me once more has – so far – kept me up to the task. I mean, I can't very well demur, or resort to alcoholic torpor when she is actually there in my presence, can I? Perhaps it's just a kind of sexual ambuscade – or am I being somewhat presumptuous? – but in any event it appears to be having the desired effect. Regressions into my self-indulgent bower are becoming less severe and less frequent, even though – as on this particular occasion – a strong fillip is still needed – and supplied – by my selfless redeemer.

The thing is, I think I'm beginning to fall in love with her again (is it possible?) and this disturbs me, as it presents fresh problems – not least being the obstacle of her current…paramour. Someone about whom I know absolutely nothing. She seems reluctant to discuss him (her?) and quickly changes the subject whenever I bring it up. So, I don't bring it up anymore. I posit that she must have her reasons, although maybe I can discern them for myself – or am I again being presumptuous? In spite of the resurgent intimacy between us, I deliberately avoid any kind of head-on confrontation with a prospect that both frightens and exhilarates me – at least while she is in close proximity. So, the thing lies at rest beneath the surface of verbal commerce, like water under wafer-thin ice. One of these days we will cut too deeply with our skates. But, until then…

Realising she is standing there, staring at me, waiting for a counterattack to her latest observation on my wayward character, I say: "Alright, what do you suggest?"

Taken aback by the riposte, she places a palm against her chest, as though she were being accused of some minor crime. "Suggest?"

"Yeah. You've exhibited enough disapproval of my lifestyle to ban me from the boy scouts; punctured enough holes in my routine to let in water; so, tell me, what form of rectification do you have in mind?"

After pausing, indecisively, she proclaims, almost in defiance: "I do have something of a…proposition for you."

"Tell me."

Taking a deep breath, she casts her eyes to heaven. "You could come and stay with me – with *us* – for a while."

"Us?"

"Yes." She nods her head, but not with any great degree of certainty, it seems to me. "With…us."

As I smile and shake my head, she drops to her knees at the side of the bed, gazing into my eyes, nailing me like a butterfly to a board. "Why not? It's accommodating enough. You could have a room to yourself. You'd have peace, quiet and time to work again. If it would make you feel better, you could pay a nominal rent from future commissions – but that's entirely up to you. If you simply wanted to –"

"Veronica," I interrupt.

"– try it for a short period, there would only be need to take the bare essentials: paints, brushes, easel, sketch –"

"Ver-on-i-ca!" I reiterate, loudly, the prolonged forth syllable concluding on a downward note. Snapping her mouth shut, she blinks at me, as though I have just slapped her in the face. "Veronica," gentler now, "my love. You are being more than kind, but…"

"But?"

"It's impossible."

"Why?" almost sullenly.

"You know why. For a start…what the hell is…you-know-who going to say about it?"

"That's been taken care of."

"Taken care of? What does that mean?

" Shrugging her shoulders, she looks away. "It means what is says: it's been taken care of. The subject has been…discussed – and resolved."

"What subject?"

"You."

"Me?"

"Yes."

"And what have you…discussed – and resolved – about me?"

"Everything."

I stare at her. "Everything? Ev-er-y...thing?"

"What's the matter?"

"Nothing. Nothing's the matter. Why?"

Focusing me with those baby-blues, the way she used to, she says: "I know that look."

"What look?"

"That look of criticism."

Reading the connotation, I lower my gaze. "It's none of my business, love."

Visibly stiffening, she rises to her feet. "Quite right," she says, and starts to turn away.

Involuntarily, as though acting of a will of its own, my hand reaches out and I have her by her wrist. "Veronica. Veronica, I didn't mean to... to..."

"It's alright," she affirms, but distantly, at the same time pulling away from me.

"Look, I'm a bit confused is all. I'm not sure what to make of..."

She stands perfectly still. There is a long pause, before: "Make of what, for God's sake?"

"You're being difficult," I tell her.

"That's bloody rich," she retorts.

"Veronica...love...let's not hurt each other...again."

"Each other? *Each...other?* Damn you; I don't seem to recall too many tears being shed your end. I don't –" She raises a hand to her mouth.

Regrasping her wrist, I pull her towards me and down onto the bed. She sits and stares vacantly into the mug she still holds in her hand. Balancing it on her knee, she lowers her head.

"I...I didn't think," she almost whispers. "The words...The words just...came."

"It's okay," I tell her. "Honestly; I understand."

"They just..."

"I know."

"I didn't mean to say that!" she snaps. Then, looking up into the skylight in dismay, adds, vehemently: "I *didn't!* Goddammit!"

"I know you didn't," I reassure her. "It's okay. I know you didn't. Forget it."

Relieving her of the mug I place it on the tray, alongside my own. But in order to accommodate this action, she has to bend slightly forward and towards me, offering me the opportunity to hold her face in my hands as I plant an affectionate kiss on her forehead. "You're much too beautiful a person to be cooped up here with me in this slag heap," I tell her – and I mean it, too.

A silence follows, in which we study each other's features. Her eyes search my face, flickering entreatingly over the countenance, and as her gaze settles on my mouth her lips part slightly, allowing me to savour the sound of air being quietly sucked in between her teeth. And in that moment, she seems to melt before me; the epidermal bravado vaporising like a spider's web in the wind. If we stay like this, I think, within this silence, then everything will survive, the adversities of the world will be held at bay. Maybe she, too, realises this, as she holds and keeps that same silence to her as if it were a possession. All I need to do to consolidate its sanctity is to place my mouth on her offered lips, which continue to open like the petals of a rose…

But, in an instant, something happens. Her face becomes blurred by its nearness, while at the same time undergoing a transformation. From somewhere in the depths of my imagination the features become dissembled, and the sudden nebulous haze redefines itself as a haunting visage of – Domino! The hitherto protective silence is shattered like a soap bubble pierced by a needle.

Pulling back, I cough quietly and blabber inanely." Listen, love, I understand that you're trying to help. I really do. And I appreciate the sentiment, but –"

Closing her eyes, she sighs and moves her head back and forth.

"What?" I ask, fatuously, at the same time accepting that the sacred silence has been irrevocably broken.

"There's no need…" she breathes, allowing the sentence to fade.

Embarrassment creates a protraction. My words come out as words, nothing more. "No need to…for…what?"

Standing up, she steps back, eyes averted. "The act. The show. Don't bother. *She* will always restrain the finality. She has totally robbed you of free will. You might as well as demolish that wall of yours now, as you have been emasculated by a ghost."

Such a mordant observation fractures my secretive cocoon. Suddenly feeling quite naked, I decide to study my fingernails.

"Anyway," she continues with false spirit, "why are we creating such unnecessary complications? Just try taking up my offer on a strictly above board, no ties basis. Think of it simply as an alternative hiding place. At least you'd get some square meals inside you."

With that, she scoops up the tray and exits quietly into the kitchen. I watch her go, almost call her back, before realising it's too late; the inclination has died even before any words can be uttered.

Climbing out of bed, I slip my feet into scruffy sneakers and heave on a pair of faded, paint stained denims. Then, after staring too long at the door leading into the bathroom, I remember the dream. The...*dreams*. As if to counterbalance any palliation in my waking life, the life of dreams has worsened, become ambiguous, diffused, overlapping the dreamworld with the real world, the unconscious with the conscious.

Was I truly awake last night when I entered the bathroom? Or not? I *had* incontrovertibly awakened from a dream – but was it to seamlessly drift into another? Could the happening behind that innocuous looking piece of wood really have taken place? If it did, then why can I not remember my exit from there, or my return to the bed? Rather than console me, this possibility fills me with alarm, because it brings into play another factor I have refused to consider until now: could these events be the result of some malignant psychosis? Am I, in fact, losing my mind? Attempting to rid myself of such a disconcerting hypothesis, I glance up through the skylight, at the enveloping welkin above. Grey clouds slide into view, and I hope they do not represent an omen of some kind.

Shuffling across to my next diversionary item only partly appeases the symptoms of my newfound neurosis, but at least the painting remains the same and does not mock me with any unexpected anomaly. So, after summoning up a diurnal response to the condition called 'nocturnal forgiveness' – whereby a total dismissal of the day's problems are counteracted by the adoption of a completely concentrated and selfish state of mind – I close the door on my doubts and fears and manifest a critical eye towards the work in question – on the exclusive illusion of mixed acrylic paint on board.

The background – a crepuscular beach with rocky, alien-esque crags scattered about its surface, and a distant rolling sea – is complete; but the hips and legs of the female figure in the foreground are still white, unpainted, primer covered board. I opine, as far as it goes, that it is not a bad representation, although the facial likeness to Veronica is tenuous. The lady of the medium has eyes that are more feline than human; while her copious breasts seem unaffected by gravity – which is intentional. But this is also a wild exercise in artistic licence, one that allows exaggeration and elaboration in accordance with the figure's supposed situation and/or location. To be honest, though, since the client is male, the emphasis is centred on nothing more than misogynistic gratification – just one more rendition of a perennial damsel in distress.

The figure is – will be – standing proud and defiant, her hair blowing in the wind; while one arm is slightly raised, as if about to ward off a (sexual?) attack by some out-of-frame assailant. Her other hand is still lacking detail, but so far – in basic colour – clutches the handle of a curved, vicious looking dagger – perhaps longer, though, more like a falchion – jutting above a leather, jewel encrusted sheath, which will – when the work is finished – be seen to be suspended from a similarly embellished leather belt that will double as a modesty line, helping to cover and conceal her – to some people's – offending pubic area.

Studying the piece for a while, I weigh up the composition – virtually non-existent around such a salient focus of attention – and scrutinise the detail, which looks to be appreciatively tight and neat. Except for a few gaudy, improbable highlights on her left side, added for an extra alien-esque atmosphere – a glow from a far-off supernova, perhaps? – the flesh tones are a suitable assimilation of the real thing. Alongside this, anatomical proportions and measurements – despite the fact that she is supposed to be a 'non-earther' – appear satisfactory. Obviously, no masterpiece, it remains adequate and relative with subject matter, acceptably abiding to the descriptive constraints and requests issued in the brief supplied by the client.

Veronica emerges from the kitchen and stands behind me. There is evidence of a return of humour as she playfully rests her chin on my left shoulder; her right arm snaking around and past my head, forefinger pointing directly at one portion of the painting. "Why don't her breasts sag – like mine?" she asks. "They look pneumatic, as though they've been inflated by a bicycle pump."

Twisting my head around as far as possible, I struggle to look at her face – so, so close – but I can only just make out the white of the end of her nose in the corner of my eye. "Lack of gravity," I explain. "The scene is set on an alien planet – remember? Besides, your breasts definitely do not sag."

"Why, thank you, kind sir." After a long pause, in which we both stand amidst our growing silent thoughts, she adds: "Sorry. You must think me a bit of a cat."

I smile. "Certainly not. I'm an ungrateful slob."

"Alien planet, huh?" Continuing as though the apologetic interjection had not occurred, she steps forward for a closer look. Adopting a series of cute wrinkles each side of her nose, she critically eyes the topic in question, insisting: "They still look like they've been pumped up."

"Will you just let me be the best judge of that?" I ask, good-humouredly.

"You're the artist," she relents. "But don't say I didn't warn you – when the guy demands alterations, I mean. You hearing me on this?"

"I hear you and I won't," I confirm. Using the mild vicissitude as a stimulant, I subjugate my fears and make for the dreaded bathroom. As an added incentive to my valiance, before I actually open the door, I glance back to where Veronica is calmly divesting her clothing before ascending the two low steps of the circular platform in the corner of the room – the corner that catches the longest period of daily sunshine. As if on cue, that old 'currant bun' reappears from behind those derisive clouds and spotlights her like a cabaret artist. Standing there, naked, she quiescently awaits me to re-pose her.

Since we first met, nudity has simply been a fact of life to her; inhibitions mere complications fabricated to uphold prudishness and false piety. The exposure of her body is no way a dissolute act, but an expression of innocence – an offering to the world of her own particular kind of truth. Such an attitude, to me, is both endearing and disarming, one that exemplifies a mode of existence that eschews society's artificial impediments; a display of personal morality – inviolate, in defiance of dissimulation or bad faith. And for the first time in a long while such an ingenuous demonstration symbolises something meaningful to me, resurrecting memories of how the sight of her body used to affect me when things were different. For strangely drawn out moments I am free to observe the present from a standpoint that can only be described as pre-Domino; while the solar glow above endows Veronica with the aura of an apparition, in which frozen instant I realise she is the true embodiment of the metaphoric light in my darkness. As I stare at her, she turns and returns my gaze, her expression frank, questioning, gradually melting into an enigmatic smile.

Under the auspices of that smile I enter the chamber of my ineffable nemesis, where I ready myself for a fight against impending panic. Riveting my gaze to the floor I close the door behind me and lean against the frame. Then, counting down the seconds until they blossom into minutes, I only half take in the black and white tiled linoleum floor with its artificial marbled pattern before me. To stare too long at them, I know, will bring on Hamlet's cloud pareidolia again – not a camel, but more vague, surrealistic shapes that jump out from the tangled skeins like cut-outs from a popup book. Creations engendered in the imbroglio of an overactive imagination. Slowly, apprehensively, I raise my gaze – past the shadows on the floor and up to the ugly plumbed pipes on the wall – until the smooth, symmetrically sculptured white handbasin materialises like a piece of debris floating around a space station. Try as I will, though, I cannot bring myself to look any higher.

And yet, in the very next moment, with a loud exhalation of pent up breath, and sudden, brisk steps, I approach the bowl and nervously turn on the taps – as if the rushing noise of the water will somehow drown out the troublesome thoughts. But it is to no avail. As I splash my face the doubts return like thunder. Even focussing all my mental energy on Veronica – and what she stands for – does not help, because the face I see is that of Domino's, now somehow representing a kind of spreading evil. It is as if the budding relationship with Veronica has become invidious. However, I can discern no reason for this, other than the fact that Veronica is alive (and once more available – perhaps?), while Domino is dead and inaccessible. Which means, yet again, that it all comes down to my own basic, contemptable selfishness: I am reaching for what is possible while disregarding what is not. Acknowledging this about myself is discomforting, to say the least, reinforcing the fact that I don't like myself much. Could it be that the dream of the sea anticipated this? Was it a warning from my subconscious self? The questions crowd in, bothering me and setting up a clamour in my skull, causing my head to start to hurt with a pain that is oddly familiar.

Response to such psychological heat from my personal crucible demands a physical exorcism, so I brush my teeth madly until there is a taste of gum blood on my tongue – which proves to be nothing more than an exercise in futility. Still averting my eyes from the area above the place of my ablutions, I – with churlish reluctance – cease brushing and spit out a toothpaste and gore composite, watching it swirl and vanish into the gaping mouth of the outlet pipe, its hues imbuing the black hole with an even greater vampiric quality than before. Prior to backing away, like a supplicant retreating from the presence of a cruel and tyrannical despot, I wait for my heartbeat to calm down a little; and as my back touches the door, I reach behind me to clutch the handle – which is cold, metallic and... real. Finally managing to actually open the door, I try to retreat through it with my mind still intact. I almost make it, too, but...

Arriving like an express train, the terror brings with it the awesome reflection of the previous night, forcing me to relive disbelief in an already questionable state of sanity. Either validation or invalidation is imperative, or else I may truly succumb to out and out madness. I must be sure. I must know.

The last things I see before I look up are the backs of my hands. I'm not certain if it's the light or faulty vision on my part, but there appears to be something...'wrong' with them. They look like...claws – large, squamous and malformed amidst the shadows.

"Are you alright?"

Veronica's voice is just a measurement of decibels vibrating in my ears, just a pulsation of sound through the synaptic matrix of my brain. They mean nothing as a coherent message or source of communication; she might as well be speaking in Arabic. And for the second time in a matter of hours my stomach flips and quivers as I absorb the visual implications presented before me.

The mirror is cracked.

Splintered in spiderweb traceries.

"Did you hear me? I asked if –"

# SOLIPSISM

\*

The sudden explosion has the deep, thunderous reverberation of a plane crash, but it goes on for too long, rumbling and roaring, more like a landslide. Rising, it howls as loud as a wounded dinosaur, before everything begins to vibrate, and the whole building feels as if it has been picked up and tossed by a gigantic hand. In a vain attempt to subdue the growing turmoil you press your hands to your ears, but the sound becomes louder and louder, suggesting the tremor of an earthquake, or the vortex of a tornado. Continuing its rise, it spreads outward and upward, muffling your voice as you cry to the heavens, imprisoned inside a world of noise and pain. Somewhere on the borders of infinity you make out Veronica's pleas for help, over and over again, rising above the boundaries of hysteria. Somehow you manage to twist your head sufficiently to grimace against the agony and stare through the now open door. She is on her knees, hands scratching at her ears as if trying to tear them off, while an indoor tempest whistles and screams around the room, as though seeking an exit – rising several octaves into a strident, tinnitus-like whine when it fails to find one. Other things happen. A chair levitates for several moments, bobbing like a cork on water, before catapulting itself into space and smashing against the wall – matchwood. Dancing, puppet fashion, the bed bumps and grinds, its blankets and sheets tortuously twisting and twirling, spiralling up to the ceiling like wraiths. Ornaments tumble from shelves, as miscellaneous pieces of glass and china – cups, flutes, saucers, plates, bowls – wing their way out of the kitchen, attacking in jet formation – before the painting, as though self-animated, flies off the easel, swooping and dipping like a kestrel. As you stare bewilderedly through the unearthly confusion, Veronica, wide-eyed and terrified, implores you to make it stop, her open mouth screeching as silently as a goldfish in a bowl. Then, with hair taking on the appearance of blustered tumbleweed caught in a prairie storm, her whole body is forced backwards under the strain, and she is catapulted across the floor, arms and legs flaying helplessly, like a doll in a maelstrom. Summoning up one, final effort, you reach out a trembling hand (claw?), while desperately calling her name, but she does not respond. As she lies, motionless and pale, a white flash blinds you like snow…

UNTIL NOW
FROM AMORPHOUS NOTHINGNESS…
FORMATION…
MATERIALISATION…
A SPECTRAL GLIMMER…
WITHIN AN INDEFINITE WOMB

Below:

Rocks. Sheer. Precipitous. Crashing waves. Swirling foam.

What if…?

What if I…stepped forward?

That would silence you.

That would make you stop.

*Futile.*

*The waters of insanity are…*

*Your own creation.*


Through a blurred, misty tunnel…faces.

Veronica is close. I think it's Veronica – although her appearance remains hazy; I cannot make out…features. But she is safe.

Another face, a different face, an older face – wrinkled, eyes bright as marbles behind rimless spectacles – studies me with professional curiosity. It retreats, becomes replaced by a hand: clean fingered, as pink as crabs, holding a syringe. His voice, gentle, modulated, echoes soothingly down the tunnel:

"That should do it. He will sleep now."


You walk towards a cliff edge bathed in gold from the setting sun, along narrow, winding tracks snaking through monolithic rocks, and over ground composed of soft, red clay beneath your feet. Out of the clay sprout sporadic miniature copses of stiff gorse and coarse grass, bowing to a hair tugging wind carrying a strong, unmistakable smell of brine – sharp, pungent, tinged with something that is unwholesome and incongruous to your expectations. But you march on, resolutely, involuntarily drawing nearer to the end of the land. Wrinkling up your nose at the odour you contemplate its source as the sound of the ocean ascends above the height of the cliffs and pounded rocks, its voice joining the wind in a kind of corybantic revelry. The booming and the hissing urge you closer, until, at last, circumnavigating one of the larger rocks, you clamber up and onto a ridge that juts out against the splendour of a breath-taking sunset. Dissecting the orange ball with the sharpness of razor blades, purple, herring-bone clouds, stretch and rest in retirement along the horizon. At the summit proper, the full range of the sickly aroma assaults your senses alongside the nebulous spray in the air. From the top of that precipice you look down and out over the sea, which appears to be adorned in a rubescent glow. At first, you think the effect is simply caused by the agitated reflection of the sun, but closer inspection reveals a terrible truth – the water itself is scarlet, dense, its foam a bilious pink. A dawning recognition – it is blood. The ocean is swollen and clotted with blood. The grotesque coverlet rises and falls like a slurping, alien lifeform, its smell putrid, clogging the back of your throat. Against the acrid bile, you raise a defensive hand to your mouth, forcing back the pervading revulsion that suddenly threatens to overwhelm you. Out there, on the surface, floats a huge, indiscriminate mass – black and glistening – bobbing across the whole width of the luminous horizon. The shape is formless, indistinct, yet intuitively obscene, writhing and twisting on the tide, gleaming and waning in the rapidly fading twilight. As it slides ever closer the stench becomes stronger, viler, carried on a westerly breeze. Lifting up your other hand, you shade yourself against the glare as the sun and reflective water meld into a singular luminescence, while, at the same time, your eyes become fierce slits against its potency, squinting at this thing drifting nearer, dark and rubbery, like a colossal, shapeshifting cephalopod – much larger, though, more like a mass of land. Now it is quite close and you realise it is a floating, organic mountain of death, collocated entirely of...bodies. Bodies of all forms, species and sizes – some in an advanced state of necrobiosis – gently ebbing and flowing with the unctuous waves. Fish, birds, animals and...humans – from all of the countries and continents of the world – from north, from south, from east, from west – from the four corners of the planet. From America, Africa, Europe, Asia, and the Arctic Circle. From Australia, New Zealand, Brazil, Greenland, Russia, the far reaches of Siberia, and all other points of the compass. As it continues to advance – a seething lump of putrefaction – details become clearer, allowing you to recognise anatomies of tortured, bloody creatures with an almost supernatural acuity. Towards the centre of this...island of flesh – as though surmounted – are the whales, bound and adhered into one giant family. From sperm whales – huge, blunt nosed and bulbous – to the small, compact susu, or Ganges dolphin. From the Greenland right whale, to the streamlined narwhal. Others you know are also there – the Californian grey whale, the common rorqual, or fin whale, the Cuvier's beaked whale, the Atlantic bottlenose dolphin – all drifting as one. On times, the island rolls, tips and temporarily submerges, making it difficult to decipher one creature from the next, as all around this monstrous mound – in a morbid parody of living nature – the smaller animals cling like parasites. Amidst such a curdling agglomeration you discern shapes only arbitrarily, picking out species almost at random. Squamous flotsam of fish – all kinds – nestle and float together. Atlantic sturgeon, bowfin, European eel, common carp, snakehead, the exceedingly rare coelacanth, yellow gurnard – along with a thousand other strains. Sharks – hammerhead, sand, tiger, Great White, basking and leopard. Rays – manta, eagle, thornback, torpedo – each one part of the dead throng approaching the shoreline directly below you. Instinct demands that you look away, but you are held, awestruck, bound by a rigid fascination of the incomprehensible, for there are even more and you feel a duty – almost a penance – to remain and identify every possible lifeform, as though obliged to compile a vast necrology. Persisting in your study, you pinpoint with strange, expert knowledge and perception, a complete universal life cycle of Earth, chronologically, in order of development and movement around the globe. From the sea, the biological death process expands outward, through the amphibians – frogs, toads, salamanders, newts – to the reptiles. There are turtles, several of which you know – New Guinea, green, side necked, giving way to the lizards – crocodiles, alligators, Gila monsters, common tegus, Nile monsters, chameleons, Komodo dragons, leading to the snakes – pythons, king cobras, adders, anacondas, cottonmouths, rattlesnakes and many more. The dreadful, devastated lineage goes on, through the animal kingdom of hunter and prey, of predator, herbivore, carnivore and omnivore – lion, kangaroo, jackal, brown bear, hippopotamus, polar bear, walrus, seal, ass, rhinoceros, giraffe, deer, camel, hare, rabbit, cat, dog, sheep, cow, goat, elk, moose, elephant, bat, anteater and tiger – none are spared. Corpses of birds are just as plentiful – owl, eagle, osprey, penguin, buzzard, ostrich, albatross, duck, swan, stork, vulture, flamingo, falcon, chicken, turkey, goose, quail, parrot, swift and even the ultimate symbol of peace – the dove. There is but one exception – for whatever reason (even though the theory goes, that if mankind disappeared, either rats, ants or cockroaches would rule the planet) – the gulls abide, swooping and diving on the drifting carcasses, tearing and ravaging, before they, too, become victims of this final slaughter. For now, under their sharp beaks, lie deceased primates – gibbon, mandrill, baboon, monkey, gorilla, chimpanzee – all having expired in multiple, variously contorted poses that mimic those of the human cadavers. People of all ages, creeds, nationalities, religions, sects and colour, some broken, twisted, spread-eagled, decapitated, limbless, eviscerated or mutilated, some whole, straight, perfect. All are mortified. After what seems an eternity, you sink to your knees under the burden. You ask yourself and the world in general, why? Over and over again – why? Why? Why? Sometimes you whisper it, hoarsely, sometimes you shout it at the sky. But no answer is forthcoming. No logical interpretation. What is done is done. The Holocaust, the Apocalypse, Armageddon, the Revelation. The End of Days – whatever appellative you know it as, has come to pass. The grisly finale has been realised. And you are the sole survivor...

I remember the lights as they suddenly fractured the darkness: their glare splitting into a million tiny splinters through the lancing rain. I had only one hand on the steering wheel; the other gripped Domino's wrist – as she had torn off her seatbelt in a fit of pique. In an instant the quarrel meant nothing. I forced myself back against the seat, anticipating the impact. Helplessly, my foot pressed the brake pedal to the floorboards. The car swerved to the side; so, did the oncoming lights. Domino screamed.

Although I did not actually see it, still, I heard the sound of her head smashing through the disintegrating glass of the windscreen – and I let go of her hand...

"How long have I been out?" I ask, blearily.

Veronica studies me for a few seconds, warily, almost as though she is expecting me to attack her with an axe. "Since this morning. How do you feel?"

"Mmmhh...Not sure, to be honest. Lethargic, weak; got this crazy sensation I'm floating."

"That's the after effect of the sedative the doctor gave you. Can you sit up?"

Taking a deep breath, I watch the room lilt and whirl a few times before managing to push myself back, my shoulders sliding up the headboard behind me. Leaning forward, Veronica puffs up my pillow and squeezes it between the nape of my neck and the frame of the bed. "Is that comfortable?"

"Yes...thank you." Incuriously, I notice that her hands are shaking.

Staring at me with frightened attentiveness, she whispers: "What *was* that? What happened? Do you know?"

I run a distractible hand through my hair. "Seemed like some kind of freak wind, or something. A...hurricane, maybe, or a tornado, or..." but my attempt at sounding logical borders on the ludicrous, even to my own ears.

"Oh! It was *nothing* like *that!*" she states with tremulous affirmation. As though cold, her body trembles, visibly, and her eyes watch my every move. I feel like a specimen in a jar. Momentarily, her expression alarms me enough for me to become fearful for her reason. "It was something much, *much* more than a natural event. It was...*un*natural...weird – inexplicable.

Not something that can be defined in everyday terms." I'm unsure what she expects me to say, so I say nothing. "What the hell *was* it? I've heard of such things – poltergeists and the like – but I never dreamed that I'd ever get to witness an actual happening. If I hadn't seen it with my own eyes…"

"Wow, wow, wow," I start. "Hold on, there. Don't you think you may be jumping to…" but my voice fades against the image of her burying her face in her hands. Apart from being aware of stress hormones in a woman's tears lowering the level of testosterone in men, and as if to further emphasise the incomprehensibility of it all, recapitulation of the awesome ferocity of the event rushes at me, breaking the residual tranquillity of the drug. It is like standing in the path of a juggernaut. Reductively, all I can find to add, is: "Jesus!"

Exposing her face again, her examinant stare is disconcerting. She looks at me as though I have grown fangs. I can only blink back at her while trying to snap myself out of this semi soporific state. "Has anything like this ever happened before?" she asks. I do not answer; I just return her gaze, stupefied. Looking away, she sighs, impatiently, almost contemptuously. "Well?"

"Hang on a second, will you? Give me time to think."

Aghast, she holds out her hands. "You need time to…to *think* – about something like *that*? God, Almighty!"

"It's this fucking drug," I retort, irritably but fatuously. "I can't seem to focus…properly. I can't seem to…formulate my thoughts coherently."

"Still –"

"*Alright!*" My intemperate snap is no more than a defensive reaction against the riveting stare that has settled upon me. "Alright…alright," quieter, gentler. "Now that you mention it…"

"What?"

"Ah, shit! This is ridiculous. I'm just trying to placate you."

"What were you about to say? Dammit! You *were* about to say something."

"Well, nothing like…on that scale…to compare with that, but…"

"But?"

"But?"

"But *what*, for Christ's sake?" Her eyes blaze and I think she's tempted to strike me – or, at least give me a good shake.

"One or two…incidents…of, erm…less magnitude, shall we say…?"

"Such as?"

"Oddities…unimportant things…"

"Such *as?* What *kind* of oddities? *Tell* me."

"Such as…as…" I rub my face in frustration as thoughts dance inside my head like mischievous imps "…cups…"

"Cups?"

"...that have...'fallen', off the table...as if of their own volition."

"And?"

"And...brushes, pencils 'disappearing' from – hey! Where do you think this is, huh – Guantanamo Bay? Ease off, will you?"

"Listen, you dawk, I'm trying to help you here – *if* you'll let me."

"Help me? Help me what? Help me how? Why the hell should *I* need help, anyway?"

"You don't *know*?"

"Know what?"

"Can't you even *guess*?"

"*What*? Guess *what*? For *fuck's* sake, Veronica! Have you flipped? Huh?"

Lowering her eyes, she nibbles at her lower lip. It's a little habit she acquires whenever she feels uncertain about something, or embarrassed. Usually, to me, it is quite disarming; but now, added to her accusing manner, it becomes a source of irritation. I do not want to be disarmed.

"Okay, listen up," I almost snarl. "I'm receiving some bad vibrations from all this shit. If I didn't know better, I'd swear you were trying to lay the blame for...for whatever the hell it was occurred, at my door – as if *I* were responsible." Raising her eyes for a moment, she lowers them again. "Christ! You *are*, aren't you?" For a few moments I am dumbstruck. "*Fuck* me! You bloody-well *are*. You actually...*actually* think that...that *I*...that *I* am res–"

"If *not* you – then *who*?" she demands to know.

"Veronica. *Veronica!* What...*what* are you implying?"

She suddenly appears calmer. "What do you think?"

"I've no *idea* what to think – believe me."

Rapidly shaking her head, her sea of hair moves like a tide. It is as if her words have rebounded on her. Taking a few deep breaths, I slow myself down, because everything, once more, is beginning to tilt and spin. "Veronica – *love*...what's on your mind – exactly? What is it you know that I don't? You're not making any sense."

Shaking her head again, she ruffles the sea of hair again. "I'm...I'm not...sure. It's...it's just too incredible for words. I mean...I mean...you... you..."

"Me...what? What's too incredible?"

Lifting an arm, in a vain attempt at semaphore, she dangles her hand limply from the wrist. "I can't...express it...properly."

"I'll wait until you can."

"You'll think I'm crazy."

"Try, at least."

"Give me a moment, okay?" I nod and she attempts to control herself, eventually gaining a state of command. Then, like a schoolgirl contemplating a tricky exam paper, she knits her brows into a frown of concentration. "When…When all…*that* was happening…When all those objects started to fly about like that…even though I was so…scared…so panic-stricken… one thing stood out…kept coming through it all. It seemed as though…as though…"

"Come *on*, girl – spit it out."

"Oh, Christ! I can't believe I'm going to say this."

"Veronica! *Tell* me!"

"Alright…Alright…It *seemed* as though it were emanating from…*you!*"

"Shit!" I growl.

"See?" she affirms. "I told you you'd think I'm crazy."

I raise my eyebrows. "What the hell else did you expect?"

"But that's not what frightened me," she muses, quietly, almost to herself. Watching her closely, I await elucidation as she glances at me – nervously? warily? – the way she had done when I first awoke. After bowing her head, she raises it; bows it again. With what seems a great effort for her, she finally confronts me, holding my gaze firmly, and for a moment I think I know how John Merrick must have felt. "It *was*…you… because you…"

"I…what? In fearful anticipation of her reply, a strange coldness ripples up my spine.

"You…you looked…*different!*" she splutters.

The coldness accelerates and stabs at the back of brain, as sharp as an ice-pick. I do not want to hear what she is going to say next – but I feel compelled to ask the question. "What do you mean…*different?*"

"I…I can't explain it," she says. "You just looked…different."

Quickly reaching forward, I grip her by her upper arms, my nails digging into pliant flesh. "In what way? In what way…different?"

Pulling back from me, she opens her mouth, wincing with pain. "Hey! Let go of me, will you? Let *go!* You're…you're hurting me."

Managing to calm myself somewhat, I relent. "Sorry." I say, as I watch her cross her arms in order to massage both abused areas: "I didn't mean to…"

"It's alright." But there is a shaky edge to her tone. Following a deep inhalation, she says: "I'm…not sure what it was – probably just my imagination – but you looked…odd."

"My face?" I ask, shakily. "Was it…my face?"

"I…I think so."

"You…*think* so? For Christ's –"

Suddenly becoming tense, she opens her eyes wide. "I don't know. I don't *know!* What can I say? You looked…different – *strange.* You looked like…*someone else.*"

Sighing heavily, I rub knuckles into eye sockets and try to relax a little. The fear is gone, replaced by a perverse sense of relief that she did not see what I had seen – in the mirror – no matter what else it could have been that she *did* see. Fright must have warped her sensibilities, I think, confused her vision.

"Like an…*animal,*" she whispers, destroying my palliative self-reasoning.

"Oh, thank *you!*" The attempted levity falls on barren ground. As I look at her, her features remain rigid, like a mask, eyes still wide open. She appears to be in a state of shock. "What…kind of animal?" I press on, riskily; only to realise her mind is elsewhere. "Veronica? Veronica! Are you alright, love?"

With a shudder she resets her gaze on me. But then she frowns again, as if trying to remember something. "Not…an animal, exactly; more sort of…animalistic – simian. And yet still…you! I'm sorry, I can't describe it any other way."

"Ah, bollocks!" I moan, contemptuously.

With a quivering lower lip, she blurts: "Look! I didn't ask for this. I didn't ask for it and I don't understand it. I'm just trying to tell you, describe to you, what I saw – and what I felt. And – Goddammit! – I felt it was coming from *you!* So, you can go to hell!"

"Veronica! Girl! Get a grip, huh?"

"Don't talk down to me. Don't you *dare* talk down to me. I'm not a bloody child. I know what I saw and I know what I felt. And I'm telling you that you were its…source, its…core – whatever you want to call it. Comprende?"

My patience snaps. "Yeah. I know what *I* call it."

"That much *is* apparent."

"Oh, come on, now. What do you expect, huh? Just listen to yourself. You spout out this crazy crap about me being some kind of frigging monster or…or whatever it is you think you saw. And then you accuse me of –"

"I – am – *not!*" she interjects, angrily. "I – am – *not*…accusing you of anything. I am simply –"

"Then what is it you *are* doing? You say I'm…I'm responsible for what happened. You say…say it was coming from me – and that I looked like… like some kind of fucking animal. Tell me, in what the hell language are those *not* accusations?"

"For God's sake! I've just tried my best to explain. To explain that it simply…*seemed* that way. That you were – are –"

"Possessed?"

"*What?*"

"Possessed. You know: P-O-SS-E-SS-E-D – like in the movies."

"Don't be so damned ridiculous."

"What else would you call it, then? How else would you describe it? Categorise it? Enter under? File next to –?"

"I don't know!" she protests, her voice rising. "I don't *know!* I don't *know!* Stop it! You're backing me into a corner! I don't *know! Stop it!*"

Raising her hands, she presses them to her ears, trying to block me, the events and the fears out; while I lapse into an exhausted silence. The room starts to whirl again, forcing me to lean back against the pillow, where I close my eyes and welcome the hiatus – even though my emotions are still running at full throttle. The whole thing has developed the illogical scenario of one of my nightmares. Is that it? Am I still dreaming? Doubts gather like wolves. Opening my eyes, I focus on Veronica, who has now lowered her hands to her lap, where her fingers squirm, entwine and loosen, like epileptic eels. In an instant the anger subsides. What a bastard I must seem to her. Frightened, confused and looking to me for support and consolation, she encounters only opposition and improbable excuses. With difficulty, I lift myself up – both mentally and physically – to take her hand.

"Veronica…" I say, my voice now tuned to sympathetic mode "…love… I think I know what you're trying to say."

"You do?" The question is sullen and distant.

"Well…perhaps not entirely, but…"

Spurning my softer approach, she sniffs and looks away. I sigh again, heavily, search the walls, the ceiling for inspiration; find none. Realising her hand feels chilled in my palm, I tighten my grip. No effect. As soon as I ease the pressure her hand slips dismissively from my grasp.

"In my opinion you're looking for a scapegoat," I tell her, gently, almost paternally. She stares at me without responding. "But if you think you're going to find it in the realms of the…the supernatural, or the… occult or whatnot, then you're deluding yourself."

"Which means you have an alternative theory, right?" she suggests, acerbically.

"Not really, no; but since we ceased living in the dark ages, there has to be a rational explanation. Don't you agree?"

"Like what? Tell me, in all honesty, what you believe could have caused something like that…on that scale – even hypothetically."

I clutch at straws. "God knows. Maybe a seismic tremor? It *could* have been, brought on by subsidence or movement in the earth's crust. There's also the possibility of a fault line, running under this whole area; an old mineshaft, perhaps; did you know they used to dig for –"

"You don't believe that – not really."

"I don't believe it was anything of a supernatural nature, either."

She eyes me, suspiciously. "You have a very strange outlook for someone who considers himself to be an imaginative artist. There's a dichotomy there, somewhere."

"Now, *you're* being flippant," I tell her.

"I don't mean to be, I assure you. It was a practical observation. You appear to be much too blasé about the whole thing – as if you're holding something back."

An eidetic flash of the mirror's featureless face pierces my mind. "Of course, I'm not," I lie. "Just trying to be realistic, that's all – place things in perspective."

"How can you be realistic about the paranormal?" Her tone is sharp, caustic, indicating that she is beginning to completely lose patience with me.

"Keep thinking that way and you'll get to believe it," I tell her. "Next stop: you'll convince yourself that I have a pet poltergeist or demon in my wardrobe."

"Or, in your bloody head!" she snaps.

Since my statement was meant as another partial attempt at lightening the mood, her incisive retort cuts me like a blade. In her defence, though, having obviously been issued with so much extemporary vehemence, she is immediately alarmed by the impact of her words. "Sorry, I didn't mean that. I'm afraid this thing is starting to get to me."

"Forget it," I tell her. "But look, love, let's put things into context, shall we? I've heard all about this same nutty stuff as you, and I know that some of it is supposed to be based on fact. Events like the – what was the name? – Douglas Deen case: reputed to have been the true story behind the 'Exorcist' phenomenon. Remember that? The hubbub: the scratching in the walls, the moving bed and chair, the obscenities in paraphonic voices? At the time, all very mystical and demonic; but now, not recognised as 'possession' or 'discarnate entities' at all, but purely as hysteria. Then there was the Cantianille affair, in France – which turned out to be a hoax. The Amityville horror, likewise. The whole syndrome is embedded in psychology. There's so much about the human brain – the mind – that remains unknown, unexplored and misunderstood." As I speak, a different case comes to memory, and I cannot resist a patronising snigger. "Hang on, how about that other one? What was it called again? Oh, yeah: the 'Rosenheim Spook' – reckoned to be a classic of its kind, and –"

"The what?"

"The Rosenheim Spook – something about a lawyer's equipment going haywire."

Once again, she knits her brow. "Yes. Yes, I think I've heard of it."

"More than probably. It was quite famous way back when. And since it –"

"– concerned a young girl," she interjects.

It is my turn to knit a brow. "Erm…possibly. To be honest, I don't remember actual details now; what I do remember is that they tried to pin it on one of your poltergeist friends."

"No!" she almost cries out, as though experiencing an 'eureka!' moment. "You're wrong. Not a poltergeist. The disturbances were created by the lawyer's secretary – or clerk – who was completely oblivious to what was going on."

Our eyes meet.

"Veronica," I say. "You can't be serious."

"It was her – the secretary's – alter ego," she enunciates, slowly.

"That's a load of horse manure," I tell her.

Taking another deep breath, she challenges, coldly: "Is it?"

"Aw, shit! Don't tell me you're actually attempting to analogise that crap with this. If so, then it means you're suggesting *I* have an alter ego – one that, by some kind of velleity, wanders about wrecking furniture, crockery, and God knows what else." Sitting there, she just stares at me. "You're nuts!" I add. "Do you know that? You must have bumped your head when you fell."

"Go to hell," she hisses.

Leaning forward, angrily, I point a finger at her. "So, what are you implying – that I'm schizoid? Nascently psychokinetic? What?"

"It would explain a number of things," she says, sarcastically. "You have all the hallmarks: you're subject to antisocial behaviour, introversion, you have a tendency to fantasise. It all adds up."

"I…*I* have a tendency to fantasise. That's rich, coming from you."

Realising her rhetorical error, she retorts: "Alright…what about the other things?"

"What other things?"

"The falling cups? The missing brushes, pencils…?"

"I would not call them paranormal."

"Then, what *would* you call them?"

I hesitate. "I'm not sure."

"See?" she declares, more confidently. "You're stumped!"

"Anomalies," I come back with. "Anomalies – of the senses. Mistakes."

"Mistakes?"

"Yes. Mistakes, for Christ's sake."

Her annoyance is obvious. "What kind of mistakes? Who's mistakes?"

"The brain's, of course," I tell her.

"You mean illusions?"

"No! Dammit! I do not mean illusions."

"Then, explain," she demands.

Frustratingly snorting air through my nostrils like a bull, I attempt to demonstrate my point. "Listen...You think you see something, okay...but you don't. Whenever your mind is occupied, concentrating on a specific subject, your vision rivetted to a particular item of interest, any movement, out of the corner of your eye, becomes distorted, misrepresented – until you take a second look, and redirect said concentration, only then are you able to discern the true reality." She remains unconvinced, so I continue: "How often have you lost things? How often have you put something down, only to discover that it's somewhere else? In the physical, material world, though, it is not somewhere else at all; it's somewhere else to where you *think* you put it. Reality passes us by like a stream, twenty-four-seven, and we accept it, but we actually remain unaware of it as a state of...being a thing in itself – out there. And because we encapsulate the world, the universe, subjectively, when the universe doesn't seem to abide by our subjective perception or understanding, we blame *it,* rather than our *own* faulty mechanisms."

"Speculative platitudes," she scorns, oxymoronically. "You've told me nothing that I don't already know, or thought about, myself. Such Berkeleian bullshit is less than persuasive. I still believe you're holding out on me – know more than you're letting on. For some reason, though – best known to yourself – you seem reluctant to expound. But you can't fool me; I've been around you for much too long to be taken in by all this...this evasive circumlocution."

"Jesus!" I exclaim. "You haven't heard a sodding word I've said, have you? You never listen to me, no matter how evincible my argument."

"But your argument is not evincible," she contradicts. "You've already everted this particular discussion, so how do you hope to convince me of your current channel of reasoning?"

"What do you mean?"

"Well, it seems to me you've switched sides. When I first tackled you about this...event, you, too, thought things were unworldly and unaccountable. Now it's as if you're standing as a bastion of logic and common sense. Where the hell did all this hard-edged rationalism come from?"

"That may have been the impression I gave you when you came at me with that fast-talking state prosecutor barrage. What you're neglecting to take into consideration is the fact that the tranquilizer was still active in my system. I mean, did you *really* expect me to awaken from a goddamned, virtual trance and be accurate, coherent?"

She looks away. "I don't know what to think anymore. All I *do* know is that I'm bloody-well confused and scared half to death."

"Aw, hell, Veron –"

"Don't patronise me!" Holding up her hands she looks as if she is about to palm off an attacker. "Do you hear me? Don't! Not now! I couldn't take it."

"I'm not being patronising, love," I say…patronisingly.

"Oh! Shit!" As she hugs herself, hands clutching opposite upper arms, her nails dig into flesh that is still red from where my own fingers had gripped. "Why do you insist on trying to dismiss this thing so lightly? You're like an ostrich; it won't go away by simply ignoring it. What happened once could happen again."

"Okay, okay, okay," I sigh, with obvious sarcasm and impatience. "You've found me out. I'll come clean. A full confession. Last night, I had a dozen acquaintances round – that's thirteen, including yours truly, of course – whereby, as demanded by tradition, we divested ourselves of all worldly attire, danced the obligatory *pas de deux*, burned black candles, inverted a crucifix, recited the Paternoster backwards, skewered the allotted virgin, invoked Old Nick himself, delivered a Pax to his hairy arsehole, after which we finished off with a few drinks – merely to be sociable – before retiring to bed. We meet again on Midsummer's Eve. As a matter of fact, the whole gang had only just left before you arrived, this morning. Does that help to explain things? I really should have mentioned it earlier."

She glares at me with utter contempt. "You finished? – because none of that was funny."

"It wasn't meant to be funny," I tell her. "But what the hell did you expect? What did you want to hear? Think about it: none of my description was any more outlandish or incredible than what you're accusing me of."

"There you go *again!*" Seizing on my statement as a kind of discursive escape route, she treats it as an opportunity to change her position from defence to attack. "As I've already said: I am *not* accusing you of anything. You can keep all that bloody paranoia for the outside world – assuming you ever decide to go there. It doesn't impress me one little bit. I'm not the bloody enemy – you know that; I'm the one who's trying to help you. Remember? Or can't you understand that? Some one – a fellow human being – is actually trying to help you. I frigging-well care about you, you idiot! God knows why – but I do."

Her disparaging speech, although tinged with meaningful benevolence, worms its way into my gut like a hungry tapeworm. I cannot let her get away with it. "And you're continually rebuked, right?"

"Right – damn you!"

"Then, why bother?"

"What?"

"Why bother? I shouldn't think it's worth the effort – having your sanctimony shot down all the time."

"If that means what I think it means…" she starts, her lower lip trembling slightly. She is desperately fighting to control her emotions. Sympathy taps me on the shoulder and bestows disapproval; but I ignore it. My unwarranted callousness persists.

"What do you think it means?" I ask.

"Oh! Go blow it up your arse, buddy!" she snarls, snatching up her jacket and handbag. "I don't have to put up with this. I have better things to do with my life," and makes for the exit.

A sudden pang of enlightenment prods at my mind like a branding iron. My future is about to walk out of the door. If I let her go, who will be there to depose the condemning spectre of Domino? Who will temper my nightmares with the reassurance of thatness? Who will save me from myself? "Veronica!" I call out after her. "Veronica! Don't be silly, girl. Come back." Halting, with her hand clutching the door handle, she stares at it, unable to come to a decision. "You know I didn't mean that." Climbing unsteadily to my feet, I sway towards her. Blood pounds in my temples like a hydraulic piston out of control. "Don't…go."

"Why not?" she asks. "You're so damned unappreciative."

"I know," I agree, gasping for breath while leaning against the upright.

"You always reject my notions, my suggestions."

"I know."

"Do you really think I'm incapable of making serious comments? Of proposing relevant solutions? Of hypothesising?"

"Of course not."

"Then why do you dismiss my opinions all the time?"

"Because I'm a male chauvinist pig, I suppose," I say, only half-jokingly.

"Look, I'm in no mood for bloody games," she moans, the tremor in her lower lip developing into a full quiver as she leans against my shoulder.

"Hey," I say, much gentler now. "I'm sorry, okay? I really am."

"Don't flatter yourself," she retorts. "This isn't about you. Not everything is, all right? I'll be fine in a minute. Bit of delayed shock, that's all."

"No doubt about it," I console, running my fingers through her hair.

"It's just that I was so damned scared. I've never known real…*real* fear before. It was like a nightmare. One that was impossible to wake from. And because I couldn't believe what was happening, I thought I was going insane. I genuinely thought I was going mad."

Lost again in my own introspective womb, the word 'nightmare' holds so many connotations for me, and oneiric images begin to dance before my mind's eye: the apocalyptic sea, the decomposing bodies, all that blood, waves rising thickly as though lapping against the rim of some obnoxious melting pot, depositing the red, oily corpses along the shoreline for as far as the eye could see. When Veronica looks up at me once more, I am only vaguely aware of her. It is the movement of her mouth that draws me back to the here and now; the sound of her voice merely a secondary condition.

"You *are* hiding something from me, aren't you?" she insists. "And you know more than you're telling. What *really* took place here this morning?"

Surfacing from the 'trance', I blink at her. "I don't know – honestly."

Since I can see that she is still not swayed by my negative confirmation, we stand in silence, the only movement my hand stroking her hair – an action carried out in an automatic, absent minded fashion – while my brain begins to float and spin. Maybe the drug I was administered is even more potent than I give it credit for – or else I arose out of bed too quickly. Perhaps both. Whatever the reason, at the moment, scenes are randomly flitting through my consciousness like some jerky, old-time, silent movie. Closing my eyes, I let them come…

*Feel so…weak…so tired. Inside…a spiritual vacuum spreads its entropic wings. It would be so…so easy to…just let go…to let everything slide away into oblivion…to divest myself of the world and its troubles…to let it drop away like a worn-out overcoat…to descend…to fall…to drift into the whirlpool of non-thought…to float in the depths of endless limbo…to submit to the…white space.*

Opening my eyes, I gaze down into Veronica's upturned face, which holds an equivocal expression. Barely hearing my own words, I'm still sure I utter them. "Don't go."

"Sorry," she whispers. "But I have to. You-know-who will be getting worried by now. If I don't…" I nod, regrettably, as she delivers a sad smile. "I will come back, though."

"It's alright, love," I acknowledge. "I understand."

And then she is gone; the door closing quietly behind her.


The clouds are mountainous configurations of soaked cotton wool. Curling and drifting like coloured dye in water, they create multiple pareidolia: faces, giant facsimiles, gods astride steeds of wind, before gradually transforming and convolving into other, more wondrous sculptures of the mind: into procreative materialisations of awakening serpents, swirling hills, castles of enchantment, and lands of magic and mystery. They are also a welcome escape from the torpidity of a reprobate artist's mind.

Three-quarters of a bottle of whiskey accompanies me over dunes and through dingles of wet and muddy sand. Like a quagmire it clutches at my sodden feet: a vast organism, seeking to suck me down into its cold, heartless bosom, squelching like a sopping chamois rag, filling my sole marks with gently bubbling slime behind me. Imprints of a passing shadow; a singular proof of an otherwise gossamer existence.

Dolefully I plough on, against a sobering wind and through frequent showers of rain, a moving scarecrow etched across a panel of grey, shoulders hunched, anorak flapping like the wings of a dying vulture, eyes permanently downcast, watching the myriad advancing ribs of sand and scattered pebbles with indifference and distain; a lone Beckettian character, searching for purpose and reason. One foot appears in front of the other with the monotonous regularity of a metronome; but the movement and motion means nothing to me; I am going nowhere.

It begins to get dark. I know not how far my peregrinations have brought me, but I care even less, remaining undisturbed by the discomfort of my wet clothes, my surround, the weather or the encroaching gloom. Apart from the spurious warmth of the liquor in my stomach, the numbness embraces me like a shroud, while an uncontrollable depression spurs me on – one that has resided within me since Veronica's ambiguous departure. With her redolence hanging in the air, spectre-like, I decided nothing short of an evacuation of the still partly wrecked studio would abate the melancholia – but I was wrong. It seems I now have two lamiae to contend with: one sucking my emotions, the other, my memories. Past and present accounted for, the future remains tantalisingly unrestricted; although pessimism strangles even that, with prospects of any kind of spiritual pacification appearing bleak, somehow tarnished; clinical anticipation of tomorrow offering nothing but trepidation. It is as though I have become the subject of a foul and irrational conspiracy, its source possessing an awesome propensity for harm, its objective arcane and undefined. What does it all mean? Am I simply acutely paranoid? Am I just imagining it all? Am I dreaming – even now? Or…insane? While, deep down, I am reluctantly able to concede there is a probable need for independent help – and can, with ease, admit this to myself – I find it impossible to confide such reasoning to another single soul. Not even Veronica. *Especially,* not Veronica! Cogitation can sometimes reveal an incongruous quirk existing within particular human relationships, for no matter how close certain couples become, personal divulgences remain bottled up and encased – disparate parts of a contrived profundity. Ergo, to me, it would be a sign of weakness to 'demolish the wall', as she put it, in order to allow her access to the penetralia of my mind. It would represent an admittance of defeat that is totally irreconcilable, creating a vulnerability peregrine to my nature. Which means, in order to beat this thing, I need to exorcise the phantoms in my own way; the neutral battle-ground must be one of my own choosing. Back there, the intramural atmosphere of the 'dilapidated sea shanty' was too claustrophobic. A vacation in the open air was called for – hence the whiskey and immoderate sojourn.

Stopping to look about me, I search the sky with jaded vision. It registers nothing. The bare sandy valleys and hillocks likewise: stark, desolate, devoid of movement and life. To the left of the high ground on which I stand – at the base of an invisible cliff – I can hear the sea. Ahead, there is a weatherworn bench.

I will sit awhile…

Trapped In a state of *acedia* you stare vacantly into darkness, listening to the moaning wind and the sighing sea. Only vaguely aware of your surround, you sit, a hunched gargoyle of rags and flesh, hair doused seaweed and feet as cold as pebbles. Your mind is cavernous, an empty void. Time passes…seconds, minutes, perhaps hours. Time passes…

Something stirs. Below the level of consciousness, something sparks and ignites into thought. A cerebration that moves your legs and stands you up. Like an automaton you advance to the edge of the precipice. Below, way below, the sand and sea kiss like strangers…

If I were to step forward…
Now!
*Futile…*
*The waters of insanity are…*
*Your own creation.*

Somewhere out there the sea has become as sibilant as a snake, while between you and it a barely discernible ribbon of sand – from which indiscriminate rocks sprout like blots of ink – stretches into a darkened, inconclusive horizon. Is it a mental aberration…or did an inkblot move? Suddenly, your eyes blaze with the intensity of laser beams in the night. Someone is walking – strolling – along the beach. Like a moth to a flame – even as a token of resistance raises its head – the motion attracts you, but this last remnant of protest dies as quickly as it forms, granting your gaze a hitherto unknown ability to be drawn and telescoped to the movement on the shoreline. Leaning perilously close to the edge gives you the impression of watching a slow-moving insect on a gravel path, and in that moment, somehow, the darkness disperses like mist, allowing your vision to penetrate the opacity, to become more clearly focussed, to function with the precision of a zoom lens that illuminates its subject of interest with abnormal clarity. It is the figure of a girl, swathed in a long, dark flowing cloak, split up the front, displaying quick flashes of white legs as she walks. Her hair, free and unnaturally long, dances and sways in unison with the voluminous, billowing garment around her. And as you watch – rooted to the spot – she stops and stands perfectly still. The wind howls, the sea hisses and the rain falls. As if becoming aware of your intrusive observation, she slowly turns and raises her face – and the hammering in your skull returns, alongside a rampant heartbeat and undignified stare. Can it be down to the distance, the miasmic atmosphere or your own sense of delusion that seems to rob her face of features?

Galvanised into action your legs pump like pistons as you run. Further along the track there is a path that sinuously winds down the cliff face to the beach, and although you cannot recall ever having visited this location before, you are sure of the path's existence and experience no sense of surprise locating it. Without a second thought you gallop down its length, snaking in and out of any number of peaks and jagged needles of rock, jumping over fallen boulders, bounding across precarious footholds, hopping and springing, descending like a startled gazelle, while all the time trying to keep the distant female figure in sight. Momentarily you panic, fear you have lost her, before a movement catches your eye, confirming she is still there. Faster and faster you follow her, gradually gaining momentum, almost out of control, mercifully oblivious to the threat of certain disaster awaiting you should you trip or stumble, as nothing matters to you outside the appearance of that figure who seems to hold the key to any number of recent riddles – not even the ripple of earth that tails you, or rocks that begin to loosen, or the gravel that stirs, shifts and crumbles, tumbling slowly, jerkily, prior to the whole cliff face moving and subsiding behind your fleet-footed steps. As it does so, it takes with it the very path along which you scamper, but you barely notice. Finally reaching the base of the escarpment in safety, you sprint out onto open terrain, completely unaware of the landslide in your wake, or of the prodigious tearing – a raking cataract of loosened clay – as the whole section of land pours down, spewing red soil over umber sand. On you race, faster and faster, heart pounding against ribs, breath burning like fire in your throat – and yet still you find yourself incapable of gaining on the apparently casually idling personage before you, who continues at a relative distance, as though within the manufacture of a dream. Only once does she turn her head sufficiently – to make sure you are still in pursuit – for establishment of the eerie fact her face is nothing more than a pale, blank space in the darkness. By now you are on the shoreline, feet splashing in the volatile waves of the ocean, whose waters have started to boil and bubble, as if somehow angered by your presence. Like a rabid hound, it rebelliously rises and snarls, snapping at your heels. But on you run. Motivated like a tortured athlete, or a hunted stag, you accelerate past images of light and darkness, and of blurred shapes of birds in flight. And as you tear on through a world that is rapidly becoming reduced to one of just sound and indefinite colour, the spouting foam spatters over you and a whistling wind buffets you, plummeting you through a vortex of disorientation, transforming you into nothing more than a careering particle in a state of motion and pain. You are lost soul, suspended between infinity and eternity, running side by side with madness…

Stop!
Breath rasps.
Pulse races.
She has gone.
Vanished.

Looking around, you view a deserted beach – as empty and as comfortless as a ruined church. Aggravated and disturbed from slumber, the sea is suddenly an explosive mass of uncontrolled energy, and you stand, silhouetted against its turbulence, like a thwarted, voracious wolf. Rain falls and lightning slashes the sky, while you await breathlessly amidst the fulgurations, hoping to catch a glimpse of human activity – but to no avail. Under thunder bombing night clouds, you search and search – but nothing is forthcoming. She has disappeared like a vaporised spirit, dissolved in the rain. Against a descending curtain of morbidity, you feel stunned, rejected and abandoned. Something solid touches your calves and you slump down onto a convenient rock, exhausted, and consternation smothers you once more. The damaged floodgates of your resistance have reopened, allowing cascading dreams, visions, nightmares, illusions and featureless faces to swarm back into you mind, threatening your reason with their irrationality. And once again you ask yourself the meaning of such things, and who – or what – perpetuates them? Are they real, or some phantasmagorical attack on weakened senses – exploitation of an overworked, anguished imagination? Perhaps, due to a general deterioration of physical health and low spiritual morale, your mind has stepped into the sub reality – the solipsism – of your fantasies. Or, maybe it is just a case – as Veronica opines – of you having been alone too long – current symptoms merely the prologue to a dreaded but not unanticipated psychosis. Ruminating on your life you burrow for clues and presages, but there are only the dreams – or, mistakes, as you referred to them – which, in isolation, present themselves as innocuous events, although, strung together as a series of…'happenings', they hint at possessing a more ominous characteristic – perhaps a potential to build up and develop into…something permanent and inexplicable? Yet, would that 'something' be real, or psychological? The incident of the indoor 'storm' was traumatic, surpassing anything previously experienced. Could such an event, on that scale, ever be fabricated in some way? Could it have *actually* been imagined? Veronica had also witnessed it – but what did that prove? Could she, too, be just another figment in a vast parade of figments? Is she, in fact, insubstantial? Her recent return had been unheralded and unexpected. So, did that mean your best and only friend is some kind of conjured up, somnambulistic hallucination? Wow! In the face of such an alarming feasibility, everything, like an out of control oil well, bursts to the surface – anger, frustration, doubt, an extreme sense of insecurity, subdued aggravation, all rising into an inordinate rage that grabs you by the scruff of the neck, shaking away residual sentimentality in a splash of red hatred – of the world, the universe, and of the self. Springing to your feet, you clench your fists and tense your muscles until nerve ends sear like the flames of a blowtorch – while, as if mimicking your explosive emotions, the sea adopts the mannerisms of some kind of feral, taunted and teased creature. At the same time, above it, clouds spit rain with venom, as lightning becomes the snapping, glittering teeth in a demon's mouth, the thunder his laughter. Flinging your hands and face to the heavens, your voice rises in verbal retaliation, joining the elemental cacophony. I refuse to submit to this! You cry. I refuse to submit to this persecution! Before sinking to your knees in desperation and exhaustion…

I lie on my stomach on a flat and desolate beach: Dali-esque, smooth, endless. Rain patters gently on my cheek, its droplets as soft as the padded feet of a cautious spider. While one eye is closed, half immersed in soft sand, the other eye is open, and through it I can see the now calm and distant sky on the horizon. Washed up seashells, grains of wet shingle and tiny pebbles cover my hand, which, from this distorted angle, seems to be far, far away.

I lie without moving.

Tired…so, so…fucking tired…

Pain…
Returning…
Growing…
Hurting…
Whiteness…
White-ness.
The glare subsides…
The pain recedes…
Darkness.

*

Turning my head, I stare out to sea. Above me, a frantic call of a gull; on the horizon, a strange glow – deep red. Memory of the dream causes my heart to leap – but the fear is groundless. The colour is not on or in the water; it is the pigment of the sky, augmenting, becoming first orange, then yellow, before spreading out from the blinding light at its centre. As it advances, slowly, I screw up my eyes against its aura. Within it, I think I can discern a shape: elliptical, smooth as polished glass. Nearer and nearer it comes, until it fills the whole sky: gargantuan, miles wide, like a secondary sun – but closer. For a brief moment I think I can make out a dark, humanoid form silhouetted against the heliacal incandescence…but I'm not sure.

Outside…pain, loneliness…
Inside…peace, tranquillity…
Freedom from the white space…
Maybe….

Voices…
From long ago. Perhaps the insemination. Perhaps…
"I'm worried, doctor. He doesn't go out much. Hardly has any friends. Spends most of his time drawing, sketching – horrible things."
"What kind of things?"
"Monsters. Monsters and things. Vampires and werewolves and ghouls and zombies – you know what I mean. It isn't natural, is it?"
"Mmmhh…"
"I mean to say – at his age: it isn't natural – not for an eight-year-old. Look at him: so pale, so thin. Not healthy, if you ask me. Not healthy, at all. What do *you* think, doctor?"
"Does he have any, erm…bad dreams, or the like?"
"Don't know, to be honest, doctor. He doesn't talk much."
"I see…"

I did tell her, I'm sure. I did. I remember, I said:
"I love you, Domino…"
"I love you, too."
"…and I will never let you go."
*Lies!*
*All fucking…lies…*

When…
When did, or will, these things occur?

*It matters not.*
*The only reality is the microsecond of...*now!

Raising yourself into a reclining position, you stare at the silent, enigmatic female figure in front of you. She stands amidst jagged rocks, facing the now calm sea, head lowered, 'watching' the waves gently nibble and chuckle around her bare feet. In the pose of some long, lost Renaissance work of art, she remains motionless, reflective, the ocean breeze gently caressing her blanket of hair, lifting it tenderly from her back as the long samite cloak beneath waltzes about her frame, moulding shimmering folds to the contours of her body. But if her stature is perfection, her face is still, to you, as blank and as white as a sacred wafer. Even so...as you ponder on the sticking point of identity, you are struck by a familiarity of stance, and by its outline cast against the flat, glistening water. There is something recognisable about the aloof, almost hostile manner that seems to be a catwalk characteristic of many truly beautiful women. Nevertheless, your interest is drawn back to the...'white blur' above the ivory pillar of her neck, as an amazing phenomenon – nothing less than a transformation – takes place. The flesh – if it can be so called – begins to move and squirm under the Daedalian fingers of an invisible master sculptor. Features become impressed and stretched, writhing, moulding and remoulding as the 'artist' seeks to create one particular portrait from numerous others. Transfixed, you stare as the physiognomy changes, not once but again and again, simulacrums of stunning pulchritude appearing and dissolving before you. As they do so, you witness – among others – personifications of the goddess Diana, of Helen of Troy, of Aphrodite, and of Circe – momentarily, you even see the startled visage of Veronica. But descriptive superlatives become inappropriate as the eyes, mouths and other constituent essences of desire form and evanesce, as though sketched and then erased on a sheet of drawing paper, while all the time you wonder...can it be? Can it, truly be she? Overcome by emotion and memories, you close your eyes – but as you do so something extremely bizarre manifests itself inside your head. It is as if your mind has sprouted wings and flown from the boundaries of your own skull. Fear grabs you, attempts to draw you back, to deter you from reopening your eyes. And yet, still, you *do* reopen them – but only to view a nightmare, one in which your vantage point has incomprehensibly altered, forcing you to observe things from a different location in space. Without having stood, walked or moved of your own volition, you find yourself staring at the girl's rear. A second ago, you were *there* – now you are *here*. The spatial aberration – like a modern-day St. Thomas revelation – brings with it an awareness of alien content, assuring you of the figure's genuine self. It *is* Domino. *It is!* And she stands before you as a true embodiment of your lost and lamented love. However, you experience no alarm at this knowledge because, somehow, both your attitude and demeanour have changed. A strength and confidence, previously unbeknown to you, surges through your very being. Gentleness, compassion and tenderness have absconded like migrating birds – leaving improbity, turpitude and baseness to rule as natural instincts. Your whole philosophical outlook has been eclipsed by a self-satisfying ponerology. Likewise, desire, for the only desire you are experiencing at this moment is one of licentious intent. A rampant satyriasis, devoid of affection, empathy or sensitivity, has you in a vice-like grip, and even though you can recognise and locate the schizoid alienation, you are incapable of controlling it, being somehow coerced into submitting to its influence, and to perceive life through the eyes of a travesty – one that betrays the inner secrets of your soul. Momentarily relenting, you allow the flames of obscenity to engulf you, before natural fear creates a counterattack – one that is not very strong, but nevertheless sufficient to rent the burgeoning perversity. It grants an instant respite in which to close your eyes and open them again, and in the infinitesimal microsecond it takes to lower your lids, you observe an image of a recumbent figure spread out on the very patch of beach where you, yourself, are reclining. Blinking fiercely, you attempt to reconjure the darkness within which the figure remains as though composed of fire, and you see his shape and solidity, his place in space and time, his look of complete bewilderment and disbelief – for it is your own personage, observed externally. Incredibly, you have been able to contemplate yourself through the eyes and mind of another, at the same time feeling the surrogate's strength, hate, and fervent, twisted carnality. Such an internal disclosure fills you with astonishment and fright, creating an aversion to the reopening of your eyes, because you know the sight that will be there to greet you. At this moment, even the dreaded psychosis you feared becomes the more acceptable alternative – at least it would be accompanied by the 'reality' of the unequivocal description of language. In actual fact, awareness of such rationality must surely render the prospect of insanity invalid – disclosing the delirium as transitory and impermanent. But this conjecture fails to stop your mind from slipping through a psychological slalom, over the unsteady stepping stones of sanity and madness, while suffusing conflicting personalities – one civilised the other bestial. Recalling the acrimonious dispute between Veronica and yourself, you wonder if her hypothesis had been correct. Is it possible that what she witnessed was this very schism you are now speculating on? Were you truly responsible for the anomalous storm back in the atelier? Surmising the heinous alter ego did show through your human guise, did *she* become aware of the vision, even while *you* remained oblivious to it? If so, how many times has it broken out before? Once – twice – many? If at all? It could be that you have visited this particular corner of hell on numerous previous occasions, only to be robbed of the intellection by self-suppression and guilt. Questions, dilemmas, schizophrenic altercation – illusions? As your head begins to pulsate, you notice a deterioration of concentration. Like some mental peristalsis, pain pumps in, forcing rational thought out. How do you combat such a thing? Being at a loss for an answer, you hide within the darkness of yourself, perhaps awaiting even a surrealistic resolution. But nothing comes…

How long you remain thus is uncertain, as the summoning of required observational courage seems to take an eternity. Eventually, though, managing to open your eyes and determine your gaze, you stare at the now accursed spot. What did you expect to see? Nebulous anticipation failed to prepare you, and the ensuing shock is as potent as it was unexpected. There, on a rock, nestled in the shadows of the cliff – from where your alternative viewpoint had been projected – resides a weird and sinister figure. Even though possessing the proportional characteristics of a homunculus – but more simian, ugly, almost deformed – there sits a…what? something composed of a dwarfish morphology? an imp? a resuscitated Australopithecus? a…a goblin? Whatever he – it – is, it is naked and it is white (although the leathery flesh appears as more of a pale grey beneath its patchy, hirsute covering), resting on his – it's? – haunches, long, muscular arms wrapped around the fronts of its drawn up legs, and great, talon fingered hands clasped like interlocking…claws about its shins. Crouching obscenely, it watches the girl with still and silent vigilance. Raising yourself up, you stare, stupefied and fascinated by the eldritch scene before you. The only sound is that of your own breathing – even the ocean has been quietened, as the nightmarish tableau freezes into a static, surrealistic incarnation. On the periphery, a little movement still flickers, here, there and about – the lapping waves, the gently coruscating cloak and slowly dancing hair of the girl – but the most pronounced disturbance is evoked by the grotesque creature to her rear becoming aware of your presence and slowly turning its head to face you. And in an instant, you realise you know that visage, recognise it from your awesome dreams as the chimera that regularly assails you from the depths of your dystopian fantasies. The head is large – slightly too large for the body – and anthropoid, tapering towards the crown, covered in thick, soot black hair, while – as though to counterbalance such an occipital extreme – the jaw is heavy and hypognathous, beneath shiny, bone coloured flesh. The mouth – a wide, froglike slit – houses monstrous, glittering teeth, standing arrayed in a rictus of permanent malice, while above this aperture, the nose is wide and flat, with gaping, flared nostrils that would be more at home on the countenance of a silver backed gorilla. And yet, such details fade almost into insignificance when compared to the eyes, which glitter like smouldering cinders – sparkling orbs of nefarious intent, gleaming and twinkling from the deep shadows of a heavy, overhanging forehead with the burning, pythonic stare of a reptile. And it is this stare that reaffirms a communication between two minds, two personalities, antilogous yet fused, harbouring similar aspirations and objectives – only the methods of achievement remain differentiated, or in opposition. However, the radical measures adopted by the particular mind of this creature are abhorrent to you, alarming you to such an extent that you are able to at least tear your gaze away from his, in order to search the dark, glinting wall of rock for the more desirable figure of the girl. But that very same wall of rock – which, in the eerie gaze of an emergent moon, has now seemingly taken on the appearance of the vertebrae of some freshly discovered dinosaur – reveals nothing but twisted shadows that encourage other tenebrous shapes to adopt similarly misrepresented identities and to disguise reality. For the Domino doppelganger has disappeared, her unexplained absence once more purposely subjecting you to the loneliness of obliterated anticipation. Disillusioned emptiness returns, but before sinking into its beckoning embrace you retaliate with an emotional gusto that surprises you. Refusing to dwell on negativity, you rise to your full height, determined to resolve this mystery by positive action. Adopting the mannerisms of a demented ant, you race along the moonlit sand, scanning the beach, searching the shallows and peering around littoral rocks, driven by the obvious notion that she must be here – somewhere. She cannot have simply evaporated into thin air. In spite of the puzzles and complexities of recent events, you remain defiant, refusing to submit to this current illusion – because that is what it is. You have been the victim of some anonymous, conjuring prankster, the hub of a series of practical jokes – the perpetrator of which can only be the faceless – faceless? why choose that adjective? – stranger who, having thought it safe to crawl between Veronica's legs with impunity, now discovers the existence of a rival. So, the time has come to put a stop to puerile games. An immediate unriddling of the riddle is called for. And yet, despite such newfound resolution, the mysterious figure of the girl – the Domino facsimile? – remains absent. Where the hell can she be? Perhaps the 'joke' has misfired – perhaps she slipped and fell into the water, where she now lies, injured, slowly drowning only a matter of feet or metres from your straining eyes. If this is so, then the imp, goblin…made-up 'thespian' or whatever he really is, must surely relinquish his role in the defunct prank and help in the quest to save her. Not surprisingly, though, your search reveals that he, too, has vanished. Returning in haste to where the thing had been perched, you can find no trace of his – its – existence. Once again, your applied practicality becomes suspect, with panic re-entrenching itself as you continue to dash hither and thither about the shore. Reaching almost a state of lunacy you sprint towards the sea, before which you drop to your knees, only to suddenly scramble to your feet again in order to pursue an elusive shadow – probably that of a low flying gull – inland, where you discover… nothing. As though of their own volition, your legs carry you once more to the water's edge, where you stumble and then crawl on hands and knees towards what could possibly be a floating body but which turns out to be nothing more than a piece of rotting driftwood. She has gone. It – he – has gone. *If* they had ever existed at all. Amidst an uncontrollable wave of anguish, as the first light of dawn suffuses the eastern sky, you rise dejectedly and slowly make your way home…

I stumble into my abode like the survivor of a shipwreck, making a direct course for the bathroom. Not caring anymore about the possible terrors residing therein, I tear off my clothes, leaving a trail of textile entrails in my wake. Stepping under the modest shower, I turn on the flow, relishing the warmth of the water as it cascades onto my ice-cold skin. Temperature adjustment allows extra heat, the stream becoming hotter – hotter still – until my flesh turns first pink and then red, like a boiled lobster.Having tolerated the burn for as long as I can, I switch to extreme coldness. The transition is startling cnough to seduce me into believing that it is not only cleansing my body but also my spirit, at the same time flushing away all the doubts, fears and neuroticism until the burdens begin to slide from my shoulders as easily as did my wet, discarded clothing. With trembling fingers rampaging through my hair, I raise my face so that the flow can sprinkle down on to my knotted features, causing me to wince as my nails scratch so severely small droplets of blood intermingle with the downpour – pink rivulets meandering erratically over my deltoids and down between my shoulder blades. I follow this with a scurrying soap scrub over the rest of my body, rubbing and scraping in a descent across my chest, down and around my abdominals into my groin and buttocks, along the length of my thighs and finally to my calves, ankles and feet. Lifting each foot in turn, as though peeling off a pair of trousers, I attempt to strip away effluvium that has become analogous with my troubles. Satisfied, I stand rock still, as seconds and minutes tick by; the only movement being the tumbling spray and the inhaling and exhaling of the tortured air in my lungs.

After towelling my whole body with determination, I march militaristically to the bed. Against the sound of loudly protesting springs I throw myself across it to lie nude and spread-eagled, squinting up at the turquoise morning sky through half-closed eyelids.

There comes an incomplete but acceptable peace.

You rise in a haze of brilliant sunshine. Its beams grope through the skylight like celestial antennae. A sensation of weightlessness abides, as though your feet are sinking into cool moss. Looking down, you observe the golden glow that surrounds you almost with indifference. Everything seems to take place in slow-motion. Slipping on a clean shirt and denims, you approach the painting on the easel. It only takes seconds for you to decide what to do. Squeezing embryonic colours from their tubes, you take up a brand-new brush and...begin.

"Wake up!"

The words crackle intermittently, like distant electrical charges.

"Come on! Wake up!"

"Mmmhh?"

"I said, wake up! Damn you! Open your eyes!"

"Wha –?"

"Jesus! Can you hear me? Wake up! Snap out of it!"

A deep warmth smothers my right cheek – and then my left.

"Will you bloody-well wake up? Come on! Come *on!*"

My cheeks become warmer, warmer – hot – gaining in intensity with each passing moment. "Whassamatter? Wha –?" Opening my eyes, I watch impassively as Veronica swings her hand from side to side. It swishes like a pendulum, back and forth in front of my vision. "What the hell are you doing?" I ask.

Throwing back her head she inhales, deeply. "Thank God for that. I thought you were a gonna."

"A...a gonna? Wha –?"

As she stares at me with a frightened expression, her breathing comes in heavy gasps, as though she has run a long way. "I couldn't wake you. You were damned-well comatose. Can you feel anything?"

"Feel...?"

"Your face, for Chrissake! Doesn't it hurt?"

"Hurt?"

"Yes, dummy! Hurt!"

"Hur-t?"

"Do we have to converse in monosyllables? Me, Veronica; you –"

"What the fuck…?"

"I've been slapping hell out of you," she explains. "You were like a lump of dough." As I shake my head in bewilderment, she adds: "I really thought you were gone."

"Gone? Gone where?"

She ignores me. "So bloody still; barely a pulse. And so damned pale – white! Have you been taking anything?" As I study her face with the mobile uncertainty of a drunken man, her hands suddenly plummet like the grabs of a crane, gripping my shoulders with a strength born of desperation. "Have you fucking-well taken anything?"

"Taken…any…thing?" My words are slurred, existing only as sounds, refusing to hold significance.

Sensing that I'm slipping away once more, she continues to slap my face – even harder. "Shit! Don't go flaking out on me again. Come on! Snap out of it!"

I ascend by necessity; the attack is becoming painful. "Will you cut that out? Jesus Christ!"

"Then, tell me."

"Tell you…what?"

She shakes me with all the force she can muster. "If you've taken anything – pills, powders, acid?"

Managing to raise my hands, I grip her wrists, while trying to clear the fuliginous cloud from my brain. "No! No pills, no powders, no LSD – no any-fucking-thing, okay?"

"Something else, then?"

"Huh?"

"Something else…You know…" she mimes the action of pushing a syringe into her arm "…You know what I mean."

"Veronica! For Christ's –"

"That's all right, then." She sighs, relievedly, at the same time reclaiming her wrists from my grip. "All…right."

"Can you get off me?"

Looking down with surprise, she realises she is straddling me, one knee each side of my chest. "There was a time…" she grunts, disconsolately.

"What?"

"Never mind." Climbing off the bed, she stands with hands on hips. "So, are you going to get up already, or what? You do realise it's eight-thirty, right?"

"In the evening?"

"Of course, in the evening. Look at the sky up there." Her brows knit into a doubtful frown. "Are you sure you've not taken anything?"

"Honestly…" I start, before hesitating. "At least, I don't think I have."

"You don't *think*, you have? You're not...*certain?*"

"If truth be known, I'm certain of sod all. I can't even remember coming to bed...although, I think I dreamed I did..."

"You *think* you...*dreamed* you did? What the hell kind of –?"

"Forget it!" I snap.

"No, no; let's not, huh? What you're saying is, you've had another one of...*those* dreams."

Sighing, heavily, I rub my face with a shaky hand. "Yeah, yeah, yeah; something like that."

"They're getting worse," she observes.

"Huh?"

"The dreams...getting worse." Touching her lips with a forefinger, she chides: "Watch my mouth: the...dreams...d-r-e-a-m-s...getting...g-e-t-t-i-n-g...worse...w-o-r-s-e...getting...w-o-r –"

"Okay, okay; message received, loud and clear, alright?"

"Seriously, though," she persists, "they are becoming stronger, more potent, more frequent. I think you should see someone."

"A psychoanalyst?"

"You hardly need a dentist."

"There you go again."

"Well, I mean, why don't you just try helping yourself for a change? Do something positive, instead of lying around the place, like some otiose –"

"Bollocks!" I remonstrate. "There's nothing fucking wrong with me."

"The patient is always the last to know."

"Meaning?"

She folds her arms. "You know damned-well what I mean. Just go take a look at yourself in the mirror, for God's sake."

"*Fuck* the mirror!" I half shout, half snarl, feeling a serpent biting into the back of my neck.

Staring at me, eyes wide, mouth open, Veronica is visibly shaken by my outburst. I lapse into silence as she tries to play it down. "There's no need to be abusive, you know. I wasn't implying that you've lost your good looks, or anything like that."

Swinging my legs off the bed, I bury my face in my hands. They tremble like dying leaves on a windswept tree. "Sorry," I say. "Didn't mean to get so heavy; purely a reflexive response."

In an instant she is on her knees beside me; her lips close to my ear. "It's alright, my love. But what the hell is going on, huh? What's happening to you?"When I shrug, unable to formulate an answer, she continues: "You can tell me, you know. You can talk to me. You can talk to me about... anything you like." Soothingly, her fingers start to smooth the hair on the back of my head. "It's not good, you keeping everything bottled up like this. Tell me…Trust me."

"The thing is…I simply don't know what's happening. I wish I did. I really wish I could make some sense out of it."

"Tell me," she coos. "Maybe I can help. You know: fresh perspective and all that. At least, let me try."

"I have no idea where to start," I tell her, truthfully. "Except to say that I…I can't seem to be able to pin down what's real anymore. It's…it's a kind of…paramnesia, I suppose; I can't make up my mind whether I'm dreaming or awake. Events have become…desultory…running into each other… overlapping…inextricably mixed up, like colours in a kaleidoscope. Maybe it's narcolepsy, and I'm just drifting off into fucking dreamland all the time. I…I simply don't…don't know anymore. Ah, shit! Listen to me, I must sound fucking nuts. '*Whom the gods wish to destroy they first make mad*', uh?"

As she watches me, intently, her face only inches from mine, her eyes are full of genuine compassion, with no hint of derision. On the other hand, there seems to be an element of relief – either because I now appear to have shaken off the torpor, or, because, at last, I am making an attempt at communication with her…a purgative explanation; once more, after all this time, I have taken her into my confidence. Is that a flash of triumph I see in her eyes? Fuck! Even now my cynicism remains ripe enough to swallow. Forget it, you arrogant bastard. (You? *You?* I *am* conversing with myself, right? It is *my* thoughts controlling this…this soliloquy, isn't it?) Emerging back into the…*real* world, I blink at her, at her nearness as she caresses my face between her hands, and the touch of her lips as they kiss my forehead.

"My poor love," she whispers.

Lowering my gaze, I continue: "I wouldn't be surprised, even at this very moment, to awaken and find myself…somewhere else. To discover that all this is…unreal. That…that *you* are unreal."

"Oh! You've no need to worry on that score," she assures me. "I *am* real. Just to make absolutely sure, though…" Her mouth approaches and captures my lips. After kissing me, long and slow, she smiles. "Any doubts?"

Knowing what she is referring to, I manage return the smile. "There's somatic reaction in dreams, too, you know."

Her expression lapses into seriousness. "Oh, I'm sure you can tell the difference." And as we stare at each other, suspended in the ineffable moments of passing time, digesting the obvious tacit concessions, her gaze drops to my mouth. "Just in case you can't, though…"

This time I take her in my arms and the embrace becomes prolonged. Her tongue pushes between my teeth and probes the inside of my mouth, like a warm snake, darting, flicking, searching, while the satin petals of her lips are soft, pliant and wet. Moving my fingers along the length of her spine, to where her shirt has pulled out of the waistband of her denims, they touch the bare skin, just above her buttocks. My other hand is buried in the full mass of her hair.

After our mouths part she is content to push her face into the side of my neck, whereby follows a silence in which we both contemplate the implications of what has just happened. Despite the hiatus, my respiration has become acute and I can feel my heart pumping and pounding as though accompanied by a section of percussionists. There are palpitations, too, the kind that come when one holds one's breath for a prolonged period. Perhaps I have been holding my breath. Or, perhaps it's just the tension, as, simultaneously, my tongue decides to stick to the roof of my mouth – a trait common to my person in times of stress or excitement – while thoughts scramble about inside my head like the start of a pigeon race. It feels as if I have been waiting for this moment my whole life.

"Thank you," I whisper.

After a brief pause, her voice rises, quietly, slightly muffled. "It's not a chore, you know." Attempting to look down at her, I move my head, but I can feel her neck muscles becoming tense, relaying a negative message; she wants to remain as we are; she wants to speak but she does not want to look me in the eye when she does so. "Coming here, I mean. It's not a chore. I don't visit for thanks or imbursement."

"I know," I acknowledge, almost indiscernibly. "And I –"

"Uh-uh." Reaching up, blindly, she touches my mouth with her fingertips. "Let me say this." Another brief pause. "I come because I care about you – because I care about what happens to you. We were always good friends, weren't we, you and I?" I nod. "Even when we went our separate ways, I mean." I start to say something, but think better of it. The tips of her fingers trace a line across my lips. "There's no need to explain," she goes on. "I understand…I understand all that occurred; and I believe that our…friendship…transcends such emotional…infractions. I say that because it does seem to have survived some serious adversity – absence, intrusion…" Another pause, during which I contemplate things I'm tempted to expound, to explicate; but again, I honour her tacit request to stay both motionless and mute. "I must admit, there have been occasions when I thought, perhaps, we had drifted too far apart, when absence had been too prolonged, when the gulf had, arguably, become insuperable – and yet, something inside me cattle prodded me into accepting that this could never be the case. Does that sound naïve to you? Romanticised?" Once more I open my mouth to speak, once more she deters me. "Maybe it does; maybe I am. I'm also convinced that when people care for each other – I mean, *really* care – then no situation is entirely insurmountable. Love, amity, adjusts to almost any situation – but sometimes it can take a while. Total irreconcilability is brought about by the chasm of indifference, not by the chasm of distance. We have suffered the latter, but – in spite of everything that took place – never the former. I'm not trying to claim that within the latter duration we have not been exposed to independent experiences that have obviously created independent memories – ones that remain as niches in our brains, lighting up when we think of them, like private peepshows of the past. It's just that they do not belong to the world of the present or to the people we have become. Ergo, as time goes by, those niches fade somewhat, becoming less illuminated, more difficult to resurrect – unless, of course, we make a constant effort to retain them; in so doing, we tend to neglect other experiences and situations which hold within them sparks of alternative, more sustainable illuminations. New illuminations, although not strong enough to eclipse the old ones, could, up to a point, parallel them. If we...allow them to...If we want them to...Do you understand what I'm struggling to say here?" Raising her face, her eyes are expectant but apprehensive.

Slowly nodding an affirmative, I tell her: "Yes. Yes, I do. I understand perfectly."

Lowering her face again, she sighs. "These...alternative illuminations can take many forms: some prosaic, some not. Travel, for example...or work...or...friendship, each possessing the seed to become more than... more than... definitional. Take...friendship: sometimes it can hold the key to transition, by palliating a...loss or...or a love that has..." at this point she hesitates, unsure whether or not to go on. It is virgin territory; I have allowed no one to step here before. A touch of my hand to her cheek grants her dispensation. She continues: "Friendship does not need to be so demanding; it eschews some of love's selfishness, some of its arrant, emotional cohesion – its desperation when things go wrong. Demands are not so extreme, as friendship does not...change gear, so to speak; it just kind of idles in neutral; there is a relaxation of mood that is not subject to jealousy or possessiveness – and things are much clearer when unobscured by jaundiced passion. Don't you think? Am I making sense?"

I give her a tight hug. "Of course, you are – and you can put a name to it, if you want. There's no call for metaphor or circumspection here; I don't mind – not when it comes from you."

The concession is fully digested, before she concludes: "So, for the time being we shall call it friendship, then. We won't try to force anything.

Nevertheless, I want you to know...if ever you feel...if ever you need something...some*one*, to help fill the void...Not now. I don't mean now...but later. Perhaps...later...

"Yes," I agree, somewhat absently. "Perhaps...later...Perhaps..."

Tilting her head way back, she looks up at me. "Who knows what the future holds, huh?"

"Indeed," I say. "Who knows?"

Sitting, motionless, we allow the penetrative thoughts to settle like dust. Finding myself unable to come up with anything meaningful to contribute – if she actually expects me to – I remain silent. However, at the same time, I cannot help wondering: was she searching for a reaction, or simply making a statement? As I ruminate on this, her voice begins again...on this occasion, low, barely audible: "The hurt *will* go, my love. Truly. And the heart *will* heal. It always does. *Before* it does, though...If I can help in some way...If you'll let me, I mean...then..."

As I forcibly lift her chin back up with my hand, I gaze down into her now tear-filled eyes, telling her: "You are such a beautiful person, Veronica, that...that I..." Involuntarily, a deep, intrusive sigh causes me to visibly shudder.(No one has ever shed tears for me before.) Releasing my grip, I drop my hand away. As I do so, she tilts her head to the side, and I can feel her eyes on my face. Gently but determinedly touching my cheek with her fingers, she succeeds in easing my gaze back in her direction.

"Don't," she says, softly. "Don't...look away, like that." As my features crack into a bittersweet smile, I exhale sharply through my nostrils. It is almost the sound of a protesting animal. "I know how much it pains you." Her fingers remain, pressed against my cheek. "I know, because I feel it, too – when I see you like this."

Taking her hand in mine, I stare at it for a few seconds, before planting a light kiss on her fingertips. "If...only..."

"If only...?"

As she lowers her head, I place a protective arm around her shoulders, running my fingers through her hair. We sit, hardly moving, until...

"What...about...you know...?" I ask.

Her reply is to reach up and gently brush her lips against my cheek. For the first time since...Domino, I feel my body stir. Her breath is warm on my face and tickles its way along my jawline and down the side of my neck.

"Veronica..." I whisper. "...are you...sure...about this. Are you...?" As she presses my hand to her breast, I look into her eyes, knowing that an expression of helplessness is shrouding my face.

"Shhh..." she breathes.

"But…"

"It's all right," she moans. "It's…all…right." Even as I hesitate, feeling like a traitor, her kisses persist. "I'm sure…I'm…sure."

Closing my eyes, I reciprocate the oral embrace.

"I can…ease some of the…pain." Her voice is like a soft breeze on a tropical night. "Let me…let me help take…some of it…away."

Nestling at the nape of my neck, her small, busy fingers send a shiver along my spine. This time I relax, capitulate, let the rising tide swallow me, pull me down into the…esoteric depths, where… your – *my* – demon of carnality squats, waiting patiently, knowing that, at long last…he is to be…freed of bondage. (What? What is this?) Entwining your – *my!* – own fingers in the lush thickness of her tresses – savagely, unlike her action – you – *I!* – turn her face up with such force that a gasp for air escapes her throat, and you – *I!* – press your – *my!* – mouth hard on to the offered, beckoning lips. (Something is wrong here. What is happening? Is this a dream? Another one of *those* dreams?) She clings to me – *you!* – fingers hooked into the muscles of my – *your!* – arms, while her mouth squirms and pulsates beneath yours – *mine! Dammit!* – her tongue licking against *your* own – tickling, teasing, urging *you* on. (Get out of my head! This cannot be! Get the *fuck* out of my head!) Moaning quietly, she moulds her body against…me? – *you!* There is a momentary retreat – as *you* relieve her of her shirt – after which *your* hand moves, at first soothingly, across her face, before descending to her silken throat – where it…*hesitates* – and *you* experience a *sudden*, overwhelming impulse to *tighten your grip – to sq-uee-ze! Through a growing tension in your groin you sense the presence of your demon, you feel his kinaesthetic influence, his goading – his proclivity for inflicting pain.* As on that moonlit beach, I – *you!* – seem to be incapable of controlling a… *perverse pleasure in violence* – but this time you – *I!* – am rescued by a physical movement. Veronica twists her torso slightly, and the conatus dies. Yet, the shadow of the…*entity* remains at my – *your!* – shoulder. Taking an offered, delicate breast, I – *you!* – tighten *your* trembling fingers, sink *your* nails into its softness – and she lets out a sharp cry! But, to *your* surprise, she immediately arches her back, pushing the flesh harder against the abusing – *claw?* – hand. This submissive act sends your satyr – *you!* – into *a paroxysm of lust as* – from somewhere deep inside, a warning voice of conscience commands you – *me!* – to desist, crying out that (this is wrong!) this is wrong, and to beware of an incomprehensible retribution. *But it is too late. You are lost, unable to dominate the engulfing surge* (Get out of my head! Now! Get out! Out! Out!) *pervading your body and mind. You have become a raging, rampant incubus. Laying the girl out full length on the bed, you are ensnared by your own concupiscence. With every passing second her flesh pro-nounces your mounting desire. You are beyond redemption. Powerless to help yourself, you invade her body with a mouth that is ravenous and hands – claws! – that are brutal.* (God! What is happening? It is a dream! It is! It must…be! Stop! Must…wake up! Must…) But even as you carry out this…assault, you – *I!* – realise the fervour is not all yours – *mine!* All I can think, over and over again, is…It has been so long…So, very, very long. From somewhere outside of *your*self *you* hear her voice, far aware and plaintive. 'My love…" she calls "…you're…you're…hurting me. You're…' *Ignoring her pleas, you succumb to the will of the wild man – to the innate beast that exists within us all. Dispensing with what is left of the emotional safety catch, you begin to understand the motivation behind the killer mind, identify with the twilight world of psychopathic intent – and what survives of your reason explodes in a blinding 'white' light.* (Stop! Leave me! Get out! Leave me! Wake up! Wake up – now!) *Ev-ery fibre of your – our – being has become alive, urgent, releasing the as-tringent serpent of frustration and fear that has been slowly smothering* us. *Raking and gouging with* our *claws – hands! – we snarl through clenched fangs – teeth! – becoming crueller and more merciless by the second, plun-dering her body with frightening ferocity.* (I am going to kill her! God! I am going to…No! No! This is not me! It is not…me!) 'Darling'…she cries '…you're…hurt…hurting…me!' *But while her entreaties mean one thing, her body means something else, as, even while crying out for*…us *to stop, she makes no physical effort to deter us – indeed, she seems to facilitate our progress by writhing beneath us in a frenzy as convulsive as our own. With little difficulty, we tear off her tightfitting denims, throwing them imperiously aside before dropping heavily upon her. Opening her legs wide to embrace us, she locks her ankles at the rear of our thighs, her hands sliding up over our back. Now, completely uninhibited, she gasps and gyrates beneath us, her tummy muscles undulating rhythmical-ly as her breath catches in her throat, and we become aware of a kind of oratorical flow – indecipherable words that tumble forth – but we have no desire or inclination to understand them. Instead, surprised by our ability to hold back – as we are in no way attempting to prolong an act we feel is designed for our purpose alone – we experience a sensation that goes on and on, becoming more acute, spreading, swarming through our whole being, sweeping up our – your – spinal column to alight at the base of our – your – skull like the sting of a scorpion. Burrowing through bone, into our – your – very brain, it robs us – you – of any abiding reason, any remaining control, casting us – you – into a world within yourself – the* *girl now almost superfluous, her body merely an accommodative chamber for – your – violent ingression. Your resistance is broken, swaying in a hammock of tortured nerve ends that are about to snap, to send you – me! – into an all-consuming limbo – into complete...*insanity! *The word pierces your – my! – thoughts like a falling comet, blazing a trail of cerebral lava...as you – I! – struggle to the...surface of* consciousness, *craving* rationality *like a drowning man craves air. As you – I! – do so, in a burning, coital thrust, it happens – done. Emitting a low, guttural groan of indifference, you – I! – hear her cry out, breathlessly, perhaps with pain, perhaps with pleasure – perhaps with both. You – I! – look down and realise you – I! – have her pinned beneath you – me! – spread-eagled, your – my! – hands manacling her wrists. She is like a specimen stretched out on a dissecting table, oblivious to her subjugation, lying almost peacefully, eyes closed and lips slightly parted – in a state of posed, post carnal contentment. And as you – I – observe her, tiny pearls of perspiration form and twinkle on her forehead as bright as body glitter, spreading to the rest of her torso, which she lifts while inhaling deeply, holding a breath that creates a concave hollow where her abdomen should be. Taking the weight on your – my – hands – still holding her wrists, you – I – push yourself –* myself *– up,* as she opens her eyes. With skin blending harmoniously into soft, tenebrist shadows, she appears like some luxuriously crucified feline. Caught in the moment, and somehow free of the indefinable terrors that had so recently possessed me, my mind suddenly abounds with prosodic thoughts and lyrical resonances – but I keep them to myself. As she stares up at me, with a gaze that is both intense and impenetrable, there seems to be no indication of any adverse response to my strange and – to me – nightmarishly schizoid performance. Of course, to try and explicate – to actually say anything at all – would be to dig too deeply within ourselves.

In the darkness of the night there is only the dimmed glow from a reluctant moon above.

I lie reclined on one elbow.

The girl slumbers at my side.

Her eyes are closed.

Her mouth half open.

Drawing back the sheet I scan her nakedness.

So soft and yet so firm.

So...vulnerable.

Of its own volition my hand reaches out.

Fingers curl around the column of her neck.

A pulse throbs at the side of her throat.

All I have to do I think is…squeeze.

Just…squeeze.

And it will be gone.

The *Atman* – the primal inspiration of life that inhabits all things – will be gone.

Swallowed by the nothingness that both precedes it and follows it.

Although for a while the flesh will remain.

The body will still be.

The object of desire still palpable.

But inanimate.

*'When we are, death is not come, and when death is come, we are not.'*

I move my hand and rest it between her breasts.

Beneath the corporal structure beats the heart.

The life stream of existence of animation.

The…reality.

The reality – the true image – of Veronica,

And with such fundamental awareness comes confirmation.

I have won.

The finality has not been restrained.

Reality has conquered doubt.

Because *this* is…reality.


It is morning.

(What the hell?)

Opening my – say *my*, eyes, I – say *I*, listen to the tattooing of a light drizzle on the glass overhead. Somewhere up there is the sun. It is. Even though, at the moment, it remains hidden, I can intuit its presence; somehow my mind is able to pass through the heavy clouds to a dazzling blue firmament beyond. Is my mood symptomatic of what is known as a 'value experience'? There appears to exist a freedom of spirit almost forgotten to me. My awareness is airborne, like a kite on a windy day – soaring, swooping and diving. The sensation is akin to the discovery of daylight at the end of a long, dark, suffocating tunnel. I can…breathe.

Beside me Veronica stirs quietly beneath the sheet. As her eyes flicker open, she smiles.

"Good morning," I say.

"Good morning."

We kiss, long and slow – until she pulls away.

"What's the matter?" I ask.

"I haven't cleaned my teeth," she explains.

I snort a laugh. "Neither have I."

"And yet you taste fine. How is that?"

"It must be my mood." I watch as she wrinkles her brow at me. "Healthy mind, healthy body. I am…aseptic…untarnished…reborn." A flicker of my own brow relays the humour.

"My God, but you're poetic this morning."

"All because of you," I tell her, seriously now.

As she watches the words move my lips, she touches my cheek with her hand, simultaneously raising her mouth, arching her throat. Taking the motion as a licence to proceed, I manoeuvre my fingers under the bedsheet, seeking out that so-called 'obscure object of desire'. Parting her thighs, she allows me access. Running my tongue along her jawline, I guide my kisses to her neck and shoulders while continuing to forage and probe below. Submissively, she just lies there and lets it happen.

"Mmmhh…" she murmurs. "Breakfast in bed."

After flashing her my best grin, I bury my head beneath the sheet, using my teeth and tongue to tickle a lambent path down the length of her body, where they meet up with my already industrious fingers.

From above she purrs, enigmatically: "You're not about to hurt me again…are you?"

"What are we going to do?" I ask her.

As the rain drums relentlessly on the skylight, she lies with hands tucked under the back of her head, staring upwards. "I don't know."

"I'll break the news, if you want."

"I don't know."

Later, she dozes, her breathing low, barely discernible. Studying her relaxed features, I think: What the hell have I done? What will become of us now? Resting my head on the pillow, beside her, I sigh, despairingly. Still watching her profile, my eyelids slowly descend and close.

Scuttling through the hair on my groin, her fingers grip me by the testicles and…exert pressure. I open my eyes with a start.

"You again," I say, grinning.

"I love you." The statement is unexpected and takes me by surprise.

"I…love you…too," I tell her, although somewhat hesitatingly.

"Happy?" she asks.

"Yes," I answer. "I think so. I was…until…"

"Will you miss me?"

"Silly question. How…How long will you be…gone?"

She shakes her head, slowly, thoughtfully. "As long as it takes, I suppose."

"Are you sure you don't want me to come with you?"

"I'm sure."

"I mean…there's no chance of violence – is there?"

"I don't think so."

"You're not certain?"

"No."

"Then I'd better come with you."

"No."

"But –"

"I said no. I can handle it…honestly."

Pulling on her denims, she sits on the bed.

"What time is it?" I ask, tracing a fingernail down her naked spine.

She shivers slightly. "About five-thirty – I think."

"Don't be…*too* long, will you?"

"God, I'll try not to be, but –"

"I know, I know."

Pulling on her shirt, she tucks its tail into the waistband of her Jeans, while at the same time easing her feet into lightweight shoes. Looking down at me she takes a deep breath – one that ends in a sigh.

"Are you nervous?" I enquire, fatuously.

She pulls a face. "What a bloody question. Of course, I'm nervous; I don't make a habit of this sort of thing, you know."

"Sorry." I watch her as she fluffs up her hair with her hands. "Veronica…"

"Yes?"

"You are positive…about this. I mean…I never really thought that you…that you and I…"

Her sudden glare silences me. Momentarily, it appears as though she is about to burst into a rage; but the expression vanishes just as quickly as it formed. Forcing a smile, she says: "Absolutely."

"Then come here," I order, and as she obeys, I look up at her while stupidly running a hand along the inside of her denim encased thigh.

"Will you cut that out?" she snaps.

"Don't go," I say.

"Oh, Christ!"

"Don't. I'm afraid that you'll change your mind; that you won't return."

In an instant her attitude softens and she leans towards me. Taking my head in her hands, she nestles my face into her stomach. "I have to. You know I do – but I will come back. I promise."

"You don't *have* to do anything – not yet, anyway."

"The sooner the better," she counters.

"Aw, shit!"

Pushing her away, I petulantly throw myself backwards onto the bed.

\*

Veronica has made her exit. Gone. Sitting stiffly on the edge of the bed, I stare at the backs of my hands (daring them to transform once more?) as if memory of the bathroom and of making love to Veronica will again create the illusion of claws resting on my knees. But it doesn't. Reality presides. The room remains free of anomaly. Empty. A quotidian loneliness swarms around me like a cloud of silent locusts, while a faint odour of her continues to hang in the air, as if her presence – or sense of it – has not completely evaporated; I still half expect to look up and see her pad in from the kitchen or bathroom. But the quietness emphasises her absence, nullifies the prospect of an appearance and consolidates the finality of her departure. Once again, I feel spiritually vacuous, exposed, vulnerable – open to attack. My sensory reaction is that of an animal in the bush suddenly catching a sense of danger, becoming aware of the proximity of a predator. Nerve ends are alive, intuitively alert, ready for any emergency; and yet my mind, as a logical, constructive entity, re- mains dulled, capable only of inconclusive reasoning. The atavistic in- stinct of the beast is controlling the man; I am ill at ease, but unable to pinpoint why. There is a tension in the air, as though a bomb is about to go off, accompanied by an aura of expectancy that pervades the am- bience, relaying a warning, one that grows with each passing moment, proliferating unease. I am restless. Standing and walking the length and breadth of my studio, I feel caged, as trapped as sure as if there were bars; and yet, visually, everything appears normal. Resitting on the bed, my eyes dart every which way, searching, searching for…what?

In an attempt to alleviate what has, by now, developed into a kind of threatening irregularity, I decide to indulge in some mundane, domestic activity – so I struggle into my tatty denims and plough through the corner cupboard for a clean shirt. Even achieving such a simple goal, though, brings little respite, as onerous clouds continue to invisibly gather about me. Once again, I pace the room, trying to ferret out this…this preternatu- ral oppressiveness, seeking to rationalise my discomfort, to nail them to some solid object or area, to attach a label to them. But it is hopeless; the thing is too imperspicuous, too much in the abstract to define.

Sitting once more, I adopt a different approach – what I call, elimination by extrasensory perception (something modestly akin to trying to emulate what Albert Einstein putatively labelled: 'thought experiments'). Sometimes this kind of thing works, sometimes it does not. As I skip through the preliminaries, memories of successfully picking the winners of several Grand Nationals float uppermost in my mind. So, taking a deep breath, I slowly exhale and close my eyes. Another inhalation, another exhalation. And again: in…out…in…out. My heart, which had been, up until now, thumping like a blacksmith's hammer, starts to calm, becoming less erratic; while my blood flow retards and my pulse decelerates. I am in command. I am…ready.

As my eyelids ascend, I stare directly ahead, awaiting a sign. I see nothing, I feel nothing. The area before me is blank, normal, inconspicuous. Mentally, I delete it from the rest of the room, like cutting away a portion of cake. Focussing to my right – likewise, nothing; a second helping of the cake disappears. But now I am becoming conscious of a certain…vibration, in the air – a disturbance in the milieu. With so much else accounted for, the…'threatening irregularity' begins to grow stronger, more concentrated, occupying an ever-smaller space. Stiffening perceptibly, and with mounting apprehension, I project all my…'psychic energy' behind me – even though I am positive the thing, the threat, the force, the influence – whatever it is – is not residing there. Still, the elimination process must be confirmed. It *is* confirmed and three-quarters of the cake is removed, leaving the remaining final quarter to veritably quiver with some kind of inimical potency. It harbours a…presence – one so absolute I can almost smell it.

Slowly, cautiously, almost fearing that someone – or, some*thing* – is going to physically attack me, I turn towards my left – further, slightly behind me. As the back of my neck crawls and seethes like a nest of vipers, a timpani drum pulse returns to throb in my temples. Twisting even further – until I am in position to view the whole corner of the studio – a minute part of me is perversely disappointed to find things ostensibly correct, as usual and as normal as they should be. Nevertheless, a kind of psychic palpitation definitely emanates from the area, like water being pumped through a faucet.

I peruse the items that exist there: the shelves on the wall, cluttered, untidily supporting the tools of my trade – spare paintbrushes, pencils, tubes of oil, acrylic, and gouache paint; a leather case, containing an airbrush; some measuring rules; a few geometric shapes; two bottles of Indian ink; several rolls of masking tape; two small jars of masking fluid; a beautiful Caithness paperweight (a present from Domino); a miniature statuette of Michelangelo's 'David'; and a selection of paperback books. Leaning against and along one wall, there are some large boards and stretched canvasses; a bijou cabinet, in which are stored countless 'reference' photographs; and the easel, holding the current, almost completed work-in-progress.

Only now, for the first time, do I notice that the painting is facing away from me, even though I cannot – before I fell asleep, yesterday – remember positioning it so. Not just that, as I stare at it, the 'force' 'threatening' me, seems to bristle, to become more potent – the reason for which eludes me. Reluctantly, and feeling a heavy sense of foreboding steal into my heart like a blade, I admit there's a need to get closer. But by now, for me, it takes a certain reserve of courage to stand and approach the seemingly harmless object.

Nevertheless, I nervously circle it, treating it as if it's some kind of dangerous animal, and as I do so, I squint along the angled width – even now realising something is freakishly wrong. Pausing a moment, I attempt to subdue a rising panic, as, incongruously – or, perhaps not – I think of the mirror. Standing there, taking deep breath after deep breath, in the futile hope that such an action will help decipher the unfathomable inconsistencies in the layers of paint, I watch the glare of the sun become refracted off the piece and towards my position of vision.

The painting is…*different*.

With a last mighty intake of air – and one formidable stride forward – I move out of the influence of the blinding sheen to stare in disbelief at the sight before me.

The background – sand and craggy rocks – remain unaltered; but the female figure is no longer an alien-esque Veronica with feline eyes. In her place now stands an almost ethereal image of the mysterious siren – the Domino-facsimile – I supposedly dreamed of. Her hair is black, long, free flowing, and levitates perfectly with the glistening silk cloak that covers most of her anatomy. Only one pale leg is visible from beneath its shadows, while an indistinct glow illuminates the ghostly likeness of Domino's dead face. The hand that was raised to deflect an attack, now holds a decapitated human head – like Cellini's Perseus – while the countenance below the hair is now that of…Veronica.

But this is not the only alteration. There is an…addition. Behind the Domino figure, residing almost secretly among the rocks, the supplementary form of the sinister, Fuseli-esque monstrosity sits, staring at me and mocking me like a vengeful familiar. And as I stare back at it, I cannot help but recall a comment made by the Norwegian artist, Edvard Munch, on the completion of one of his pieces:

*'Could only have been painted by a madman.'*

Ouch!

As the room suddenly becomes hazy, a kind of psychic whirlpool rises up around me, only to suck me down into its gullet of incomprehension and confusion.

And I tumble like a stone…

TRAPPED STILL
LATENT STILL
DRIFTING WITHIN
PARAMETERS OF LIQUID SPACE
NIHILISM
A WILL WASHED
BY INFINITY

The 'white' glow fades slightly and tiny specks of black appear, like conglomerating ants. Restlessly tossing and turning in half slumber, your troubled mind is bombarded by questions that swirl amidst ineffable visions and mysteries. From a blurred montage of colour and movement, a scene emerges, one which you, an astral interloper, must observe...

The sun – a great, flaming, Cyclopean eye – sinks behind purple crags, leaving a saffron tinted landscape to the mercy of a quietly moaning wind. Dim lights of the old city blink like glow-worms along the stucco, flat-topped buildings in the distance, while, close by, the silhouette of the man hanging by his neck from the arachnid tree stands etched against the glowing twilight sky, the ends of his robes fluttering quietly about his ankles. Looming a metre or two from the tragic tableau, a male figure – tall, slender, longhaired and faceless – silently surveys the corpse as it slowly turns towards him. Simultaneously, from somewhere overhead, a high-pitched whine penetrates the evening stillness. It is accompanied by a weird elliptically shaped glow that appears as if from nowhere in the sky. Materialising into solidity, it descends to hover near where you and the stranger stand. As a hitherto undetectable aperture appears in the object's side, a second, tall, longhaired figure emerges. Like the first figure, he is dressed in a flowing garment, the capacious folds of which slowly undulate about his frame like some gelatinous organism. He, too, has a face that is featureless. It is done? he asks, his voice composed of pure thought. It is, the other answers. After 'looking' at you, he again turns towards the suspended cadaver, 'studying' the scene in silence for several moments. At last, he 'speaks', saying, So, the drama has been played out, let us hope the natural progression of events will unfold in accordance with the proposed eschatological model. Time alone will tell, comments the second figure, although I must confess to experiencing a certain sense of foreboding. I, too, telepathizes the first figure, all went as planned at the trial? It did, confirms the second, with the appropriate result. Then there is nothing more to be done, states the first figure. Nothing, agrees the second, except to await the forthcoming event at the sepulchre. The first figure nods. Then the amelioration of these otherwise impercipient primitives will begin, he says. Hopefully, 'sighs' the second one, and both figures cast their 'faces' in your direction. Uncannily, you can feel them 'stare' at you from the blankness of their masks of flesh. Then, as if on cue, like two applauded thespians, they bow, cordially, before 'walking' back to where the glowing, transparent ellipse levitates. On 'entering' it, the first figure turns to look again at the hanging wretch. He will become known as mankind's most infamous villain, he says, but without him none of it could exist or be perpetuated. As the aperture closes, his 'voice' adds, Farewell, my hapless friend, we regret having used you so. As the 'craft' disappears into the very air around it, you are unsure if the comment was addressed to you or the dead man.

Twisting and writhing, you mumble incoherently in a heat of slumber so unbearable you can smell your own sweat. Although vaguely aware of your surround, you keep your eyes tightly shut, so as to allow images to flit and rise from the substratum of your mind, where they dart and jump in protean confusion. Eventually, though, everything becomes still...

The sea is as calm and peaceful as a millpond. Across its vitreous surface, the orange sun, just above the horizon, and its elongated reflection, shimmer like an inverted, astronomical exclamation mark. Waves, as mischievous as sprites, gently ripple and corrugate against the shore, while voracious gulls dive and weave about the sky, their strident calls piercing the otherwise silent atmosphere. An idyllic, unspoiled scene, frozen as though on a holiday postcard. Sitting on a rock, you welcome the mood that wafts over you, relaxing and dispelling fears that are gradually becoming less extraneous, allowing your mind to sink into blissful lassitude, where a rare state of optimism resides. Maybe things are not so bad after all – now that the amatory relationship with Veronica has been re-established, now that it has again started to thrive, to blossom into something salubrious and endearing. Affections reaffirmed are mutually alienable, creating a state-of-being you never again thought possible. Whereas you had previously been obstructive of any ascendant desire, now, under the influence of this current indulgence, you have become consolatory, your newfound drive helping to eradicate the lamented memory of Domino. Although, something still overshadows the fact that – on occasions – the infatuation remains, by design? monomaniacal, almost contrived, in order to fill the void and to procure contrition. Yet, allowing for this constrained, if spurious peace, Veronica arises as a true saviour. She is sustenance for your resurgent sexual hunger, an obsession with which to fill the emptiness. Her presence has anaesthetised the impact of frightening vagaries, and helped to expatriate them to an alternative realm of existence. As a movement catches your eye, you glance across the expanse of sand, at the casually advancing figure of your lover. Completely naked, she saunters, languorously, along a gentle slope, step idle, face turned contentedly towards the rapidly diminishing glare of a retiring sun. As you watch, she raises a lazy actioned hand to run her fingers through her hair, before coming to a halt, standing with one leg slightly bent at the knee, like some sensitively sculptured Emilio Fiaschi statue. Narrowing your eyes against the still effulgent sunset renders her appearance almost supernatural, reflecting off her skin as though her body were made of gold. Becoming aware of your perusal, she turns to offer a friendly wave, and you nod your head, returning the gesture with a smile. For the first time in a long while you are in denial of the 'attraction' of a personal demise, as a warming aura of wellbeing permeates you, banishing such contemplations to the outer regions of schizophrenic mania. This is the other side of the self-loathing coin. It is the fabled but difficult to achieve 'peace of mind' you have heard so much about. Dropping your forehead onto arms that rest across your knees, you close your eyes and – perhaps – slumber…

Shorter and squatter than usual, with broad, white, velociraptor-toed feet forming alternating prints in our wake, we amble, apelike, across the wet, sandy beach, all the time becoming more and more conscious of the burgeoning surge of power and strength of will inside us, while outside us, affixed to a long, muscular arm, our right hand swings like a pensile club, as opposed to our left hand, which is raised, clawed fingers curled around something soft and fragile in its over retentive grip. Before us, the ocean begins to boil and crash, as though subject to some kind of sentient inner commotion, but we laugh at its rage and look up at the delicate object in our hand – which is also a hand, one so disparate to our own hirsute, taloned paw, that it resembles a rose in the presence of a sledgehammer. Lifting our gaze, we observe the slender arm to which the hand is attached – higher, to where the smooth skin is lightly tanned and covered in a soft pubescence of a paler shade, suspended from a curvaceous shoulder aslant a proud and beautiful profile. Beneath the profile and below the flawless neck, her breasts jiggle slightly with every condemned step she takes. Our concomitant stroller is a vision of loveliness…and it fills us with evil delight that she is about to die.

Quickly raising your face, you squint up at the luminiferous sky, seeking the threat which has seemingly developed out of the very air around you. Whatever it actually is, it rents the halcyon scene as clean as a meat cleaver, and is closely followed by a sudden wind from nowhere, skidding through your hair, causing the strands at the nape of your neck to stand to attention, like the arched back of a cornered cat. An almost identical sensation to that which preceded the incident at the easel prevails, the same fear, the same panic and the same presentimental awareness – a psychological contiguity of an inimical presence. Looking to your right – away from the apricating figure of Veronica – you somehow know what – *who* – you will find there. The Domino facsimile stands in stillness and in silence. Only her hair moves, as slowly and as sinuously as kelp caught in a gentle current, so long, so thick it beckons you to scoop it up in handfuls, to comb your fingers through its volume, to feel its weight and to bury your face in its mass. But still you sit, motionless, seemingly encrusted to the rock, barely able to breathe. And there, too, she remains, chin slightly raised, staring fixedly, looking, if not through you, then passed you. Forcing a cursory glance in Veronica's direction, displays her as oblivious to her rival's manifestation, as she deliberately alters course, in order to meander towards the sea – which is becoming more aggressive, any surviving reflections of the sun now blurred, creating nothing but indistinct impressions on the agitated surface of the water. Returning your attention to the inscrutable vamp, you half expect her to have disappeared again, but she is still there, a ghost of a smile playing among her beautiful yet anachronistic features. Features of a wonderous but terrible spectre, one who should no longer exist, even though the aforementioned features are an almost exact replica of Domino's own – straight nose, moulded cheekbones, firm chin, and seductively petalled mouth. But not her eyes. The genuine Domino's eyes were dark, lucent and alive – the facsimiles' eyes are dull, soulless and lustreless, appearing to have no pupils at all. And such an imperfection invalidates an otherwise perfect illusion, exposing the face as cosmetic, lacking mien, as if it has been created from wax or stone. Yet, still you are drawn to her, drawn in the wild hope that, in spite of the flaw, it is truly she, and that, by some divine miracle or trick of fate, has been returned to you. Nevertheless, above all else, confirmation is still demanded, because from confirmation will come absolution, for if she now lives, then she could not have died – you could not have killed her. And if you can cling to this belief, then surely deliverance is at hand – guilt, remorse and self-denunciation will be eradicated. You will become whole again. So, all that's required is the elusive confirmation – of identity, which, once established beyond doubt, will end the nightmares forever. Therefore, you must speak with her, you must hear her voice, experience an audible truth, in order to undisputedly demonstrate her resurrection. (Why does that word resonate in your head?) But you fail to induce communication. Moreover, afflicted by a strangely inopportune aphonia, you just stare at her, jaws agape, struggling to translate your thoughts into speech. The consequential enormity of the confrontation inhibits you so much that doubts escalate, flying like scattering bats, and you think – what if her voice, her answers to your questions, her vocal inflections do not comply with expectations gleaned from prior intimacy and conversational knowledge? What if her oration and opinions differ from those of the lover hitherto deemed dead? The abyss looms, dark, deep and wide, re-entry an irrevocable one-way trip. Then, in the midst of this torment, something stirs and tugs at your senses. The facsimile seems to feel it, too, and as her pupil-less eyes glitter in the darkness, focussing fully upon you for the first time – she smiles. And it is because of that smile you become confronted once more by…reality. As the smile broadens into a grin, to reveal teeth that are much too white, it constructs an effect counter-productive to a smile's purpose, so uninviting and disturbing that it causes you to retreat from its influence. With the help of the rising wind, and coruscation of her ensconcing cloak harmonising with the turgescent ocean waves, you concentrate on the re-establishment of an ability to reason – which stabs you with a shock so severe it spins you around to fearfully search for Veronica. At the same time, the wind – as though sensing your panic – rises in velocity, to become a derisive howl, or a mocking exultation. Scanning the churning waters, you mercifully espy her slow-moving frame silhouetted against the ever-weakening flickers of a dying twilight. Quickly enshrouding the diurnal world in nocturnal gloom, the sunset serves as a kind of symbolic representation of your predicament, obscuring her image among swirling waves and foaming froth. But why is she there at all? Why does she continue to confront such a tempestuous sea? Even as its conditions worsen moment by moment, she persists in walking on with the temerity of one who is about to attempt a swim. God! There is no chance of her conquering such thrashing monsters. She will surely drown. And yet, still you hesitate, hoping, even at this late stage in proceedings, that she will cease her slow but resolute step, that she will stop and turnabout. But she does not. Almost at the water's edge now – so small, so frail and defenceless against the uproarious turmoil – she offers no indication of wavering in her purpose, marching steadfastly on like a prisoner to the scaffold. At last, the constriction in your throat abates sufficiently for you to shout to her. Veronica! Veronica! But your cry goes unheeded. Lost in the increasing storm. Muffled by the wind. Carried to nothing within the inordinate cacophony. Veronica! Come back! Come back! And it is at that moment, just when you are about to leap down onto the sand to give chase, you notice an extra shadow where before no shadow had been, and recognition of it freezes you in impotent rage. Having adopted the mannerisms of a zombie, Veronica wades purposefully into the boiling cauldron of brine, her torso twisting one way then the other against the rising, turbulent force – but she is not alone. Keeping pace with her is a squat, muscular, almost deformed shape – human yet inhuman – an ambling phantasm, with long arms, somewhat stunted legs and tapered skull. With an oversized, raised, taloned hand, it grips the girl's submissive fingers, leading her like a malformed offspring leading its mother. As you watch, spellbound, a huge wave rears up in front of them. Like a lizard about to lick up and army of ants, the mountainous mound curls and readies itself, before surging down on them, engulfing them in an aqueous blanket of oblivion. And they are gone. Too late, you rediscover your voice. Veronica! you shout. Veronica! While your stentorian entreaties die amongst the rampaging elements, from behind you, a low, sibilant chuckle can be heard – like the hiss of a snake in the night.

As though from outside of myself, I hear a voice: "Veronica! Veronica!"

"It's all right."

"Veronica! Come back! Come…back!"

"I'm here. It's all right. Wake up."

"Oh! Christ!"

"It's all right; you were dreaming."

"Oh! Christ! Christ, alive! What? Dreaming, you say? Dream-*ing?*"

"Another one of *those* dreams, by the sound of things. But it's past now. I'm here."

"I dreamed you were drowning," I gasp. "I dreamed you were drowning and…and I couldn't save you."

Pulling my face into her bosom, she nurses me like a frightened child. "Huh-huh," she soothes. "You don't get rid of me that easily."

"When did you do this?" Veronica asks.

"I'm not entirely sure. It was before you came – before you had trouble rousing me. But I didn't know it at the time."

"What do you mean?"

"The truth is, I simply thought I was finishing off the existing painting. I didn't approach it as a *pentimento*; I just got out of bed, looked at it, knew what was required for completion, and *ex tempore*, set to work."

"And this is what you came up with?"

"I'm afraid so."

After looking thoughtful for a few moments, she nods her head in knowing fashion. "No mystery, of course." Gazing down at my feet, I await her to state the obvious. "She's still here – in this room. She's still with you, clinging to your remorse and pseudo guilt. But you don't need *me* to tell *you* that. Right? Nor do you need me to diagnose an attempted exorcism."

Narrowing her eyes slightly, she points a wary finger at the diabolical familiar in the background. "What about...*him*, though?"

Ignoring her remark, I try working around it. "That isn't how I first saw her – in my dream, I mean. Initially, her face was a blank – featureless. The likeness of Domino was created and sculpted before my eyes. One minute, a de Chirico mannequin...the next – *her.*"

"And that...that thing..." she persists "...what about him?"

I offer a counterfeit shrug. "God knows."

"So, do you, too...I think."

"Aw, shit! Let's not get into that alter-ego crap again, huh?"

She also shrugs, but her shrug is genuine. "Okay, have it your way. However, there's someone a lot more awe-inspiring to confront now, isn't there?"

"Oh? And who the hell is that?"

"The guy who commissioned the damned thing, of course. He's going to want to know what's happened to his investment."

"How did it go?" I ask.

Hesitatingly, she lowers her eyes. "I'm...not sure."

I watch her, carefully. "How come?"

"Erm...There wasn't anyone home."

"Then there's no way that –"

"Probably...by now. I left a note."

"I'm sorry, love."

"Don't be; can't hit a bull's-eye every time, right?"

I grin, sheepishly. "That's a novel way of looking at it. It's just that all this weird shit is getting to me; I feel like I'm sinking in mud. I have...the *rats.*"

"The what?"

"The *rats.* It's an expression my grandfather used, when he couldn't explain why he felt anxious, uneasy or depressed – you know: like Churchill's 'Black Dog'."

"Very apt, I'm sure."

"Don't mock it. There was this one time, when I was quite young, my parents took me for a day out, at the seaside or somewhere. On our way back, we had a minor accident, in the car – no one injured, but it delayed us for a while. When we contacted him, the following day, my grandfather claimed he had experienced, the previous evening, a premonition that something had gone wrong. He had had the 'rats', he said. I think I'm suffering from them now – portentous, like a bad omen."

Poking me playfully in the ribs, she says: "You're such a happy soul, aren't you? You really should kick back now and then."

"Kick back?"

"Yeah, you know: against these moods of yours. Try gritting your teeth for a change. Try saying no to the dark, and yes to the light."

"Easier said than done," I tell her.

"See what I mean? Morose to the end. Listen to me: I know you've suffered some…bad experiences lately – we both have – but they're done with now. Finished. As long as we're together again, we can…lay the ghosts to rest – if you'll forgive me for putting it that way. So…how about we…go somewhere?"

"Go somewhere? Where?"

"Anywhere. Just the two of us. Take time out, as the Americans say; go someplace where we can allow ourselves a hiatus in the chaos. What do you say, huh?"

I look at her in surprise. Such self-assertion, such confidence is new. "What is this, more of your amateur psychology?"

"No. Just an observation of symptoms, that's all – plus, possible treatment."

Through a deep sigh, I say: "You could be right, I suppose – a change of environment, and of scenery, may be the answer." Looking around, I add: "This place is too full of memories – and regrets. They abide here; and ergo, make it difficult to form comparisons. They tend to throttle all ascendancy to gratitude."

"There you go," she agrees, a little too patronisingly, perhaps. "You have me now, a *femme nouvelle,* as the French call it."

"*Femme*…what?"

"*Nouvelle – femme nouvelle* – new versatile woman: model, pseudo agent, lover…housewife?"

"Housewife?" I question, humorously. "Some chance. You're an even worse cook than me."

"Alright; how about…domestic help?"

"Domestic help? Are you serious? That doesn't sound at all…modern – *or* new – to me."

"Really? Then who the hell do you think tidied up this place, after that…bloody storm or earth tremor…or whatever it was?"

"Ah," I say. "I'm afraid I'd forgotten about that – the cleaning up bit, I mean. Apologies."

"I should damned-well think so, too. Only a moment ago you were talking about gratitude."

"Yeah, I was, wasn't I?" After kissing her gently on the forehead, I lie back and stare at the ceiling. The word 'gratitude' forms a picture in my mind, and I am almost overcome by its sudden relevance. Not only am I grateful to Veronica, but also, unbelievably, for…my own existence. When this becomes coupled with the other reference to 'comparisons', there is a turning of memory's key and I am transported back a number of years.

"A penny for them," she says.

"What? Oh, I was thinking about my past."

"Shady, I'll bet."

"Not half as shady as I'm sure you're assuming," I tell her, with a grin.

"Ah! Spoilsport." Her voice sounds huffy, but it doesn't stop her planting a kiss on my cheek.

"I was actually thinking of some-*one* in my past."

And it is at that very moment when she almost blows all the accumulated, hard-earned, good will out of the water. "Oh! Not another female, *please!* I don't think I can cope with…Ohmygod. Ohmygod, I'm so, so sorry…" firstly she glances away, but almost immediately looks back at me with a guilty eye "…I've…I've got a big mouth sometimes. I…"

After pausing for no longer than a moment, I quickly choose not to succumb to either a state of anger or maudlin sentimentality. Instead, in order to deny Domino's possibly damaging access back into our lives, I decide to totally ignore Veronica's slip of the tongue, and simply continue with what I am about to say. "Actually, it wasn't; it was a male – a boy, who lived not far from my family and I, and who suffered from some kind of glandular disorder – very fat, obese, even – with the whole of the medical fraternity prognosticating a short life of only sixteen, maybe seventeen years. His heart would just give out, they said; the strain would be too great. Even though I saw him infrequently, his condition bothered me, and I often found myself pondering on its futility. Why did he exist at all? For what purpose? Since everyone was aware of the fact that he was soon going to die, anyway, what was the point of him being born in the first place? I felt there just had to be some consolation or expiation for that shadow of mortality hanging over him like the sword of Damocles. And then…I found out about myself."

Veronica looks puzzled. "You? What could you possibly have had in common with…?"

"One day, I happened to bring up the boy's condition – and my troubled reaction to it – with my dad, who simply said: 'What about you?' I told him I had no idea what he meant, so he related something to me that I've never told you or anyone else before. Apparently, when I was about one year old, and living – along with my dad (my mum spent long periods of time in hospital) – in a somewhat remote area with my grandparents, I contracted what turned out to be an obviously serious and usually – for infants, at least – fatal complaint (meningitis was later hinted at, but never confirmed) which resulted in me not being expected to survive the night. An 'old time' doctor – whose surgery was the closest port of call in the event of an emergency – was sent for, but, alas, was deemed…'not available'; which left a distant A&E department the only alternative. Since there was no guarantee as to how long it would take an ambulance to reach our location, my dad and grandparents were left with a dilemma. Until my grandmother came up with an idea. For many years, she had been very friendly with a district nurse, who lived not too far away, and who had only just returned from a warzone where she had witnessed an attempted genocide, and was currently recovering from PTSD. The story goes that, in the middle of the night, my dad ran all the way to the nurse's house and pleaded with her to come and see me – which, to her credit, she did, bravely getting behind the wheel of her own car for the first time since arriving back in the UK. On viewing my condition, it was she who diagnosed whatever it was that was ailing me, declaring my situation as critical if not terminal. What happened next can – as far as my dad and grandparents were concerned – only be put down to the horrific experiences the nurse had gone through beforehand, as she, against all medical and Hippocratic rules, decided to administer a – to this day an unknown and unverifiable – medication specifically manufactured for adults, eventually taking her leave with the caveat: kill or cure by morning. The rest, as they say, is history, but the result has plagued me ever since."

"Why?" Veronica asks. "The kind nurse probably saved your life. Without her somewhat questionable intervention, you would not be here now. We would not have met, and you would not be…who…you…are-ah!"

"Precisely," I say. "So, at last, you understand the connection, right? I would never have existed, not as a natural, neurotic, and dangerous influence; you would never have ended up getting hurt by or because of me; and Domino would never have been…never have been…Listen! The simple truth of the matter is…I should *not* be here."

"Just like the fat boy, huh? Oh, come on, now, listen to yourself – don't you realise how conceited and egocentric that sounds? Surely, you cannot consider your existence as having such an important effect on events – negative or positive. There *are* more factors than just *you* involved here, you know – namely, among myriad others…Domino and myself. Besides, there's a state of being out there that's a lot more philosophically digestible than the one you're proposing. Something that actually rules us all, universally, from cradle to grave. I know theologians, scientists and most philosophers attempt to dismiss it, but, like it or not, absolutely everything is subject to, and encompassed by it: religion, and even the broadest interpretations of metaphysics are at the mercy of a cosmic impulse called…determinism, which functions as a diametric opposite to your conception of a self-obsessed solipsism. And, in the process, cancels out, overrides or assimilates all efforts to lay claim to any kind of 'rupture' by preordination. It's something that just…'is' – that always *has* been, always *will* be; that occurs before our eyes, day after day, even second after second, with all events irrefutably caught up in its eternal matrix – and *no* one escapes its eschatological resolution. End of story."

The word 'eschatological' suddenly rears up as though highlighted in red letters, while the diorama, consisting of the hanged man and the twin 'alien' figures, from my dream, rushes at me like an 'X' factor image. Rapidly shaking my head, I attempt to get rid of it.

"What, now?" Veronica asks.

"Nothing," I say, unconvincingly.

It is her turn to shake her head, only in a slow, almost exasperated manner. "There you go again, scuttling back inside yourself. I thought we were having a meaningful, one-to-one discussion at long last."

"No discussion required," I contend. "You just stated: 'end of story'. Well, that's all it was I told you – a story. Metaphysics, deterministic or otherwise, have nothing to do with it."

"Oh, I disagree," she argues. "Your…non-metaphysical 'story' must mean much more to you than that. Why else, after all these years, would you decide to bring it up now?"

"Because…" I start, before some obscure, involuntary compulsion causes, what can only be interpreted as iconic words, to fall from my lips "…I've…just invented it."

She frowns at me. "You mean it was a lie?"

"Maybe…maybe not. Let's just say…it *could* have been."

"I'm afraid statements like that are a little over my head," She says. "In my book, you either made it up, or it's true."

"Truth, like life, is relative," I announce, pompously.

"Then what about existence itself?" she asks. "Have you thought about the possibility of the unanswerable?"

"In what way?"

She shrugs, offhandedly. "Well, perhaps the answer cannot be, simply because there is nowhere to go."

" Nowhere to – What the hell do you mean?"

"Maybe…" she offers, slowly "…the fat boy did *not* die."

And that's it. Right there. The crunch. Because the fucker didn't! He *didn't* die. In spite of all the negative medical diagnoses, he's still alive. Why, for fuck's sake, did she have to say that? Why? Shit! I cannot let her get away with it. My rebuttal is weak, but it's all I can summon, under the circumstances. "He must be by now," I insist. "Even if my info was incorrect, I –"

"That's not what I'm getting at," she interjects. "What I am getting at is…what if, what…*if,* deterministically, no one dies?"

My tone is only gently sarcastic. "I'm afraid such statements are a little over my head."

"I'm serious," she retorts. "Just suppose that life, existence, is analogous to that old theory about the pebble."

"What old theory? What pebble?"

"You know…the one that suggests a pebble, when dropped, can never actually reach the ground – because it always has to travel half the distance that's left."

"So?"

"So, maybe life, existence, works on the same principle. If a living, thinking being can never come to terms with the prospect of its own demise, then perhaps that is so because the final instances have to be lived, and relived, over and over again, *ad infinitum* – like Nietzsche's eternal recurrence – but compressed further and further into shorter and shorter periods. After all, there's a…kind of precedent, isn't there? Is it not claimed that a drowning man relives the whole of his life in the last seconds before he expires? Ergo, what if, each time his life is played out, as it approaches its finality, it has to be replayed, in ever briefer microseconds, again and again – forever!"

As we stare at each other, I remember the other dream, the dream of the sea: *Death is the only independent absolute. A singular, definite fact on an otherwise indefinite journey.* Can such an axiom be wrong? Slowly, a mischievous smile hovers around the corners of her mouth, before she once more prods sharp fingers into my ribs. "Had you going there, for a mo, didn't I?" she chuckles.

The dream sea evaporates, but a serpent uncoils in the regions of uncertainty, hissing doubt into my ear like a temptress. "Yeah," I admit. "Just for a mo, you did."

Even though her half-joked proposition is obviously untenable, I still wish she hadn't said it.

It is sometimes the small, prosaic things that seem to count for so much. The intimate, almost inconsequential things: the affinity, the touching, the knowing smiles, the understanding glint in the eye – all the little things that exist between two people who care for each other.

Leaning against the upright frame of the paint flaked doorway, I watch the waltzing roll of a mist covered sea. Everything is tinted with various shades of grey; even the sand has a pale tinge, lacking primary stature, imbuing it with a faraway look. To me it has the appearance of a painting that has been sprayed over lightly with an airbrush.

Standing behind me, Veronica, with arms encircling my waist, rests her chin on my shoulder. As she breathes softly into my ear, her explorative fingers burrow beneath my sweatshirt to caress my abdominals. "You're very quiet," she says. It is a statement, not a question, so I make no comment. As the ocean's swell continues to heave and sigh in its fashion, she adds: "It's so peaceful here. I do understand your attraction to it. It's as though the rest of the world has passed us by. Almost primordial or ghostly, like we're trapped in time, intruders in another realm. It only requires a minimal imagination to visualise its inhabitants – a stegosaurus here, an iguanodon there – as they clamber cumbrously over those dunes, hills and rocks. As a matter of fact, from this distance, those gulls could be mistaken for Pteranodons or pterodactyls. Don't you agree?"

"Mmmhh…Might even be an odd Australopithecus, huh?"

With a deep throated laugh, she light-heartedly corrects my anthropological/palaeontological attempt at misaligned parody. "Don't be silly, the Australopithecines did not appear until much, much later – and you know it."

Lying in the semidarkness of the room, my back resting against the headboard of the bed, I stare in ill eased wonderment at the moon kissed painting on the easel. As, yet again, I ponder over its mystery, selenic rays appear as separate prongs, picking at the thing like discriminating torch beams. On scanning the picture, with what I consider to be a professional eye, I can recall knowing what to do in order to complete the work, but afterwards there is only the dark, fathomless void of forgetfulness.

At the moment, though, there are more mundane concerns to occupy my thoughts. Most importantly: what the hell am I going to tell the buyer when he gets in touch? – something I am expecting to happen any day now. How do I explain the whereabouts of his long-awaited fantasy painting, 'starring' a nude portrait of Veronica (which, in my opinion, was the sole reason the topic was chosen by him in the first place – or am I just being bad minded)? Fuck! How do I explain it to myself?

Anyway, staring at the damned thing like a mesmerist fails to uncover a single clue from its stubborn layers of acrylic paint; so, I give up and slide under the sheet, where the warmth of Veronica's body awaits me. And I close my eyes…

"It cannot be your real name," I said.

She laughed. "Of course not; I was christened Dominetta, after my grandmother. But everyone calls me Domino."

"It's…Italian, right?"

"Yes. My mother was Italian; my father was English."

"Was?"

"They're both dead now."

"I see. I'm sorry."

Her face, having clouded over for a moment, quickly brightened again. "So, which ones are yours? Show me."

Turning on my heel, I pointed out two paintings hanging in a somewhat shadowed alcove. "Over there."

With a casual familiarity that took me by surprise, she gripped my hand in hers and guided us through a throng of people pretentiously discussing the stagnation of twenty-first-century art. Coming to a halt in front of the indicated pieces in question, she inclined her head, before remarking: "Not bad. I like your use of colour, and I admire your compositions – but your female figures are too male idealised."

"They are?"

She eyed me sceptically. "Of course, they are – but you already knew that."

"I did?" Laughing again, deep and throaty, she kept her eyes on mine, as I added: "Do you think I would be able to recognise why, though?"

"You wouldn't be much of an artist if you couldn't," she said, I thought, with tongue-in-cheek. "But I'll stress the obvious, if you want me to."

"Go ahead," I told her.

Taking a step back, while thoughtfully touching her lower lip with a forefinger, she said: "That one: her breasts would not stay so pronounced in such a pose. You've painted her as though she were sitting in a more upright position. There again, that's probably more appealing to your inbred gender drive, is it not?"

"I did use a live model," I said, defensively, at the same time thinking of Veronica. "That is pretty much as she looked to me."

"Indeed?" Her smile seemed rather wry. "Then, either she's a truly blessed young lady, or else it's as I suggested: you…subconsciously, maybe, male-idealised her." Was there a gesture of defiance, or even pre-conceived jealousy, about the way in which she tossed her long black hair like a…a cloak? "So, which is it?"

Somewhat fatefully, I said: "I suppose it's going to make me sound like – to use an overworked, pre-#MeToo phrase – a male chauvinist, whatever I say, huh?"

"Not…necessarily," and she smiled. "Let's agree that you have a specific way of looking at things, shall we?"

"Subjectively, you mean?"

"Is there another way?"

We both laughed at this, before reaching for *vernissage* free drinks off a passing tray. Feeling a little nervous about the topic under discussion, and fearing I would overstep the mark and offend her – what seemed to me to be (and therefore probably validating her observations of my work) – strong feminist sensibilities, I wondered if I should discontinue with the line of conversation. But I need not have worried, as, rather than demur or attempt to change the subject, she actually used it to seize the initiative. With an unwavering eye, and humorous sigh of resignation, she said: "Of course, there is but *one* way to demonstrate my point, isn't there?"

"About what?" I asked, hoping not to overdo the nonchalance.

"Breasts…in that kind of pose."

"Erm…yes," I said. "I suppose there is."


The sound of the wind penetrates my sleep-numbed brain like a Buzzsaw.

It is becoming louder.

Louder.

I open my eyes.

I look about me.

The whole building is vibrating.

Veronica is asleep at my side.

I shake her by the shoulder.

She does not awaken.

I shake her again.

She does not awaken.

I throw back a bedsheet that floats in slow-motion.

I climb into my denims and sweatshirt.

I return to Veronica and lift her torso.

Her head hangs back like a rag doll.

The wind becomes even more vigorous.

The roof seems as though it is about to fly off.

I stagger to the door and open it.

A cloud of sand blows in.

It sprinkles the floor with myriad grains.

I must sweep them up in the morning.


Outside, the wind is a tormented tiger, goading you away from the sea, inland, over dunes and hillocks, towards the flat-topped buildings of the city. The sand is as dry as a swarm of insects, spraying flesh and eyes with brittle torrents, while tempestuous gusts tug fiercely at your hair and cloth-ing, forcing you forward and onward, like some vicious slave driver. And as you are thrust along by this blustering zephyr, you stumble over clumps of dried, coarse grass, scramble out of deep sandpits, and fall heavily into drifting dunes before picking yourself up to resolutely march on as though incapable of doing otherwise. Ahead, you espy a group of people, huddled together within a high, sand ridden enclave. They are looking down at the ground before them, their robes flapping like wings of dying birds, and as you approach, they turn towards you, multi-eyed as a mutant spider, before parting to grant you access to their object of attention. In the parched ground there are two rectangular, freshly dug, grave size holes, and you peer down into the shadowed depths of the nearest hole with curiosity. At the bottom lies the cadaverous frame of a naked man, limbs sprawled in a grotesque assemblage, as though he were thrown in there carelessly, without consideration. The skin is leathery, obscene in its nudity, lacking coffin or cerement, and the head is twisted to such an awkward angle that the neck must be fractured or completely broken. Attached to it, the face is a rigid mask of horror, with hanging jaw and cracked, yellow teeth grimacing in rictal evidence of a pre-death beating. Eyes, immobile glass marbles, stare from their sockets, as loose sand cascades into the open grave, half burying the ghastly features from your gaze. While standing amidst the howling gale, you hear a voice behind you, saying, Poor, misguided fool, He should have known better than to trust those lying bastards. Looking at the speaker, you find yourself confronted by a young, bearded face set among madly flapping folds of a burnouse, eyes as scintillant as diamonds in a sun scorched countenance. I knew they would not free him once the people had chosen the death of the other, mutters another voice, older, weaker, in the twilight of its years. The other? You ask. Aye, says he, the one they called the Nazarene – whose grave is there, next to this one. Moving a little to your right you stare down into the sandy pit, to one side of which rests a large flat rock. But it's empty, you state excitedly. It is, agrees the younger man, Graverobbers moved away the stone and made off with the body. Rumour has it that it possessed special properties, informs another voice, from the back of the throng. They say he called himself the Son of Man, explains the older figure, and that he was holy. The Messiah? you enquire, hopefully – Did he also claim to be the Messiah? Some say so, aye, the younger man says. But you do not believe this? you ask. Some even called him the Son of God, declares the older man. If he were the Son of God, argues the younger man, then would he not have saved himself? Would he not have struck his tormentors down with a flash of celestial fire? Watching the man as he speaks, his display of intense belligerence makes you wonder if he is a Zealot, and just for a moment you contemplate remonstrating with him, but the arrant expression on his face dissuades you. Instead, you murmur words that form in your mind as though projected there by some external means, And Jesus answered them saying, The hour is come, that the Son of Man should be glorified. What say you stranger? the zealot demands to know. Shaking your head, you say, Nothing, I was merely thinking out loud. But now the eyes are watching you, flickering malignly over your whole frame, scrutinising your appearance with suspicion. You are dressed oddly, friend, comments another voice, low, gruff, minatory, From where do you come? You seek out the speaker's face but it is hidden within the tenebrity of a heavy cowl. From the west, you answer. That is a somewhat unspecific reply, continues the voice. His accent, also, is strange, points out another, as a sense of hostility spreads like the hood of a cobra before you. Moving as one, the start to encircle you. Do you think he could be a spy? asks a different voice. Perhaps he is the very assassin of our own brave comrade, there, come to confirm the internment, suggests another. No! you deny. No, for I am a stranger in this strange land, come to witness proof of the Resurrection. The Resurrection? several ask at once. Yes, the rising of the one called, Jesus, you reveal. To show that he died and rose for our sins – for the redemption of our souls, And the living confirmation is there, Look – the empty grave. An empty grave, protests the younger man, proves nothing, friend, other than the fact that what was once there is now gone. At that moment, there is an interruption, and an alien voice, low, sonorous, as if echoing down a tunnel, says, You must leave this place, pilgrim, for you have already spent too long in the company of these natives. Turning to view the yawning cavity – which may or may not be the disturbed inhumation of a – the – Messiah – you see two of them – perhaps the same two you last encountered – one standing at the head of the grave, the other at the foot. They are both alarmingly tall, straight-backed, garbed in white flowing robes that seem to swirl of their own volition and not of the wind's. Their hair is shoulder length, golden in colour, framing faces that are blank, lacking eye, nose and mouth. Make haste, says the nearest one, You have so little time. Glancing back to where your protagonists stood, you discover that they have disappeared. Hurry, continues the resonant voice. With a last, fleeting glimpse of the sepulchral scene, you follow the directing hand of one of the weird figures, and scramble up the steep slope of a loose running dune. At the top, you turn for confirmation of destination, but both figures have vanished. There are only the slowly filling graves.

Above you, the sky is dark and inclement, as great clouds, like thunderous dragons, race madly across its crepuscular expanse. Standing and straining against a wild simoom, you dither over your choice of direction as you scan apparently endless, drifting mounds of a topography that is as empty and desolate as the moon. There is only one indication of anything of interest – a vague aura, or atmosphere that seems to beckon? from the east, and, even though it represents but a minor disturbance in the milieu, it is at least something – a guiding light, perhaps, or a beacon? Deprived of any optional incentive, you feel it working on your intuition, stirring you into action. So, you follow its influence, on and on, over dune after dune, ignoring the rasping breath in your lungs, and the ache in your legs, until, just when you are about to give up, a figure appears, moving slowly, etched against the skyline like an animated paper cut-out. Summoning hidden reserves, you didn't even know you had, you break into a trot, clambering up a stark hillock, to give chase to the person who walks steadfastly on, oblivious of your approach. It is a woman, attired in a voluminous white garment that covers all but an open slash for her eyes, from where her pupils sparkle above an unsteady hand holding the material in place across her nose and mouth. And as you confront her, your attention is drawn to a strange red mark, directly between her eyes. With lungs heaving, you stare at her until she seems to notice you for the first time, and is momentarily startled. But as she lowers her gaze to take in your own flapping robes, she relaxes, her vision concentrating on your forehead, from where a comforting sensation emanates like a tepid balm. Follow me, she says, and you numbly step aside, letting her pass before nestling into her wake like an obedient neophyte. Without you initially being aware of them, others join you – all garbed in white – ascending from desert dips and hollows like spirits from a necropolis. Behind them, even more arise to walk with you, their number proliferating into a multitude, accompanied by a low moaning that harmonises with the wind. An antiphon, delivered with funerary reverence, floating out of mouths as a Gregorian chant, rising and falling, modulating with the soughing breezes. And as the crowd continues to grow, the chant becomes more vociferous, all-consuming, the ground losing its barren blanket of sand, giving way to a slow encroachment of grass and vegetation. Trees, although thin and sporadic, begin to mushroom from the dust, and a verdant carpet spreads itself across the prior, dying sandscape like an unfurling scroll. It is as if a border, or demarcation line has been crossed, and a paradise, cut from the wilderness by some numinous hand, has been entered. Striding through this newly formed landscape, that is both beautiful and fertile, you watch in wonderment as the sky begins to clear itself – ominous clouds, vaporising like ghosts in daylight. Helios being reborn to illuminate a rapidly expanding and autonomous oasis. With a sudden cessation of the chanting the silence seems almost deafening. Looking about in amazement you observe that you have arrived in what appears to be an uncircumscribed orchard or garden, decorated with a profusion of bushes and plants, some of which are lush, tropical, unexpected and incongruous to the country in which you find yourself. Strangely, the name of the country eludes you, but you instinctively know where it is, its geographic location and significance in the world. And it is among such an exuberant terrain of colours, shrubbery, and exotic flowers that the crowd comes to a halt, *en masse*, robes hanging like soft willows from their bodies, standing as still and strategically positioned as statues in the grounds of a vast estate. Each and every individual faces a spot directly ahead, until, as if on a given signal from some invisible, omnipotent conductor's baton, the heraldic voices begin again, hauntingly sad, a canticle flitting through the luxuriant arboretum like a living entity – a descant, swooping, gliding and gently penetrating your eardrums with the rhythm of a romantic poem. Entering your brain as a fragmentation of a dream, it instructs an awareness to burgeon in your mind – so, you look around for...*her*, and your eyes meet. Standing beside you, she issues a gentle smile before lowering her gaze, while you vaguely become aware of the throng as they disperse, pairing off, each one moving slowly and purposefully towards their allocated partner, one or both of which is superbly beautiful, physically flawless, bordering on the angelic – all bearing the red marks on their foreheads. Holding hands, in order to consolidate the pairings, they appear almost as twin parts of single entities, before – with the precision of a well-choreographed chorus line – they drop to their knees and bow their heads. Following their example, you take her by the hand, experiencing a calefacient smoothness as her fingers rest in your palm. Cautiously casting a sideways glance, you take in the celestial profile of a goddess, as, close up, she is even more wonderous than you could possibly have imagined. It *is* Domino – but it is *not*. It is more of *a* Domino, one with skin that is creamed perfection, lacking even the slightest blemish. A Domino whose facial outline has transcended the authoritative structure of a princess. A Domino sublimated to the role of seraph. And yet...in spite of these obvious attributes, the eyes are still...'wrong', remaining white, pupil-less, with a slight, unnatural inclination at the corners, relaying an almost Oriental appearance, or of Asiatic, possibly even Polynesian extraction. The hair, however, is finer and longer than you remember – as black as a raven's wing, shimmering with a blue haze whenever caught by the light. Like a sable, rippling cataract on her back, it contrasts sharply with the now pure white of her robe (as opposed to the sparkling *domino* of your previous encounters) presenting a vision of delight, and creating an angel that provokes within you the ambivalent drives of both protector and ravager, fusing an agonising synergy of paternal jealousy with urgent, libidinous intent. Once more the hymnal chanting ceases, and the accompanying soundlessness enables you to audibly discern the soft hiss of her breathing, coupled with an accentuation of an interior thunder in your temples and behind your eyeballs. Then, at that moment, as if from the very sky itself, a voice lacerates the created peace. We are gathered, it booms, for the final time before the Event – for the final introduction and indoctrination of the final convert. A low murmur of approval from the multitude. He, continues the voice, alongside his designated intercessor, must advance to the Presence. With a squeeze of hands, and with mounting trepidation, you both rise to stand somewhat unsteadily as the low, melodic notes begin again. Flashing an encouraging smile, she turns far enough towards you to confirm that the smile has been much modified – no longer the emotionless grimace you witnessed on the beach. Relievedly, it has been reconstructed into a welcome endearment, sympathetic and enticing, as though a spiritual sculptor has executed a potent emendation. With fingers that curl and stiffen in your hand, she gently pulls you forward, weaving a path through the servile congregation, and a haziness fills your mind – a lethargic warmth, lading your limbs with the heaviness of viscous slime. The effect causes everything to float, as if in slow-motion, while the surround starts to fade, becoming indistinct and blurred, acting as a backdrop against which is focussed a prosilient object – in this case, the girl – whose image is now the only truly defined one, drifting along before you like an earthbound sylph, her grip featherlight but as strong as a mousetrap at the end of an arm that appears elongated and out of proportion. Vaguely, it occurs to you that perhaps you have been ministered some kind of hallucinogenic drug, but somehow it does not seem to matter if you have, even as the arm before you stretches further and further, to become longer and longer, creating the sensation of being restrained by some unaccountable force, like a stone in a slingshot. If its hold on you should be released...If...It *is* released and your mind breaks free, to become levitated like a summer butterfly, to float on a warm breeze like an eagle, to soar and drift on thermal waves so light the experience unfetters you, raising you higher and higher above ground, way above the hunger of gravity, to become the spray of a cascading waterfall, or a fluttering dragonfly wistfully coiling and suffusing with the air itself, a disembodied spirit, a random chord in an unfinished symphony, participating in its flow and nuances, its unrestrained intangibility, a rose petal on a pellucid pond, the scented aroma of newly mown hay, a softly whispered salutation from a paramour's mouth, an astral blossom in a distant galaxy, a spectral droplet of perfumed liquid, a phosphorescent glimmer in a starless night, a sublime thought in a philosopher's mind, the blue/violet glint in an amethyst quartz. As the singing becomes more resonant, the melody flows consonantly, canalising through the synapse of your brain, urging you to follow your charcoal haired angel, whose flowing robe appears as a series of rolling waves on a lacteous sea, the motion becoming hypnotic, coruscating into festival pennants on a windy day, so you nestle in the wake of this guiding star, eyes rivetted to the undulating, magnetic movement that has you in tow, only to see it suddenly unmould, like reversed smoke dwindling down into a funnel, swishing to one side, rippling to stillness, and you kneel beside her, staring at the hem of a silver cloak gently swaying before you, and her grip tightens on your fingers and you realise that she, too, is frightened, because you can feel the relayed tension from her body as a heartbeat, badly timed, erratic, bumps within you, and your throat is dry and the palms of your hands are wet with perspiration as something touches your head, resting upon it, creating a tingling sensation, like vibrating static or mild cramp, crackling through your nerve ends, transmuting into enlightenment, into revelatory thought, so, you twist your head to look at the girl as she kneels, head bowed, eyes closed, like a Madonna at prayer, and at the long fingered hand resting atop of her head, throbbing with unearthly light, impulses of energy illuminating the skeletal x-ray structure and vascular anastomosis beneath the skin, every pulsation regular, monotonous, like a synchronised fountain inside your head, creating visions, splashes of effulgence and colour that thump from obscurity to definition, caught only by your subconscious receptibility, indecipherable and unintelligible to your surface awareness, your brain becoming like the storage bank of a computer, receiving and compartmentalising fractal images and shapes for some abstruse future use, casting you in the role of medium, compiling, cross-indexing, latent, until the time for its transference elsewhere, but how or when this will take place is uncertain, the only certainty being the relevance of everything to a yet to come subject to monumental happenings, to radical change in the structure and existence of humankind, when the state of things will become manifestly altered forever, when cosmical disorder, followed by sequential cataclysmic events, unprecedented in the annals of recorded history will occur, fulfilling the prophecy, and with this knowledge comes a retardation of the pulsations, preceding imagery that becomes less desultory, more comprehensible, and you stand, an impartial observer, watching the history of the world of reason – albeit greatly misused – disclosed before your eyes like pictures on a vast, universal page, as, from somewhere – either on inside or outside of your head – a rambling, logorrhoea accompanies the astral sojourn...

*...blackness, into which erupts an astronomical explosion, endless, nebulous, effulgent light, boundless, expanding, spreading infinitely, eternally, in every direction, a celestial cornucopia in the void, a kaleidoscope*

*of heavenly dust, of bodies, of forms, among them an infinitesimal particle, earth, to which a zoom-lens vision races, selects, identifies, pans across molten matter, evolving, tongue licks of fire, rising, jagged mountains of rock, austere, forbidding, raging, infertile oceans, becoming fertile giving life, single celled amoebic creation, evolution, proliferation, accretion, amelioration, biological birth, biological development, biological sophistication, biological culmination, humanity, images of humanity, images of its progenitorial incarnation, the ultimate objective always inherent, perpetual, constantly evidential, within the burgeoning forms, within insemination, viewed, as was decreed, piscine-human, amphibious-human, creature-human, animal-human, primate-human, human-human, human as learner, as hunter, as builder, as instructor, as mentor, as nomad, as settler, as developer, as innovator, as friend, as benefactor, as philanthropist, as altruist, as companion, as competitor, as rival, as lover, as opponent, as coveter, as protagonist, as deceiver, as enemy, as conqueror, as destroyer, as killer, as victim, creation, nullification, destruction, desolation, for most, but not for all, humanity will survive, by change, by adaption, by transfiguration, by biological transmutation, by genetic selectivity, by divine inspiration, by divine aspiration, by divine realisation, humanity will become its own creator, its own god, humanity will be human-like, it will become homo deus, become its own complete god, by intervention, by guidance, by submission, by subjection, by humility, by love, by acceptance, by sequacious resolution, by devotion, by implantation, by admission of the omniscient state, by ingenuous supplication, by un-recusant loyalty, by veracious obeisance, all this, analogous to that which has already come to pass, to that which already exists, humanity toiling in a world of content, of shape, of light, of darkness, of colour, working the land, sowing seeds, reaping, sowing, erecting abodes, fortresses, castles, conurbations, defending the home, the land, the home-land, loving, hating, propagating, living, killing, dying, post-death, matter dispersed, dust in the ground, dust of land, land cultivated, sown with seeds, harvest born from dust, from humanity's rotted flesh, from blood dried, from clay, food of descendants, humanity that was is humanity that is what humanity becomes, its own heritage, its own existence, its own future, the way, which has been, which would be, unless, until now, until interjection, until the Theophany, from which will come cerebral acceleration, cerebral divination, not from goodness, purity, guilt, conscience or edict of right or wrong, promulgated by misguided theologians, for humanity intrinsically remains animalistic, it is not within its spiritual or intellectual capacity to realise this objective alone, but from a benevolent, extraneous source, which has striven across millennia to perfect an absolute mutation, by patience, by appliance, by appropriation, by assimilation, by dedication, hence the sporadic appearances of the guiding lights, incongruous giants of intellect, innovation, erudition, possessing the knowledge to show the way out of an individually appointed period, gathering the faithful for the journey forward, not the faithful of spiritual life springing forth from death, the requirement being faith in the ultimate physical morphology, and intellectual objective of the imminent human semi-deity, which is the basic, protoplasmic, chemical foundation for the nascent god, not the fabled, ethereal god of myth, of legend, but a god of flesh and blood, of corporeality, a god that occupies space and time with physical substance, able to transcend the human prison of life by means of thought and by awareness of what is, not what might be or what could be, a god who can, by design, manipulate the continuum to the benefit of the seed, which is to come, possessing ever greater understanding as progression succeeds progression, for this you have been chosen, selected, for this you are privileged, granted an exegesis, an enlightenment, and to this purpose are you supplied with the definitive paramour, appointed to go forth, to exemplify your descendants, who, through this will become closer to godliness, a final seed allowed conception among the civilised barbarians of this inconsequential part of the galaxy called earth, for the time of its conclusion is at hand, the Beast stirs, is becoming awake, the embryo of destruction readies itself for the bursting of its amniotic shell, for being let loose upon this sphere to rent and burn that from which it is born, the Beast spawned by residue of the cosmic juxtaposition, by the moulding together of particular molecular patterns, a synthesis formulated within parochial, myopic minds that have been used and misused by insidious, avaricious demagogues and despots to impose upon others chauvinistic ways and social/political acceptances of said despots, of their puissant synthesis, coercing the victims of the threat to submit their lands, their produce, their energies and personal wealth sources to the sometimes subtle, sometimes blatant totalitarian law, which is simply the law of the tyrant, the oppressor, the strongest, for they that possess it have power absolute, making them the authority to inflict such laws, and their avarice, their unquenchable thirst for command has brought about the birth of the Beast, which is evil incomparable, being born from evil, from their evil, and will bring about the demise of this insignificant spheroid, and of all life upon it, an irony primarily created by the ongoing separation, sectarianism, racialism and conflict of beliefs that cause antipathy and hatred between creeds, tribes, societies, cultures and civilisations who differ in those beliefs, while the whole time representative factions remain involved in seeking the very same goal, the same falsely promised redemption of their respective invented deities within separate believing cultures, but because all roads that lead to this cata-*

*lyst are diverse and legion human hearts have become incapable of compromise, unwilling to adopt a syncretism, thus causing the downfall and termination of this doomed planet, so, chosen ones, you have need for great haste, for by your own union shall you take a step towards the sanctity and partial survival of humankind, towards a complete freedom, even one that demands a forsaking of the birthplace of the species, however, necessity rules, as the original quest and intention to tutor them in the way, the destiny, of this existence failed, they were presented with the concept of the Lamb, which was rejected and repudiated, cast out in favour of more worldly things, of scientific, empirical, self-gained knowledge, that led to arrant logistics, which, in turn, led to the ultimate self-assertion, conceit and pre-eminence of a supreme egoism, that dictated humanity as ruler and keeper of its own fate, as its own god, by the directive of hard, fast, unbending secularism, it has come full circle, passed through all the phases, but has learned nothing, continuing to believe that the human creature is free to do with this world as it pleases, its overall soul remaining unredeemed, having become one with the serpent, the Evil Entity, raising its status to that of victory, which, although complete, shall be shallow and short-lived, for the very seeds of the Evil Entity have formed to compose its own nemesis, the Beast, for they are one and the same, a bifurcation of twisted desire, of uncaring ambition, denying that a need to dominate does not accord with a need to destroy, the latter being that which culminates in the road to self-destruction, the Babel doctrines are doomed, and soon the self-inflicted genocide will begin...*

The narrative ends, and the hand is removed from your head, but a temporary numbness persists until an arrowed thought pierces your mind, forcing you to enquire of yourself, over and over again, Why me? Why me? By what, or who's recommendation have I been chosen? By what criteria? How and why do *I* qualify for such knowledge? As you shake your head, desperately trying to rid yourself of the confusion, you feel a pressure against your cheek, gently easing your face to your right. With her cool fingertips touching your perspiring skin, you look into the white, lifeless eyes that seem to be attempting to communicate something through their awful blankness. In order to accompany and support such a non-stirring of emotion, almost as compensation, her lower lip begins to tremble slightly, and she tentatively leans towards you, kissing you full on the mouth. This is followed by a kind of electric charge that flashes inside your brain as the hierophantic voice continues, You must not tarry, Go now, time grows short. As your lips part, she takes your hand in hers, and you rise up together, eyes lowered. When it is done, the voice goes on, When it is confirmed, your intercessor will come to you and the exodus will begin. Slowly, apprehensively, you raise your gaze to where the oratory originated, up the length of the resplendent silver robe enshrouding the body, to the face, from which the features are already starting to fade. Before they actually disappear, however, before the flesh completely unmoulds itself into the featureless state, you catch a glimpse of that which had been there – eyes, emitting an expression of utter, desperate sadness, surveying you with the intense sympathy reserved for a wounded, endanger-listed animal, set in a face, long-drawn, ascetic, with angular cheekbones beneath pale, insalubrious flesh that contrasts sharply with what could only have been the unshaved shadow of a beard and moustache adorning jaw and upper lip of a straight, thin, mouth. The main speciality of the whole visage, though, is one that sends a shiver up your spine, for there, before your disbelieving eyes, dotted across the forehead, are a line of scars, red and livid, an archipelago of blood, swallowed up at each temple by a dark jungle of curls tumbling down, like a baroque frame around a ghostly, icon portrait. Then, in the final, dying instants of transformation, a faint smile touches the corners of the mouth and the head executes a condolent nod. Bowing your own head once more, you grip the girl's hand even tighter, before slowly retreating from the emotive presence. Somehow, the situation strikes you as comparable to the time you sought to back away from the bathroom mirror without gaining knowledge of what its reflections held. As you contemplate this, the figure raises its hands slightly, palms up, as if reluctant to let you go, and you are possessed of a fundamental understanding...

With the dream having ended, I sprawl almost in a state of shock. How long I have remained like this – eyes closed but awake – I do not know. Pondering and recapitulating I have analysed and reanalysed the oneiric contents – the strongest yet – over and over again. Projected so clearly and vividly, they seem to be more in accordance with a memory of actual events, rather than with a subconscious release of the brain's captured energy – which is, after all, what dreams are supposed to consist of. Alternatively, terrifyingly, could the incident really have taken place? If so, how the hell did I *get* there – wherever it was? How did I get *back*? And why am I unable to properly address even the most basic elements of the hallucination – if, indeed that is what it was? Moreover, every other episode – seemingly the ones that were meant to count: every location, every note of the chants, every slanting shard of light, every feature of the faces – or lack of – stay fixed and rigid, etched into my otherwise spurious memory, like molten metal cooling in a mould.

And what is to be made of the awesome, presiding figure dressed in the silver robe? *Prima facie* implications are too monumental to contemplate. Although I will never forget that fading countenance – so saturnine but sympathetic; those eyes; the scars – even post acknowledgement of it causes me to break out in a cold sweat, one that demands a cessation of further conjecture. I have to mentally bury it – or at least circumnavigate it until it is deeply and hermetically entombed inside the core of my dubiety. By smothering it so, there is always a forlorn hope of it either detracting of its own accord, or else resolving itself into a more clement and acceptable explanation – one that is admissible to the utterly confused distemper that grips me. As things stand, the supposition is too alarming, too repercussive to accept, so I search for a surrogate theory that will refute the 'evidence' in my head. Inevitably, I fail; intuition and remembrance again and again coming to the same trenchant conclusion.

But I must resist it. I must continue to doubt, to ask myself: was not the incident merely yet another episode within the creative boundaries of *those* dreams, as Veronica refers to them? They must be. They *have* to be, and it is absolutely essential that I believe that, otherwise...But *If* I do believe, then why the troublesome inquietude? Why the post-somnial malaise? Such fallacious consternation is unbecoming in one of such Voltairean secularism. A conviction that it was simply a fantasy, a nocturnal dramaturgy spun by a persecuted imagination, must be maintained. Nevertheless, even when given the benefit of the doubt – that they are, indeed, just phantoms – the fact remains and cannot be controverted, that my recurring sojourns into oneiric catacombs *are* becoming more frequent and potent, demanding more attention, more credibility, manifesting a greater possibility of them being real. Incidences of where I find myself at a loss to speculate positively whether or not the memories fulgurating in my brain are those of dreams or actuality are increasing. In the no-man's-land that exists between them I am persistently haunted by chimeras and succubae – some benign, some malign; some charitable, some malefic. Also, I am threatened by winds, storms, and hostile oceans that may or may not be substantial. I am even mocked and provoked from within my own id by a demon of potentially uncontrollable iniquity.

Of equal or extra concern, of course, is the re-materialisation of the girl – or, at least, an ectype of her – so convincing that, if it were not for the anomalous eyes, I would be completely ensnared by now. I mean, how could such a skilful creator make such a blatant error? It must be added to my desperate interpretation of the dreams being dreams and nothing more. Nevertheless, she seemed so...real. Enigmatic, and apparently blessed with profound insight and Gnostic purpose, she led – leads? – me through the surrealistic landscapes of my own psyche, luring me to some indeterminate destination like a pneumatic Lorelei.

Raising a hand in the darkness, I wipe away perspiration that has re-formed on my forehead. My reaction to these mental occasions is becoming more physical; perhaps the whole evocation is, as theorised earlier, purely pathological, and I am suffering from some rare kind of fever or delirium. Is it possible that these mind-blowing events could really be traced back to a truculent, microscopic bug that had ambushed me from a reheated piece of meat or sausage roll? Such an a-priori is certainly a prospect I would welcome at the moment, suggesting an acceptable and practical solution, holding in its summary no more retribution than a dose of antibiotics. Maybe a simple inoculation would, indeed, send the hurtful little bastards packing. It is a warming thought.

Opening my eyes, I stare up at the skylight above. The firmament beyond is a void, with just the odd movement of cloud, made even more vague by the rivulets of water running down the glass like melting fingers. It is raining, and its gentle rhythm breaks the silence of the night, only to intermittently become scattered across the panes, injecting the monotony of the beat with a kind of reptilian hiss.

With eyes that have become accustomed to the shadows I turn to my right: Veronica sleeps peacefully at my side, oblivious to my neurosis. Her mouth is open just wide enough for me to be able to make out the minute glint of her teeth between her parted lips, while the rapid movement behind her eyelids conveys an unconscious mind exercising Freudian fantasies that are, hopefully, more agreeable than mine. At the same time as I listen to her breathing, I watch her breasts rising and falling beneath the single sheet that covers her. In her slumber she has thrown back a large section of it, leaving one pale arm to rest, limp and free, fingers of the hand relaxed like an open flower. And while I watch her, I count down the seconds as I perversely will her to evaporate, or to burst into flames, or some other silly extravagance that will confirm her incorporeality – but, as if to defy my worst fears, she remains there at my side, her presence denouncing me as paranoid.

Reaching out, I stroke the smooth, cool flesh of her cheek, while half expecting her to awaken – as she used to – and for her eyes to open and search me out in the gloom, her smile widening invitingly from the pillow; but there is no response, her awareness remains locked within the tightly closed shell of sleep. Tenderly, I move her arm, place it under the blanket, before covering the rest of her body up to her chin. Then, lying on my side, facing her, I watch her profile, and as I do so, I run the fingers of my free hand through her hair, as thick and unkempt as Medusa's coils.

Above, the rain continues to sprinkle the glass with its fluid tap-dance; below, our heads rest, side by side on the pillow, like pebbles dropped into a snowdrift.

I sleep…I think.

"I recall telling Domino: "I'm going to miss you."

Leaning out of the railway carriage window, she kissed my eyes. "I'm going to miss you, too." Then she smiled that smile I had come to know so well. "I won't be gone long, I promise; I'll be back before you know it."

"Every bloody hour will seem like a day," I told her, earnestly.

Between the sounds of doors slamming, and an indecipherable vocal message reverberating around the interior of the station, she said: "Now, now, Mr. Einstein, you take care of yourself, alright?" Tracing a line down my face with a well-manicured fingernail, she added: "At least you'll have some peace and quiet to work while I'm gone."

"Is that supposed to be consolation?" With a barely discernible movement the train began its silent slide. Walking along beside it, I grunted: "How the hell am I going to create anything minus my muse?"

"Pick me up here, when I return," she said, ignoring my query.

"Of course."

"I'll give you a call, let you know my time of arrival."

"I'll look forward to it."

Perceptively, the carriage gained speed, moving away from me. As I quickened my step to keep up, she leaned further out of the window, stretching her neck. Clumsily, we managed one last kiss, this time on the lips, and she was on her way. As she raised one hand to wave farewell, the other clutched a small, glinting crucifix at her throat, which, for a breathtaking instant in the diffused morning sunlight straining through the grimy, overhead glass, it illuminated a golden 'X' on her face, as though she were being 'crossed' out.

"Don't worry," she called, still just in earshot. "I'll come back. I'll always come back to you."

Even after the train had disappeared from view, I continued to stand there on the empty platform for much longer than the occasion demanded.

The silence is strange.
Not quite…right.
I open my eyes.
It is still raining.
Veronica continues to sleep at my side.

Something awakened me.
Something.
A shiver ascends my spine.
My heartbeat is erratic.
There is a…presence.
I know it.
I can feel it.
There is someone else in the room.
I am afraid.

Raising yourself up on your elbows, you scan the surrounding darkness. To your left, on the bedside table, rests a glass of water and the dormant rattlesnake shape of a silver strapped wristwatch. To your right lies Veronica, hair spread out like a sunburst on the pillow and arm once more exposed on the top of the sheet that blends into a shadowed penumbra at the foot of the bed. All is still and silent, until the light, sprinkling rain suddenly intensifies into the sound of a million ant's feet scuttling across the panes of the skylight, before, just as suddenly, subsiding to its former pedestrian state. What was it that disturbed you? Awakened you? Wrenched you from an otherwise condition of relaxed insensibility? As you await on an echo of whatever it could have been, your pulse accelerates, creating a crawling sensation on your skin, one that seems to signal the approach of something. And a knowing feeling abides. With the saliva in your mouth drying to sand, a strange paralysis clenches the nerves in your stomach. Straining your eyes, you peer into the very fabric of night, searching confirmation of your suspicion. At first, there is nothing…but, gradually…you see it. Initially no more than a disturbance in the air, it begins to shimmer in the atmosphere, forming a prefiguration of a shape that becomes movement, motion and a soft rippling swish of material. Consisting of mass and of density it occupies space. You wait, suspended, unable to move, anticipating an appearance. And she glides towards you, one step. Soundlessly, her disembodied face unfurls from the darkness, followed by a sigh, as muted as a rose petal drifting to the ground on thermal waves. Underneath the face you can just make out the details of the same consuming cloak she had been wearing on the previous occasion you saw her. It flows from her shoulders like a frozen waterfall while some of the loose strands of her black hair rest among its folds. Staring at you with those soulless, lifeless eyes, she seems to hover at the foot of the bed like a vampire awaiting a welcome. Still unable to move a muscle, you hear the soft pad of a bare foot on the floor as she takes another step forward. After a moment's hesitation, she advances one step further, until she is close enough to look down at you. And you look back up at her – two opposing figures encapsulated in a Dutch old master. Slowly…ever so slowly, her hand materialises from the shadows to rise like a cobra from waist to chin. Mesmerised by its movement, you gape as delicate fingers unhook the clasp at her throat. The material slides from her shoulders with the gravitational speed of melted snow and she stands before you, naked. Above, another sibilant downpour cascades across the skylight and dies away. The subsequent retinal impasse between you is broken by the lowering of her eyes and the bowing of her head, before one final step gives her access to the bed, from where she reaches forward, pulling away the sheet that covers you. Imperiously casting it aside, she watches impassively as it floats across to land as a shroud on the sleeping figure of Veronica. Questioningly, you confront the succubus looming over you, who whispers, Do not concern yourself, she will not awaken. It is the first time you have heard her voice and its modulations serve only to confuse you more than ever, qualifying nothing. It *sounds* like Domino's speech patterns – and yet it does not. But you are immediately robbed of your sense of wonder of her, as, without further ado, she first straddles you and then lowers herself onto you, like a hen onto an egg. To your surprise there is a resistance, a constriction obstructing the way, one that forces her to rise up, before lowering herself again. This action is accompanied by a profuse lubrication, and, at last, entry is achieved. Now, thrusting your pelvis upward, you seek to coordinate and facilitate her movements, but, as you do so, her gyrations cease long enough for her to clasp your wrists tightly, guiding your hands to her breasts. Continuing as before, but now with greater acceleration, she bumps and grinds, arching her torso until her thrown back head disappears above a white, smooth, throat. This is followed by a shudder and then by a strangulated gasp that freezes her in the Rodin-esque pose for almost a minute, before her body subsequently collapses forward from the waist, her hair falling in the manner of a final curtain, over both her face and the preceding carnal act. Gradually, as her breathing retards she places a hand each side of your chest, leaning close enough for her eyes to take on the illusion of distant, pinpoint stars against the silhouette of her head. After kissing you once, almost distractedly, she straightens her spine, sits up, and stares across at the still sleeping figure of Veronica. A smile, comparable to the one witnessed at the beach, rather than the one at the oasis, widens the corners of her mouth to expose teeth that gleam with the same malign luminosity as her eyes. It is a smile that disturbs you, not so much as the first time you witnessed it, but enough to plant the seed of doubt in your mind. Who are you? You ask her. The empty eyes refocus on you. You are not who you appear to be, you say, You look like her, you speak like her, you even have some of her sexual predilections – but you are not her. The smile remains, fixed, teeth still glinting like pearls, as she answers, I am the one you most yearn for, the one you most desire. Not wishing to offend her, you hesitate, but still conclude you must say that which must be said – before the situation escalates to a point where nothing exists but the abyss. I…am not…sure anymore, you stutter. For a moment or two it remains set, but then the smile is erased, vanishes as the pale gaze flickers back to the fair-haired Veronica beside you. I see, she says, more to herself than to you, We feared as much, therefore something will be done…soon. As she utters the final word, her gaze returns to meet yours, and you feel it bore into your very soul. *Someone once described to me the effect of hypnotic suggestion, of the awareness of reality, but of the inability to cling to it – the will becoming subservient to the directives…*As though imbued with enlightenment, her vocal register seems to instil within you a profound understanding and, just for a few moments, everything makes sense, as though you have suddenly been granted a bird's eye view – despite a conscious realisation that, deep down, it stems from nothing more than a desperate longing for a return to order and normality, to peace and stability, so you allow yourself to drift with the flow, to accept specious promises of wellbeing, like an impoverished member of the electorate being swayed and duped by a mendacious, smooth-tongued politician. Yes, you hear yourself agreeing, almost with indifference…soon. With that, seemingly of their own volition, your hands move downward, sliding around to grip peach smooth buttocks, while, at the same time you ease yourself up until your face is level with her breasts. What else can you do? Whether she be angel or demon, confronted with the prospect of losing yourself in the soft contours of this dream lover's charms, it is so easy to give in, to shed the doubts and fears, to let slip the burden of responsibility, and to seek psychological succour through physical gratification. *The road to excess leads to the palace of wisdom.* While bowing her head to smother you in a shroud of hair that feels like aromatic cobwebs, your extremities begin to ferret, as quick as rodents, over and into her body. Such priapism is a rare experience for you, but somehow it does not seem strange, since your mind has become blind –. or blinded – to logic. The only thing that matters is the aseity of now, in whatever form it takes, in whatever reality or…fiction. As if to consolidate this abandonment of reason, she draws you into herself, fingers scrawling up and down your spine, nails as soft and sharp as the clawed paws of a kitten. And as you fall back onto the bed, supine, you pull her down with you, holding her gently but firmly, the motions of your body in unison with hers, creating a climax that is smoother, more intimate, and less spasmodic...human.

When it is done, you both recline there for a long time without moving, conscious only of each other's physicality, of its smell, aura and occupied space. Next to you, Veronica, as a living, breathing entity, means nothing.

Perhaps you dozed, perhaps she did, perhaps you both did. Nevertheless, what you are presently aware of, is her retreat from you. Sliding away like a vapour she stands and throws her hair back from her face, before bending to collect her robe from the floor. Re-immersing herself within its mysterious folds she looks down at you and smiles – but this time you are not even aware of the expression, because your gaze has become distracted to a point past where she stands, up towards the rectangular skylight above, and waves of fear and disgust engulf you. There, on the roof, squatting like a gargoyle, is the peccant scavenger of your psyche, and as you shamefacedly scramble to cover yourself from its diabolical inspection, it grins, hideously, while nodding its head with a knowing affirmation. Exhaling a loud cry of rage, you raise your clawed hands with murderous intent. But the creature merely laughs at you and keeps on nodding, pinning you down with its glaring evil eye, until you feel like an impotent baby in a crib. However, as the rainclouds disperse from the sky the twin sparks of light fade from the cacodemon's red pupils to become just two more distant stars in an otherwise star-ridden night sky. Simultaneously, you realise the Domino facsimile has also disappeared, so you await the fresh metaphorical darkness that is about to descend on you with a mixture of resignation and despair.

"Are you going to answer that?" Veronica asks, irritated.

Lying on the bed, fully clothed, hands clasped behind my head and legs crossed, I listen impassively while the telephone screeches like a tormented parakeet.

"I said –"

"I heard you."

Marching in from the kitchenette, she stops and stares at me sourly for a moment before lifting the receiver. "Yes?"

With scant interest I watch her as she tries to make excuses for the delay of the painting – which I have not even glanced at since the last time I showed it to her. The thing has ceased to have any significance for me. Gripping the telephone with one hand, she gesticulates wildly with the other, uncomfortable and embarrassed, attempting to reaffirm her stand against the obviously invective tones on the other end of the line. Replacing the receiver down with a clatter, she storms off, back towards the kitchenette. As she reaches the door, she turns.

"That was –"

"I know who it was."

"Then you'll damned-well know what they wanted," she hisses, almost venomously.

Sighing loudly and demonstratively, I throw my legs off the bed and shrug my shoulders. Feeling her eyes burn into the back of my skull, I find I am at a loss as to what to say to her. I do not even know what to do next. Wary of having to face yet another argument, I rise to my full height and approach the door.

"If you go out again..." she warns, as I take down the dark overcoat from its hook on the wall. "If you leave me here on my own once more..."

Standing with my back to her, fingers curled around the door handle, I stare at the pale skin on the back of my hand.

"Did you hear me?"

"I heard you," I confirm, and quietly leave the room.

For hours I have wandered over hillock, dune and sandy ridge – a figure in a landscape. At the moment I am standing on the edge of a precipice, a sheer escarpment, staring vacantly out to sea. The water is muddy-looking, restless, like squirming rats in a canvas bag, as waves spit at rocks with contempt.

If I were to step forward...
Now.

On the horizon, a black, pencil-shaped tanker gropes its way over a gunmetal ocean like a slow-moving slug against the canescence of the sky. I watch it and I watch it until it melts into the slowly infiltrating evening gloom. Starting out on my way back home, a fine, misty rain descends to keep me company.

Grey on grey.

Throwing off my sodden overcoat, I enter the small kitchen, where everything is unusually clean and orderly – post-Veronica. Thoughtfully, she has regimented every piece of cutlery and dish away in their respective drawers and cupboards before leaving; it will take only a minimum effort on my part to clutter them up again. The place is quiet, lacking personality and character, like returning home from school to discover that your parents are not there. Already I am filled with regret and self-loathing, missing not just the salutations of a lover, but also the exacting tones and imprecations of a saviour. I am fully aware, of course, that I should not have treated her so; I should not have let her go. But things had gotten out of control – *I* had gotten out of control – or, at least, my *mind* had. There was an aura of chaos in the air, casting us as bathers swimming against a tide of emotional slime. It had to end. Just when victory was in sight, too – just when I was beginning to feel like a human being again. But now the hope, the budding optimism and incipient happiness has evaporated, allowing old acquaintances – reclusiveness, misanthropy and loneliness – to resettle like homing pigeons in their coop. Once more I discover that, I – say *I*, am imprisoned inside my own head, courting phantoms and ghosts of my own making. How the *fuck* could a hallucinatory visitation – a *wet dream* – have been so convincing.

The anger that grips me is sudden and uncontrollable, causing me to throw open doors, only to throw them shut again, followed by a bull-in-a-china-shop forage until, at last, I find that which Veronica had tried to hide from me.

Selecting a bottle from the cache, I unscrew its metal cap, place the open neck to my lips and...swallow deeply. Coming up coughing like a sot, my throat burns as though scraped raw. But I just grin; that was simply a lack of recent practice. So, before giving myself time to recover from the alcoholic onslaught, to even think about what I am doing, I repeat the process, again and again and again, until...tearing off my clothes with one hand, I manage to stumble towards the bed, where I collapse into blissful indulgence and...escape.

I have no idea how long I've been out of it – how many days, that is – because, once again, it's dark outside. My semiconscious – or unconscious – state has been protracted and deep – although obviously not protracted and deep enough, as the headache still clings to the back of my neck like a rabid bulldog, its bite exacerbated by the half empty bottle still clenched in my jealous fist. However, despite my unrecognised desperation of the situation, and without a second thought, I pull off the cap in order to minister even more helpings of amnesia, drunkenly reasoning that a rear-guard dose will also act as an analgesic, sending me back into peaceful, dreamless oblivion. Of course, this prescription can only result in an even greater excruciating pain when I reawaken, but such self-claiming facts are currently as useful to me as a chocolate kettle; they're all too much too far away – somewhere in the distant future. Back in the present, one more mouthful almost completely quells the presiding burning effect because my sensory reaction is by now numbed, my receptibility dimmed to that of waves of static on a broken radio channel. And yet, amidst this torpor I can still hear the distant boom and hiss of the sea, helping to introspectively confirm my recidivism, and to acknowledge the redonning of the reprobate overcoat. This means that the degenerative personality is back in the driving seat, relegating the principled brick – emancipated by Veronica – to inconsequentiality or absolute nullity for the foreseeable future. Even so, from somewhere unplumbed inside me, a minute, common-sense resistance attempts to start a revolution, and is momentarily successful – guilty thoughts and associations flitting through my mind like Lethean pigeons – but a further spot of 'medicine' not only regains control, it also, to my surprise, contravenes that control, by helping me to remember an applicable condolence, an explanation theorised by Carl Gustav Jung – about the *soi-disant* unity of consciousness being illusory, and about alternative complexes existing within a single mind. Complexes possessing a willpower and ego of their own, creating a condition of schizophrenia, releasing themselves from conscious control – becoming personalities unto themselves. His particular demonstration was illustrated as gradually darkening circles, representing different spheres of the mind, circles that decrease in circumference, until becoming a central black hole of collective unconsciousness. The subject's conscious authority surrenders to the unconscious, and when this happens the unconscious part becomes galvanised, augmenting until gradually subjugating the conscious. The subject sinks completely into unconsciousness, to become dominated by the newly formed authority of the central black hole. A fantasy takes over, with one or more of the multiple personalities gaining prominence. Wow! Does that sound fucking familiar or what? So, conclusion: Veronica must have watched this happen to me – eventually realising that the situation was irredeemable – before leaving. This time probably for good.

What the hell did I expect? Did I really think she was going to stay here, sacrificing her time and life, while I allowed phantoms to rule mine? Strangely enough, however, now that she has gone, so have the phantoms. I have not suffered a single dream since her departure. That could simply be down to the excessive consumption of alcohol, of course, but heavy drinking had never deterred my nightmares before. So, I suppose that must reveal something profound about me – God knows what, though. All I am certain of at this moment is…I'm alone again, with only memories and regrets to keep me company. A state of reality – finally realised – swathes me in its bundle of facts, bitterness and truth, persuading me that the dreams were just that – dreams – and nothing more. The actuality of my life is unconnected with mysterious or romantic theories. I am here; the dreams are there. I exist here – separately, obviously, uncomplicatedly. Who was it said, a momentary revelation is worth more than a lifetime of not knowing? Perceptive fucker, whoever it was.

Shaking my head, I force a further mouthful of liquor through gritted teeth. Some of it spills down my chin, issuing a warning of repletion. Reluctantly, I screw the top back on the bottle before dropping it beside the bed. Closing my eyes, I watch the visions pulsate behind the lids, awaiting them to start to whirl and oscillate, signalling a bilious attack. On the other hand, they may just diffuse and die – dissipate into the darkness of…sleep.

Ah! Fuck it! So what? Bring it on, Hypnos. Come, you bastard of oblivion – I can confront anything you can create.

You look into a void that is ink black, like death. A cold and empty state, a visible core of loneliness. It is what theologians and fools call a soul, inside which your consciousness churns like a microbe, drifting in blood, helpless, aimless, powerless to negotiate its flux and currents. Carried along its fluvial path, you bob and float, feeling its chill, its substance, its volume, its icy caress around you, until, out of the blackness and the blindness, you perceive faces. Some rush at you quickly, and are gone even more so, screaming silently, their eyes and mouths filled with the ebony ichor. Others swirl among the eddies for a while, still more hover like hawks on the wind, mouths open, words smothered by the spatial density, impotent tongues waggling. All become swept along by effluent surges. Only the odd few remain to defy the influences long enough to project recognition. Two faces in particular. Veronica, her skin pale, the underparts of her eyes darkened by fear, stress and tears, asks you, over and over again, Why did you do this to me? Why did you do this to me? While Domino's features come and go transiently on a visage of white flesh, contours forming and evanescing in unison with a pulsating mouth, saying, The seed must be expedited, There is so little time. The seed must be expedited, There is so little time. But you are only able to watch the images with numbness and incomprehension, as the words become, first audible, then distant, then audible, then distant again. Slowly, gradually, the countenances fade and evaporate into darkness until only the words abide. Eventually, they, too, drift off into obscurity, leaving you with Veronica's alone, her question now a statement, echoing silently from the limbo, You are killing me, You are killing me, You are…

Opening your eyes, you sit up, jerkily, like a puppet suddenly stirred by a bad-tempered puppet master. Momentarily, a blindness persists, but only until you realise it is simply the natural darkness of the room. In a similar process to photographs developing on plates, shapes mould themselves out of the shadows while Veronica's entreaties continue to ring in your ears, plaintively whispering down a long, empty tunnel. But since the voice is confined to the inside your head, the silence of reality overtakes it, swamping it, until it becomes transmitted into just the drip, drip, drip of subdued rain pattering on the glass above, or a distant gurgle of residual water chuckling from the mouth of a drainpipe somewhere outside. Further away, the sea is reduced to nothing more than a soft sigh in the heart of no-man's land. Surprised by the absence of a hangover, pain or the urge to vomit, you lie there, thinking and waiting for the debilitating morbidity to gather its forces for an all-out attack. But nothing comes. Effects of extreme alcohol abuse appear to have been swallowed, digested and magically disposed of while you slept. There are no sorry consequences at all. On the contrary, you actually feel quite vigorous and fit. Easing back the bedsheet, you gaze down the length of your naked body and you smile a smile of recognition, because you can sense the presence of your nocturnal temptress. She is here. You can hear her breathing. Rising from the bed, you approach the platform in the corner of the studio. Above the skylight, the clouds part to allow the gleeful face of a full moon to blink through, nocturnally spotlighting her in the same way that the sun had diurnally spotlighted Veronica. She is naked and sits like an eastern goddess in the centre of the dais, legs crossed in a full lotus, exposing the thick triangle of black pubic hair. With arms bent and palms pressed together, she sits as if in prayer, head bowed, long tresses hanging each side of her face. As you watch in silent awe, she slowly raises her head to look at you. I remain barren, she says, we must try again. Nodding in the affirmative, you reach out and take her hand, observing the almost reptilian motion of her limbs as she uncoils herself to stand, pressing her body against you, tummy muscles undulating like a nervous belly dancer. This time, she says, I will stay until it is done, until we are sure, as I am now able to look within myself, and will know the precise moment of conception. Again, you nod, leaning to kiss her mouth, slowly, languidly, in order to savour the taste of her, your hands meandering over her body with a touch normally reserved for rare works of art. Easing herself about, she leans back to recline among the haphazard folds of the bedsheet, from where she guides you in – at first gently – before spoiling the mood somewhat by moving prematurely, hindering you, disturbing the equilibrium. Very quickly, however, you manage to resolve the situation by manoeuvring her into a position whereby her spine rests on the very edge of the bed. From there you are able to thrust forward with a new accessibility, taking the weight on your hands and staring down into her…manufactured? face as you move. As if reading your thoughts, she both closes her eyes and opens her mouth, breathing more rapidly and forcibly, causing you to stop for a moment, fearing something is wrong – but she continues to writhe beneath you, unaware of your concern. As a matter of fact, her breathing becomes even more nasal and shallow, its rhythm in unison with the increasing tempo of her hips, making it difficult for you to counterthrust, until, for a second time, you momentarily cease. Opening her eyes again, she closes them again, before gasping loudly as you now succeed in coordinating your movements with hers, the alacrity required temporarily deflecting any realisation of a kind of regulated prolongation of the expected finality. It feels as if you have lost control of your bodily functions, and that you are being physically manipulated in some way. As this awareness dawns on you, though, she, at that moment, arches her back and pushes down hard, an action meant to herald an end to what has come about, as though planned and orchestrated by some strange, external force.

It is over. As you rest, supine and spent, staring up at the clearly defined lunar orb in the sky, a movement to your right causes you to turn towards the beautiful, unworldly profile beside you, where small jewels of perspiration on her forehead and upper lip cast an ambiguous spell on your on-off interpretation of reality. This is no dream. It cannot be. It is *not*. She *is* substantial. Such painstaking details of perfection neutralise the 'error' of the eyes – now closed – rendering her presence indisputable, and slamming the door on any Jungian, pseudo psychological escape route into the land of fantasy or make-believe. The dark, magic, central circle bullet has been exposed as a fallacy. She still exists – in spite of your mindset remaining as solid as the furthest outer ring – corporeal and seductive, a deliverer of absolution and somatic delights. It makes you feel as though you could stay like this forever, contemplating, remembering and reliving conversations and silences gone by. But, suddenly, you wonder just how long you have been engaged with these thoughts, as something strange seems to have taken place. Where is the moon? Where has it gone? The sky remains cloudless, and yet you can no longer locate its selenic influence in the heavens. It takes hours to pass across the complete panorama of the skylight – but it appears to have done so without you noticing. And your mood darkens. The answer is obvious, of course. You were wrong. The lovemaking had been nothing more than a single episode wrapped within the package of one of *those* dreams. A fucking *wet* dream, no less. Jesus! None of it had actually taken place. With a sense of despair and disappointment falling like the shadow of an eagle over a helpless lamb, you exhale a sigh that is almost a sob. But wait. What is that? Can it be? Yes! It is the touch of her fingers on your arm. Stirring like a lioness she closes in on you to plant a gentle kiss on your cheek. Be patient, my love, she whispers, Have faith, You must wait while I meditate, while I confer with a higher order. With that, she rises to revisit the dais in the corner of the room. There, she sits at its centre in a readopted full lotus, immobile, silent, barely breathing. You watch her for as long as you can, heart now as light as a drifting balloon, before the shadows arrive to gather about her as an aphotic halo, whereby, either your eyelids droop and you succumb to slumber, or else she slowly disappears…

Looking around, even though you can still smell her fragrance and sense her presence, you are alone. It is raining heavily once more, and you hear its volume increase to a torrent on the glass above. Raising somewhat unsteadily from the bed, you shiver in your nakedness, while quickly searching out your discarded denims, slipping them on alongside a shirt from inside one of Veronica's recently tidied cupboards. Ambling about the studio in a kind of stupor, you touch things, pick things up, before putting them back down again, your actions culminating in a visit to the kitchenette, where you idly stare at the utensils therein, before making an exit. Following that, you step into the diminutive bathroom, where you urinate, wash your hands and return to the area of the bed without knowing why. Although now, for the first time, you notice that the door leading to the outside is open, and that a strange light is penetrating through the aperture. It is not the blue light of the moon – still missing – or the reflected glare of any internal light, it is much brighter, a rufescent light of…alien quality. Like rippling torch beams, its rays probe the interior with fingertip deftness, while you, cautiously, step forward. Opening the door wide, you stare out into the weirdly lit night. There she stands, with her back to you, naked in the rain, legs together, arms straight, raised slightly from her hips, head back, the glow from the sky illuminating her body like red chalk scribbled on a blackboard, motionless, an unswaying image not even emanating any sign of exertion or breathing. She is like a shell, or husk, who's life source has been completely sucked out. Looking up into the obscurity of a dense sky, you observe that the object, or light, is ill defined, just an anonymous glare in the dark, just something blurred by falling rain. Filled with trepidation, you approach her, staring at the long black hair that cascades down her back, almost to her buttocks, which are firm, muscles as rigid and as tense as a marble statue. Either she ignores you or she is unaware of you, because she does not move. Her body is as stiff as a mannequin – a de Chirico mannequin? – and you step so close to her that you could, if so inclined, reach out and touch her – her shoulder, her hips, her arms or her hair. Her…hair. There is…something strange about it. Standing and staring at it for – how long? – you try to absorb the nonsensical evidence on display before you. Apart from the rain and the distant sea, there is no sound. Apart from the light and the girl, there is no other visual image. So, there can be no ambiguity, no misrepresentation or anomaly of light. What you can see, you can see. What is…is. Raising your hand, you slowly reach out. Place your fingers on her head. On her hair. And there is no doubt. Immediately your hand begins to shake. Not from the cold – although it is cold – but from disbelief and incomprehension. How can this be? It can*not* be. Such states only exist as verbal abstractions or as symbols – there is no place for them in nature or even in the world of experimental physics. But the reality is…*She is dry.* Again, and again you run your hand over the shimmering tresses hanging there before you – and they continue to confound you. They remain devoid of wetness, or even of moisture. Somehow, they are repelling the falling droplets as though protected by some invisible forcefield or undetectable membrane. Elsewhere about her person is the same – her shoulders, her hips and legs are all as dry as parchment. Even though your hand is soaked, bespeckled by a thousand tiny liquid jewels, her flesh remains immune from the downpour. A sudden clamour – one not unfamiliar to you – sets up station inside your skull, inflating like a ball of flame in your brain, followed by an agonising prickling sensation, sizzling up your spine, swirling around the back and sides of your neck to your jaw, where it proceeds to clench your teeth into a vicelike rictus – your tongue becoming adhered to the roof of your mouth with the suction power of a limpet on a rock. And at that moment, she moves. Emitting a long, loud sigh, her arms jerk outwards, her back shivers and her breasts rise with a following great intake of breath. Watching her tilt her head forward, you await the terrible inevitability of that which is going to happen next. As the wind rises, her hair begins to swirl and dance about a head that turns towards you with the kind of slow-motion, single frame action used for dramatic effect in movies. It is only half turned when your worst fears are realised. The flat profile – suspended in time – continues to 'click' around, each tiny motion, each millimetre bringing it closer. Unable to move, afflicted by an unrelenting grip of paralysis, you stand there and stare, mesmerised by what you see before you. She has no eyes. She has no nose. She has no mouth. There is just a white, blank, impassive mask of flesh surrounded by waves of thick, flowing hair. A void. A…white space, from within which comes the sound of a voice – her voice – existing only inside your head, saying, It is done, now we must part and wait for the time to come, then I will return to you, my love, I will return to summon you…before the… Event…

SOMETHING
AN OCCURANCE
AN INCONGRUITY IN THE VOID
IN THE UBIQUITOUS VACUITY OF NON-EXISTENCE
A DISTANT MOTE
A PARTICLE OF…SOMETHING

"Domino!" I snapped. "For Christ's sake!"

"But you have been seeing her!"

"I have *seen* her. I have not been *seeing* her."

"That is *not* what I heard."

"I don't give a fuck what you heard. I'm telling you the truth."

"I don't believe you."

I stared at her, my brain ablaze with anger.

"It would account for things," she persisted.

"What things?"

A loud sigh. "You know what I'm talking about."

"You're clutching at straws," I told her.

"Am I? Then why are you unable to make it lately?"

That shut me up. I could not answer – not simply, not conclusively, not in a way that would appease her indignation. In spite of the invective, I did not want to hurt her. But I could not really explain it, either, could not describe the sudden, intrusive feelings that had started to attack my subjectivity, that laid bare a sense of absurdity dogging me halfway through the act – the momentary flashes of myself from a point suspended somewhere just below the ceiling, revealing my actions and mannerisms as those of a demented, wind-up toy. There was no way I could think of to gently elucidate my recognition of her Judy to my Punch. Ergo, I had to treat the symptoms on the basis of temporality – something that had been brought on by tension and worry. The tension created by the worry and wondering about how the hell I was going to carry on living without a source of income, now that the Veronica induced commissions had dried up. Frantic phone calls to old clients had proved fruit-less. The unreliability that had become attached to my name like a label put them on their guard. No one was prepared to take a chance anymore. Even though Domino's presence continued to spasmodically blinker me, under-neath, deep inside me, concern for my career was steadily eating away like a cancer. Hence the guilt complex and ephemeral impotence.

"Listen," I said. "I'm not in the habit of lying to –"

"Stop seeing Veronica, "she interjected, "and you won't have to – will you?"

With reconciliation thwarted, I lost my temper again. "How many times do I have to say it? I have not been seeing, meeting or screwing

Veronica – at least, not since I met you. And, even if I had, I don't see what right you have to…"

Something happened then, behind her eyes. As she watched my face, it was as if a curtain had dropped, veiling the expression and locking out reason. Her voice, when it came, was low, sibilant.

"Oh, I have a right," she hissed; adding after a short pause: "A right that can – and will, one day – be exercised."

This morning I almost did it. Almost. I got up, entered the bathroom, took a long, hard look at my face, at its sallow complexion, its expression of inane sensibility, and opened the door of the medicine cabinet. I had gotten this far before, of course, in the dark days following the accident: I had taken down the bottle and perused it somewhat longingly. This time, though, as calm as you like, I unscrewed the top, poured the contents into the palm of my hand, filled a tumbler with water and actually placed two pills on my tongue. Watching myself carefully in the maculated mirror, I closed my mouth in order to better appreciate the acrid tang on the back of my throat. But when I raised the tumbler to my lips, I…just remained there, like that, until the tablets gradually dissolved by natural process. What stopped me, I ask myself, from carrying out the procedure fully? Why did I demur yet again? It would have been so easy to simply deposit the rest of the deadly little mites within the consenting orifice, to lubricate the way with water from the well-used receptacle, and then just to have sat there and waited. Everything was in place, stage set, conditions ideal. I was completely alone, with no likelihood of anyone disturbing me, or reviving me from the ensuing coma. It would have been all over and done with by now. And yet – after a severe coughing bout – I'm still here. What was Aristotle's question again? '…if water itself sticks in a man's throat, what do you give him to wash it down with?' Because all I did, eventually, was to swallow…water. Goddammit! Such crazy fucking thoughts. My fucking head is full of them. Even more of them are at work at this very moment, bugging me like a swarm of mosquitoes. If I had really intended to go through with it, then this morning would have been the most propitious time. A state of absolute despair presided. There were no excuses. Which means…what? That my intentions were ungenuine after all? Or did I just postpone the inevitable – once more? Who knows? The word 'intention' has so many connotations. It is… ambiguous. Even the philosopher, Ludwig Wittgenstein had problems with it. Perhaps it would be more apt to label it…ambivalent. Let's just say I have…ambivalent feelings towards the act. Mind you, there have been stories of other frauds, too: people of the same disposition as myself, who have manipulated time and locations to coincide with discovery of the dirty deed, resulting in no damage being done. And then there are others, who, having administered a lethal dose, impassively changed their minds before journeying to the nearest hospital, where they had the whole lot pumped out again. Of which section of human depressives am I a member? Am I simply just one more of life's pitiful teasers? Or is there, lurking beneath a mound of neuroses and self-loathing, an actual, *bona fide* intention?

Fuck knows.

The truth of the matter is: I stopped. I stopped, stared at my pathetic image for a long time, before eventually re-screwing the lid back onto the bottle and replacing it in the cabinet. There was no hurry, I told myself. Remember the lady poet? Like her, I had the power to call that guy with the scythe anytime I pleased, and he was dutybound to obey. So, tomorrow, then? Maybe. Maybe I'll go through with it tomorrow. Or, maybe not. Perhaps I'll keep returning, day after day, swallowing one or two pills until the bottle is empty. Who knows? Who fucking-well cares? More crappy thoughts. More cerebral shit to be churned. What a waste of time. Look! I tell myself, either you're going to do it, or you're not. I *will* make up my mind – soon! Until then…Oh! Shit! Here I go again. How long have I been mulling this load of bollocks over and over in my head? How long has it been? Days? Weeks? How long has it been since Veronica left? I'm not sure. Think back, you prick! Think back and try to formulate some sort of order and sequence from the vacuous mist of the…recent? past. Details remain sketchy, all lost in one, long, apathetic cloud of incapacitation and inebriation. Thoughts, memories and any creative ability I still possess have atrophied to an alarming degree of inaction and somnolescent suspension. I mean, look around the studio at this very moment. What registers? Some large and current cobwebs hanging from three out of the four corners of the ceiling; a thin film of grey dust adorning nearly every object on the shelves; some discarded bedclothes curled up on the floor like a washed-up poulp; pillows, sporting dark stains where my unwashed hair has abraded the cotton; and countless, empty alcohol bottles lying about the place like the husks of dead insects. What's more, my larder is completely devoid of food. Christ! It must be even longer than I first supposed. As long as a… month, perhaps? Can it be? Or, two? Could it be as long as *two* months since Veronica went away? No. No! Not two! It cannot be *that* long. Rubbing my face with trembling hands detects a substantial growth of beard on my cheeks and chin. When was the last time I shaved? It is *bloody* disturbing to realise that I do not know. Also, I have not washed or showered since…Jesus! I have no idea of that, either. An unreasonable – by that I mean too late – panic alights on my heart like a scavenging vulture, and discursive thoughts run amok in my head – the most salient being: why hasn't Veronica at least telephoned me since she absconded? Is that too much to expect of her – subsequent to what happened? I don't know. No doubt, maybe the last, acrimonious incident was, after all, the final straw, allowing her a complete, emotional excision. And yet, knowing her as I do – did – I cannot bring myself to fully believe that. An annexed panic: there is something wrong – she is ill, has met with a serious accident, has been assaulted or attacked. The words of the dream come flooding back: *'You are killing me. You are killing me.'* The panic increases. I must do something.

Jumping much too quickly to my feet, I bravely confront and combat the rising vomit and dizziness with a new resolve, at the same time grabbing for the telephone like a drowning man clutching at the grasses on the bank of a river. As I dial the number, I am unable to stop myself from swaying and almost toppling to the floor; only my grip on a small table supports me.

The line is dead.

There is no sound. No dialling tones. No engaged signal. Nothing.

Replacing the receiver, I try again, reasoning that I am quite as likely – in my present condition – to have dialled the wrong number as the correct one. I wait. Nothing. Silence. Staring at the thing with suspicion, I hang up. Suddenly, somehow, the shape of the phone reminds me of skull and crossbones. Marching up and down, I deliberate with a growing unease. Should I get in touch with…? I have the number written down somewhere. Veronica left it 'in case of an emergency', as she had put it. No! Fuck it. If she thinks I'm going to go ringing around all over the place…Sighing, resignedly, I begin to pull out drawers.

Eventually locating a crumpled piece of paper, I stretch it flat with the palm of my hand and dial. The silence is absolute. An even further panic. Have I been cut off? It's a possibility. Paying the bill is something else I cannot remember doing. After first restudying the scrawl, I repeat the process I had carried out with Veronica's number.

Again, nothing.

Standing with the receiver clutched to my chest, I accept the fact that no communication is forthcoming. Placing the thing back on its cradle, I sit on the bed, where the worry perseveres like toothache. Now that concern has become embedded in my brain, I will achieve no peace of mind until I know for sure she is all right – even if it means acquiring a black eye from her intransigent paramour.

So be it.

On entering the bathroom, I clean myself up in a similar manner to that which I would adopt to overhaul a car, probing and scrubbing until all moving parts are functional again. By the appearance of my well-worn visage, a disguise would not go amiss, either, so I trim – but do not completely shave off – my beard, before washing, and then drying my hair with the only clean towel I can find. Padding back into the other room, I discover some unused clothing still hanging or folded where Veronica had left them. As I dress, I glance out of the window, towards the sea, which looks to be at high tide, like a lead plate beneath an iron grey sky. That means it's an overcoat job. After a brief search, I find the garment on the floor, behind a chair, and quickly mop it up to cover my shoulders like a duffle bag.

Before I leave, though, there is something that must be done. Walking up to the easel, I stand and stare at the painting still residing there. To me, it definitely seems to radiate a kind of – if not evil, exactly – sense of unease in the viewer. Such a sensation cannot be explained, however, but the piece appears as a catalyst, embodying an insoluble mystery within its layers of applied acrylic colours. Its main influence, the Domino figure, gazes out insouciantly from the flat surface as though silently mocking my confusion and fear; while, in the background, the squatting imp, goblin or – as Veronica would have it – my alter ego, appears to possess a secret and separate meaning within itself – the hideous grin a further appurtenant symbol of derision.

So, calm and self-confident in my decision, I lift the thing off the easel, place it across my raised knee, and slowly exert enough pressure for it to first crack, and then snap in two. Taking each piece separately, I repeat the action twice more, before stacking each piece, one on top of another. Strolling across the room to the already overfilled plastic bin, in the corner, I drop them among a cache of empty bottles and accumulated rubbish. For the first time in…God knows how long…I manage to summon up laughter.

I am still laughing – hysterically? – as I stamp into the blanketing drizzle of the outside world.

Anticipating that someone may still be inside, injured, I rush forward, but as I get closer, I realise the car – half inclined in the roadside ditch – is empty. The front wheels are partly submerged in sand, while the rear wheels remain adhered to the solid tarmac of the unusually empty highway. Both doors are open wide, as though the occupants had vacated in a hurry.

Warily circumnavigating it for a few minutes, I look about me, casually, searching for any sign of life. Maybe the driver had suddenly been taken ill, or had been drinking, or had experienced a near collision with another vehicle or animal; since some people can be upset by such episodes, maybe he – or she – had wandered off in order to calm nerves. Standing there, I await a return, but no one appears. The only movement is the grey rain falling from an even greyer sky. Not a sound or a movement anywhere; just silent hills, dunes and grass coated sand on either side of a road that winds between them like an unctuous serpent, whose head and tail are swallowed up in each direction by misty distances.

Cautiously peering into the car's interior, I observe that the key is still in the ignition. Being a two-door model, the front passenger seat is tilted forward, probably to allow someone to climb out from the rear. On the floor, lies an abandoned child's shoe – a girl's – so I reach down and pick it up. Consisting of a dark brown colour and made of imitation leather, its buckle remains secure, prompting an elicitation that it could possibly have been pulled off during an act of resistance. Idly staring at it, only half concentrating before searching further, I notice, on the back seat, a shopping bag, lying there with its contents spilling like entrails from a slaughtered calf. Below it, on the floor, there is a loaf of bread and a carton of milk – plus a newspaper, which rustles quietly against the draught from the open door. Retrieving the organ, I flick through the contents with only minor interest.

Dated a couple of days previous, it sports the usual headlines of injustice and political unrest, so, I turn the pages in perfunctory manner, until an item catches my attention – and the words seem to scorch the very paper with their significance.

*'Strange radiation readings located at the north pole.'*

Beneath such an enigmatic statement is printed a short, almost cryptic account of incongruous heat levels emanating from the centre of a major ice flow, followed by:

*'The progress of ice ablation is accelerating rapidly. Speculation by leading scientists and geologists in the sector predict substantial flooding of both hemispheres if it continues unabated and at its present rate.'*

But it is the final few lines that cause the hairs to bristle on the nape of my neck:

*'There have also been reports of sightings in the North Sea of masses of corpses – both aquatic and landlocked species – drifting south. It is suggested that the sheer weight of numbers indicates a sign of some cataclysmic event having taken place in the area. As of yet, it is still uncertain if the two incidents are connected.'*

Slumping down in the driving seat, I re-read the piece several times, until the words become intermittently blurred, the vision of my dream illustrating them like an accompanying travelogue. I cannot help but wonder as to what has happened in the meantime – since the account went to print; and I reflect on the high tide I witnessed through my window, before I left. Slowly but surely it dawns on me that it is the 'wrong' time of year for such an occurrence to have taken place – the 'wrong' season. A flash of inspiration guides my hand to the ignition key which, in turn, will switch on the radio. As the engine coughs into life, the radio reception consists of nothing but pure static. (More background noise from the Big Bang, perhaps?) Madly, I twist knobs and press buttons – but to no avail. Like the telephone back in my atelier, communication does not exist.

Getting to my feet once more, I look about me. The weather is deteriorating at a speed of knots, and a thick fog joins the rain, drifting in from the coast. Switching off the engine, I stroll around the car, still half expecting an appearance of driver and/or associates. When no one arrives, I decide to self-organise a search. The sand is soft hereabouts; there must be footprints.

At last I find them: two sets of adults, one infant. The smaller pair exhibit alternate indentations of shoe and barefoot, heading off into the mounds of wet sand, where they become obscured by the elements.

Demurring, and still half expecting – hoping – someone will turn up, I reluctantly resort to following the trail. Pulling my overcoat tightly about me, I plod alongside the fresh, inconsistent prints, observing here and there that they seem to be interrupted by signs of a slight skirmish – a number of the concavities veering away from the destined track. There is also evidence of the sand having been kicked up, and of the smaller feet being dragged? leaving behind marks like scars through tufts of coarse grass and gorse, ultimately determining a one-way direction. For some distance the child's track disappears altogether. Maybe she had been carried for a while.

With time seeming to stand still, I am now unsure as to how long I have been in pursuit of my still unseen 'prey'. Although, just ahead, I can see that their trail leads to somewhere behind a large hillock, about twenty paces from where I stand. Once more, I hesitate, pulling up the collar of my overcoat, only to push it back into place again; somehow, the rain trickling down the back of my neck helps me to concentrate and continue my search. Following that, after first plunging my hands into my pockets, I withdraw them to rub my palms together in an effort of self-encouragement. Finally, looking around, I first squint into the thick atmosphere, then at the imprints before me, and lastly at the desolate valleys and dunes that surround me. From above comes the stentorian call of a gull, swooping and gliding invisibly through the murk; while all else remains motionless and silent. But there is this persistent…prickling of apprehension, which disturbs me. Nonetheless, I have come this far…

Almost without my brain's consent, my feet start ploughing on, and I approach the obstructing dune with mounting trepidation. Even the thickness of my attire fails to prevent my spirit from sinking into an ice-cold state of anticipation, where further procrastination urges me to seek the sky, the mist or any other available reason as an excuse not to go on. But I cannot turn back now. So, taking a deep, fortifying breath, I spurt forward, and around the base of the acclivity – to where I see them.

The bodies of the young woman and the child are almost together, the separation having been brought about solely by the force of the shotgun's blast. They had probably been standing together – perhaps cuddling, as loving mothers and offspring are inclined to do when confronted by adversity or danger – before the impact tore into them. The woman – mother? – lies, slightly to the child's – daughter's? – right, on her back, arms thrown out from her sides, head twisted towards me. Her face, in life, must have been attractive, but now it is spattered with blood and wet sand; her eyes as still and as glazed as china balls with inkblots at their centres. Most of her torso is mutilated by the buckshot – like a damaged, overripe tomato.

The little girl is mercifully half turned away from my P.O.V., sprawled somewhat higher up the side of the bank – more than likely because of her lighter weight. A tumble of auburn hair covers her features, while just below them is spread a copious, incarnadine stain. On one foot there is a twin shoe to the one in the car; the other foot is bare and pale and still.

Uncomprehendingly, I swivel my gaze to my right, past the now harmless piece of technology that is the gun – further, to the corpse of the man. He was probably thirty-plus before the explosion blew most of his head away – I posit this from the style of his clothing and what is left of his dark hair. Actually, there is not much else to go on; from the shoulders up, there is just a revolting splash of crimson. Further conjecture: the way the almost headless upper body is positioned suggests he must have held the weapon directly under his chin before pulling the trigger.

Burying my face in my hands appeases nothing; white skin and red blood remains etched behind closed eyelids, as vivid as a technicolour film. To make things worse, the images begin to move, regressing to the events that preceded the tragic and terrible sight before me. Transfixed, I observe the resolute march of the stricken trio as they seek a location of acceptable privacy, as they take up their positions, as they administer last farewells and utter absolutions before setting about the fateful task. In my mind's-eye, each accepts their role with grim determination – even the child, who must have been completely and uniquely overawed and subdued by the pathos of her 'parent's'? mood, and by the occasion.

What motivated such drastic measures? How desperate had conditions become to warrant such an extreme and deadly action? How – why – could a compact family unit decide to finalise their mortal existence in this way? Obviously, careful thought had gone into the result; it had not been a spontaneous act, or one of passion or rage. To have walked all this way must have taken a special kind of resolve – *'a special way of being afraid no trick dispels'?* – a gesture that honoured a profound and irrevocable cause. How many causes could demand such an ultimate sacrifice? Surely, not something so speculative and distant as a clipping in a newspaper.

And yet, thinking back, the deviated footprints, the open doors of the car, the forsaken shoe, must represent evidence of at least a token of dissent on the part of the little girl. Whatever the reason, though, and whatever the compulsion, it was sustained by the parents? guardians? relatives? to such an extent that they were able to override all of the infant's protestations. And it is this particular element of the situation that urges me to deduce they must have been a family – father, mother, daughter – as the expediency and execution was of such a trusting and intimate nature. The sheer will it had taken to uphold such a definitive motivation, to see the dreadful act through to the bitter end, could only have been guided and driven by love.

Reflecting on my own, pathetic half attempt, I compel myself to, one last time, look upon the result of such a mode of thought – and I am filled with sorrow and self-contempt. If I had been so truly inspired as the unfortunate souls splayed out before me, I would now be sharing their peace and their silence. Instead, ironically, I am cast in the role of their only witness, their only sympathiser, their only mourner; a reluctant and compromised paraclete who cannot bring himself to turn on his heel and leave them like this, offered to the elements, the birds and the worms. My nature – as imperfect and self-obsessed as it is – still commits me to tie up the loose ends with – albeit modest – ceremonious solemnity.

Using the handle of the gun – another irony – as a spade, I eventually manage – with as great a physical effort as I have ever expended in my life – to remove sufficient sand and pulverulent shingle from the unstable slope of the dune to create a makeshift grave.

*(But it's empty, you state, excitedly...)*

Now, task completed, I remain on my knees while attempting to summon up the required courage to actually touch and move the stiff limbs of the cadavers. A great effort of composure and assertion on my part is needed to perform such a duty.

On my feet again, I take several deep breaths before – averting my eyes as much as possible – dragging and tumbling each of the three bodies into the hole in the ground. Somehow, the most difficult and emotional part is the tossing of wet sand and soil on to the exposed but mangled features. There is something repelling about hearing the dull, flat sound of the shovel loads hitting the rigid surfaces of flesh; but I at last succeed in covering them completely before slouching, panting and staring down at the mound, this anonymous tumulus, which will, hopefully, serve as their undisturbed garden of eternal sleep.

Now that the task is done, finished, I wonder why in hell I had not simply relinquished obligation, made my way straight to the nearest public telephone – I do not, never have and never will, own a smartphone – and reported the incident to the authorities. It would have been the obvious and correct thing to do. However, deep down, I know the answer. The self-inflicted mini massacre had been clearly meant as a personal rite – something governed by their own reasoning and conviction. To post-inflict upon their demise the procedures and preponderances of the establishments that may very well have helped drive them to it in the first place, would be a kind of sacrilege; after all, are they not entitled to the peace and solitude that they, themselves, chose?

Partly leaning on the upright, previously discharged shotgun, the instrument of their destruction, I feebly attempt some kind of threnody – but the utterances that pour from my lips take me by surprise – (the memory of my incongruous, messianic search within my dream storms at me like an out of control express train) – and as they disrupt the silence they alienate me, cast me once more as observer, robbing me of the gift of participation. Immediately deciding the role of elegist is unsuited to my character and conscious beliefs – or, lack of – I shut my mouth and simply bow my head. But when I close my eyes, the visages of the three corpses gather about me like the witches from Macbeth.

Looking up, I realise it's beginning to get dark; once again I am experiencing difficulty in identifying time. Is it really twilight already? With the gun still clutched in rigid fingers, I suddenly become consumed with anger and revulsion. Swinging back my arm, I throw the thing as far away from me as I can. After which I retrace my steps back to the road, in order to continue my journey in search of Veronica – now elevated to the status of a quest.

One that must take precedence over all else.


On reaching the car, you find it as you had left it – did you really expect anything to be different? Climbing inside the cab, you huddle into the driving seat like a bird into its nest, losing yourself in a morbid thanatopsis, where the corpses continue to race at you from the darkest recesses of your mind. The contrasting colours – ashen flesh, vermillion gore – become more and more stark with every pulsation. Forcing yourself to snap out of it, you look down only to discover that you still retain the small shoe between bleached bone fingers, each as cold as arctic compass points. This causes you to once again pull up the collar of your overcoat, before trying the radio several times – only to hear the voice of the universe reduced to a mundane, uninformative crackle of static. Remaining thus, half dozing – in order to invent reasons and/or excuses not to put the car in gear and drive to the city – your mind gradually empties itself of any creative thought, until you find yourself, fugue like, counting off the passing seconds, as though you are waiting or expecting something to happen. Even after each sixty seconds become a minute, and even after sixty minutes flow into an hour, you remain as you are, oscitant and listless, staring ahead into the dimness, the will to venture on decimated by ineptitude and sorrow. Insidiously, the inertia blankets you to such an extent that you close your eyes, succumbing to the encroaching slumber as deep as a brown-throated sloth on Valium. But it is not a relaxing slumber, being filled with wild, spinning images of dead and mutilated people and animals – some in a state of semi metamorphosis. Fish, with human heads, arms, legs and other protrusions sprouting from their bodies, twist and wriggle alongside misshapen, indescribable anatomies whose limbs are growing from places where limbs should not grow. Agonised, glaring eyes seek you out within red or pink agglomerations of carnage, as though accusing you of their abominable predicament, until, after what seems to you to be an eternity, a fleshy montage, slithering and slurping, converges into a single, living Lovecraftian monstrosity, its tentacles and other obscene appendages groping and snapping at you with needle sharp teeth and oversized, vengeful claws. Emitting vile noises, like bubbling lava or slime, the hideosity crawls and slithers towards you, a slopping, writhing mass, and you are unable to move as the loathsome entity scoops you up whole, like plankton swallowed by a basking shark. Becoming as one with it, you feel its pain and torment, as if the suffering of the world has entered your heart wholesale. Thousands of years of civilisation and experience has yielded nothing, it has taught humankind nothing, it has learned nothing, the agony remains, as it has always been – self-inflicted. Awakening, you look about you in post nightmare fright. The gloom has been joined by a thick, curdling mist that engulfs the car in a caress as repulsive as an anaconda's coils. It's opacity cold-kisses the windscreen, isolating you in the void, and creating such a sensation of complete and utter aloneness, it feels as though you have been reduced to a single living entity in the vastness of the universe – a perfect solipsism, filled only by dreams and fantasies – an existence compiled of nothing but self-constructed illusions. Except one. One seems to be substantial, and breaks through the silence by scratching on the glass. Slowly turning your head, you peer out, but the thing, whatever it is, remains so indistinct – a mere movement – it causes you to wonder if you are still asleep. Until you see it more clearly, as it swirls out of the fluidity of the atmosphere, gradually taking shape – and you recognise it for what it is. The white, leather-skinned features of the hobgoblin – now much larger, as massive as a silver backed gorilla – are being pressed against the pane, eyes twinkling as bright as polished rubies from beneath the heavy, over-hanging brows, wide grin splitting the osseous jaws like a sword slash. And with it comes a great weakness, as though your strength – and even your very spirit – is somehow being drained from you, to be transferred into the creature outside. Falling beneath the spell of its malign, hyp-notic stare, you feel yourself begin to sway – or is it the face that sways, oscillating like a pendulum in the turbidity? – before a hand appears, as coarse and leprous as the taloned claw of an eagle, beckoning with a hooked finger that curls in slow-motion. Powerless to resist, you open the door and step out into the impenetrable opaqueness, circumnavigating the car to stand on the spot where your terrifying familiar had stood. But you discover that he, it, has vanished. As you search the dense, vaporous melange, the swirling motion increases, curdling, creating shapes and patterns within itself, and you once more find yourself at the mercy of your own somnambulance, caught in a narcoleptic grip, robbed of cona-tion, carried through time and space, nothing more than a spectator – and as you drift, you become transported through portals and across physical boundaries, spiritually, unconfined by bodily restrictions. Abducted by esoteric influences, and guided by abstruse, unperceivable forces, you are, in a way, privileged, as you are about to enter the unknown...

Lifting our gaze from the ground, we immobilise our ambling gait. There is a kind of absence. The mist dances about us, its coolness possessing a con-ticent pleasantness that soothes us, placates the violence within us, controls us, appeases us, while granting us a rare state of self-cognition. It detaches us from the usual drive and instinct that dictates our metaphysical existence, freeing us into a temporary coalescence with the antithetic, schizophrenic entity we are burdened with. For we are binary. Casting a glance over our shoulder, we observe, through the grey blanket, the entranced figure stand-ing there, motionless, mindless, anaesthetised, as still as a mannequin. This is the first time we have contemplated his presence without antipathy, as he represents, to us, all that is weak and useless in the human condition. Alone, he could not exist in such an indifferent world, and it is difficult to allow ourselves such quiet objectivity, being perpetually locked in conflict with his legislative guilt persona. So, the contempt abides, but stretched thin enough for abstract identification. We stand thus and peer at him over hunched shoulder long enough only to contemplate a mutual anamnesis – for the end is now in sight. One of the purposes of the Event is subjective annihilation. Before that, though, there is much to be done. We march on…

Plummeting through a spinning tunnel, you spiral down into the aloneness of self. Like falling into a black hole, you are being stretched, elongated at the event horizon, as though strapped to a rack. Nevertheless, this awareness of physicality is somehow objective, separate, enabling you to observe yourself from 'outside', from a position of 'apartness'. You are as you are to the external world, an observant shadow, a bestial entity, and, ultimately, as a more obscure… 'thing', nascent, a single link in an infinite and eternal existence – an insemination of something more, a microcosmic particle in a greater whole. But even though this knowledge fills you/*us* with calmness, the final ties with corporeality have not been completely broken, you/*we* can still feel the body's reactions to the descent, that nauseating rise of the hypogastrium – similar to driving a car at speed over a humpbacked bridge – as it assaults you/*us*, followed by a tingling sensation in where *our* genitalia should be, rising rapidly along *our* spine, like an ice-cold comet, to alight on *our* brain, wrapping it in a blanket of numbness. Having no option but to succumb to its influence, *we*, at last, lose contact with any material confinement, becoming monadiform within the swirl of the will. And as *we* float and somersault with the lightness of a leaf on a windy day, the surround condenses into solid blackness, and from its depth of silence come whispers and then forms, like wraiths, circling and vying for attention and recognition. Watching them and listening to them, impartial and aloof, *we* deign to 'feel' only when *we* consider it necessary – before *we* see her. Discarding the last of her clothing, she stands, facing *us* as though looking in a mirror, fluffing up her hair with her hands. Realising that she cannot see *us*, *we* smile behind the simian mask, until she obliviously turns her back on *us*, granting *us* an opportunity to approach like Nimrod, and, within an instant, she is supine, and there is water, into which she falls, a look of terror on her face, and she is struggling and thrashing and fighting in her death throes, like a helpless kitten in a sack. Liquid swirls and rushes into nostrils and down throat, blood pounds thunderously through arteries, while heart thumps impotently against ribcage. Suspended in those final moments, *we* view images of the past – those of the girl as she was when *we*/you first met her, young, vivacious and carefree, now, as lover, naked, locked within an introspective bower of passion and self-indulgence, now, as maternal friend, soothing away *our*/your puerile and pitiful sorrows, now, as protagonist, confronting you/*us* from an opposing end of an argument or disagreement, now, as a distant singularity, an invisible representation of longing, and now, finally, as a terror-stricken mortal – facing termination.

Eventually, the apoplexy subsides and her mind slips silently into nonexistence. Even though immured in a state of ataraxy, *we*/you 'feel' the arrow of destiny wing its way onward, recording a passing of something. *When we are, death is not come, and when death is come, we are not.* Memory of the words means nothing to you/*us* – reduced to nomenclatural symbols, they remain unaccompanied by images or emotions. Synonymity with perception is no more, language has ceased to be needed as a 'tool' or source of communication. You/*we* have risen above such concepts. Knowledge now comes to you/*us* directly, in its purest form, dispensing with intermediate correspondence of any kind. Things and situations just are, and you/*we* know them to be so – and with the knowing everything flows, acting in accordance with what should be. So, the wild, simian persona retreats and sinks within you, having temporarily fulfilled its purpose. With its departure comes a momentary loss of strength and psychic puissance, but it passes, leaving you ready for what comes next.

Slowly burgeoning out of the aphotic surround, a nebulous glow, like a regulated stage light, illuminates a group of figures, a couple of whom turn their blank visages towards you with mild curiosity, before quickly 'looking' away again – down at their object of interest. As they stand in a semicircle, in the manner of surgeons around an operating table, the sound of heavy breathing can be heard – rapid, nasal, followed by a loud, piercing cry. The movement among them suddenly becomes filled with a sense of urgency, preceding another bout of loud suspirations, followed by a second cry, followed by…silence. Subsequently, an emanation of joy radiates from the group, and, as one, they step back in order to observe their handiwork. Then, from their midst, arises the Domino facsimile, visibly trembling, unsteady on her feet. When one of the figures attempts to support her, she wards him off with a declining hand. As though preparing herself, she stands perfectly still for a few moments, before approaching you with wary steps. Totally naked, she carries something in the crook of her left arm, the white of her flesh contrasting sharply with the incarnadine stain between her legs. Beckoning to you with her free hand, she tentatively, somewhat breathlessly, smiles an oasis smile, whispering, Come, my love, and bear witness to the future. Looking down, you observe a new-born child, covered in blood and postnatal fluids. Wiping some of it away with her hand exposes an infantile face, devoid of eye, nose or mouth – the head as smooth and as shiny as a freshly laid egg…

It was raining – heavily. I could hear it drumming on something hollow and metallic; and my face was wet, although I instinctively knew it was not from the downpour. On trying to move my head, I found that I could not. I could not move my arms, either – or my legs for that matter. I could not move – period. Oddly enough, this did not strike me as alarming; but I was vaguely annoyed by the constriction of my lungs. Something heavy on my chest pinioned me like a heavyweight wrestler demanding a fall, granting me only short, sharp, rasping intakes of air. Whenever I attempted to take a deeper breath it was accompanied by a bubbling sound from somewhere in my lower thorax; also, there was a taste of blood in my mouth. In the distance, I could discern noises of activity: a low hum of machinery – perhaps of a compressor – alongside a loud clicking sound, like teeth catching in a cogwheel, regular and monotonous. There was movement, too, as though I were being jerked upward slightly – every jerk synchronised with every click. And there were voices, seemingly far, far away, indecipherable, lost in abrasive static, so that the only word I could make out clearly was 'over', punctuating the crackling like an exclamation mark.

As I lay there – for how long I don't know – just listening to the sounds and feeling the wetness spreading over my face, I eventually let my curiosity get the better of me, by deciding to try and climb out of my somewhat comfortable cocoon. So, I opened my eyes – but immediately closed them again against the overwhelming glares of light that penetrated my retina, leaving me puzzled as to how unprepared I was for them, since the spectrums remained behind my eyelids like giant sunflowers. All the time the rain continued to patter down, and I continued to lie there – for what seemed like hours – just accepting the situation while trying to summon up the will and strength for another attempt. When I did, eventually, succeed, I flickered up my lids with a rapid, rear-guard, blinking action – in order to avoid all the glares attacking me at once – only to discover that the blobs of luminosity were way up high, creating an impression of a scene from 'War of the Worlds'. And yet, as I squinted at them, the brightness became slightly diffused for a moment, as the wind gusted the rain across the beams, causing them to sway, gently. Then they all swayed together, like faces in a chorus line, and I realised it was actually a fault of my vision, which was attenuating rapidly, and to such an extent that it seemed as though I were peering down a long funnel of some kind. And it was at that moment when darkness began to swarm over me, like a rippling coverlet of black satin; but before I became completely smothered by it, an object caught the corner of my eye – situated to my left, and slightly elevated. A mound of some sort, partly obscuring the glares, with a shape that did not make sense to me. It had a strong colouring, though, and I remember thinking about it in the context of a piece of abstract artwork:

blue, dissected by pink, and arbitrarily splashed with red. I wondered whether it had been painted in oils or in acrylics...

The oleaginous road, like a serpent in the night, slithers towards me out of the rain-soaked landscape. Leaning forward in my seat, I squint at the dizzying array of tickertape cat's-eyes while trying to ignore the impediment of a slightly frayed windscreen wiper, which restricts my vision somewhat – but not enough to allay my disquiet concerning the images and scenes of an almost apocalyptic nature fleetingly illuminated in the beams of the headlamps. Further impressions of widespread dereliction and destruction prompt me to keep the accelerator as near to the floor as possible, easing off only when access to my route becomes difficult – or downright impassable. On several occasions I have had to reverse and circumnavigate fallen rubble, abandoned cars or overturned lorries and coaches – periods of deceleration and delay that allowed me to observe multiple burnt-out buildings, broken windows, looted arcades, doorless hallways and scattered debris. Smashed TV sets, computer laptops and music systems lie spread out among splintered tables, legless chairs, axed wardrobes, damaged washing machines and fridges, and ribbons of torn clothing splayed among a million fragments of glass and china adorning the streets like fallen stars. In the distance, behind the superimposed high-rise apartments, offices, stores and corporate mansions, saffron auras light up the sky with the luminosity of numerous minor sunsets. From somewhere over there come the stuttering echoes of mayhem and devastation as petrol tanks explode and window panes fall to the onslaughts of sand bricks and sledgehammers. Closer – maybe a single street away – men's voices ring out in both terror and laughter, while women and children cry. Who was it said: *'Civilisation has only ever been as successful as the madmen who ruled it'*? Hobbes was right: morality *is* just a veneer. Urban madness abounds.

After negotiating a sharp corner, I find myself confronted by a burning truck set at an angle in the middle of the road – so I stop the car and kill the headlamps. Flames dance merrily, peppering the slowly billowing smoke with fountains of orange sparks, while demented silhouettes leap and hop like crickets. And as I watch, something heavy belches out of an upstairs window to crash down only yards away from where I am parked, blasting glass and metal in all directions.

Slamming the gearstick into reverse, I catapult the vehicle back from further danger. Then, with tyres screeching and spinning prior to me being thrust forward once more, I renegotiate the gearstick directly into second, propelling the car down an intersection blanketed by shadows. Removing a hand from the driving wheel, I switch on the headlamps once more.

After the chaos of the main street the protected facades of residential semis appear incongruous in their uniformity and silence, as though having been granted territorial dispensation. And yet, even here there is a blatant anomaly: not a single light probes the darkness from living room or bedroom, and all streetlamps have been extinguished, standing like rows of redundant warriors. Even so, I welcome the state of what can only be labelled 'specious peace' as I cruise along, slowly, while allowing my heartbeat and presiding panic to recede a little...

With no idea as to how far I have come from or progressed to – it feels as though I've been driving around for days – I remain still unable to discover a way out of this nightmare stronghold; whichever direction I take seems to lead me into the company of yet another raving bonfire party. All exits are blocked. Other than go back the way I came, there appears to be no alternative but to try and run the gauntlet of some crazy, saltatory mob.

With headlights off, I sit in the darkness of the car and stare ahead in disbelief at the crackling, leaping flames of an umpteenth conflagration. Hoots of derision and screams of fright echo into the night sky, accompanied by the sound of splintering and shattering glass. Occasionally, like someone with a nervous, stuttering cough, quickfire blasts – perhaps of gunfire – can be heard reverberating through hollow, empty buildings, followed, again and again, by loud, maniacal bursts of laughter.

Society has broken down completely and I can only theorise as to the reason/s why. My immediate conjecture is that a kind of nuclear holocaust has taken place (did some bat mad bastard really get around to pressing that fucking big red button?) but dismiss this on the grounds that I should not have escaped its consequences unscathed, even if my abode of hibernation had been constructed of bombproof material. Adding to this supposition: I have not travelled that far a distance; to have slept – no matter how stuporously, like some latter-day Rip van Winkle – through such a monumental event would have been nigh on impossible. Also, there was that newspaper report of numerous bodies floating in the North Sea, and the highlighting of rising heat levels at the polar cap – caused by melting ice on the Olkiluoto Island in western Finland, perhaps, where massive amounts of nuclear waste are buried for, supposedly, a hundred-thousand years? Yeah! Right! Although it would invalidate the hypothesis of war, it would not cancel out the possibility of any number of other...'accidents' having taken place. But there is no evidence to connect such a catastrophe with that confronting me at the moment. So, something more localised, then? Could the current ethological insanity have been the result of an incident – a fire or explosion – at a germ warfare research station? Or an escape into the atmosphere of some kind of nerve gas – or even a virus? If so, perhaps this whole thing is not macroscopic at all, and I am trapped in a labyrinth of lunacy, cordoned off, but still close enough to the forces of law and order under instruction to contain it?

Any of these speculations could be perceptively genuine, of course, but are of little use to me in my present situation. Whatever the cause may be, the result is nothing more than a reversion to territorialism. No matter how chaotic the situation appears on first inspection, behind them exists an underlying system. Each and every roadblock represents a boundary, or demarcation line, separating one district from another. And these districts are diligently guarded and defended; 'outsiders' seeking access to shelter, or to make claim on indigenous provisions are set upon, beaten, and/or killed. Such sectarianism has resulted in a complex network of no-man's-lands and no-go areas, rendering any attempt at ingression, or integration, or, indeed, even communication, futile.

So, what to do? I can either retreat – in which case the chances of ever seeing Veronica again are pretty slim – or I can attempt to ram one of the blockades. Surprisingly, and in spite of the obvious danger, the latter seems to me to be the better bet. I posit that, even if I fail to get through, I will still be able to abandon the car in the ensuing confusion, and lose myself in the turmoil before the 'guards' realise what is happening. Darkness is my friend. Rumination on this takes but a few minutes before I finally decide. Actually, there is no contest. Not even a craven, such as myself, could satisfactorily return and spend the rest of the future – if there be one – wondering if, and hoping that, she is, somehow, safe and well. I must go on.

*I can't go on, I'll go on.*

As I sit here, closer inspection reveals a gap in between the flames of a burning barricade and the wall of a terraced house. If my approach could be executed with surprise, there will be just enough room to squeeze through.

Taking a series of long, deep breaths is only marginally helpful, so, I start up the engine, place the car in gear, and move slowly forward. My plan is to gain speed surreptitiously, advance as quickly as possible before, at the very last moment, switching on the headlamps. Hopefully, this will create a state of panic, disorientation and disorganisation.

And yet, as my scheme unfolds, the panic comes, not from them, but from me. I cannot see enough of the road – even by the light of the bonfire – so therefore cannot prevent one of the front wheels from hitting the kerb with a bone jarring crunch. My nerve fails me and I find myself switching on the headlights much too soon. Still in second gear, *I* know that *they* know I am coming. Momentarily pressing the brake, I quickly change my mind, jump on the accelerator, aim the bonnet at the aforementioned gap, and watch in horror as it becomes smaller and smaller as I hurtle towards it.

It is too narrow!

I will not make it!

On viewing me, there is instant alarm, followed by shouts and curses. Roughly a half dozen shapes appear, as if from nowhere, to fill the entrance between wall and fire. Clubs and/or other handheld weapons are wielded, bottles are thrown, and a sand brick – as red as the flames – arcs towards me, twisting and turning like a space satellite. Seeing it bounce harmlessly off the bonnet, I urge maximum revs from the protesting engine. I am now in third gear and speed towards them at about forty miles per hour. If I assumed that they would scatter I was wrong.

Standing as firm as a Roman *contubernium,* the figures calmly watch my approach. Huddled so close together, silhouetted against the glow, they seem to adopt the appearance of a single entity: a multi-legged, multi-armed, multi-headed creature of mythology, guarding the way like Cerberus at the gates of Hell. As my thoughts race, my courage evaporates. What shall I do? To carry on regardless would be to run them down – injuring or possibly even killing at least one of them.

Get out of the way, you crazy bastards!

Let me through!

My mental constitution, being what could be described as weak, is crowded with doubts and uncertainties; but a weak state of mind is a cowardly one and will, when not dwelt upon and analysed, adopt a natural sense of preservation. All my prior thoughts of self-termination have come about following prolonged contemplation; in an extemporised situation I have no time for such luxury – my foot stays resolutely pressed to the floorboards.

Racing at them with the impetus of a bobsleigh, and with the image of the access having now disappeared, I can only guess as to where I should be aiming – so, I brace myself as the front of the car bounces and jars, half mounting the pavement. The engine roars. The creature screams. I can actually see its black tongue protruding from its centre: straight, long and shiny. From where I am sitting it looks like a…a *shotgun*!

Within a split second I throw myself across the passenger seat, my right hand gripping the steering wheel, guiding blind. The gun's blast explodes through the windscreen, directly in front of where I had been sitting, sending down a cataract of glass. In an instant the vehicle momentarily slows, as though ploughing into a snowdrift, before lurching forward again. Raising my head, I wipe away the flying shards as I desperately try to regain some control. Ahead of me, at a rapidly diminishing distance, I see two black holes superimposed on a blanched face – one eye screwed up, the other focussing on me along the length of the barrel.

As he pulls the trigger, I am upon him, and the buckshot spouts harmlessly into the night sky. Its report is followed by a sickening crunch, along with a scraping sound to my left, and a red fulguration lights up terror filled features that are being pitched towards me. At the same time the other figures disperse like birds before a ravaging cat. One throws himself over the terraced wall to my left; another one dives backwards, away from the propelled bonnet; while a third tumbles sideways, into the leaping flames of the bonfire.

Executing a kind of sedentary rugby swerve, I hunch myself against the driving side door as the gunman lurches through the smashed window, his head scrunching against the top of the metal frame – probably breaking his neck – and his shoulders twist under the impact, projecting him away from me, into the passenger door. He still manages to collide with my upper arm, though, causing a pain to shoot up into the side of my jaw. This deflects his trajectory somewhat and he flops over almost onto the passenger seat, raking a path through the ruined windscreen.

All this takes place in mere moments, but I view it like a stop motion film, as though time has been slowed down, and as this registers in my subconscious I seem to catch an instantaneous glimpse of an old man with a shock of dishevelled white hair and soft, sad eyes nodding knowingly and smiling a wry smile. During this vision, everything really continues to rush at me with the unfolding velocity of single frames, and I realise that the car is still speeding onward.

I am through.

Since the incident at the bonfire, I have been continuously driving around, afraid to stop or even slow down, letting the darkened streets, back lanes, alleyways and open commons flash by with zoetropic speed, unrecognised and/or unnoticed. And it is during these periods I remain completely unaware of steering or changing gear, my hands and feet executing their own operations and choreography on wheel and pedals with independent cerebration. Eventually, though, as if rising up out of some psychological quagmire, my brain suddenly sparks into life, directing me to observe my surround – whereupon I find myself cruising down a relatively 'safe looking' side street, which appears to be deserted – not a squirrel, wild fox or even a rat in sight – so I pull over, stop and kill both the engine and the lights.

This is a chance to dispose of my unwanted passenger. To dislodge him, to touch his corpse, to feel the crumpled, bloodstained clothing; to imagine the process between primary flaccidity and rigor mortis already taking place beneath ghostly white skin; to lift him, to be aware of his weight, volume and density, and to become accustomed to his occupied space. But my initial reaction is to just sit in silence, perusing the object for what it is: a mound of flesh and textiles, an empty dwelling place, one that is even now beginning to decompose into a fetid slime, and eventually into an evaporating gas; the corporeality slowly rotting into remains. And as I study it, as it hangs there, half inclined through the shattered window, it seems to take on an aura of familiarity that I cannot readily identify or pin down. The torso seems misshapen, like a discarded guy on November the fifth, while, from somewhere below the pensile head, the sound of dripping liquid can be heard. Peering into the shadows I am able to make out a black pool spreading across the leather upholstery of the seat, meandering among the patterned creases as freely as an oil spill, overflowing, at several low points, on to the floor.

Pulling myself together, and with a trembling hand, I take a firm grip on the hair – in order to raise the surprisingly heavy head – and a loud hiss, like a punctured tyre, exhales a necklace of gore from the slashed throat, pouring down over handbrake, gearstick and, finally, over my left leg. One of the upstanding splinters of glass must have lacerated an artery when the body was launched into the cab. As though bitten by a snake I withdraw my hand, at the same time pressing myself back into my seat, attempting to put as much distance between the thing and myself as possible. Then, with growing trepidation, I lift my foot, place it against the lifeless shoulder, and push.

My reluctant hitch-hiker slides halfway down the bonnet, leaving rivulets of blood over the paintwork, before…coming to a stop. A piece of his clothing has caught on a metal protrusion, suspending him there, encrusted, like a desperate mountaineer clinging to an overhang, eyes glinting with accusatory hatred at the one who had let him fall.

For long, drawn-out moments I am unable to move, rivetted by that unholy expression. The face is wax white, luminescent in the darkness, like a shell-peeled egg on spilt beetroot juice. Features are frozen in exaggerated surprise, the mousetrap mouth open and distorted by the weight of the jaw pressed against the metalwork. But it is the acid drop eyes that hold my unwavering attention, hypnotising me into a realisation that I am, once again, responsible for a death. I am, once again, a killer. Being someone who loathes to even step on a spider the revelation explodes inside my brain like a phosphorous bomb. I think it was Albert Camus who postulated that artists are the least likely candidates to commit murder – although, I suspect, the homicidal antics of Messrs Adolph, Paul Joseph and Hermann Wilhelm go some way in invalidating that theory – but knowledge of this merely seems to exacerbate the situation, as it makes me an exception of percentages, a contradiction in terms: a creator of destruction. And the thoughts immobilise me, gripping me in a vice of self-awareness while assaulting me with the vengeance of angels.

Glancing down at my hands, I watch them shake and tremble in the gloom. If I am not careful, I may find myself succumbing to a state of total shock. Ergo, I repeat what is becoming my mantra: that I must pull myself together – take control. I mean, am I not suffering enough trouble with my conscience as it is? Anyway, this whole situation is different. This was not murder. It was not even negligence. Far from it. The choice was his. He could quite easily have stepped aside and let me pass. Instead, he decided to stand firm in an attempt to kill me. He had stationed himself there of his own free will, coldly taking aim down the sights of the gun, before firing, knowing there was a strong possibility that his action would result in my – the anonymous driver's – death. So, what does that make me? Interloper? Protagonist? Enemy? Victim? Certainly not a murderer. It was not even a conscious act of self-defence. After all, I had no intention – there's that fucking word again – whatsoever of deliberately running him down. On the contrary, it would have been far more convenient for me, if he had simply moved out of the way. It had been blind panic – when confronted with the threat of the shotgun – that had kept my foot glued to the accelerator. It had been purely an act of survival.

Augmented by this self-reasoned mitigation, I stretch a leg through the broken windshield – ripping my denims slightly on the array of glass teeth as I do so – and position the heel of my boot against a pale cheek. A sharp kick is all it takes, and the face retreats, allowing me but a fleeting glimpse of the marble eyed stare as it disappears over the curve of the bonnet. Retrieving the limb, I sit in the shadows of the cab and attempt to decelerate my erratic heartbeat. There must be a way of calming this still burgeoning hysteria. The pulse in my forehead seems set to burst clean of the temporal artery, granting *carte blanche* to the cold fingers that grip my brain, squeezing out pitiful memories like juice from a grapefruit. Images of Domino become interlaced with the countenance of the recently deceased gunman, pulsating like flashbulbs in a camera. Faster and faster, brighter and brighter, until the whole of my body twitches as though afflicted by chorea; while at the same time pain spreads out in waves from the base of my skull, until…here we go again:

My head hurts. My head hurts. My head hurts…my head hurts…my head hurts, my head hurts, my head hurts, my head hurts,  my head hurts, my head hurts, my head hurts, *my head* hurts, *myhead hurts, myheadhurts-*

*myheadhurts-myheadhurts-my head hurts , my head hurts, my head hurts, my head hurts, myhead hurts, myheadhurts, myheadhurts-myheadhurts-myheadhurts-myheadhurts, myheadhurtsmyheadhurtsmyheadhurtsmy...* fuck-ing *head hurts...*

With no more than a split second to spare, I throw open the door and watch the watery vomit splash out onto the dark roadway...

Blinking myself awake, I stare up at levitating metal rectangles punctuated by a criss-cross pattern of tiny holes. Through the holes I can see sable shapes moving across a solder grey background; while, in the foreground, wedge-shaped blocks slide into the scene like giant monoliths. Above them, the profile of a dragon's head snarls its way across from right to left, followed by a snub-nosed whale floating amidst monstrous fronds of kelp; just below, a puma leaps, claws outstretched, towards an indeterminate prey – the whole thing, a paralysed frieze, drifting slowly across my line of vision like a banner trailing in the slipstream of an aeroplane.

Blinking a couple more times deprives me of my pareidolia, and presents me with the fact that I am lying on my back beneath a wrought iron fire escape, behind which the darkened outlines of high buildings stand in relief against a curdling, cloud filled sky. A wet spot, landing on the back of my hand, warns me of imminent rain.

Turning my head to the right, I view a concrete alleyway, protected by a high, red bricked wall daubed with aerosprayed graffiti. At the base of the wall several cardboard cartons lie scattered amongst overturned trashcans, mounds of wastepaper and other miscellaneous litter; while overhead piercing cries of scavenging birds echo through damaged structures of iron, stone and glass. Under my cheek I can feel the coolness of one of the cartons, folded double into a makeshift pillow. Another is spread flat under my back, while a torn plastic bag acts as a make-do blanket over my torso – the role of which is only marginally successful, as it fails to deflect a tremor from wafting over my whole body, as cold as a winter welcome. Yet it must have been adequate to a certain extent, because, against all the odds, I have, somehow, succeeded in attaining another dreamless sleep.

With the rain droplets becoming more frequent, many of them are now finding their way through the metal maze to land on my face. A low wind, moaning like a gentile's breath through a Jew's harp, scours the alleyway, disturbing some of the maverick pieces of rubbish, and lifting cartons high enough off the cement flooring to scrape along with the hesitancy of manta rays suffering from glaucoma. The sound is accompanied by something else – a piece of canvas, perhaps, or an item of heavy clothing being dragged along the floor – and I become aware of a presence. Quickly raising myself up onto one elbow, I look around.

"Don't try anyfink, mistuh," he warns.

He cannot be more than ten or, maybe, eleven years of age, dressed in a cut down adult raincoat, as enormous as a bell-tent hanging off his narrow shoulders. His face is small, with pointed chin and huge, black eyes; while on each side of a still infantile mouth streaks of dirt decorate his cheeks like warpaint. From inside the mouth comes the sound of teeth chattering as loud as castanets – either from the cold or from fright.

My awakening must have disturbed him from purloining the carrier bag – containing most of the bread, which I still have with me from the now abandoned car. Raising myself slightly higher causes him to retreat a few steps, and a vicious looking blade sprouts between his delicate fingers from within the capacious sleeve of his raincoat.

"I'm fuckin' warnin' yu' – I'll fuckin' stick yu,"

"It's alright, sonny," I tell him. "I won't harm you."

"Too fuckin' royal!" he snaps. "Don' fink I won' use 'iss."

"Oh, I wouldn't doubt it for a second," I assure him. "But there's really no need."

Since my back is stiff from a supine position on the hard surface, and cramp is attacking my legs, I feel it requisite to placate him. At the moment any sudden necessitation of self-defence could prove to be quite a formidable task for me. I need time. As he eyes me, warily, he executes several experimental stabbing motions with the knife.

"Look," I offer, "why don't you put that thing away and take shelter under here, with me? You'll get soaked out there."

The rain is now pattering heavily on the concrete, maculating the grey with dirty brown. Its accelerating intensity also sticks his tousled hair to his forehead, and causes the grime on his face to run like tearstained mascara.

"Huh! Yu mus' fink I'm fuckin' stupid or somefink," he declares.

"Not at all; I'm just trying to be practical," I explain.

" Shit on 'at!" he snaps. "Besides, I been wet before."

"I dare say," I acknowledge. "Doesn't mean you have to be now, though, does it?"

As he impatiently shuffles his feet, his fingers clasp and unclasp the handle of his weapon – which, I notice, is constructed entirely of wound-round adhesive tape. Obviously homemade, the blade still glints malevolently, honed and sharpened to a fine point.

"Wha' do you care, anyways?" he demands to know.

"Because I do," I say, trying to sound and appear as benign and unthreatening as an older brother. "So, if you'll just give me a chance to –"

"Stuff i'!" Jabbing the air like a duellist, he narrows his eyes in an added attempt to intimidate me. "Jus' gives us wha' yu' go' there an' I'll fuck orf."

"Take it easy, will you?" I tell him, raising my hands in a gesture of submission – an action he immediately interprets as a threat. With a shaking hand he dances back a few steps, before holding out the knife at arm's length, as though taking aim down the barrel of a revolver. "I'm sure we can sort something out, here," I add.

"No need to sort anyfink'," he argues. "Jus' gives us tha' fuckin' bag – or else."

I am piqued by his tone. Even though I had decided within the first few seconds of the confrontation to offer him a share of the bag's contents, his belligerent manner is beginning to poison my altruistic…intention. Feeling that it would be a mistake to expose any signs of weakness, I offer him: "If you want it, then you'll have to come and get it. Okay?"

Shifting his weight from one foot to the other, he licks his lips, nervously. Then, with his pupils dilating, he prods his weapon at thin air – but makes no attempt at a direct attack. A confusion of emotions flicker across his face like a frame-by-frame film show.

"What are you waiting for?" I taunt.

Feigning a forward lunge, he realises I am unimpressed, so shies away again.

"What's the matter?" I ask. "Scared?"

Pushing out his chest like a feather duster, he lifts his shoulders while snorting out a forced laugh. "Wha' – of you? Scared of…*you?*"

Having, up to now, been unaware of my appearance being so unprepossessing, it does not deter me from holding out my hands, palms up, while enquiring, acidly: "Is there anyone else here?"

"Yeah," she says, in almost a whisper. "There is."

Turning my head, I watch as a young girl steps gingerly out of – what is to me – a previously concealed doorway – one that must lead to a basement or cellar. She is about twelve years old, with long, straggling hair that moves in the wind. Her face is drawn and pale – much too lived-in for her age – emphasised by the dark rings under her large eyes, and how her thin, mauve lips quiver beneath a pert, retroussé nose. In better times she would be considered pretty; but now, standing against the backdrop of downpour and dinge – dressed only in a damp, soiled dress and torn cardigan – she looks like a rag doll that had been left out in the rain. As I stare at her, she clutches her upper arms and shivers, allowing – while her presence distracts me – the boy to rediscover his courage.

Pouncing like a cat, he slashes in a downward motion with the blade. Only just managing to jerk out of the way, I throw myself to one side, simultaneously raising a protective arm in defence. There is a tearing sound, followed by a searing pain scorching across the back of my wrist, the manoeuvre causing me to stumble and fall to one knee.

"You sneaky little bastard!" I yell.

No sooner have I yelled than he's at me again, this time spearing the weapon at my face. Smartly hunching back against the wall is the only thing that saves me from the point of the knife piercing my cheek. Pinned under the obliquity of the fire escape, I crouch like a frog and glare at him.

"Cur it ou', will yu?" orders the girl. "There's no need for tha'."

"Bugger orf, sis," he retorts, warming to his task. "I'm goin' to fuckin' stick 'im, I am."

"Leave 'im be!" she insists.

But he ignores her. In full throttle, now that he has drawn blood, he throws caution to the wind and lunges at me. The knife curves up in a long, wide arc, forcing me to squeeze myself back as far as possible into the wall. As I do so, though, I lift my arms in an attempted parry, and my overcoat swells out a little from my body. The move probably saves me from serious injury, as, fortunately, the blade becomes entangled in the thickness of the material – and in the instant it takes him to try and retrieve it, I grab his arm and swing him around, hoping to pull him closer, so that I can disarm him. However, he is an inch or two too tall and his head cracks against the ironwork. There is a dull 'thung' and he collapses in a heap. Raising a potentially murderous fist, I am about to bring it down on his unprotected features, when the girl reaches out and touches my elbow. Her action is so natural and fluid that it stops me in mid pose, its deftness immediately bringing me to my senses.

Shaking his head, the boy scrambles away from me. There are tears in his eyes, but he does not cry. Instead, he turns on his sister, complaining: "Now, look wha' yu done, sis. If yu 'adn' tried to stop me, I'd a' 'ad 'im."

"Aw, give it a rest an' all," she tells him.

"I woulda'," he insists. "I'da fuckin' 'ad 'im."

"I said shu' it!" she enjoins. After glaring at him for a few moments, she bends under the fire escape to look at me. "Yu alrigh', mistuh?"

Clutching my arm, from which tendrils of blood meander out of the cuff of my sleeve, I look back at her. "I'm not sure. But you'd better keep that little bugger on a leash, or, believe me, something bad is going to happen – to the two of you."

She laughs at this, hard and brittle, as though trying humour for the first time. Joining me under the steel steps, she kneels like a geisha girl, prising my fingers away to contemplate the wound.

"You'll live," she assures me, dismissively.

"Thanks for nothing."

Behind her, the boy sniffles and retrieves the knife. Scowling at me he mimics a stabbing motion in the air. Catching the look in my eye, the girl twists around to face him. "Pu' 'at thing away, alrigh'?" she orders. He hesitates, still glowering at me. "Did yu 'ear me?"

"I don' trust 'im," he mouths, silently, as though I am incapable of translating his mime into words. "I still fink we orta do 'im, before–"

"I won' tell yu again."

"Bu', sis –"

"Jus' leave 'im to me, will yu?"

"Bu', sis, I –"

"For Gord's sake!" She is obviously angry now. "Piss orf, will yu?" After stamping his foot, the boy strolls off into the rain. Glancing back, he reluctantly ensconces the blade in his oversized pocket. "Besides," she adds, "there's ovver ways."

"I won' be far orf, if yu needs me," he calls over his shoulder, defiantly.

Tugging up my sleeve, I take a dirty handkerchief from my pocket and attempt a spot of first aid. The girl watches me with those huge eyes and reaches forward.

"'Ere," she says, "le' me." Wrapping the material around my wrist, she ties it into a neat bow. As a dark stain spreads like ink, her small fingers pull the sleeve down once more. "Don' be too 'ard on 'im," she adds.

"Why not, for Christ's sake? The little runt tried to skewer me."

Another hurt-filled laugh. "'E wouldn 'av' – nor really." Immediately after I raise my eyebrows in disbelief, she continues: "I promise, alrigh'? 'E's 'ungry, 'ass all – an' 'e's scared."

"*He's* scared!" I echo, sarcastically.

This time, a smile. "Ger away wiv yu. You're a bloke – twice 'is size. Yu coulda taken 'im anytime yu liked."

Secretly, I would be happy to accept her assumption of my prowess; it's not exactly ego building to think that I could have ended up dead in this stinking alleyway, felled by a ten-year-old urchin. Even so, reflecting on the incident I have to admit there was a strong element of luck about my so-called victory. If the blade had not become tangled in the voluminous material of the overcoat, there's no way of telling what the outcome would have been. On the other hand, the little prick did have the element of surprise on his side; an adult does not generally expect to be attacked by a pre-adolescent – no matter what kind of ethological imbalance exists. Mentally, I adopt this somewhat spurious excuse and sit on it like a disingenuous usurper on a throne.

"I'm glad you think so," I tell her, with more than a little acerbity.

"Yeah, well, I wuz only sayin', like."

"Nevertheless, I'd rather forget about it, if you don't mind."

"Okay, mistuh, anyfing yu say." Her voice drops several octaves as she stares at me with a flintlike expression. "It's jus' 'a' we 'aven' eat'n in days, ass all."

My instincts tell me to relent and hand the bag over to her; but my hackles are up, tilting my judgement off centre. In fact, my pride has been hurt. There's a lesson to be learned here; roles to be played. The puerile attitude nudges me into adopting my most pedantic standpoint – if that's not a contradiction in terms.

"I can appreciate that," I say, condescendingly. "It still doesn't give you the right to go about behaving like a juvenile Bonnie and bloody Clyde, though."

To my surprise, she does not remonstrate; instead, she just bows her head slightly. "I know."

"All you had to do was…" I start, but as she raises her face to give me an eye-to-eye, my words falter away into silence.

"Ask…" she finishes for me.

"Erm…Well…yes," I agree.

Pulling a face, and exhibiting a degree of physical discomfort, she shifts her position a little, explaining: "Cramp…in my knees."

"There was no need for you to…" I press on, while feeling her fingers slide gently along the collar of my coat.

"Course no'," she accords, without really listening to what I'm saying.

"If either of you had simply asked, and not…and not…you know…I'd have…"

"I realise 'at now, mistuh," she whispers, her fingers entwining themselves in the hair on the back of my neck, her breath on my cheek. "From now on, I'll make sure 'at…"

Her contiguity alarms me, so I push myself away from her. And as I look hard into her face, the expression I see is one of strained enticement. Her hand remains where she had placed it.

"What the hell are you doing?" I ask.

"Nuffink, really," she coos. "Jus'…askin', yu know…like yu said."

"Like I said?"

"Yeah…Like yu said. Look…"

With that, the pressure on the back of my neck gently intensifies, guiding my face down. At the same time, with her free hand, she lifts the hem of her dress above her waist. She is wearing nothing underneath.

For a second or two I just gape, digesting her proposal with stupefaction; and suddenly her fingers feel like the soft pads of a spider crawling along the base of my skull. Pushing her away, I squeeze past her and step out into the rain, where I stare up into clouds cast against a grey welkin, like elements of an animated slate engraving. Relishing the droplets as they refresh my disturbed sense of morality, I hear, from behind me, her almost mocking tone as she enquires:

"'Ey, mistuh, wassa matta wiv you, 'en? Yu bent, or somefink?"

Thrusting hands deep into my overcoat pockets, I look back at her, over my shoulder. "No. No, I'm not...bent – or somefink."

Squatting there, on her knees – still holding up the dress, exposing her-self – she seeks to adopt a different tactic. Tilting her head to one side, while 'seductively' sucking on her thumb, as though it were a lollipop – or 'somefink' – she winks at me. Jesus! Where the hell can she have learned such mannerisms?

"Look," I tell her, resignedly. "Just take the damned thing and go. Okay?" She frowns. "Wha'?"

I indicate with a nod. "The bag: take it and go."

Glancing at the carrier bag, she then looks up at me, before looking back at the bag again. "Yu mean i', mistuh?"

"Of course, I mean it. It's yours."

Picking it up, she momentarily peers at the contents, before staring at me with suspicion. Slowly emerging from the shelter of the fire escape, she comes to stand next to me in the rain – which plasters her hair to her forehead and runs down her cheeks like thin, pink worms. With a toss of her head, she blinks rapidly, flicking tiny jewels of water off her eyelashes.

"Now, what's the matter?" I ask her.

"I'm...nor sure," she says. "I don' fink I trus' yu."

Through a sardonic snort, I laugh at her. "Don't *trust* me? You...don't *trust me*? Christ! You just offered me everything you've got; what more could I be after?"

As she rolls down the top of the bag, using the surplus as a handle, she continues to eye me, warily. Then, a non sequitur: "Where yu been, mistuh?"

"What?" The question takes me by surprise.

"Yu been 'iding ou' somewhere or wha'?"

"Why do you ask that?"

"Dunno, really. There's jus' somefink odd abou' yu, ass all."

"Odd? What do you mean?"

"Yu don' fit," she says. "Yu're no' like 'em ovvers."

"What others?"

"All 'em ovver ones, yu know. Yu're no' like the res' o' 'em."

Images of dereliction, destruction, burning vehicles and leaping silhou-ettes flash through my mind, followed by the ashen features of the gunman, as he slides, jerkily, down over the bonnet of the car. And I know what she means: I *am* different – but not because I exist on a higher ethical plane, but because I am new to all this; I am a stranger who has not yet adjusted accordingly – a social novice.

"You think so?" I say, almost absentmindedly.

"Yeah…I do."

"Why, exactly?"

"Well, no one gives fings away now-days – 'specially food."

The rain falls even heavier, droplets as big as a glass bead curtain swaying in the wind, and we stand, facing each other, like a father and daughter awaiting that certain conciliatory gesture required to eradicate the bad blood of a generation gap disagreement.

"I suppose that's why you tried to knife me," I suggest, only half teasingly.

She looks shocked. "*I* did'n' try to knife yu. Anyways, i' was yu're own fault."

"It was – really? How do you figure *that*?"

"O' course, i' wuz." Defiantly now. "If we can' steal fings, wha' we gonna do? Iss the only way for us, inni'?"

I lower my gaze from her face. "Not the only way, apparently."

"Uh?" But then she catches my drift. Glancing down at herself, she allows a wry smile to slither from one corner of her mouth, and she almost blushes – but not quite. "Yeah…well…"

We both laugh at this, nervously, not because the situation is imbued with humour – it isn't – but because it just seems be the only appropriate way to react to it. However, in a matter of moments the appropriation suffuses into a sense of the idiotic, so, in order to cover my/our embarrassment, I suggest we re-shelter under the iron framework.

"Just until your brother returns," I tell her. "Where the hell could he have got to, anyway?"

"Don' worry," she says, reassuringly. "'E's nor far away, Watch 'iss."

With that, she places two fingers on her tongue and creates a whistle so loud and strident, it resonates through the silent concrete corridors like the call of a nighthawk. Almost immediately, the boy reappears, still brandishing the knife.

"Wha's up?" he asks, first glaring at me, before glancing at his sister, and then glaring back at me again. "Didn' try no kinky stuff, did 'e?"

"Don' be daft," she says, defensively on my part. "'E's alrigh', 'e is."

"A bi' quick, though," he mutters.

I stare at him, incredulously. "What?"

But he has spotted the bag and leaps to his sister's side. "'Ere, yu gor i' 'en! Gis a bi', uh? I know wha's in i'. Attempting to snatch it from her, he adds: "Aw, come on, sis. Jus' a bi', yeah?"

Dancing away from him, out into the rain, she hides the bag behind her. "'E give I' to me, 'e did. I'ss mine."

Advancing upon her, he reaches around her from the front, pinioning her arms to her sides, their wet noses almost touching. "Aw, come on, sis. Stop pissin' abou', will yu? I'm starved."

"Nor now," she tells him, seriously. "We gorra keep i'. We gorra pu' i' wiv the res' o' the stuff. I'ss gorra las'; yu knows tha'."

For a few seconds, as he digests what she has told him, they just stand in silence, toe to toe and nose to nose. When his words do come, they are in the form an exhalation of despair.

"Aw, sis," he groans.

With a lump beginning to rise in my throat, I decide to walk away. My mind reels and I cannot help but think of Veronica, of Domino, and of the tragic family back in the dunes. This is not happening, I tell myself. This is *not* fucking happening. I am asleep. I am asleep, and any moment now I will awaken to find myself safe and sound, back in my 'dilapidated sea shanty' – all this being nothing more than an episode in another one of *those* dreams.

"'Ey, mistuh!" the girl shouts. "Where yu goin'?"

As I look back at them, the boy whispers – loudly enough for me to hear: "Leave 'im be, sis. Le' 'im go; I don' trus' the bas'ard, I don'." Ignoring him, she approaches me, squinting up through the ever-worsening precipitation.

"I have to go," I tell her.

"Where to?" she asks.

"There's someone I'm trying to find."

"Who?"

"Just…someone."

"Who? Girlfrien'? Wife? Who?"

"A friend," I say. "Just a friend."

She laughs that same brittle laugh as before. "Nor many of 'em abou', now-days."

"No," I agree, with a smile. "I don't suppose there are."

"Wha's their name, 'en?"

"Whose name?"

"The one yu're tryin' to find, silly."

"Why do you want to know?"

"Dunno, really; maybe we knows 'em, 'a'ss all. Maybe we can tell yu where they lives, like – or somefink."

"*You* won't know them," I state, more than a little pompously. At once mentally reprimanding myself, I add: "But thanks, all the same."

"Sor-righ'," she says.

I smile at her, but she does not smile in return. Instead, she grimaces against the cold and pulls the wet cardigan more closely about her shoulders.

"Will you do me a favour?" I ask her.

"Whassat, 'en?"

With a slow movement, so as not to alarm the boy – who watches me reproachfully, still with knife at the ready – I shrug out of my overcoat and present it to her. "Take this, will you?"

With the boy hissing something between his teeth while stepping forward, she holds up a restraining hand, making no attempt to receive the offered item.

"Why?" she asks, warily.

"Why not?" I answer, issuing her with what I believe to be a propitious grin.

Sidling nearer, the boy stands at her side: the two of them staring at me as though from a grainy Victorian daguerreotype. As I watch tiny rivulets of water dripping from their cheeks and chins, I am consumed by a social anger that can no longer be placated or satisfied under present conditions – if it ever could be – and remain, rooted to the spot, saturated overcoat hanging from my fingers. It is at that moment I ask them what I had wanted to ask them all along:

"What the hell happened, anyway?"

After looking at each other, and then back at me, in unison they ask: "Whaddya mean?"

I gesture around me with my free hand. "All this. All this urban mess. All this destruction and violence. All this…madness – how did it start?"

The girl pulls a face. "Dunno, do we? Jus…'appened, didn' i'?"

"But how?" I persist. "What…caused it?"

She tilts her head to the side, a knowing look in her eye, and I hope she's not about to pull that trick with thumb in mouth again. But she just delivers a kind of half smile.

"I wuz righ' abou' yu, wasn' I?" she says.

"In what way?"

"Yu *'ave* been 'idin' away somewheres."

"Not…exactly," I reply, non-committedly. "But I have been…out of touch, shall we say, for quite a while."

"Tha's a bloody laugh," she retorts. "Yu mus' 'ave been sleepin' on anovver planet or somefink."

"Or somefink," I agree. "So?"

"So, wha'?"

"So, what if I have? Tell me what happened – while I was…away."

141

"'Ow the fuck do we know?" answers the boy. "One day, everyone jus' started…yu know…'avin' fun, like."

"Fun? What do you mean…fun?"

"Well, everyone jus' started takin' wha' 'ey wan'ed, yu know?" says the girl.

"But…how? Why?"

Her expression implies I must be stupid. "'Cause, there wuz no one 'ere to stop 'em, wuz there?"

With the quote: *'Catch 22 says they have a right to do anything we can't stop them from doing,'* buzzing in my brain, I ponder on feasibilities that could, in truth, prove to be nothing more than banalities. Had all this just been one gigantic, socio-political fuck-up, after all? A revealing vomitory ignominy of the age? A result of national, perhaps international – (or, God forbid! *alien* intervention; the observance at the oasis suddenly taking on new relevance; but, surely, hadn't that been merely a…*dream*?) – snake oil, governmental idiocy? It wasn't as if the semiotics didn't point that way – even before I decided to wash my hands of society and become a recluse. Such retrospection of western incompetence and eastern ambition pales in comparison to what happened in my personal life, of course: the death of Domino persistently overshadows all and sundry – a (for me) cataclysmic event that both subsumed and relegated the geopolitical to the furthest corner of my interest and concern. However, after dwelling on possible reasons for this current apocalypse, I still feel compelled to ask: "What about the authorities?"

"Thu wha'?" asks the boy.

I sigh. "The police, the army – whatever?"

"Oh, 'em." The girl shrugs, raising innocent eyebrows. "Dunno, really. 'Ey jus'…didn' bovver to come roun' no more, s'pose. Some armoured cars, an' 'at, came for couple o' days – an' took some people away, like; killed a few ovvers; bu' 'en 'ey jus' wen' away again. Don' see 'em no more."

"And now there isn't anyone – to enforce law and order, I mean. Or anyone to look after the likes of…you."

Another brittle – but this time world weary – laugh from the girl – before the boy spouts with venom: "*No* fucker ever looked after *us*, did 'ey?" Casting a glance at his sister, a momentary glimmer of sorrow and sympathy wells up in his eye. "Did 'ey, eh, sis?"

A low sigh. "No," she agrees, quietly, as though ashamed. "No one ever did."

With my heart feeling as heavy as a stone inside my chest, I attempt to combat the burgeoning depression with a physical act – so I wriggle my hand about, shaking the still offered overcoat. "Okay, let's try and do something – however insignificant – to help change that, shall we?"

"Whaddya mean?" asks the girl.

"Take this," I tell her. "Take it as a gift – from me to you."

Leaning closer to her, like the snake in Eve's ear, the boy says, eagerly: "Go on, sis – take i'."

Still mistrustful, the girl reaches out a hand to accept it. With a deft movement she drapes the garment over her shoulders, pulling the overlap about her narrow frame as though wrapping a parcel. I swear I can hear her teeth chattering; but she seals her purple lips as tight as an oyster shell, proudly sticking out her chin like a royal. Reanimating myself, I step up to her and nestle the lapels of the coat tight against her throat. As I do so, the boy raises the knife a few inches, but immediately lowers it again. Looking down at the front of the overcoat, the girl says: "Thanks, mistuh."

"You're welcome," I tell her. "Just sorry it isn't more *haute couture*, that's all."

"Is'n' wha'?"

"Never mind. Tell me: what will you do now?"

In dramatic fashion, the boy places a finger to his lips. "Say fuck all, sis. Don' tell 'im nufink."

Motioning with her head for him to shut up, he adopts a sulky expression, but on realising he is not going to remonstrate, she says: "'Ere's 'iss place we knows – secret, 'o, so can' tell yu where i' is, righ'?"

"Of course," I comply. "I understand, and I don't want to know; just as long as you have *somewhere*, that's all."

"It'll do," she says. "For now, anyway."

"Good. Then I strongly urge you to go there as quickly as you can. It's beginning to get dark; you could catch your deaths hanging around in this weather."

But, like Vladimir and Estragon, they do not move, and the three of us continue to stand there, just looking at each other, unable to think of anything further to say. Eventually, though, keeping my eyes on them, I slowly make my retreat; and since I am still a little unsure of them, I cannot help but remain somewhat reluctant to offer them my back. But the girl simply tugs the lapels even tighter under her chin, while the boy places, what could be construed as, a melodramatically protective arm around her shoulders. As their heads come together, he again whispers something in her ear, and she giggles, before playfully pushing him away.

Reflecting on the resilience of childhood – someone once claimed that infancy is the matrix of humanity – I turn on my heel and march resolutely towards the alleyway's exit, at the same time, wondering how far I have to go and how dangerous my quest is going to become. With dusk settling like an eagle into its nest, the encroaching shadows will help serve as camouflage, at least until/if I manage to locate a refuge when/if the occasion arises. Despite the minor hair-raising encounter with my pair of juvenile muggers – plus the slash on my wrist – I still feel slightly uplifted and refreshed from the sleep I had prior to their 'educational' interruption. And it is just at that moment, as I approach the opening to the street, that I hear the boy's voice assailing me from the depths of the lane.

"'Ey, mistuh!"

Stopping in my tracks, I look back over my shoulder, half expecting a repentant 'thank you' or at least a friendly wave. "Yeah?"

"Look a' this!" he calls out. "Look wha' yu missed, yu stupid fuck!"

Standing side by side, they nod, as though counting in the beat of a tune or a previously rehearsed choreographic movement, like American football players. On the final count, the girl flings open the coat, and the boy reaches across a hand to lift her dress above her waist. With a violent jerk, she thrusts her pelvis towards me.

"Fuck-in' sucker!" they recite, together, syllables rising and falling as in a nursery rhyme. "Fuck-in' sucker!" Throwing back her head, the girl laughs hysterically, while her brother slaps her on the back in helpless mirth with his free hand.

And then they are gone, their footsteps and voices echoing into the grey twilight, like the cries of a distant schoolyard at breaktime. Listening until the sounds fade to silence, I push my hands deep into my trouser pockets before walking away a much sadder but wiser man.

It is dark. Hidden within the secluded shadows of a shop doorway – the windows of which are boarded up, the floor spattered with glass, wood and concrete detritus crackling and crunching beneath my feet – I peer at my destination on the opposite side of the silent, rubbish strewn street. The block of dilapidated maisonettes – housing the address I seek – is tall, dark and angular, exhibiting only sparce evidence of movement therein. A flight of well-worn stone steps leads up into the vacuous maw of an entrance that boasts only one operative door – the other has been ripped off and leans against the wall like a drunken sentry. Along the expanse of masonry there is very little sign of life – window illumination on the ground floor being completely nullified by wooden planks or sheets of corrugated iron; while most other fenestra on the first floor and above are either in total darkness or curtained by materials expansive enough and/or thick enough to disguise occupancy. However, here and there on the remaining floors, high enough and safe enough from potential vandalism, faint glows can be evidenced, flickering like elliptic coronas around sharp mullions. And they imbue me with a minute ray of hope.

Hunching my shoulders against the nocturnal chill, I massage my upper arms. Mercifully, it has ceased raining, but a bitter wind persists in taunting me like a playful tiger, penetrating my damp jumper with icy needles. Already I regret the naïve benevolence that prompted the giving away of my overcoat – my need currently proving to be far greater than that of the pre-adolescent villains who now possess it – as, after all, didn't the girl tell me they actually had somewhere to go? Such heart bled stupidity deserved betrayal. Stamping my feet a few times on the splintered glass, I project my head out of the safety of the doorway. In the distance the familiar flashes and sounds of destruction spark into the night sky like steel blades against dry rocks; but the immediate vicinity remains totally depopulated.

Deciding that now is as good a time as any, I dart across the roadway, to where I locate a suitable retreat on the upper steps of a basement bedsitter. This residence, too, is boarded up and emits no sign of activity. Making sure I am still alone, I proceed along the pavement, ducking from doorway to doorway, like a circumspect rat, until arriving at the first step of the stairway that – hopefully – leads to my goal. Gazing up into darkness, an overbearing sense of foreboding seems to sweep down on an ill wind towards me; nevertheless, a single glance over my shoulder satisfies me that my clandestine foray has, this far, gone unobserved. So, I bound up the steps, two at a time.

Inside, it is as black as a church bell, and I have to wait several moments before my eyesight becomes conditioned to the surround. As I do so, I strain my ears for any indication of a foreign presence, but there doesn't seem to be one. Gradually unfolding shapes in the umbra inform me of a passageway to my right; while to my left there is a wall sporting two elevator doors – one of which looks as if it has recently been burned with a blowtorch. Straight ahead, there is a flight of stairs, carpet-less and barren. Obviously, the lifts are out of order, so I scamper up the steps to the first-floor area, where I stop and look around me. There, in front of me, is a doorway with a small, circular window situated at eyelevel, and I squint through it to view an empty, impersonal corridor. To my right, the stairway doubles back on itself, ascending to the next floor, and as I raise my face to peer around the bannister, a sound, like the rustling of dry, autumn leaves, floats down through the aphotic haze towards me.

Frozen to the spot, I listen intently for a repetition, but all I can hear is the beating of my own heart. Is there someone up there, on the next floor – or is it just my imagination? It makes little difference now, though, as there is no going back. The reason being, there is nothing to go back *to* – not alone, anyway. Whatever catastrophe has befallen society or even on the whole of civilisation – and ever-growing evidence points more and more to it being, if not on a macrocosmic scale, then at least on an international scale – must also affect me. All influences concerning my existence – work, food, drink, domestic activity – have been abrogated. To backslide – to renegotiate a successful journey through the urban carnage and madness – would only lead to a resuscitated condition of inertia, psychological mortification and ultimate death. Granting the latter prospect oppresses me less than it would most members of the human race – although, under present circumstances, that is debatable – I still feel it an obligation to establish the whereabouts and/or fate of Veronica. If dissolution is both imminent and ineluctable, then perhaps it could be made more comforting if we were to meet it together; after all, Pascal said that the heart has its reasons which reason knows not. Which means, I owe her that much – providing, of course, that she is prepared to acknowledge a reciprocal debit. Providing that she is here at all. Up until now, I have consistently refused to consider the possibility that she would not be. God! What the fuck will I do if she is not? What the fuck will I do if she *is*? And, evil of all evils, what the fuck will I do if she simply spurns me in favour of her present company? Pangs of regret at my obtuseness alight on my heart like mocking vultures. What the fuck do I do if he – or *she* – opens the door? Hi, there. I've come for Veronica; thanks very much for taking care of her these past weeks – months? – while I remained wrapped in an alcohol ridden state of self-indulgence and self-pity. Or: You'd better come with me now, darling, because I've decided I need you after all. But come *where,* for Christ's sake? How will we manage to get by – even if she *is* compliant with my demands? A vague, half-baked notion of somehow procuring sufficient supplies and returning to the sanctuary of the battered, tumbledown 'sea shanty' floats about within the medley of intent like an amoeba in repellent waters. Having, up until now, been somewhat preoccupied with insistent pressures of self-survival, I find myself lacking any other adroit purpose or direction; nothing is concrete or formulated, and the immediate future hangs before me, a nebulous mass of ill-founded, indefinable considerations. I have no plan.

My reverie is again disturbed by that self-same rustling sound from above. Craning my neck, I review the gloom. The noise ceases – to become replaced by a low swish, identifiable as the pneumatic decelerator of a swing door – and I speculate whether or not, whoever it was, has now departed from the above area or if they have been joined by someone else. Remaining here, holding my breath, I await confirmation, one way or another, but there is none forthcoming. Positing that there is little to be gained by holding my position, I cautiously ascend the almost invisible stairs to the next level.

Here there is nothing but a duplication of the area below; so, I come to another stop, half expecting to hear charging footsteps, followed by the physical presence of an attacker. But there is just stillness; the single persistent sound being that of a throbbing pulse in my temples. Looking through the window of a swing door twin to the one on the lower floor, I am confronted by another long, dark corridor: featureless, except for rows of blank, paint flaked maisonette doorways.

Carefully, so as to allow only the merest sibilant disturbance, I ease open the door and enter the passageway, my fingers retaining their grip on the handle until the aperture is completely sealed shut behind me. Stepping forward, I attempt to make out the numbers on the doors, only to discover, to my dismay, that some of them are missing. On the first entrance there is just the figure two; on the next, a five; while the next exhibits...nothing. So, should it be twenty something – or, fifty something? Creeping along to the fourth door, I again discern no clue as to the number of the address. Although remaining fairly certain of the floor, I have no idea how far the corridor stretches. Maybe there's another way into the building, and I should have approached it from a different direction.

Ahead, there is further swing door and I bear down on it as determinedly as a cuckolded husband on the trail of his rival. Behind me, shadows crawl across my traces like past times, until I am squinting through another window – this one broken – of an adjoining door. With the same dexterity as previous efforts, I open and close the obstacle with barely a hiss. Approaching the first residence in this corridor extension, I sigh with relief, as it boasts a clear fifty-six in silver numerals. That means the apartment I seek is just two doors down, and within a heartbeat I am positioned outside it, acknowledging to myself that this is the moment of truth. Inside, there is either salvation or expulsion.

Tapping quietly on the scratched veneer, I stand back and wait. No response. Another knock – this time a little harder – produces the same result: silence alone stirs behind the now seemingly impenetrable barrier. Almost willing an appearance – by now not caring if it be of a benevolent or inimical nature – I look both ways along the passageway: but at nothing, other than respective voids. In spite of my disappointment, with hands thrust deep into my pockets, I stroll short distances in each direction – but the half-hearted perambulation conjures no forthcoming inspiration. Retracing my steps, while spitting obscenities through clenched teeth, I scowl darkly at the dim sheen of number fifty-eight.

Now, what do I do? This is a predicament I had hitherto denied would happen. Arrival at Veronica's threshold had precipitated a resurgent instinct for survival, seen me through dangerous, even potentially fatal encounters, with anticipation of the here and now serving as a fillip, a self-forged spur, instilling within me a fresh will and determination to keep going. To what ends? The featureless door before me tells me that my efforts have been in vain; I have come all this way for nothing. Desperation subsumes acceptance of such a negative conclusion, so I contemplate alternative reasons for the internal silence. She has gone somewhere – simple. *They*...have gone somewhere – not so simple. Nevertheless, a solution: I will simply await her/their return. Is such a stand tenable? If it is, then precisely how long should I wait? Until when? What must occur – or not occur – in order to influence alternative thinking? What if she/they have moved to a different residence – in a different sector? What then? Obviously, my vigil will become pointless. Would it be possible to track them down, though? Taking into account that I don't have the resources, surely, someone – a neighbour, perhaps – must already know where they have vacated to. There has to be a trail that leads... *some*where. To take it up I need to overcome my natural misanthropy and instigate a search. With this in mind, I warily eye the doors on either side of number fifty-eight. Both appear just as impassive and unhelpful. And yet, before adopting a departure, I decide to continue a while longer with a more orthodox approach. It's possible that she/he/they are in there, but – understandably in these unpredictable and dangerous times – are reluctant to open up to a...'stranger'. Pressing my cheek against the wood, I first hammer on the surface, before calling out – loudly:

"Veronica! Open up, love! It's me!"

Still no response. Stepping back, I confront the obstruction as though it's a deriding enemy, to such an extent caution becomes belittled by a growing rage that urges me to raise my fist once more – which I do, before pounding as heavily as an angry debt collector.

"What's all the row there, soldier?"

The enquiring voice, low and rough, conjures up an image of car tyres on a gravel path.

The door directly to my left – with a single seven hanging slightly askew – has groaned open, allowing a face to peek through the crack. It is a thin face, an alarmingly long face, with a pointed, stubbled chin, and a nose, as large and narrow as a crescent moon, hanging above a small, almost lipless mouth. The cheekbones are high, with pale skin stretched almost to breaking point over the angular bone structure beneath; while the eyes, burning out of sunken sockets, look like beads, holding that sharp, glassy stare of a parrot. The whole visage cries out to be de-anthropomorphised into an eagle or, more appropriately, a hawk. It levitates, at about a height of six feet, underneath a battered black bowler hat, supported, in part, by a pair of very long, prominent ears.

"– all the row there, soldier?"

The accompanying voice is high-pitched, melodic in its effete inflection, but definitely male in origin. It belongs to a face that suddenly manufactures itself directly below the other: oval, ruddy complexioned, with glacier-iced, porcine eyes glinting fixedly from each side of a bulbous, upturned nose, into which the nostrils have been bored, large and pink, leaving that undefined central piece of flesh between them seemingly to act as a single mannequin string, suspending the bow of the upper lip in the shape of a coat hanger. And because this characteristic is so pronounced, large teeth are set permanently exposed in the centre of the mouth, like the twin grinders of a beaver. Below the teeth, the chin is as grey and as wet as a sharpening stone, glistening with uncontrollable spittle that dribbles from the slack jawed mouth, as fluidal as frogspawn. Finally, above these glove puppet features – as if to purposely ridicule its owner – a similar but precariously perched bowler hat balances amidst a mat of red hair, as thick and as tangled as coils of loose tropical ivy hanging from a tree.

Not being sure about which face to answer, my surprised eyes flicker from the top one to the bottom one, and back again. Before I can get a single word out, however, the first voice continues:

"It's enough to wake the goddamned dead, it is…"

"– wake the goddamned dead…" mimics the second voice.

"…and we don't want that, do we, eh?" A long, bony finger protrudes from the gloom to scratch the side of the huge beak. "'Cause there's already too many of the bastards!"

"– too many of the bastards!"

As both heads nod with the unity of ventriloquist dummies operated by a single mechanism, my reaction to them wavers from apprehension to humorous deprecation – while the twin pair of eyes, like berries on a bush, return my view with identical expressions of malign curiosity.

"You could be right," I agree, as I recapitulate my experiences of the violence and carnage on my journey. "There's probably a great deal of –"

"All that *fuckin'* din!" interjects Hawk-face, with a scowl. "What the *fuckin'* 'ell was you playing at, out here?"

"– playing at?"

Even though I'm not in an apologetic mood, I feel it wise to placate them in order to glean information. "Look, I'm sorry if I disturbed you," I say. "But I'm trying to locate someone."

"Locate someone?" repeats Hawk-face – in the form of a question.

"– someone?" re-repeats Beaver.

"Yes. Erm…a girl. I've been led to believe that she lives here."

"A girl?"

149

"– girl?"

"By the name of –"

"Do we know any girl?"

"– any girl?"

The top face looks down; the bottom face looks up. They remind me of a pair of indigent vaudeville clowns, who, perhaps, once upon a time, were some kind of double act; such timing could only have been developed over a long period of close proximity and/or constant rehearsal. As the banter continues, though, I cannot resist a loud sigh.

"Don't think we know of any…*girl*, soldier," says Hawk-face, ignoring my obvious frustration.

"– of any *girl*, soldier," says Beaver.

"…or…do we?"

"– do we?"

As they again stare at me, unwaveringly, like chimps in a cage, I consider my patience has outstayed the merit of the situation, therefore, I start to explain: "Look, I have it on good authority that this is her address. So, do you – or do you not – know if she –"

"'ave we seen a girl round here?"

"– girl round here?"

"Mmmhh…Not sure about that, soldier."

"– not sure about it, soldier."

"Aw, come on!" I exclaim. "She'd be your next-door neighbour, for Christ's sake!"

Reprising previous action, the two heads look at each other, and back at me, followed by Hawk-face's voice dropping more than one octave, conjuring an image of an even heavier tyre grating on a thicker layer of gravel. "A neighbour, uh? A neighbour of ours, you say?"

"– of ours, you say?"

As a dull ache of fatigue sets up station in the base of my skull, the voices begin to get on my nerves. After all I've been through, this Pickwickian drivel is the last thing I need.

"If she be a neighbour of ours," continues Hawk-face, slowly widening the aperture with the toe of a heavily scuffed boot, "then I feel we would 'ave observed her." Sidling out of the doorway, he leans louchely against the upright of the frame.

"– would 'ave observed her," echoes Beaver as he cautiously squeezes past his companion to stand in the corridor, covering any line of retreat to my left.

Below the sartorially ludicrous bowler hats, the frames of the two men are completely hidden within huge, oversized black greatcoats, suitably voluminous for the concealment of almost any kind of weapon – a presumption given further credence by the imperceptibility of hands, which remain ensconced in deep pockets. Beaver's coat is untidily trimmed so that the ragged hem drags along the ground when he walks – obviously the rustling sound I had heard earlier. Hawk-face, smiling a sinister smile, drones:

"Would 'ave...met her..."

"...'ave...met her..."

"...would 'ave...talked with her..."

"...talked with her..."

"Or, at least, would 'ave exchanged...'good mornings' and the like."

"...and the like."

Insidiously, the voices have taken on the intonation of a derisive anti-phon, and I step back while raising a placatory hand – but lower it again on the indicated 'advice' of a Beaver cocked eyebrow. The initial humour – if, indeed, there had been any – has dissipated under the emergence of blatant intimidation, and I now expect the worst.

"Look..." I start.

"Yes, soldier?"

"– soldier?"

"If you're thinking what I think you're thinking..."

"If we're thinkin' what you think we're thinkin'..."

"– what you think we're thinkin'..."

"Then you're making a big mistake," I finish.

"We're makin' a big mistake," iterates Hawk-face.

"– a *big* mistake," reiterates Beaver.

"I've got nothing," I tell them, shrugging my shoulders and lifting my hands, palms up.

"You've got nothin'," states Hawk-face.

"– nothin'," confirms Beaver.

"No money."

"No money."

"– money."

"No smartphone."

"No smartphone."

"– smartphone."

"No valuables."

"No valuables."

"– valuables."

"Absolutely...nothing."

"Absolutely...nothin'."

"– nothin'."

"What you see is what you get."

"What we see is…"

"…what we get," Beaver completes, uncharacteristically.

A silent confrontation ensues, in which I take a step back; only for the two men to take a step forward. As I retreat further, until my shoulder blades touch the wall behind me, the duo edge so close I can now feel their breath on my face. Thoughts race through my head like disturbed bats in daylight. Should I attempt to make a run for it? What if I suddenly pushed my way past them? It's possible I could make it to the door, slam it shut so violently in my wake that the vital extra seconds gained would allow a descent into darkness and safety. But memory of the slowly operating pneumatic doors, plus a menacing fidgeting motion from somewhere inside the fathomless depths of Beaver's greatcoat, dissuades me from attempting to carry out such a plan.

"You know what, soldier?" Hawk-face queries, breaking the impasse to survey me with that hawk like stare.

"– know what, soldier?"

"What?" By now I am wishing for something – anything – to happen, just to clear the air, so to speak.

"I do believe you 'ave the wrong impression about us."

"– wrong impression about us."

Returning the stare with as much bravado as I can summon, while cautiously retaining the image of Beaver's movements within the periphery of my vision, I reply, sarcastically: "Really?"

"Oh, without a doubt, soldier. Without a doubt."

"– without a doubt."

"In what way?" I enquire.

The avian eyes narrow into human slits. "Because you think we're out to do you a mischief, don't you?"

"– a mischief, don't you?"

"To…rob you, for instance?"

"– for instance?"

"I have nothing for you to rob," I tell them, again, almost wearily now.

"Or…commit an assault upon your person?"

"– assault upon your person?"

"Or…even…" the threat hangs in the atmosphere, unsaid.

"…even…" also, unsaid.

"I can't imagine why I should consider such things," I say, introducing a surprising – to me – acidic strength into my apprehension. "I mean, you're such an affable pair of fellows, are you not?"

Hawk-face rides the jibe with distain. "You obviously don't know who we are, do you?"

"– do you?"

"Or, more specifically, *what* we are?"

"– *what* we are?"

I manage a wry, mocking smile. "I have my own ideas – but I dare say you'll enlighten me if I'm mistaken, right?"

"Too true, soldier," confirms Hawk-face with a sardonic snort. "Too *fuckin'* true."

"– *fuckin'* true."

And with those words – the inflections of which hold a chord of finality about them – his unwavering gaze momentarily disengages from my own, to settle on Beaver – who grins a mighty beaver grin. When the accipitrine eyes swivel back to focus on me, the narrow mouth below them begins a slow, deliberate pronouncement of seemingly random numbers:

"Five, nine, twenty-six, forty-four…"

This time, instead of an echo from Beaver, there is unison recital, his wet lips writhing duplications to his partner's verbal emissions – and it takes several moments for me to recognise the little act as a coded communication. Too late, I realise it's a countdown to a previously rehearsed offensive procedure.

As a quickfire image of the two urchins in the alleyway, carrying out something similar, comes into my head, Hawk-face winks an eye at me, stamps his right foot noisily on the floor, before ejecting his hands from his pockets with such speed they appear as blurs ascending towards my head. But to my amazement, he simply alters their bearing, grins, and lifts his bowler hat.

Confused by the sudden irrelative sequence of movements, my own hands reflexively follow suit, creating a defence for my upper body. With exact anticipation, the moment my lower body becomes exposed, Beaver jabs a brass knuckled fist into my solar plexus.

The instant I double over and drop to my knees, they are upon me. My arms are pinioned behind my back and, through the pang of pain, I hear the metallic click of locking handcuffs. As surprised by this as I am by the swiftness of the assault, I find it inconceivable that these two clowns are policemen or members of any particular kind of even para-law enforcement agency. Almost with the same fluidity as I am felled, I am hoisted to my feet and thrust, face first, against the wall. After which a prolonged search and – what seems to me to be a purely gratuitous – pawing is carried out, before I am unceremoniously pivoted around to gawp once more into the hawkish countenance. The whole incident has taken place so quickly, and with such apparent ease on their part, that all I can do is gasp silently through the discomfort, while the gravel voice interrogatingly growls:

"Now then, soldier, let's find out why you were *really* tryin' to gain entrance to the 'ome of a superior officer of the United Urban Militia, shall we?"

Without warning, Beaver delivers another vicious blow to my already abused midsection and my body agonisingly jack-knifes once more. The attack is immediately followed by something hard crashing down on the base of my skull, causing a million tiny lights to explode inside my brain.

Although still semiconscious, I fleetingly succumb to the dissonant buzz that swarms over me. I feel as though I am floating, or resting face down in a hammock, divorced from anything solid – not unlike freefall before the opening of a parachute. But reality becomes reinstated by the pressure of supporting hands under my armpits and by the scraping of my towed feet. Somehow managing to control an urge to vomit, I realise the assailing wall of noise is being dissected by the singular sound of a key turning in a lock. From its direction I roughly determine my position in time and space, and comprehend that I am being half dragged, half carried over the now fully open threshold of number fifty-eight.

So, there is someone inside after all. My mind suddenly becomes fertile ground for a wave of ambivalent emotions. One of them is a feeling of relief at the prospect of, maybe, actually meeting up with Veronica again – of being able to talk to her, to explain why it has taken me so long to contact her; mixed with dismay that perhaps she will not understand, and the 'chasm of distance', as she called it, has finally been replaced – on her part, anyway – by the 'chasm of indifference'. And yet, to simply see her one more time, to look into those 'clear pools of emotive sparkle' would be ample consolation compared to the experiences of my recent past, and I find it impossible to project my thoughts beyond the vision of our reunion. This is because a stubborn conviction that I can still persuade her to resume our relationship persists, and it presides over all hypothesised adversities – except one: and that is the possibility I have mistaken the purpose of the buildings, and now face – if the implications of Hawk-face's words become true – an indefinite cross-examination by a violent and preponderant, civil or pseudo military bureaucracy.

Failure to lift my head high enough to scan my surroundings results in me becoming temporarily fascinated by the click clacking heels of a pair of polished boots leading the way about a metre ahead. The dim passageway, along which I am being transported, eventually catches the illumination of a sharp rectangle of light from an open door, through which I find myself being dragged before being deposited on an upright wooden chair. However, curiosity of my whereabouts takes a backseat as I gratefully double over, suspending my head between my knees. Gradually, the retching motion in my stomach subsides to the level of discomfort, and I am able to concentrate more on the voices floating above me.

"Got the little shitbag," Hawk-face announces, gleefully.

"– shitbag," repeats Beaver, just as gleefully.

"Before 'e managed to piss off again."

"– piss off again."

"You're sure it's the same one?" A third voice, flat but authoritative, belongs to the owner of the boots.

"Oh, fuck, yes! Sir!" confirms Hawk-face. "Even if 'e does seem a bit better lookin' close up."

"– better lookin' close up," agrees Beaver, emphatically.

"I that case," says the flat voice, "you are duty bound to write out a report – on paper; not just recorded out on your phones, as – and you don't need me to tell you this – half the time, there is no reception. Is that clear? Good. Then, follow me."

The three men make their exit and leave me to contemplate my position. Glancing round the room – which is practically bare, except for the chair on which I sit, and an identical chair situated on the opposite side of a small, wooden desk – I can see that, on the desk there is an ashtray, a notebook, a pen, a pencil and two, large, brown envelops. The walls are completely devoid of wallpaper or any other kind of decoration; it looks more like a converted cell rather than an office – for which, I assume, it is currently being used.

Sitting with my eyes closed for a while, I take several deep inhalations, awaiting relief in my midsection, while the taste of stifled bile burns in the back of my throat, along with a nagging pain hovering around the base of my skull. (My head hurts. My fuck-ing head hurts!) However, these sensations pale into insignificance when I think about how close I came to actually soiling my underpants. Not from fear or cowardice, but from a purely physiological weakness. In the past diarrhoea has been suffered even as a result of the consumption of particular food, or from too tight a belt; repercussions of severe blows to the stomach do not bear thinking about.

With eyes open again, my gaze idly roams up to the ceiling, from where a small red glow to my left attracts my attention. There, confronting me like some curious mechanical Cyclops, is the cold, penetrative optic of a surveillance camera, its baleful, accusing presence causing me to involuntarily recapitulate, and to self-scrutinize my body language for signs of betrayal. No matter what, though, I refuse to categorise myself as a criminal, despite what has gone before – including the episode with the gunman and the car – so I straighten my back in an attempt to relay an attitude of unaffectedness through the glass lens, and beyond, to the hidden observer behind it. But realisation, under the circumstances, that such abstract resistance is both futile and stupid, prompts me to look away and to consider my situation from a more introverted standpoint – although, not for long.

The door opens and two men enter.

The first is huge in stature, obese, with tyre thick neck and savage eyes. He is dressed in an ill-fitting military uniform which barely encompasses his bulk, the material stretched to such an extent around his massive girth that certain areas of pale flesh have become exposed between strained buttons. From a prodigious leather belt, as long as – and needs to be – an anaconda, hangs a holster, containing a 45. automatic handgun, and a long, highly polished baton, painstakingly decorated and embedded with screwheads, nail heads and metal staples. Scowling at me, he folds his mighty arms over his chest and leans with his back against the wall.

His colleague is shorter, slimmer and more delicately constructed – but obviously of superior rank. His uniform is neater, cleaner and more tailored to requirements, with knife edge creases in the trouser legs and almost luminescent shine on the hitherto observed leather boots. His head is surprisingly large, the surface shaved to a blue/grey sheen, balancing on narrow shoulders as precariously as a pumpkin on a fence pole. The face is wide and heavy looking, with enlarged, mobile eyes that flicker from behind magnified spectacles, their gaze surveying me with presumed guilt candour; while the small, infantile lips below a slightly aquiline nose, are pursed into a permanent expression of opinionated condemnation. Crossing the room with the rapid steps of a neurasthenic, he sits in the other chair, interlaces his fingers under his chin and flashes a counterfeit smile.

"Why have I been brought here?" I demand to know.

"First things first, my friend," he says.

"Why have I been abducted – attacked?"

"All in good time. We'll just begin at the beginning, shall we?"

"I want to know what the *fuck* is going on," I persist.

Deliberately ignoring me for a few seconds, he opens the notebook, produces a pencil sharpener from his breast pocket, and proceeds to do what needs to be done with the pencil's lead. Carefully, after brushing the shavings into a neat pile on the desktop, he replaces the sharpener in his pocket, and holds up the pencil, point at the ready.

"Name?" he says.

"Erm…Pencil and paper?" I mock. "Really?"

"Name?" he repeats.

"Not until you tell me why I'm here."

The giant shuffles his feet, impatiently.

"Name?"

"Look, I've just told you –"

"Address?"

"Wha –? What? Look, have I been arrested? If so, I want to know what the charge is. I –"

"Occupation?"

"Who the hell were those two goons, anyway?"

"Age?"

"Jesus!" I exclaim, on the point of losing it now. "Will you just *tell* me what the *fuck* this is all about? What's happening? What *has* happened…" I toss my head, indicating to just about everything and everywhere "– out there?" But the man simply smiles at me, like a passive fish in a tank. "What…what *is* it I'm supposed to have *done*? What's so fucking damned-well important it takes precedence over such…such sociological bedlam? What possible felony demands the attention of…of…I don't even know who the fuck you are."

There is the sound of a heavy footstep, behind me, followed by a searing pain shooting up the side of my head – (my fucking head hurts!) – one that also spreads rapidly down over my shoulder to my arm. After the formidably decorated baton has bounced off my trapezium muscle, it becomes horizontally lodged under my chin, held each end by hands as strong as wheel braces. Pulled tight, it restricts my breathing, and I gasp for air, simultaneously attempting to pitch myself backward, away from the pressure – but an obstruction, in the form of a bulbous abdomen against the nape of my neck, prohibits such a move. The piscine eyes, opposite, blink through the milk bottle lenses and the smile disappears like chalk erased from a blackboard.

"Listen to me very carefully, my friend," he says, quietly. "I dislike flatulence. Also, I dislike hysteria. Flatulent hysteria I dislike even more than the now obsolete 'right to silence'. Therefore, when I ask a question, I expect an answer. I do not expect – and will not tolerate – a flatulent or hysterical tirade." Glancing down for a moment, he picks a minute piece of loose skin from a fingernail. "However, in order to save time, and to establish some ground rules, so to speak, I will attempt to explicate what appear to be sticking points." As the baton is jerked tighter, he raises an enquiring eyebrow, levitating it until I, at last, succeed in producing an affirmative nod. "Good. So, firstly: you have *not* been abducted; you accompanied two members of the S.M.S. – Special Militia Squad – in order to…*voluntarily* submit relevant information concerning a particular offence. Secondly: you have *not* been arrested – yet; you are merely 'helping us with our enquiries', to quote a somewhat trite, perennial phrase. Thirdly: *no* attack against your person has taken place; you simply underwent a standard, preliminary search, in the name of security, before being granted an audience with yours truly: R, C. – Regional Commander – of the United Urban Militia. Is that clear?"

Once my windpipe is freed slightly, I cough out heartfelt but stupid comments – at least, as best I can. "No! No, it is not! You haven't the right to do this. From where do those sadomasochistic shitheads derive such authority? And what is this so-called 'voluntary' information supposed to consist of? 'Helping with enquiries' is such a well-known euphemism, I won't even bother to interpret what I think R. C. should stand for."

Again, the stranglehold is intensified, this time for a much longer period, causing me to rock about on the chair as I desperately fight to alleviate it. My eyes feel as though they are about to pop, and my mouth opens as wide as a full-blown yawn, while the image of the R. C. begins to blur and dissolve into a haze of flesh tones and grey. This impairment of vision is accompanied by a great rushing sound inside my head, and my lungs start to burn like hot cokes. One of the flesh tones – I assume a hand – ascends slightly and the choking slackens enough for my interrogator to resume definition. Leaning forward, the oversized optics appear to leap out, as though from a three-dimensional film, before he inclines his face slightly, daring me to go on.

"You were saying?"

As I cough again, I shake my head, giving the impression I am deferring; but inside me a growing anger swells like a balloon being filled with water, eventually taking the form of obstinacy and recalcitrance. From behind their balustrades I watch the R. C. patiently place pencil point to paper for a second time.

"Name?"

"Dumpty," I tell him.

"Mmmhh...Christian name/s?"

"Humpty."

Lifting his eyes, he pierces me with that exaggerated stare. "O-kay... Address?"

"Upper Brick Wall. Brick Wall Avenue. North Brick Wall Estate."

Well, Mr, Dumpty, if you don't mind me saying, you look like you've lost weight."

"I haven't been well, lately."

"Really? What's been the problem?"

"I had a fall – and I haven't been right since."

A hint of humour escapes through the lenses. "That's too bad. Occupation?"

"Unemployed," I declare. "But hope to soon be taking up a position as –"

"– fairy-tale eggs-ecutive?" he finishes for me.

Blinking, I half smile, realising I have probably underestimated this man. Sitting motionless behind the desk, he regards me with an expression of mild amusement, while from the rear comes an aggressive scrape of a boot on the floor; the thick fingers clenched around the baton becoming as restless as maggots. Nodding towards his subordinate, the R. C. says:

"You are more than fortunate, my friend, that our third-party companion is not so well versed in classic literature."

I remain silent, but accept the droll yet tacit connotations left hanging behind the spoken words. The huge guard is obviously disposed to acting on impulse, rather than waiting for direct orders. Whether or not this is because he has unspecified authority to do so or because he is simply out of control is difficult to glean; the R. C. glances down at the desktop rather than answer the awkward question in my eyes. When he looks up again, the unverified temporary entente is gone, and he straightens his spine, reasserting both rank and distance.

"So, Mr., erm…'Dumpty'…why have you come back?"

The query takes me by surprise. My brain races, repeating the words so that they penetrate the furthest reaches of my mind, as though searching for indication of familiarity. Alienism is self-confirmed.

"I don't know what you mean," I say.

"It's simple," he explains. "You were here; you went away; you came back. Why?"

"I've never, in my life, been to this place before," I protest. With shoulders hunching of their own volition, I expect further treatment from the guard; but the R. C.'s hand restrains it.

"Then what are you doing here now?" he asks.

"Looking for someone," I tell him, truthfully. "But, evidently, I've come to the wrong address."

"Who is it you're looking for?"

"A…friend," I say. "Just a…friend."

"Name?"

I emit a groan of despair. "Oh, Christ!" Let's not start that again, huh?"

A tightening of the baton is again deterred by the motion of his hand. "You really are tempting providence, my friend."

I sigh – as much as I am allowed to. "Look, it doesn't matter who it is. The person I'm referring to has got nothing to do with any of this."

"Any of what?" Obviously, the change of approach means he is hoping to trick me.

Casting my gaze around the room, I say: "Any of...this."

"I...see." Leaning forward, two hands gripping the pencil in parody of the baton, he adds: "Tell me... 'Mr. Dumpty', do you have a brother?" Momentarily, his eyes become obliterated by a flash of light reflecting off his spectacles, concealing any possible visual explanation for the non sequitur.

"Erm...What? Brother? No."

"Is there anyone in your family who could conceivably be mistaken for you?" His line of reasoning is lenient but regrettably unhelpful.

"No," I tell him, seriously. "I have no family."

He sits back. "In that case...'Mr. Dumpty', I consider it only fair to inform you there are witnesses who are prepared to swear under oath that you were seen on these very premises just two nights ago."

"They're mistaken," I say; but my self-assertion is somewhat undermined by his tone. "I was many kilometres away from here two nights ago."

"You can prove that, of course."

There seems little point in fabrication. "I doubt it," I admit.

"Then I suggest, unfortunately, that you may be batting on something of a sticky wicket, my friend."

"So, it seems," I reply.

He frowns, quizzically. "Is that all you have to say?"

"Until you explain to me why I'm here." I retort. "As far as I know, I've committed no crime – unless, of course, you categorise survival as such." A sudden image of the gunman being catapulted through the windscreen almost detonates my self-proclaimed innocence, but I manage to supress it. "Therefore, for the moment, I regard it prudent to exercise a little verbal restraint. To be honest, it seems inconceivable to me – in light of what's occurring all around us – that any single offence could merit the importance you are currently administering to...to whatever you think I'm involved in."

Tossing down the pencil, the R. C. clasps his hands behind his head and tilts his chair onto its two back legs. After rocking gently for several moments, he says:

"Try murder."

"Murder of who?" I ask, defiantly. "Anyway, even murder pales into insignificance when compared with the mayhem taking place...out there. Or, is it simply a case of: every stranger is an enemy?"

Dropping his chair back onto its four legs, the R. C. slowly shakes his head with bewildered amusement. "What, from fairy tales to Levi now? I'll say one thing for you: you've got nerve."

His remark puzzles me, but he does not elaborate further. Instead, he picks up one of the large brown envelopes from the desk, peeks inside it, and drops it down again. Picking up the other one, he opens it and slides out several enlarged photographs. Holding them up before him, he asks:

"Did you know you've been under surveillance since you entered this sector?"

"No. No, I didn't."

"No idea that you were *allowed* to arrive at this location unchallenged?" Spreading the pictures out, side by side, on the desk before him, he motions for me to survey them. Some are of me ignominiously shuffling along empty streets or hiding in doorways; others depict me in the ground floor atrium, on the stairs and peering through corridor doors. All shot in infrared. "This...person you're searching for," he adds, as I peruse the copies before me. "Wouldn't be a...young lady, would it?"

"Perhaps," I offer, as enigmatically as I can. "Why?"

"It's just that our bowler hatted friends told me you were enquiring about a girl when they disturbed you."

"Disturbed me? What are you implying?"

"You *were* attempting to gain entrance," he says.

"But I knocked on the door," I point out. "I was not trying to break in."

"Yes," he muses. "That is why I am somewhat perplexed – especially since you are already aware of an alternative access." His resumed fishlike stare seems stern enough to bore into the very penetralia of my brain – and, without diverting that gaze for an instant, he opens up the other envelop to slip out its contents in front of him. This time, face down.

Returning his stare with a frown, I argue: "Alternative access? I know of no other access than that of the main entrance. How could I have, considering I've never visited this area before? I was actually unaware that this was/is a Militia establishment." Lowering my voice, I append, almost to myself: "I didn't even know there *was* such a thing as a fucking Militia."

"So, *you* say," he counters, tersely. "However, those self-same members of the S.M.S., on reviewing the photographs, immediately recognised you as the person spotted on the fire escape, at the *rear* of this building, the night before last."

"Impossible," I deny. "What, in the name of all that's holy, would I be doing on the bloody fire escape, two nights ago – or at any *othe*r time?"

"We're more interested in what you were doing *before* that," he says, icily.

"*Before* that?" Automatically, my eyebrows arch in surprise. "How the hell could I –"

"Are you a practicing nudist, my friend?"

Closing my mouth with a snap, I open it again, before closing it and opening it once more. With eyelids flickering madly, I gawk at him, stunned. "What the fuck kind of question is that?"

"When you made your escape," he explains. "Those two swear you were...unattired. In their words: as naked as a sheered sheep."

"I've never heard such fucking cra –"

"They also said you have unusually pigmented skin – very white – and that you have a remarkable covering of hair on your body." Nodding to the guard, he suggests: "I think we'd better have a look for ourselves, don't you?"

With that, the giant behind me relinquishes his grip on the baton and laughs out loud – although the sound is more like a snarl than an expression of joviality. Before I can make any kind of move to resist, he grabs my sweater by neckline and shoulder seams and tears the material apart. As I attempt to stand up, he forces me back onto the seat. His strength is awesome, and I feel like a child before him. Without further ado, he tugs the remains of the garment all the way until it becomes wrapped and tangled about my forearms, painfully wedging one of the handcuffs against my still wounded wrist.

"Satisfied?" I demand to know, as the R. C. regards my exposed torso with mild curiosity. "Now, what do you have to say about –?" but the words are cut short by the repositioning of the baton underneath my chin.

Pressing palms together and touching fingertips to pursed lips, the R. C. observes: "Hardly hirsute, I grant you – but your skin *is* very pale."

"Oh, really?" I gasp. "Sorry about that; I'm afraid I've not been able to afford my usual continental holiday this year."

Dropping his hands, he scoops up the prints already seen by me, and slips them back into their envelop. Holding up the remainder, he stares at them, while issuing the caveat: "You are in no position to be flippant, my friend." Removing the top photo and placing it at the bottom of the pack, he refocuses his large eyes on the second one down. "Nevertheless, let us get back to the subject of this young lady, in whom you appear to be so interested, shall we?"

It's the strange way in which he glances from the pictures to me and back again that creates my burgeoning cold sweat, and for my heartbeat to accelerate in concert with the throbbing pulse in my temples.

"What about her," I ask.

"Who is she?" Sliding the top image to the bottom, he scrutinises the third in the pile. "What is her name?"

"I've already fucking told you, okay? She has nothing to do with this. Therefore –"

"Ver...on...ica, is it not?"

The cold chill that descends on me establishes the fact that I am not at the wrong address after all – and a state of panic ensues. Struggling against its effects only enforces the rigidity of the baton keeping me in place, its pressure almost nullifying the pain in my wrist which should have, by now, become excruciating – but hasn't. On gritting my teeth, something wet erupts over my lower lip, causing my words to suddenly sound…garbled.

"What do you want to know about her?" I…growl? my tongue feeling as if it's beginning to swell. "Where is she, anyway?"

The R. C. watches me as my whole body starts to tremble. He probably assumes that it is the result of the cold – but it isn't. I am not cold; I am hot. My muscles are inflamed, and blood flows through expanding arteries like miniature express trains.

"She isn't here," he says, from a distance, as though speaking through a megaphone. "Well, at least, not anymore."

The final words are delivered with a descending inflection, emphasising a kind of terminal quality. Then, after studying the print in question for a few moments, he places the whole pack – again, face down – on the desktop; and a sensation of nausea overtakes me. Closing my eyes against the surge, I observe the colours that are beginning to form and dart about behind my lids. Pulsating splashes and glows take shape and I watch them become more and more discernible. At first, they are mere blobs palpitating in a darkness as black as deep space, along with other amorphous, inchoate globules of light which quickly coalesce into a single form – and a voice, low and guttural, demands:

"What do you mean…not anymore?"

Initially, I imagine it is the guard, speaking for the first time; but the silence that follows persuades me to open my eyes and gaze at the R. C., who seems somewhat taken aback by something. After his jaw momentarily drops, he goes on:

"Oh, I think you know exactly what I mean. Also, I think you now fully realise you were not mistaken about the address of your so-called friend. Moreover, you knew, too, that this is the personal residence of a much esteemed and respected officer of the United Urban Militia."

"That's a load of –" I start, before coughing to clear my throat, at the same time accepting that the prior guttural tones had actually but incredibly been manufactured within my own larynx. As I restart and finish my hitherto incomplete sentence: "…a load of crap," an odd look develops in the narrowed eye of the R. C.

"Is that…right?" Fingering – a trifle nervously, it seems to me – the edges of the photographs, he adds: "So, you categorically deny having visited these premises two nights ago."

I genuinely try to answer him, I really do, but my tongue appears to have swollen even more, verbally disabling me. Closing my eyes again, I suddenly jerk back in my seat with such a powerful exertion the guard is forced to emit a low curse through gritted teeth. The visage – now a clear, distinguishable K-Factor image – races towards me at the speed of light, projecting features – bone coloured flesh, hypognathous jaw, froglike mouth, glittering teeth, flared nostrils and smouldering eyes – that assail my senses.

"Of course, I do," growls a voice, as though from inside a cave. Reopening my eyes, I attempt to accompany the reply with a nod of my head, but the baton regains its position, impeding me from doing anything other than squirm in my seat.

"Also…" continues the R. C., "…that you climbed the fire escape…"

"Yes."

"…forced the latch on the bathroom window…"

"Yes."

"…gained access…and then hid, until…"

"Yes!" the voice rumbles like thunder.

"…the young lady, whom you now claim to be searching for…"

Straining against the stranglehold, I can feel the veins erupt on the side of my neck, while, somehow, its constriction seems a little more relaxed than before.

"…and who just happened to be the sister of the aforementioned officer…"

The word 'sister', along with the preterite, 'happened', burn into my brain like branding irons.

"…entered."

Vigorously resisting the hitherto incapacitating hold, I succeed in shifting my position slightly – at least enough to goad the guard into grunting a further obscenity. As this takes place, I glance across at the R. C.; something about my face appears to be bothering him: his large eyes have widened more than ever, and the colour looks to be unaccountably draining from his cheeks.

"You…you then…" he stammers "…attacked her and…and…"

A wet stickiness spreads out, painlessly, from my wound, while my back, shoulders and arms, like snakes in a sack, succumb to rapid, kinaesthetic spasms.

"…and…"

At once, a great, lavaform heat sears through my body like an electric charge. I am on fire. Around me, the room becomes hazy, ill-defined; and as the R. C. tries to speak, fleeting glints of spittle become visible within his open mouth; they are, to me, the only clear images in an otherwise indistinct milieu.

Now managing to move more easily, I sense the guard behind me strain and pant as the handcuffs physically tighten about my wrists, leaving the chain linking them together to stretch as freely as a damp leather thong drying out in the sun. The deadened pain that should be intense in my arm does not even matter anymore. Slowly prising my hands apart, I feel my captor's grip ease and slacken to nothing.

Pushing himself back in his chair, an expression of alarm filling his face...*you see her*...the R. C. drops the envelops in an attempt to stop the table vibrating. As I straighten my legs and lock my knees, the huge guard again swears – this time louder – while the R. C., his cheeks now ashen with fear, frantically tries to gather up the photographs...*she is discarding the last of her clothing*...while behind me the curses become more desperate and vehement as the ogre fails to constrain the liberation of my enraged inner self. In a cluster, the pictures fly from the R.C.'s grip to flap about the desktop like frightened swallows. Slamming his palms down, as though squashing marauding ants, his eyes probe the thick lenses with rapid, panic-stricken nictations...*you/we watch as she stands, facing you/us, fluffing up her hair with her hands*...Turning about, I/you see the guard step up, baton raised to attack my/your head, but his mouth gapes and he looks *up* at me/you, goggle-eyed; he cannot believe what is happening, and a high-pitched gurgling sound escapes his lips; the taloned hand has him by the throat, lifting him easily from the floor, and his legs dangle, executing a bike peddling motion as though his life depended on it. Twisting my/your body around, I/you/*we* investigate the cry of anguish emanating from the other side of the desk...*she cannot see us and we smile behind the simian mask*...where, still sitting in his chair, the R. C. becomes propelled backwards, crashing against the wall, followed by the desk, which hovers until tilting at an angle, before smashing into his chest with the velocity of a battering ram. Slumping to the side, he collapses in a heap, blood pouring from his mouth, his head hitting the floor with a sickening crack, and his spectacles splintering into tiny, spiderweb patterns...*obliviously, she turns her back on us, allowing us to approach like Nimrod*...while the pensile guard becomes still, his ungainly mass swinging gently below the black face and protruding tongue, as I/you/ *we* regard him impassively. His death means nothing to *us*, he being just another microbe floating aimlessly within the will, so the clawed hand releases its grip, and he plummets to the floor, a bundle of life*less* matter and of a *life* that was but is no more. Consequently, in the haze that surrounds *us* like mist or a filter over a camera lens, control has gone, *our* mind acting subserviently to outside directives...How did *we* get here? Where are *we*? Where is this place? Lowering *our* gaze to the body before *us*, an extraordinary sensation enters *our* head, and a kind of rhythm, like fingers squeezing and relaxing *our* brain, calms *us*, and as *we* look, the clawed hand descends to retrieve one of the discarded photographs... *now she is supine, and there is water, and she is falling away from us, a look of terror on her face, and she is struggling, thrashing and fighting against the death throes*...raising it up through a series of stop motion frames until *we* can make out the image of a girl lying in a bathtub full of water – and *we*/you– *I,* cannot breathe, *we*/you/I am choking; the girl is gently afloat, arms loose, palms up – but her...her head is...under the sur-face...*liquid swirls and rushes into nostrils and throat*...and *my* chest is tight...*blood pounds thunderously through arteries*...*my* head hurts, MY head hurts...*and heart thumps impotently against ribcage*...as I realise, at the precise moment the snap had been taken, either the angle or the effect of the flashbulb, had manufactured a blur or a gleam, exactly over the dead girl's face – robbing it of...eyes...nose...and mouth!

An explosion!

Whiteness...White-ness...White...
Lightness...Light-ness...Light...
Brightness...Bright-ness...Bright...
SIGHT!

Like a nemesis, the smooth, featureless visage blindly 'stares' up at ME from its watery grave – robbing ME of the last vestiges of true imagery. But I can still hear her voice:

*You are killing me...you are killing me...you are killing me...you are killing me...you are killing me...you are...killing me...killing me...killing... kill...*

EXISTENCE
A PHENOMENON
A DISRUPTION OF NOTHINGNESS
CREATION
DEFIANCE OF NON-EXISTENCE
A DISPLACEMENT
AN INFILTRATION IN THE IMPERVIABLE VACUUM
A DRIFT
A QUIRK IN NIHILITY
SENTIENCE

I floated up through liquid blackness: a dense, oppressive substance that rendered me immobile. Nevertheless, I remained conscious of a glow beckoning to me, as remote and solitary as Turner's beacon in a storm. By concentrating, and by applying that concentration, I found that I could ascend towards its influence. However, a mere instant's relaxation caused either me or the glow to recede – even as it granted me a power I couldn't understand. So, for a while I rose and fell, like one of those toy submarines operated by a tube and a hollow rubber ball, each climb gaining ascendency over each fall, allowing me to drift up, nearer and nearer to the burgeoning radiance, until, after eventually succeeding in rising all the way up…I opened my eyes.

It was still raining. I could hear its fingers drumming incessantly in the background; and the lights continued to sway, way up there. But this time they did not shine so severely – maybe because the intensity of the downpour diminished their brilliance – and I found I could look at them for longer periods than before. Noises persisted, clattering and clanking somewhere up, over and around, their metallic resonances and shouting voices reminding me of a busy restaurant kitchen: activities heard intermittently through swing doors opening and closing, a flight of fancy requiring only a minor further effort to envisage the comings and goings of snappily dressed waiters hurrying and scurrying about with their orders.

Then – who knows why? maybe because something had dripped directly on to them – I reclosed my eyes, only to sense the passing of a shadow between the brightness of the lights and myself. Reopening one eye still seemed to be a task that was achievable for me – so, like a pirate without a patch, I lifted a single lid and squinted up into the face above.

It was a wide face, a heavy face, with any number of crags and furrows scrawled into its surface like hieroglyphics, allowing tiny rivulets of water to run down them like streams on an asperous mountainside; while the eyes, with the luminosity of reflecting pools in a rough terrain, glimmered each side of a broad, hillock shaped nose. From somewhere towards the lower end of this landscape of features a cavernous mouth opened, giving access to inhalations and exhalations of breath that sounded like the rising and falling of a wind whistling through crevasses of rock.

"Hang on in there, mate," his voice, as rough in intonation as the face was in texture said. "We'll have you out in no time."

The words were meaningless to me, registering nothing, just baritone decibels falling out rather than in, through the event horizon of a distant black hole – in the rain! Blankly returning the gaze of the reflecting pools, I was only vaguely aware of them squinting for a few seconds, as though reassessing their objective, before blinking up to a spot situated above my own, somewhere in the region of my forehead. An expression of concern caused the valleys in the face to deepen, trapping minute droplets of precipitation like dewdrops on a spider's web.

"Shit!" Turning away from me, the craggy landscape, partly obscuring one of the glares, became a silhouette below a tall, misshapen head – like the head of Mekon from a vintage Dan Dare comic strip. "Hey, Doc! Doc! I think you'd better get over here." Facing me again, the craggy terrain grinned a craggy grin; above it, in contrast to all the rugosity, the Mekon head made more sense as a high, white, shiny helmet – especially when I noticed the thick, elasticated strap encircling the chin, holding the whole thing in place.

A moment later it disappeared, and I just stared at the lights some more, now accompanied by another glare from a more animated source: a blue, coruscating luminosity emanated from somewhere over to my left – past the abstract piece of artwork still sprawled there. Attempting once more to move my head – so as to achieve a clearer view of the damned thing – I found that the muscles in my neck refused to respond, challenging me to explore by sight alone. Just out of range, the shadowed form remained a tantalising enigma in the furthest corner of my vision – but I knew it was blue, dissected by pale pink, and somehow fragmented with a maculation of crimson. However, there the speculation ended. While still puzzling over the problem, I became aware of an approaching presence, and a face projected itself almost against mine.

Small, twinkling eyes, set among multiple criss crossings of pink skin, stared down at me from behind rimless spectacles, balanced pinz-nez-like on the end of a sharp, triangular nose. And I felt that I knew that face; I had seen it before, but failed to decompartmentalise it into a specific period of my life. That said, I simply knew I had seen, met, even talked with its owner at some time in the past. The brows – white, with hairs sprouting like pampas grass – knitted themselves into tight flutings on what could have passed as the surface of a carmine sponge, while the optical pebbles underneath glinted from within slits of flesh, studying my face for a prolonged, quiet interval. Then, as the newcomer turned away from me, I watched his profile: watched the movement of his lips, and the way the flesh of his neck was stretching out from his stiff, white collar, like the creases of a shirt tucked into the waistband of a tightly belted trousers; and how droplets of rain cascaded from his head of grey hair, down onto pink cheeks, as though from a freshly opened bottle of champagne.

"I need to get in further," he said. "I can't tell if it's safe to move him from here." Refocussing on my face, the eyes first rose to my forehead and then higher, finally to scan an area above it. "This here…" there came the sound of a hand banging against metal "…can it be removed?"

With the elderly face doing a disappearing act, it became replaced by the prior face, the one with the mountain streams. After looking about, it withdrew again, but its voice was clear. "I think so. Those supports will have to be burned away first, though. Where's Charlie? Tell Charlie to bring the oxyacetylene. Now!"

As the older face recomposed itself before me, it said: "I'll give you a jab, old son. Is that okay? You won't feel a thing. When you wake up, you'll be out of here. Alright? Good."

I tried to answer him, but I couldn't control my tongue, which had become swollen, almost filling my mouth. However, the face seemed to spot my effort, proofed by its smile and condolent nod, before retreating into the rain once more. Voices drifted on the wind from distance, and I listened to the crackle of communication between them against the persistent snare drum solo of the downpour:

"Charlie? Where the fuck has Charlie got to with those bottles? Ah! Charlie! Look, leave that. No! I said leave it! Get over here, will you? For Christ's sake! Yes. Yes, I fucking-well know that – but the doc wants this seen to first. Look, don't give me that shit, will you? Just get your arse over here – right away! There's one inside that's still fucking breathing. Okay? Right!"

Up to my left, the mound continued to intrigue me, and I rolled my eye-balls as far as I could in its direction. This time, allied by common sense and extrapolation, I succeeded in building a true picture of what it was. It was a human figure. A female human figure, and it wore a dress – a blue one. The intersecting line of pink was, in fact, an arm: a bare arm, hanging limply back towards my left, which, for a while, made it difficult to make out, because its angle was all wrong. Consequently, I decided the reason for this was because it must have been broken, or, at least, dislocated; to lie in such an awkward position was evidence of that. Satisfying myself that this must be correct, I then postulated, rather indifferently, that the dark red blemishes could be nothing else other than…blood.

Manifesting itself once again, the senescent face said: "Alright, old son? Good. Then here we go." With that, his hand compressed a syringe, spouting a thin fountain of liquid in the opposite direction to the rain. "Soon be all over with."

And he was right.


I am cold. I squat on a doorstep, hugging my knees tightly with my forearms. What has happened to my clothing? Why am I dressed only in denims, socks and shoes? I cannot remember. All I can remember is the image of Veronica, lying – floating – with her head just below the surface of the water – and of the terrible whiteness of her featureless face, caught by the glare of the flash. Desperately, my mind replays the scene of the taloned hand holding the photograph closer for me to study. Was it just a dream – like the others? I hope against hope that it is. (*Unlikely; Camus said: 'All the misery of men comes from hope.'*) Still, maybe, just maybe, what has supposedly taken place was simply one more crazy creation of my madness. In my mind's eye I will Veronica to rise up out of the water, alive and well – to rise up and laugh at the mischievous prank she has pulled on me. But she does not. The image of stillness presides. I drop my head on to my arms and close my eyes...


*What's happening to you?* I raise my face, eyes boring into the darkness. *You can tell me, you know. You can talk to me about...anything you like.* I stand and look around me. The street is deserted. A sudden explosion, coming from somewhere near, does not perturb me. *It's not good, you keeping everything bottled up like this.* I walk a few yards, hunting shadows. It starts to rain once more. *Tell me...Trust me.* A cat squawks and darts across the roadway, angry its refuge has been discovered. Stopping on the opposite kerb, it arches its back and shows me its fangs. *You've no need to worry on that score.* Spinning around on my heel, I race in the other direction. More doorways. More shadows. *I am real.* "Veronica," I whisper. "Veronica, is that you?" But her silence reaffirms her absence.


The wind rises and skids along the barren sidewalk, swirling about me, trying to get inside me. Shivering violently, I look up, towards the heavens: clouds move slowly, like ink in water between the vast grey blocks of concrete and glass. Diving between them, an avian form is instantly swallowed up by the tenebrous geometry.


Why didn't you tell me it was your brother? Why? If you had told me it was your brother you were living with, even if he was – is? – a high ranking officer in the Militia, things could have been – would have been – different. Things would have been so, so different. Damn you, Veronica! Damn you! Why the secrecy? Did you think I would have been influenced by his position? Did you? Jesus! You knew I've always been apolitical; I wouldn't have cared. But was that what things were truly all about, though? Was it something more basic, more personal? Was it simply to try and make me jealous? Or was it revenge for my attraction to Domino? Was that the real reason? Was it, after all, merely a sexual ambuscade? Was I right to think that?

Damn you, Veronica.

Damn you!

Rain cascades from the sky in torrents, soaking me, while my shoes squelch on puddle strewn tarmac, across the surface of which large holes gape like craters of the moon. Full with glutinous black water, they reflect nothing but blackness back. Walking along, an unseeing, uncaring zombie, I know not where I am or where I am going. *Total irreconcilability,* she says, *is brought about by the chasm of indifference, not by the chasm of distance.*

It is also brought about by death.

Sit...squat...wrap arms around knees...lower head...drink in the darkness...the cold...and the emptiness...Breathe out the lifeforce... breathe out...breathe out...out...out...out...

Die, damn you. Die, damn you. Die, damn you. Die, damn you. Die, damn you. Die, damn you, Die, damn you, die, damn you, die, damn you, die, damn you, die damn you die damn you diedamn you diedamn you diedamnyou diedamnyou diedamnyoudie diedamnyoudie diedamnyoudiedamn diedamnyoudiedamnyoudiedamnyoudiedamnyoudiedamndiedamnyoudiedamnyou. Die, damn You!

Fuck it! Fuck it! Fuck it! Fuck it! Fuckit! Fuckit! Fuckit! Fuckitfuckit! Fuckitfuckit Fuckitfuckit! Fuckitfuckitfuckitfuckitfuckitfuckitfuckitfuckitfuckitfuckit...FUCK IT!

*Wake up!*
It does not work.
*Come on! Wake up!*
It does not work.
*I said, wake up! Damn you! Open your eyes!*
It does not work.
*Will you bloody-well wake up? Come on! Come on!*

It...does...not...work!
Apnoea does not work!


Who am I? What is my name? Where do I come from? What am I
doing here? Where is this place? Where am I? Is this death? Am I
dead? How did I die? When did I die? How long have I been dead? Did
I bring death on myself? Did I succeed? Or not? Am I not dead? Am
I alive? Am I still living? Is this living? Where is this place? What am I
doing here? Where do I come from? What is my name? Who am I?


In a state of ague, the shivering is uncontrollable. I am like an epileptic.
Arms shake, legs shake, body shakes, head shakes, eyelids flicker, teeth
chatter, lips tremble...
A landed fish...drowning in the air...
*I'll give you a jab, old son. Is that okay? You won't feel a thing...*


Cold...
Empty...
Outside: pain...loneliness...
Inside: peace...tranquillity...
Freedom!

When?
When did, or when will, these events occur?
*It matters not...*
*The only reality is the microsecond of now.*


*As she stares up at me, with a gaze that is both intense and impen-*
*etrable...*Veronica...*To try and explicate – to actually say anything at*
*all – would be to dig too deeply within ourselves...*Veronica... *We feared*
*as much, therefore something will be done...soon...*Veronica...*Like a*
*nemesis, the smooth, featureless visage 'stares' up at ME from its watery*
*grave – robbing* ME *of the last vestiges of true imagery...*Veronica...IT
was created to...kill you.


Buildings: huge, black rectangles; geometrical shapes: obelisk-like
from ground level; broken windows: eyes of the dead. Charred skeletons
of burnt-out vehicles and...bodies...

Man, who is born of woman, and is wretched...Die, you bastard! Die,
damn you! Or...wait! There is always the waiting. Time to wait. Time *is*

waiting. The totality of life. One, long wait. A descent – from open cunt to open grave. Amen.

Mounds of refuse, scattered, strewn over vast areas, like flocks of felled birds; rodents, spurting, darting, tiny paws pattering, claws scratching among debris and broken glass; forlorn, lost dogs, sniffing, howling, barking: canine orphans of the wind...

Happiness – the conceptual folly of happiness. There is no such state of being. There is only ignorance of the truth. Awareness of truth strangles happiness. To be happy is to be oblivious – to be ignorant. The key to happiness is ignorance. But there is no going back. The loss of ignorance is the loss of innocence. And it is the lot of humankind to suffer from knowledge. Knowledge the destroyer...

Grimalkins...spitting and mewing, hunting grimalkin prey; silhouettes cast against fires that – at long last – purge both squalor and affluence alike...

The life of humankind is but a flickering candle in the darkness of death. It is lit...it burns...it is extinguished. Who morns it...and why?

Savage, itinerant mobs, wrecking and killing; dancing, screaming maniacs; starveling hoards; pitiful wretches; victims, crippled, anchored by the weight of shit and other bodily wastes, adorned in putrid rags...

Who knows God? The person who knows God is the person who, when they close their eyes, do not feel alone. The person who is conscious of nothing but their own consciousness is surely damned...

Corpses – some eviscerated, some bloated – sprawled, spread-eagled, like swollen, poisoned sacs; masses of the living dead, racked with post-living pain; bodies, medallioned with sprouting tumours and suppurated sores, pillaging the remaining squalid abodes of the once was...

On and on – purging, spewing, farting, belching – until some good will come of it. Is that possible? No such luck; nothing is that easy. It's just like saying 'fuck' until you're exhausted...

The remnants of mankind, caught in the pandemic death throes of a pitiless, metaphysical will. The last vestiges of an avaricious cancer on the skin of the world. And now, the suffering of nature's cure is at hand...

# SOLIPSISM

*

Charon, you bastard, I grow weary of waiting on Acheron's shore...

Although you have walked openly and in total disregard of safety, you have experienced no assault or even serious importunity on your person. Your peregrinations have infiltrated the most purulent, inhospitable regions of a collapsed society's cloacae and slums, where you witnessed the abject depths of human dissipation and degradation. Yet, you remained unharmed, free to meditate on eschatological profundities, like a protected, untouchable historian peering down through the channels of time. You have rubbed shoulders with vagabonds, harlots, beggars and murderers. You have been party to brutalities and cruelties unknown outside the deathcamps of megalomaniacal regimes. You have looked upon the utter desperation and dissolution of a lost and damned populace. A walking chronicler of the holocaust, a sole observer of the *Dies irae*, you alone, seem exempt from the ultimate hecatomb...

Raising your face, you look about you. Ahead, there is a dead-end. A high brick wall – Humpty Dumpty's, maybe? – with a faded rectangle painted on it, barring your way. There is something vaguely familiar about the design, something you barely remember, but it becomes lost in the rapid confusion of thoughts bombarding your mind. The paint must have been too thinly applied, as long stalactite rivulets hang from the horizontal line like amputated, skeletal fingers. Staring at the obstacle, running your gaze along its muriform structure, it's as though you're expecting it to somehow evaporate, or for a hole to appear somewhere along the surface, granting you access to the street beyond. Because all you want to do is to walk, and to carry on walking – anywhere. Just to feel your feet stamping – *one foot appears in front of the other with the monotonous regularity of a metronome* – on and on, aimlessly, in order to pathetically persuade the physical exertion to subsume the rampant lamentations in your heart. To keep moving, and moving, so that you do not have to look at things for too long, as looking at things is to think of things past, and to disinter memories that should be forgotten. Too many sorrows lie in such provinces. Approaching nearer to the wall, you peer up at the broken glass embedded along the top, as sharp as an array of glittering teeth, and you wonder, if you were to stand on tip-toe, whether or not you could locate a spot easy enough to climb – but there does not seem to be any such finger or foothold; the wall of bricks is too high, too flat and too smooth to negotiate. Pressing your cheek against the cold expanse, you slide down until you end up in a foetal ball, curled against the wind and the lazily drifting litter.

*...what if, deterministically, no one dies...*Die! Die!*... because the final instances have to be lived and relived...all...gone...now...finished...compressed into ever briefer microseconds, again and again – forever?* My head hurts. My head hurts. My fuck-ing head hurts!

"What's that you're sayin', soldier?"

The exordium scythes down through the void, a grating comet of sound in the silence of space. Following it, the inevitable echo pierces the ambience like the screech of a night owl.

"– you're sayin', soldier?"

Cosmic noise in the fathomless concavities of nothingness. Self-perpetuating impulses of electrochemical energy. Condolences of introversion. Resultant sparks of something flickering between the physicality of matter and the spirituality of thought. Pulsations of past reason probing the insanity of the present. Anomalies in the psychotic morass. All gone now. I am alone in the universe.

"You're a difficult man to track down, soldier."

"– track down, soldier."

"But no one escapes *us* for long."

"– escapes *us* for long."

"Us, bein' the professionals what we are."

"– professionals what we are."

Something touches my shoulder – grips it in an iron vice. There must be discomfort, I suppose, but I am beyond such things.

"Come on, soldier, up you get."

"– up you get."

I am lifted to stand unsteadily, my back against the wall, and a vague outline – pink and elongated – hovers before me. About two thirds of the way up its surface, twin pinpoint blots glitter as black as obsidian gems in snow, and are suddenly accompanied by a larger blemish situated below them, growing and widening before dematerialising again. Reanimated, it writhes and squirms, and I realise its movements are concomitant with the acoustics that are assaulting my eardrums.

"What the fuck was all that shit back at the flat, then?"

"– that shit back at the flat, then?"

"What 'appened there, soldier?"

"– 'appened there, soldier?"

My temples throb with a more than familiar regularity, and an attempt to shake away some of its obfuscating clouds only results in my head being slammed back against the bricks behind me. An indeterminate sensation – which my dulled brain interprets as pain – spreads up and over my skull, from occiput to sinciput, causing my vision to become even more indistinct than it was.

"And 'ow the fuck did you manage to vacate the premises without bein' spotted, uh?"

"– without bein' spotted, uh?"

I shake my head again, this time with incomprehension. "Wha'? What?"

"You 'eard me, soldier. Bit of a fuckin' mystery, wouldn't you agree?"

"– you agree?"

"One what needs to be gotten to the bottom of, I think."

"– gotten to the bottom of."

The elongated pink outline is joined by another pink outline – round and heavy looking, decorated with similar black blemishes as the other – and the two images float before me as both lower blemishes move, coinciding with the – to me – phonemic noises.

"So, that leads us to you, soldier."

"– to you, soldier."

Something hard and cold is pressed against my cheek, superimposing itself on the rouged visages, and seems to separate them from me, suspended like a long, out of focus, black bridge across a ravine.

"Along with a need for some answers."

"– some answers."

As my head clears a little, a slow, dawning recognition formulates in my mind, and I glare from one dirty face to the other, de-anthropomorphising their alter egos into my consciousness. Both Hawk-face and Beaver watch me in disbelief as I laugh out loud.

"What the 'oly fuck's so fuckin' funny, soldier?"

"– so fuckin' funny, soldier?"

As the hard object is pressed even harder against my cheek, I feel it probe into the flesh just above my jawline. "Just piss off!" I snarl, instantly killing off any merriment from continuing during this bathetic banter. "Piss off and leave me alone."

Hawk-face grins a lopsided grin. "Not the most judicious comment you've ever made, soldier."

"– erm…comment you've ever made, soldier," half comments Beaver.

"Not with me 'oldin' this little toy, 'ere."

"– little toy, 'ere."

Gradually, the two pink hazes lose their blurred edges, stabilising their faces into clarity. Observing me from the other end of the metallic tubes of a sawn-off shotgun, Hawk-face brutally screws the weapon further into the side of my jaw. "Make a real pretty piece of Pollock on the wall behind you, this would," he says.

"– a real pretty piece of bollocks…" paraphrases Beaver, before realising he has blundered.

For a moment Hawk-face glances at his partner with contempt, and then: "Shame you wouldn't be able to appreciate it, though – you bein' a fuckin' artist and that."

"– a fuckin' artist and that."

The remark scatters my inertia and I blink questioningly at my two antagonists for a moment. "Who the hell told you that?"

Hawk-face frowns. "Told us what, soldier?"

"– what, soldier?"

"That I'm an artist."

"Oh," smirks Hawk-face. "We 'ad ourselves a little chat with our R. C., we did – back there. Seemed to be in a state of shock, 'e was. Told us all about you, though, 'e did."

"– all about you, though, 'e did."

With that, the Hawk-faced countenance twists into a wicked grin. "Did you know 'e 'as a file on you, soldier?"

"– a file on you, soldier?"

"Told us all about you and that little girl what got 'erself drowned, like. 'Er fuckin' brother bein' such a bigwig in the fuckin' Militia, and all."

"– such a bigwig in the fuckin' Militia, and all."

"Oh, God," I groan, as the image of Veronica's blank face comes back to haunt me – again. If they didn't have me pinned against the wall, I believe I'd collapse on the spot.

"Showed it to us, 'e did – the file, I mean."

"– the file, 'e means."

"Couldn't fuckin' stop 'im from goin' on about it, we couldn't. Some crazy artist, 'e called you; and some kind of 'uge fuckin' creature, or somethin'."

"– 'uge creature, or somethin'."

Raising his free hand, Hawk-face knowingly taps the side of his temple. "Mad as a fuckin' 'atter, of course."

"– fuckin' 'atter, of course."

"What, with 'im stutterin' and stammerin' on about it like that…Well, my partner, 'ere, 'ad to give the motherfucker somethin', didn't 'e? Just to shut 'im up, like."

Beaver laughs a wet, toothy laugh. "– to shut the 'im up, like."

"Never seen anyone in such a state, I 'aven't. Can't blame 'im, mind you – 'im 'avin' been stuck in that room on 'is own with that fuckin' big, 'ulkin' corpse, like, 'uh?"

"– with that fuckin' big, 'ulkin' corpse, like."

I moan to myself as the memory rushes at me in the form of another K-factor image.

"What beats me, though..." Hawk-face goes on.

"– beats us, though..."

"...is 'ow the 'ell you managed to get the better of that big, fat bastard."

"– big, fat bastard."

Their intrusive presence rides roughshod over my luxury of remorse, disinterring my most darkened sarcasm. "Oh, I work out – several times a week, actually."

"Ah! That's fuckin' funny, soldier," jibes Hawk-face. "*Fuck*-in' funny."

"– *fuck*-in' funny."

"You're a goddamned laugh a minute, you are."

"– laugh a minute, you are."

"Can't resist getting' those gums of yours round a joke, can you?"

"– round a joke, can you?"

"Never know what a funny cunt like you is goin' to come out with next."

"– come out with next."

"Let's just 'ope that sense of 'umour of yours lasts until they execute you – you crazy, 'alf-arsed bastard."

"– crazy, 'alf-arsed bastard."

Once again, I confound them by laughing out loud. It is a strange laugh: high-pitched, as brittle as breaking glass. As it dies away, it simultaneously protracts into a low, gurgling sound, mimicking the water dribbling out of drainpipes.

"Got another joke comin' on, 'ave you?" enquires Hawk-face; while Beaver grabs my arms in order to re-handcuff them.

"– comin' on, 'ave you?"

"Well, fuckin' laugh *this* off, soldier."

"– *this* off, soldier."

Taking a fresh grip on the gun, Hawk-face clubs me over the head with the handle. The pain does not register as pain, but the effect is just the same as if it had: my knees buckle and I fall to the ground.

"That'll fix 'im," snorts Hawk-face. "Look at 'im, the crazy cunt bastard!

"– crazy cunt bastard."

"Fuckin' wanderin' about like that – in this weather." Leaning over me he slaps my face a few times. "Got somethin' against attire, 'ave you, soldier?"

"– against attire, 'ave you, soldier?"

"Don't seem to go in for it much, from what I can see."

"– from what we can see."

"This is the second time we espied you denude of fuckin' weeds."

"– denude of fuckin' weeds."

With his gun hand hanging loosely at his side, he stands next to his partner and stares down at me. Managing to twist my head sufficiently, I stare back up at them: two ragged scarecrows etched against the darkening sky.

"It's a fuckin' wonder the silly twat doesn't catch 'is death," comments Hawk-face.

"– catch 'is death."

"'Ave to be quick about it, though," he adds. "Since the fucker's goin' to be dead pretty soon, any-fuck-in'-way."

"– dead pretty soon, any-fuck-in'-way."

Throwing back their faces to the heavens, they both convulse with laughter, until Hawk-face's merriment rattles off into a muciferous bout of coughing.

"Ohmigord," he groans. "Come on, let's get the fucker back to base, so's I can 'ave a fag and a shot."

"– a fag and a shot, yeah!"

As the echo of Beaver's voice fades, they both lean over me like hungry hyenas. Picked up, I find myself once more being half carried, half dragged along by this duo of deadly vaudeville clowns, and I wonder if they intend on transporting me this way all the way – however far that may be – or if they have a vehicle of some kind parked nearby.

We turn a corner and there stands what was once a Land-Rover; now it is something more, encrusted with armour plating, wire netting, purposely welded sharp edges, chained wheels and protected headlamps.

Glancing about him somewhat nervously, Hawk-face opens a rear door and bundles me inside. Landing hard on my back on the bare, unforgiving, metal floor, a streak of pain – felt at last – jumps like an electric current from my wrist, and a small part of me finds this reassuring, confirming the reality of the situation, having half expected, up until now, that all this could just be another extract from one of those dreams; an abiding rational part of me, however, despairs of such a self-same reality because it again reinforces the conviction of my guilt. (Blow it up your arse, Albert).

Squeezing in beside me, Beaver delivers a hefty kick at my ribcage with his boot, and I cry out loud, as the pain does now actually exist in its own right, registering in my brain as well as in my flesh; sensation becoming more and more internalised. With the boot retracted, Beaver plants his rear-end on a makeshift seat constructed over the interior curve of the wheel casing, and stares at me, porcine eyes glinting within the Land Rover's interior.

After the driver's door closes with a bang, Hawk-face instils life into the engine, while I watch his hand between the gap in the front seats slam and ram the gearstick with the same aplomb as he appears to run the rest of his life. Jerkily, the vehicle starts to move away from the kerb. In the back with me, Beaver adjusts his bowler hat, and spits on the floor, right next to my face.

"Won't be fuckin' long now, soldier," he says. "Then you'll get yours."

It is the first time I've heard him utter an original sentence.

You lie on the floor of the Land Rover, feeling cold metal beneath cheek, shoulder, arm and hip. Drawing up your knees, you attempt to erect some kind of bodily barrier between yourself and the itchy, threatening boot resting mere inches away from you. It is a rough boot, unpolished, with scrapes and scratches on the rounded toe, and ragged laces dangling like mini nooses from the holes. Just above it can be seen a tattered sock, as ruffled as a squashed concertina below the calf, which, in turn, is swallowed up by the mouth of a frayed trouser leg. Twisting your head, you look up at the portly body – revealed to you for the first time between the open fronts of the oversized overcoat – and higher, towards the underneath of the permanently wet, flabby chin, from where pensile strings of spittle glimmer like diluted glue in the darkness, the discharge trickling freely down over the pulpy throat, below which a once starched collar sports a ridiculously soiled bowtie. The man looks as though he had once dressed scrupulously for high tea, only to henceforth never subsequently bother to change back into his day clothes. And now he sits there, elbows resting on his knees and face turned towards the windscreen, from where lances of saffron lights pass like railway sleepers viewed from a speeding train. As each illumination crosses his face his pupils glint in anticipation, his right hand, with its pudgy, almost childlike fingers, wandering lovingly inside his coat to caress the strobe lit butt of a heavy revolver hanging in a shoulder holster under his left armpit. With the vehicle bumping along, its suspension seemingly impervious to any strewn rubbish or fallen masonry scattered over the streets outside, you raise yourself slightly, seeking a glimpse of the passing scenery. Looking at you and grinning – his central incisors even more pronounced against the flickering orange glows – Beaver places his foot against your shoulder, wedging you between it and the opposite wheel casing. Now, don't go tryin' anythin' funny there, soldier, he says, Otherwise, you may not even make it back to base, is that clear? Looking away once more, he stares ahead, the imbecilic rictus slashing his face like a gridiron. Sounds of explosions – although muffled by distance, along with the roar of the Land Rover's engine – reach your ears, and Hawk-face snarls something to his partner over his shoulder. Leaning closer, Beaver listens, eagerly nodding his head in compliance. Standing, as best he can, hunched against the roof of the vehicle, he slips the gun out of its hammock, before glaring at you and reissuing his earlier caveat. As I said, soldier, no fuckin' funny business, okay? Then, pushing upward with his free hand, he slams back a hitherto unobserved gun turret, letting in a gust of freezing cold air to swoop and dive inside the cab like an inquisitive bird. As he forces his head and shoulders through the opening – while desperately holding onto his bowler hat with his other hand – you, from your position on the floor, watch him as he squints against the oncoming wind velocity. Just slow down a bit, he calls to Hawk-face, There's another gaggle of the fuckers up ahead. With curiosity getting the better of you, you struggle into a sitting position, in order to achieve a clearer view through the wire netting of the front window, and out to the road beyond. As instructed, Hawk-face reduces the speed of the Land Rover, and in so doing, catches, ahead in the beams of the headlamps, a group of pathetic figures, looking like Old Testament lepers seeking alms. There are four of them, adorned in soiled and torn beggar's raiments, two of whom appear to be fairly young, supporting an older member between them, with a fourth hobbling behind on a makeshift crutch – all emanating graveyard pathos. Slowing the vehicle to a crawl, Hawk-face, shoulders hunched, peers forward as though taking in every detail of the unfortunate quartet's situation, as, hesitatingly, the figure with the crutch raises his free hand, exhibiting a tremor that can be seen even from this distance. Entreatingly, his mouth opens in hope, but, coughing out more of what appear to be random numbers, Hawk-face slams his hand on the steering wheel in excitement, just before Beaver shoots the helpless cripple through the right eye. In sudden panic the two bearers drop their burden, and attempt to make their escape into the anonymity of the night, although the concussions sounding from above assert the futility of their action. Screaming with maniacal laughter Hawk-face thumps the dashboard with his fist, and is immediately joined by a high-pitched jubilation from Beaver, who indicates that the beggar being carried has been abandoned, his emaciated body dropped into the roadway, still alive. This news encourages even greater merriment from Hawk-face, who eases the Land Rover almost to a stop, before creeping it forward, as slowly and deliberately as possible, mercilessly bumping the four wheels over the condemned survivor – twice. As screams of terror and then agony rent the air, Beaver bangs the top of the cab in exultation, causing you, without a word of protest, to return to your position on the floor of the vehicle – where you close your eyes in an attempt to seek shelter from the persistent infamy of humankind.

Maybe you actually dozed for a while, as the street noises had become muted and more distant, subsumed by the raucous, monotonous drone of the engine. At the moment, though, you are lying as still and curled as a nervous caterpillar, partly against the cold, but more so against any impending assault from the now repositioned boot. So, whether it was the rapid deceleration of the vehicle or the sound of Hawk-face's loud profanities that woke you, you suddenly find yourself aware of an all-consuming presentiment. Beaver seems to sense something, too, as he glances at you oddly before almost tumbling towards the front of the cab. Quickly restabilising himself, he enquiringly squints over the shoulder of his comrade-in-arms. Wrenching up the handbrake, Hawk-face sits, breathing heavily and listening to the now low hum of the neutralised motor, saying, Crazy, fuckin' bitch just stepped out in front of me. Instantly forgetting whatever he had felt on his questioningly eyeballing of you, Beaver attempts – but fails – to issue a saucy whistle through non-negotiable, pursed lips. Making sure you are not drawing unwanted attention to yourself you manage a stealthily ascent far enough above the driver's shoulder to observe the girl caught like a nightclub artist in the Land Rover's antennal radiance. She is young – no more than eighteen or nineteen years of age – with a face as blank and beautiful as a Matisse line drawing, framed by a forest of long, wildly ruffled hair, and she stands, smiling fixedly and unblinkingly into the white beams of light as though in a trance. Could she be under the influence of drugs, you wonder, or is there something more going on here? A sudden respite in the night's surrounding violence lends a strange and ominous quality to her unexpected presence, and as the wind rises somewhat, lifting the hem of her belted trench coat, a particular scent develops in the air, like the aftermath of a lightning strike. Exposed by the wind's disturbance of her garment, a bare, shapely thigh proves to be flawed by streaks of dirt and scratches, and punctuated with, what look like, recently inflicted bruises. Despite her obviously tender years, her appearance is more like that of some broken down sex siren from a bygone *film noir*. Exchanging lustful glances in the reflected light, Beaver asks his partner, Whaddya think, 'uh? Wrinkling his huge beak, Hawk-face scans the outside of each window in turn, perhaps in expectancy of some kind of trap or ambush, before ambiguously shrugging bent-over shoulders. I reckon we should give the slut what she's askin' for, he says, and Beaver giggles like a naughty schoolboy. Yeah, he repeats, Give the slut what she's askin' for. So, saying, he climbs over into the front seat, opens up the passenger door and jumps out. Be motherfuckin' careful out there, warns Hawk-face, as Beaver advances to sidle up to the girl, who remains as motionless as a Stone Age dolman. Revolver in hand, Beaver casts nervous glances around and about before presenting her with his famous Beaver grin. As his lips squirm like leaches in a bag, the girl slowly turns her attention towards him, her own smile as rigid as the painted-on smile of a circus clown. Stretching forward, Hawk-face taps the windscreen with a long, crooked finger, and Beaver waves an acknowledging hand, simultaneously leaning closer to the girl, in order to whisper something in her ear. Looking towards the Land Rover, she lowers her face conspiratorially, while Beaver – still clutching the gun – persuasively extends his hands until they are about ten inches apart, obviously indicating a measurement of some kind, before pointing directly back at Hawk-face. As her eyes follow Beaver's directive, the girl's smile widens – although more than a little falsely, it seems to you – while Hawk-face snorts, Bastard! before tapping the glass again, this time with more urgency. Get 'er in 'ere, you stupid prick! He calls out, Get 'er in 'ere first. Beaver, acknowledging for a second time, lifts his gun hand, places his other arm round the girl's shoulders, and continues to whisper in her ear. She, nodding slowly, takes hold of the lapels of her trench coat, seductively pulling them apart, offering Beaver a chance to cheekily try and push the barrel of the weapon inside the décolletage. Teasingly shaking her head, though, she immediately tugs the lapels tightly together again under her chin, before, with a toss of her head, hinting at a growing interest in the Land Rover. Capitulating with a giggle, Beaver guides their return to the vehicle along the fixed beams of the headlamps. And it is at that moment an alarming portent of danger seizes you, one that escalates with every footstep of the approaching couple outside. Apart from the fact that, only a short time ago, you were actually willing self-dissolution, now, suddenly, you seem incapable of arresting an overwhelming drive for survival. *Don't…*let her *in here!* you shout, while stretching upward and forward. Without looking round, though, or even turning his head slightly, Hawk-face fells you with a wide arcing, backward blow to your temple, wherefrom, in your precariously balanced position on your knees, you have no chance of retaining your equilibrium, reeling and rolling to the rear of the vehicle, until you head smashes into the unforgiving metal of the closed door. Through a cloud of pain, you yell, Don't you *understand? Don't* let her in here! *Don't! She must not come in here!* But your warnings go unheeded. The door swings open, allowing Beaver to usher in the strange young woman, who, after settling into the passenger seat, offers a licentious grin in Hawk-face's direction. Slamming the passenger door, Beaver saunters to the back of the vehicle, whereupon opening the rear door, only just manages to catch you before you involuntarily tumble out. A momentary glimpse of a dark and lifeless street is all you're allowed before he roughly bundles you back inside. Tryin' to get away, 'uh, soldier? He says, No fuckin' chance, pal, no fuckin' chance at all. With that, climbing in, he slams the rear door behind him – but, you notice that the handle is not pulled all the way down. The door is *not actually locked*. Viciously kicking out at you as he passes, he scrambles towards the front of the cab until he is positioned directly behind the new arrival, whereby, without ceremony, he, with a rough, clawing motion, clumsily grips the girl's chin, forcing her head back and around, at the same time attempting to deliver a slobbering kiss on her mouth. Diving his other hand into her cleavage, he drools, Wow! Just look at this, pal – not a fuckin' stitch on under 'ere, not a fuckin' stitch. Like a flash of lightning, the searing vision crackles inside your head, and you roll on to your back, raising your bent legs in anticipation of action. Look at this, Beaver goes on, offering the girl's body to his partner, Wait a mo., though, let's get this thing off 'er, first. However, on hearing the movement behind him, he quickly twists around, reaching for the gun again, and it is unclear whether or not he intends to shoot you – but you do not wait to find out. Summoning up every remaining ounce of strength within you, you kick at the rear doors – and as you do so, you once again experience that old, familiar sensation of time distortion, where everything seemingly moderates, extending – on entering your mind – split seconds into minutes. As if in slow motion the doors swing outwards and – carried by the lazy momentum of your effort – your body gradually slides into the outside world. At that very same instant Beaver is reaching for you, gun hand raised, and Hawk-face is engrossed in slipping the trench coat off the girl's shoulders, saying, Come on, sweetie, let's see what you've got there, shall we? – followed by, 'Oly shit! She's fuckin' wired! Half turning his face, and freezing every muscle, Beaver repeats, Fuckin' wired! and Hawk-face desperately grapples with the door handle. Before you hit the ground, the final tableau you witness is one of Beaver, gun hand poised, face turned – and Hawk-face, one ineffectual arm raised as a shield, the other clawing for the exit handle – and the girl sitting in profile, calmly looking down at her exposed torso with that same, blank, fixed smile of inevitability...

The raw, cadmium explosion, followed by a rapidly spreading concoction of human elements and inorganic matter, disintegrates the front half of the Land Rover, sending individual chunks of metal, glass, plastic, rubber and flesh out into the night sky like a manmade super nova. The rear half is propelled backwards for many metres, along with your own string-puppet frame as it cartwheels through space to land as ungainly as a sack of spanners on the solid tarmac of the roadway. Bouncing and sliding a few times, you come to rest on your side, facing what is left of a once armoured Land Rover. Somewhere over there a snowfall of broken, tinkling glass precedes a heavy, metallic crash as one of the rear doors descends from way above, buckling, parcel-like on impact. After rolling along of its own volition, a chained wheel rotates slower and slower like a child's whirligig losing momentum, until eventually dropping flat besides the now inert body of Beaver, whose limbs are as spread-eagled as a landed starfish. Incredibly, you remain conscious, but inflicted by integral palsy, retaining only eyeball mobility, casting you as a captive observer, watching events unfold before you, as flames leap from the charcoal carnage in the shape of dragon's tongues, licking, crackling and spitting myriad sparks into the billowing diesel black cloud that obscures the sky. From who knows where, figures appear, apparently emerging from hidden side streets, subfusc refuges, camouflaged doorways and deep manholes, walking, limping or dragging themselves into the circumference of flickering light like an army of the damned. Some are crippled, some are maimed, some legless, some armless, some completely limbless, being carried or towed on makeshift stretchers and trollies – some without eyes, some without tongues, some without genitals, some holding intestines in place with claw like hands, some carrying their livers, kidneys and bowels in leather pouches, circuitries of tubes and pipes attached, and various other metallic or plastic medical contraptions, stumbling, hobbling, creeping, ambling, shambling, slouching, shuffling, staggering, tottering, lumbering and trudging in their hundreds, forming a wider and wider circle around the post explosion scene. Blinking your eyes, you experiment with signs of kinesis of your limbs, but the sole response is numbness, even though awareness and cognition remains, trapped, incarcerated within an inanimate frame of powerless flesh. Beaver, miraculously still alive, twitches in unimaginable agonies as he lifts a bloodstained hand towards the sky, pointing at something, as though witnessing the arrival of the golden chariot descending from heaven. As his torso convulses, he lolls over onto his stomach, dropping the hand with a loud, wet slap, before extending his fat neck, trying to pull himself along the ground, fractured, bleeding fingers ineffectually hooking into cracked and crumbling tarmac. Opening his saliva ridden mouth as far as he can, he screams in torment as his upper body slithers forward over a surface of gore, unfortunately leaving behind his whole right leg, and it is with a certain measure of indifference that you notice he now possesses just a single Beaver tooth. A moment later a little girl, about five years old, dressed in rags and bandages, and incongruously wearing a linen patch over one eye, steps forward out of the multitude. Limping towards the choreic killer, and dragging a thin, grey leg amputated at the ankle, she stands over him, staggering slightly while trying to keep her balance – but Beaver seems distinctly unaware of her as he doggedly and twitchingly continues his attempted escape from whatever it was he saw in the firmament, his eyes bulging and his mouth gaping, mottling the roadway with small, uneven, pulpy lumps of matter and bloodclots, like raw pet food. The child, still tottering, produces – from somewhere – a large handgun – a Smith & Wesson 44. Magnum revolver – as massive as a cannon in her small fingers, and she aims it at the back of the man's bowler hatless head of orange hair. Lifting her other hand, she grips her gun hand wrist, steadying it as much as she can, but the weapon is too heavy, gravitating both her arms, until she is joined by a small boy, who helps her to raise the gun up again, sharing the weight as she measures her aim for the second time. Oblivious to what is about to take place, Beaver perseveres with his 'ascent' up to the very moment the tiny finger succeeds in pulling the trigger. The recoil propels the two youngsters backwards, the boy losing his balance and falling over, the girl landing on top of him, but the bullet is true and blows away most of Beaver's head, encouraging a loud cheer from the mouths of the throng as the victim's nervous system sends the otherwise lifeless body into throes of spasmodic jerks, before gradually lapsing into a cessation of movement altogether, to lie as still as a miniature island in a reservoir caught in a rubescent sunset. As if to the raising of a conductor's baton, the crowd surges forward, pulling and tearing the dead man's clothing like voracious animals, before shouts and cries rent the air as a second explosion bursts from the skeleton of the incapacitated Land Rover, cascading showers of glittering flames down onto the heads of many of the rampaging beings below. Ragged garments catch fire and several people leap and fall about, rabidly attempting to extinguish themselves, rolling on the floor, yelling, screaming, as others jump or vault over them on knife whittled walking sticks and crudely constructed crutches, kicking the human obstacles out of the way with contemptuous irritation. Amongst all this, the tiny female murderess is hoisted shoulder high, to be triumphantly carried across the heads of the crowd like a cork bobbing across a windswept lake, but just prior to her disappearing into its depths, she turns, points at her amputated foot and shouts out to you, You stole my shoe, mister, you stole my shoe. Once again you try to move, this time with a little more success, and you raise yourself into a sitting or slouching position – which is as far as you get. No matter how hard you struggle further action is unforthcoming, your hands seeming to just flap about of their own accord, while your feet simply refuse to carry out the instructions fed from your brain. All around you the frenetic swirl of motion intensifies as people's behaviour continues to become stranger and more shocking, dancing and leaping like demented ants, out of the midst of which steps a figure to stand before you. Don't worry, old son, says the doctor, Nothing more than a spot of ataxia, soon pass. Tapping you on the shoulder, he unzips his trousers to produce a syringe from where his penis should be. I'll give you a jab, he goes on, okay? Everything will be fine, You won't feel a thing. Micturating through the syringe, he finds himself confronted by a man wearing a large, shiny helmet. Don't waste it, doc, the man says. Taken a little off guard, the doctor raises his fluffy eyebrows. Damn, I'm so sorry, old chap, Didn't realise you were in short supply. With that, he redirects his flow into the shiny helmet the man now holds out in front of him. When full, the man acknowledges the doctor's generosity with a nod. Thanks a lot, doc, he says, This will be more than enough. Disappearing into the crowd, he is pursued by the doctor, who hops and skips uncomfortably as he tries to replace the instrument back inside his trousers. Just then, a young woman steps forward, her face and shoulders nothing but a mess of blood and loose, ruffled flesh, to stand arm in arm with a man who is minus his head. That was my daughter, you know, she announces, proudly, pointing to where the little girl has been swallowed up by the horde, You stole her shoe – and our car, Joyrider! What's the problem, lady? Asks Hawk-face, looming there with residual smoke and flames decorating his oversized overcoat like glowing medals. This shithead stole our car, accuses the young woman, and our daughter is expecting us to join her for the finale, Hawk-face 'glares' at you from empty eye sockets and burnt, twisted flesh of his still Hawk-like face, Oh, yeah, 'e would, he says, Just fuckin' typical of 'im, that would be, Raising his conflagrating bowler hat, he bows low while extending a handless arm, Allow me, he offers, I will personally transport you in my very own authorised vehicle, Straightening up, he loops his good hand under the young woman's arm and the trio saunter off, Hawk-face explaining, 'Aving a spot of bother with the transmission, Apart from that, though, she runs fine, Runs fine, echoes Beaver, as black as a monstrous, cooked maggot, wearing nothing but his bowler hat and dragging himself on one leg, utilising a shotgun as a crutch, and leaving a spattering of sticky, liquescent clots and loose entrails in his wake, Come on, mistuh', cajoles the young girl, whose straggling hair moves like live eels in the wind, Come on, or yu'll miss the main attraction, Aw, leave 'im there, sis, says her brother, 'e's a fuckin' sucker, 'e' is, Lifting the hem of her dress, the girl thrusts her pelvis forward and back like a bump 'n' grind artist, Suck on 'iss, she provokes, dancing away into the squirming mass of moving flesh, hand in hand with her sibling, who tries to poke her up the anus with a huge, gleaming knife, Cu' tha' out, she reprimands him as the crowd parts like the Red Sea and you stagger to your feet, lurching onward through the opening to where there is a lot of cheering and clapping and people lifting their faces up towards a high ledge of what remains of a once fashionable apartment store, And now, ladies, gentlemen and children, bellows the R. C., dressed in the attire of a circus ringmaster, An act of daring and faith, and he points towards the ledge, The young lady will venture to the centre of the tightrope, from where she will attempt to solve a philosophical puzzle, When dropped, does a pebble ever reach the ground – or does it always have to travel half of the distance that is left? Veronica, naked and still wet from her bath, holds out her hands, pivots like a ballet dancer and takes a tentative step out on to the tightrope which traverses the street, Her foot slips and a great oooooaaaah-hhh arises from the audience like gas and the sound of an explosion is heard from somewhere over there while the R. C. calls to the huge, obese guard with the blue/black face and lolling, purple tongue, Go and put a stop to that, will you? She needs absolute quiet for this, and the guard nods his head before arrogantly pushing his way through the crowd, swinging a long, polished baton, while above, Veronica has edged her way almost to the centre of the rope, standing and balancing gingerly, an expression of supreme concentration holding her features as rigid as though injected with Botox, before looking down at you and laughing, No sudden storms, now, she warns, taking another step as the spectators look up as one in anticipation, waiting for her to stop, which she does, before bending over to grip the tightrope with her hands, from where she slowly unfolds herself until she is hanging by her fingers, remaining like that for several seconds, composing herself, prior to bending at the waist and thrusting her legs upwards with a swinging motion, hitching the backs of her knees over the wire, from where she unfurls like a snake until she is suspended upside down, arms spread wide, And now, ladies, gentlemen and children, booms the R. C., our fearless performer will demonstrate the truth – or the untruth – of the aforementioned poser, and he beckons with an expectant hand for Veronica to kick herself free – which she does – to plummet to the ground like a stone (pebble?) whereby a loud multivocal cry erupts from the mouths of moonlike faces, eyes wide open, following her descent that ends in a sickening, wet thud and subsequent silence that is gradually broken by low murmurings before Domino makes her entrance, dramatically lifting Veronica's battered head from her broken corpse, only to approach you in order to exhibit it for your approval, as the eyes of the decapitated head spring open above Veronica's mouth, blood drooling from its corners, droning the monotonal words, You see, I told you no one dies, I told you no one dies, I told you no one dies…no one dies…no one dies…no one…

He…I…(who?) – let us say 'I', awake/s with a jolt. (back to the symbolic counterpoint) His…my – let us say 'my', eyes pierce the darkness of the room. A pulse pounds in my temples and my heartbeat accelerates to staccato. Gazing down the length of my torso, above the thrown back bedsheet, my flesh looks almost blue amidst the eerily gathered moonbeams fingering through the large skylight. Sweat glistens on my chest and, as I raise my head, I can feel its sticky wetness in the folds of my throat. A nervous wipe of skin dampens a palm and is...held by another hand.

Turning my head, I look up into a pink, oval face, behind which subdued lighting reluctantly escapes from a couple of naked bulbs suspended from the wall. Above, through the rectangular roof window, dark, scudding clouds play hide-and-seek with the moon.

"How are you feeling?" asks the nurse, tugging the bedsheet high enough to protect my modesty. I blink, I frown, I try to answer her, but my thorax is as dry as desert dust – so I begin to cough. "It's all right," she assures me, fluffing up my pillow, raising my head and placing the rim of a plastic tumbler to my lips. "Here, drink this." The liquid mostly flows down over my chin, and I cough again. With a reprimanding tone, she adds: "Sip it. Just sip it."

Lowering my head back down, she places the tumbler on a small cabinet at the side of the bed, and sweeps a lambent hand over the blanket that covers me, tucking it tightly under the mattress.

"Where...Where am I?" I ask.

"St. John's," she answers, brusquely, as though I should know.

"St. John's?"

Straightening up, she brushes down the skirt of her uniform and squints at a miniature watch dangling off her breast pocket. "Hospital, of course. Try and get some rest; you've been through a most traumatic experience. Complete rest is the best treatment for you now."

"You mean sleep," I grunt. "That's a bloody laugh."

Casting me a puzzled look, she gently pats my arm. "Sleep would be beneficial, yes. But I have to go; if you need anything, just press that button, there." Motioning with her head, she indicates a lead attached to a small red disc.

"Will it work?" I ask, dubiously.

"Work? Of course, it will work." Waving a hand towards the wall lights, she qualifies her point, proudly. "We do have our own generators, you know."

"Really?" I respond, but only to her back as she clip-clops away on unsuitably high heels along the – in places, cracked or broken – tiled floor. Wearily closing my eyes, I am immediately forced to reopen them again as Veronica's disembodied head smiles a Medusa smile – one that stabs into my very soul like a stake into a vampire's heart. Stifling a further bout of coughing, I lift my gaze to look around the hospital ward. It is an expansive area, but filled to over capacity with too many beds, some of them improvised, hastily constructed from spare mattresses or – here and there – even just folded blankets. Patients, in various states of infirmity or disability sprawl about like war victims – which, perhaps, they are – with most of them decorated with splints and bandages, offering further evidence of injuries rather than fevers or maladies. Some moan quietly or cough out loud; some weep openly in distress. It reminds me of a scene from an old war movie, one in which a thespian Florence Nightingale, plus oil lamp, appears to administer soothing yet scripted speeches at bedsides; but the current nurse's uniforms remain stubbornly modern, if somewhat well-worn and soiled – or even downright tatty.

Attempting to relax only creates a greater tendency towards tiredness, a tiredness that will demand a complete submission to sleep – where the images will continue to race at me like Grand Prix turbos, decimating any accompanying luxury of slumber, leaving me mentally exhausted, staring up at the 'skylight' with wistful nostalgia for the tranquillity and mindless torpidity of life in that 'dilapidated sea shanty'. At the moment I am at a loss to know whether or not such a place exists or ever existed, being stranded in uncertainty and suspicion about each and every experience, memory or dream that assails me. The past, up to the present, seems to be nothing more than a vast kaleidoscope of incoherent and alarming sounds and visions, the validity of which may only be present inside my own head, thus rendering me – from an objective point of view – *non compos mentis* and doomed to unpredictable fugue.

Above the glass, set in the high ceiling, dark clouds part once more to reveal a bright, clear constellation, and it is this brightness that makes me think of the real Veronica – the Veronica I knew. Is she truly dead – or was my witnessing of her demise, also, just a hallucinogenic creation or a further bout of paramnesia? The gulf between wakefulness and slumber is becoming more and more indeterminate, offering grains of both hope and despair within polarised 'realities' I can but cling to, eclectically accepting the verity of that which is desirable over the decanting and disposing of elements I find most lamentable. Maybe time will expose the proof or falsehood of such an open-ended conception; presently I can produce nothing to incite either an acceptable or – to me – unacceptable resolution, and remain a nomad amidst the input of my own senses.

My morbid reverie is disturbed by the swing doors, at the furthest end of the ward, opening to allow a small retinue to burst through like a sandstorm. The group – headed by a tall, elderly figure in spotless white coat and an adopted manner as flash as new false teeth – moves in hurried fashion from bed to bed – feeling foreheads, measuring pulse rates, inspecting eyeballs and placing thermometers under tongues – with all the mechanical precision of pre-programmed robots in an automobile factory. At intervals they actually step over some of the more anonymous looking patients, seemingly having previously condemned them as terminal cases or simply not worth bothering about. Apprehensively I watch their advance with something approaching guilt, because it suddenly occurs to me that I am not disabled or injured in any way. In order to confirm this, I lift the sheet that covers me and peer down the length of my body. Where are my dressings? Where are my scars – lacerations – bruises? Sharply raising a hand, I touch the redeeming bandage around my head with a perverse feeling of relief. One strip of frayed material grants justification of presence and access to amenities; it also allows me the right of exegesis.

In no time at all they are at my bedside and there is a guarded consultation – low and in the exclusive medical fraternity mode – before any formal acknowledgement of my existence is endorsed. Looking up into the flat, bland faces of administerial benefaction with a kind of submissive detachment, I refuse to be intimidated.

"Well, now, Mr...erm..." says the pompous, elderly man in the white coat, carelessly eliding my name. "How are you feeling this evening?"

Even as I open my mouth to answer he is turning away to receive a paperclipped chart on a board. One of the bland faces closes in on him and whisperings ensue, floating terms like 'absence seizures', 'sensory instability' and 'paranoia' about in the air like buzzards. More bland faces converge over the chart, studying the linear abstractions concernedly, intermittently interjecting with pseudo erudite observations. The man in the white coat glances down at me, flashes a patronising, dentist's smile and continues the recondite conference. More medical jargons drift overhead – all in adjunction to the overriding noun 'psychotherapy' – until, at last, the conferring buzz ceases and the man looms over me, basking in his directorial stature.

"Tell me, Mr...erm...ever take mescaline? Lysergic acid diethylamide?"

"What are you implying?" I ask, indignantly.

Consulting the clipboard again, he raises his long eyebrows and peers over the top of his spectacles. "How about Demerol, methadone?"

"What have they got to do with psychotherapy?"

"Paracodeine? Dionine?"

"They're opiates," I tell him. "You'd be better off asking about hallucinogenic drugs."

"Think so?" he enquires, bluntly. "For your information, L.S.D. is a hallucinogenic."

"The others aren't," I retort.

"You seem to know a lot about such things," he comments, accusingly.

"They're just words in a book," I explain. "You don't have to be a druggie to be able to read."

"Have you ever been diagnosed as paranoid?"

"Certainly not."

"Schizophrenic?"

"No."

"Psychotic? Neurasthenic?"

"Piss of," I say.

"Psychopathic?"

"Since you've already achieved the response you sought, just cut the crap, okay?"

"A psychiatrist as well as a pharmacologist, eh? Perhaps you'd care to step up here, and join us on our rounds?"

"No, thanks. But I wouldn't mind hearing a diagnosis of my injury. You know, the one I suffered in the accident."

"Mmmhh," he mumbles, resorting once more to esoteric consultation with the sycophantic blurs at his shoulder.

After a few seconds of being occluded, I ask: "So?"

Deigning to confront me again, he says: "We first have to study the results of your tests."

"And what tests would they be?"

"The ones we've already carried out," he proclaims, as if it was common knowledge.

"And then what?" I demand to know, as he turns away once more. "More tests? More consultations? When the hell are you going to administer some actual treatment?"

He glances back, over his shoulder. "Just as soon as we know what we need to treat. In the meantime, Mr.... erm...you get as much rest as you can and leave everything to us." A low hum of concurrence from the blurs.

"Oh! Thanks a bunch," I spit; but my voice is lost amid the retreating clicking of heels and rustling of clothing, as they respond to some indiscernible Pavlovian command. Lying there, staring up at the 'skylight', I listen to their inaccessible dialogue ebbing away in the distance, gradually to become subsumed by the more prosaic sounds of coughing, weeping and cries of anguish.

It is said that knowing what to expect is half the battle, so, deliberately closing my eyes again, I manage to temporarily negate the oncoming visions by simply staring at the darkness behind my eyelids and concentrating on nothingness. Because darkness – blackness – is a friend to the creative spirit; white is the enemy – a terrifying archetype. Black is a haven of peace and serenity; white is confusion and fright. Black is the armour of defence against the rage, the garishness, the greed, the arrogance, the madness, the evil melee of humankind on the march. It is a refuge from the stampeding herd; a place to live outside the hive. It is the container in which to ensconce one's *weltschmerz*. It separates the shadow from the coyote. An oasis.

However, as usual, the approach is efficacious for only a short period of time. Unable to sustain nothingness, the human brain cannot help but absorb afterimages of reality, while merging with, and transforming into, memories already in residence. The desultory confusions that develop create even more impressions of Veronica, who extols the interminableness of life from a floating, bloodstained head, attacking me over and over again, like some insane quizmaster.

"Time for your capsule," says the oval faced nurse, shaking me by the shoulder and thrusting a small, plastic bullet under my nose. It looks like a suppository and I shake my head.

"What's that for," I enquire.

"Doctor's instructions," she says, as if further explanation is superfluous.

"But what's it for?"

"Simply a calmative," she assures me

"I am calm," I tell her.

"That's because you've already had some of these," she persists.

"When?"

"When what?" Picking up a tumbler, she proceeds to fill it with water.

"When did I last take one of those?"

Sliding her hand under the back of my neck she lifts my head off the pillow. "Let's see…This will your third palliative, so…four hours ago. Now then, no arguments, please; you have to take this and that's all there is to it. Okay?"

"I don't want it," I say.

"None of that, if you don't mind – or I'll have to report you to the doctor."

"Lady! You can do what the fuck you like."

"I…see." Removing her hand, she straightens up and regards me with a smirk. Replacing the receptacle on the bedside cabinet, she nods in knowing fashion. "They said you'd be difficult."

"Who did?"

"Never you mind." With that, she turns on her heel and clip-clops away, calling over her shoulder: "I'll be back, though." Her voice is both melodiously and threatening. "And the next time it will be an injection – so don't say you weren't warned."

A weary looking old man in the next bed eyes me with distaste. "Wouldn't get on the wrong side of that one, if I were you."

"Oh? Why not?"

Propping himself up on one elbow, his face radiates 'hospital wise' knowledge. "Liable to give you a bloody enema, she is – just for the fun of it."

"Better up my arse, than in my mouth," I tell him.

Looking at me sourly, he says: "Wouldn't count on it; at least you can see what they put in your mouth," before painfully turning onto his back and closing his eyes.

*"I'll just give you a jab, old son. Okay? You won't feel a thing."*
A snigger of satisfaction from the oval faced nurse.
"Bitch!" I hiss. "You crept up on me."
"That's right," she confirms. "I did warn you. So, you can go back to sleep now."

Whiteness...white-ness...white...vast areas of white...distance... height...space. lightness...light-ness...light...floating globules...drifting through gigantic conduits...channels of glass. Brightness... bright-ness... bright...stinging...singed vision...until...
SIGHT!
An enormous suspended structure of glass and light...hovering...descending...
Like Jonah, I am swallowed.

Somewhere within, part of it, a metaphorical cog in a metaphorical wheel, a physical presence inside the will, been here...so long, existing in pre-existent form, a something that was to come, resting in the womb of time, until it became something that was, that is, something that will be, again and again – but without order or sequence, there are no straight lines in nature, so why should space and time be linear? because they are not, they are haphazard, perhaps forever – a part of the always been and the always will be – a part of when there was nothing, when there was only gas, before the universe exploded, before it expanded, moulding itself around universal laws, of lava and volcanic life, violent seas, a single cell becoming something plural, fish growing legs, dinosaurs shaking the earth with their preserved footprints, after which monkeys fought for bones, lighting fires to illuminate caves, tectonic plates drifting, causing mountains to ascend into the sky, valleys nestling in oceans, nomads settling, rectangles forming pyramids, to the birth of the 'Son of Man', his death, before or after Khan conquered the known world, or when Alexandria lost its priceless scrolls, and Cleopatra's nose was not long enough, to Napoleon 'vacationing' on Elba, to when Waterloo was not the name of a station, when London burned, when white roses were red with war, when Hopkins grilled human flesh, when William spilled the lovers' blood, when Dickens sang a carol, when Melville drowned Ahab, when Earp sinned behind a badge, when Giovanni Giacomo regurgitated fucks, when Bathory took health baths, when Stoker breathed life into the legend, when Gilles rode beside a saint, when Sade rotted with his morals in the Bastille, when Custer cut his hair, when the Mayflower sailed and the Titanic did not, when Homer 'saw', when Machiavelli schemed, when Michelangelo chiselled, when Adolf dreamed of being an artist, when Magritte created dreams, when Stalin buried the evidence under the ice, when Nietzsche burned with the fever of perception, when Hegel viewed it all, when Jesse rode the footplate, when Blackbeard dug in the sand, when Sir Francis hit the 'jack', when Moses struck the rock, when Judas pursed his lips, when Mary constructed a nightmare, when Fatty ruptured a bladder, when Nero fiddled, when Caligula did not, when Bluebeard lit both kinds of fire, when Passchendaele was red, when Lenin was not, when Joyce rearranged the cyclops, when Sam retreated to that room, when Ludwig was not deaf, when Charles ordered free abortions, when an 'Iron lady' torpedoed ironclads, when Christine took the role of Pandora, when Capone sang opera, when Bonnie said 'yes' to Clyde, when De Gaulle said 'non' several times, when Kong loved Wray, when the six-hundred could not ride, when the Wrights walked, when John put quill to parchment, when she said 'I will', when she bared her breasts and opened her legs for the first time, when the membrane broke, when all that had gone before died – or did it? – when the past was extinguished – or was it? – when realisation of the present meant – means – all, when the future splits into multiple dimensions, when the existence of death was/is questionable...forever... because thought never dies...it is only... ever...forgotten...

A waiting lion of silence.
Existing in its own right.
In its completeness.
In its soundlessness.
I open my eyes.
There is...someone...near...

The wall lights flicker, allowing impending darkness to minimise the penumbra into a soft, localised halo around the bed. Propping yourself up on your elbows you stare, wide eyed, into the void beyond, and initially wonder if you have developed glaucoma of the iris, but the image materialising at the foot of the bed disqualifies such a diagnosis. Come, says the Domino facsimile, we must vacate this place – now! Standing amid the shadows like a spectre, she is attired in the same white rob as at the oasis, and from somewhere among its folds, a hand appears to beckon you nearer. Involuntarily casting the bedsheet aside, you eagerly obey, whereby she takes *your* hand, guiding it beneath her robe to press the palm against her evidently tumescent stomach. See, she says, proudly, I am with child – but such an announcement puzzles you. Could this mean that the birth dream was just that – a dream? If so, then Veronica's fate could have been just a dream, also. As if reading your thoughts, the Domino facsimile smiles, sympathetically. You are perplexed, she says, and seek an ultimate truth, which is the fact existence in a quantum universe is non-linear – as of yet still at odds with the theory of relativity – one that arranges or rearranges time and space as though in a current but perpetual state of flux, whereby there is no future, there is no past, there is just the microsecond of now – which has gone. It is where the young can be old and the old can be young – each remaining unaware of each other or of which is which and when is when. Regarding the birth of the infant – it has either been born or is about to be born, depending on the spatial and cosmic dimension you presently occupy. Therefore, chronology, as it is known, cannot be relied upon. When *you* observe the world, it becomes personally distorted, aligned with *your* point of view – as it does with your memory. Hence, the pejorative legend, 'lying like an eyewitness'. Berkeley's *esse is percipi,* but bound by the laws of a multivalent cosmos. So, the death of Veronica can be true or false, I say, glumly, and was or wasn't oneiric – as the poet said, 'For now he was awake and knew, No one is ever spared except in dreams.' Smiling again, her eyes still glittering with albescent luminosity, and the red spot in the centre of her forehead glowing with equal clarity, she says, If that is what you believe to be true, then so be it, But such things are a luxury destined for speculation elsewhere or on an alternative plane, for the coming of the Event is near, and we must make haste. So, saying, her other hand appears, holding a robe similar to the one she is wearing. After quickly slipping it over your shoulders, she leads you with silent determination between rows of beds on which unconscious occupants dream their own falsely true dreams. As you approach the locked doors, they swing open of their own accord, only to swish back together, relocked, once you have passed through them. Outside the ward, the corridor is almost pitch black, but the alabaster shape of your succubus lights the way like a drifting beacon. Without a sound you descend several flights of stairs before exiting into a cold and deserted street where fallen masonry and broken glass lie scattered alongside crumpled, rustling newspapers, and plastic food cartons that crackle and scrape on nocturnal breezes. Venturing on, you encounter dark, reclining bundles that, before your eyes, become transformed into discarded or abandoned corpses, around which your mysterious pathfinder carefully steps, pulling you in her wake like a reluctant pet. Looking up into a clear, moonlit sky, speckled with empyreal lights that now seem to burn with an indefinable significance, you experience a yearning for what the Germans call *heimwech* – a longing for one's home – dragging at your heart. Close by – maybe in the very next street – a massive explosion reverberates through disused architecture and a saffron aura bathes the heavens, superimposing blackened debris like airborne pieces of Chinese puppetry. It is followed by screams of terror, shouts of desperation and echoes of incongruous, insane laughter. Several windows crash to inanimate oblivion and the sound of automatic gunfire chatters like an ogre's teeth in winter. In spite of the mayhem, you walk on without hesitation, apparently travelling along an inviolate path. For a while a large armoured truck rumbles alongside you, but even though the armed guard surveys his surround from an elevated gun turret, he either ignores you or does not see you. Slowly the vehicle pulls across and turns left at an intersection, from where you watch the maw of the street devouring it, leaving only the tiny red slits of its rear lamps as evidence of it having been there at all. Above what survives of a public house a faulty neon sign fizzes erratically, its twisted bars of light like the death throes of a fatally wounded glow worm, its intermittent flashes strobing a timid mongrel dog who sits and whines for an absent owner's affections. From around this minor tragic scene the desolation spreads its tentacles of despair and hopelessness far and wide, probing dormant structures with its poison and its silence, abandoning time displaced teletransmissions, unfulfilled dreams, raptured births, lamented deaths and children's joy to the social memories of survivors – if there be any – for it is now rats, earwigs and woodlice that claim occupancy of these domains, presiding over insect and rodent infrastructures – all threat and hindrance from human civilisation having ceased, its population regressing to anarchy and barbarism as it expedites its own self-destruction by means of ignorance, arrogance, greed and mass ethological dementia. Realisation of all this is difficult for you, as it coincides with an emptiness that washes over you, recreating the dream of the sea and of your own fatalistic acceptance of its inevitable conclusion. How easy it would be now, to adopt such an attitude, to cease this obviously futile sojourn, to let yourself float and drift within the tides of kismet, and to simply smother beneath whatever mantle of disguise it chooses. As though telepathized, the defeatist doubts mould a frown from the hitherto encouraging smile of the Domino facsimile, who urges, We must raise the pace, for the Time draws close, There will be opportunity for contemplation later. Somehow you manage to cast off the intransigent chains and continue to follow her, at the same time feeling the grip of her fingers on yours nervously tighten. More detonations splinter the night, followed by several tons of bricks and mortar crashing to the ground only yards from your predestined path, but volition persists and you navigate with impassivity, the girl's cloak swelling about her frame like the wings of a bat's ghost, and you nestle behind its protective cover. On and on you journey, through tenebrous subways, partly lit avenues, deflorate gardens, echoing chambers, deserted arcades, bombed out esplanades, firelit backstreets and sequestered alleyways. And as you go, you witness wholesale carnage and destruction, watch the populace convolve like a rattlesnake to turn on itself with unprecedented violence and hatred, observe the rape and murder of innocents, the roasting of bodies and execution of controlled, sectarian pogroms. Everywhere there is rubble, shattered windows, desecrated churches, smouldering vehicles and mounds of vomited detritus. Chaos rules with a capital 'C', creating within you such spasms of oxymoronic disgust and sympathy, that you are about to abandon your indeterminate quest when the beautiful doppelganger slows her stride, easing her grip slightly. Following the direction of her raised hand, you watch a group of people approach in the single file of mystic priests, their feet invisible beneath white flowing robes, creating the illusion of pneumatic transportation. Moving slowly, they stare directly ahead, comfortably alienated from the self-inflicted annihilation, cutting a swathe through society's ordure and blood like a clear blade slicing through a freshly slaughtered carcass. Silently they pass you by, legion in number, totally resolved, and the Domino facsimile stands, facing you, holding your hands in hers. Come, she says, we must join them, It is our destiny. But, caught in the throes of guilt, you cannot bring yourself to move. Where are we going? you enquire. Wrinkling her brow again, she tilts her head to the side. We go to obtain salvation, she answers, and the sanctification of our descendants, For this we have been chosen. Wearily, you motion in the negative. And if we do not? you ask, What then? Dropping your hands, she takes a step back. Then we will die, she says – and our child will die, also. Staring at her, at the gorgeous but artificially constructed features, and at the strange, luminescent eyes, you say, I do not think so. After observing you in silence for a few moments, she whispers, I do not understand, and a dull ache begins to throb in your forehead, but you smile at her through welling tears. Haven't you heard? You say. No one dies. Feeling like a traitor, you take her hand and lead her alongside the enigmatic multitude. There has been so much suffering, desolation and death, perhaps the survival of an unborn – your unborn – could rectify things by just an infinitesimal amount, and leave – as a great man once said – a stain on the silence. It is within your power to do so...

*

Strong but gentle gloved hands lifted me, accompanied by grunts of exertion and growls of malediction, each exclamation only as loud as an infant's sneeze punctuating the hiss of the rain and the groan of heavy machinery. Something hard and flat and straight slid under my back until, moments later, leather straps were looped over my torso, hips and legs, securing me and rendering me immobile, trapped like an animal awaiting vivisection.

Over there, to my left, the blue lights continued to rotate their urgent message, while the huge iridescent glows swayed like sea anemones behind my eyelids. A slight ache in my arm reminded me of where the needle had penetrated; but not even the tangible wetness of the downpour could diminish a sense of unreality that grew to attack my sensibilities.

"Easy does it there," came a voice, saltatory, trammelled by the Doppler principle. "We don't want any more cock-ups. So, Sam! Move your arse; take the other end. Okay?"

A far away reply: "Okay, got it."

"Right, guys! Altogether now: h-e-a-v-e!"

A grating of metal on metal – followed by clicks of teeth catching in a cogwheel.

"Wow! Wow! Hold it! Hold it! It's caught on something! Bob. Bob! Can you fix it your end?" A pause. "Good! Okay! Fuck me! Alright... again! H-e-a-v-e!"

From somewhere else: "It's coming...It's coming! Gently does it, though. It's...coming."

A sudden jolt and I was floating in the air, supinely twisting and turning like a faulty propeller. Falling in even greater volume the rain doused my face with an icy persistence that relieved me somewhat, adjuring me on to a greater effort – so, I opened my eyes and squinted through the sparkling droplets at the distorted glares of the massive spot lamps that drifted slowly one way as I drifted the other, spinning with all the dignity of a dead fish on a weighing scale.

"Okay! Okay! He's free! Just hang on a minute. You hear me, guys? Hang on."

Another voice answered in the affirmative, passing the message on to someone else, who in turn shouted a further affirmative. Just lying there, twirling in the rain, I forced myself to relax and let the rescuers get on with whatever it was they had to do. From somewhere down below the raucous sound of buckling metal and splitting glass helped to keep me in a state of semi-consciousness, as though the injection had not been truly effective – suggesting the administering of a painkiller rather than a sedative.

After a while, the loud clicking started up again, synchronising with the slow accompanying jerking movement as my cradle was lowered. When this happened, my head involuntarily flopped loosely to one side, so that I could see the tangled wreckage of the car compressed against the warped underbelly of the huge articulated truck: all glistening blackly in the rain and the artificial lighting. For a few moments the motion ceased – while gloved hands gripped the rail at my side, in order to swing me into the required position – before the descent began again.

This new perspective enabled me to see clearly for the first time, not just a bundle or shape or an arrangement of colours, but a salient composition of abused flesh and torn clothing, crushed and twisted by the impact of unyielding metal. She had been thrown forward through the windscreen and lay – legs still inside what was left of the cab – with torso sprawled over the misshapen wing like a rag doll. Her one arm was dislocated and remained crookedly suspended from the shoulder, while her head was twisted so that her cheek rested on the rain soaked, bloodstained hood, facing me. In comparison, her features were ghostly white; her mouth pulled down slightly at one corner, offering the impression of a half-smile at the other, exposing just a glint of teeth between the shadow of her lips. Her long, dark hair was splayed over the top of her skull and adorned with red streaks from glass inflicted lacerations; while her eyeballs – as though carried by their own momentum, even after the sudden impact – were rolled upward in her head, hidden beneath her open eyelids, disturbingly exposing the sclera only. And as I was gradually lowered below her level, the pupil-less stare rivetted me with white hatred and an unearthly accusation, seeming to follow me like a painted portrait until I was 'out of sight'.

"Okay, guys, well done," said a faraway voice. "Get him into the ambulance, while I attend to the girl."

Lifted once more, I was transported towards the flashing blue light, while the darkness of the night covered me like black silk, suspending me between a world of reality and a world of dreams.

They both welcomed me as a friend.

A SURROUND
EXTERNALISATION
OBJECTIVITY
AWARENESS OF
SEMINAL ACHROMATISM

There is a snipping sound. Snip. Snip. Snip. Movement between myself and a source of light. Something dark hovers over me. I think I open my eyes. Maybe not. There is only grey. A blur. Partial sight. Even so my imagination gives it shape and form. Moulds an anthropomorphic semblance from the shadow. From the shadows. A hand holding a scissors appears. Beyond it a face. Eyes. Nose. Mouth. Jaw. Hair. Protrusions of ears each side of a head. From the mouth noises. Garbled. Echoing down a long tunnel like wind through winter boughs. It is accompanied by a low throbbing heartbeat that resonates within my own shell. Regular. Paced. Sustaining the lifeforce. A lifeforce that by right should have ceased. Should have been terminated. Should be a thing of the past. (*If there be such a thing.*) But on it goes. Bump. Bump. Bump. Insistent. Determined. Something in the nothingness. Part of the eternal mystery. Plaguing reason with its ineffableness. Provoking knowledge like a mischievous demon. Resistant. Persistent. Forever outstaying its welcome.

What if…no one dies?
Say something.
Something from the void.
From *out there*.
Release the monadic chains.
Set me free.
Set me free and let me…*feel*.

But does it matter? Did it ever matter – even to the 'leaders' and the 'demagogues'? For if all ends, then all that has gone before is meaningless, pointless, absurd. Everything is – and always has been – for nothing. A great, cosmic, universal nothingness. Memories of a single species, divisible by billions of separate, subcortical, neuronal perceptions, themselves, in turn, divisible by billions of internal, synaptic receptions and conceptions, all convolving and folding in on themselves and their own created universes – terminating individually – thus destroying the external universalisation in its most basic form. Nothing creates nothing but fleeting punctuations in the maybe, like commas, full stops, colons, semicolons, exclamation marks and question marks amid the unintelligible jumble of language or comparable symbols of languages. At – and for – the moment I find myself at its centre, awake and aware of the Cartesian 'I am'. Soon, though, I will be no more and nothingness will rule supreme. As it did before, and as it will do so…forever…

What if I…stepped forward?
Now?
That would silence you.
That would make you stop.
*Futile.*
*The waters of insanity are…*
*Your own creation.*

When?
When did or will, these things occur?
*It matters not.*
*The only reality is the microsecond of…now!*

The sun looks misshapen, elliptical, flattened at the 'poles', spreading golden reflections on the surface of the ocean like liquified honey, and bathing countless floating bodies in shades of yellow and sienna, as though monochromatically filtering and parodying colour with civilisation. On the horizon spidery flashes of lightning crackle amid sulphurous cloud forma-tions, resembling some artificially created atmosphere in a Brobdingnagian retort or slow-motion film of a nuclear explosion, minus the sound effects. To my right, as pious as a papal icon, stands the Domino facsimile, pre-saged natal bulge evident beneath the folds of her robe, while the amassed multitude of 'chosen ones', dressed in white and exhibiting their marks of passport on foreheads and palms, gather in sanctimonious complacency, indifferent to the spectacle of the lifelessly natant charnel house that sur-rounds them. No one moves, no one speaks, every last soul locked within separate, ingressive bowers of expectancy, patiently awaiting the coming of the Event – awaiting personal deliverance. All appear so secure in their faith, so confident in their uncontested sublimity, that doubt seems sacrile-gious – and yet, I cannot accept such individuals have been singled out as paragons of salvation or for the transfiguration of mankind. By what crite-ria have they been ordained? Who – or what – has selected them to the exclusion of the rest of civilisation itself? Brooding on the death of Veronica, on the apparent suicide pact in the dunes, on the hapless gunman crashing through the windscreen, on the moribund young siblings in the alleyway, and on the mutilation of the real Domino I am filled with frustration and guilt. That very same source has also exalted me – an egocentric, self-indulgent reprobate and inadvertent killer. The familiar throb in the base of my skull heralds the start of a neurosis that has become something of an old acquaintance, challenging our credentials of 'meekness', our right to inherit anything – never mind some unsubstantiated mythical Elysium. Looking about me, I actually see nothing but bastardisation – a soulless evocation of some cheap science-fiction book jacket. Can beings so devoid of compassion, so wanton in elitist preservation, really be qualified for beautification? To me, mannequins poured from cryogenic moulds of sus-pended emotion seem unlikely candidates for progenitors of a chosen race. And yet such seems the reward granted to the inheritors of sequestered lives and bequeathed influence, for here congregate ex-dwellers of pro-tected domains, ex-residents of impenetrable bubbles of privilege – figures perennially untarnished and untouched by worldly privation. To whom do they owe this dispensation? Is there a patron saint for plutocrats, capitalists and corrupt political grotesqueries? Maybe the text should read God and Mammon? Or is this simply the reactionary viewpoint of a lone miscreant transporting personal heresies across new, uncharted borders? After all, isn't it true that a sane rebel in an insane world will be regarded as insane? In that case, am *I* insane? Am *I* the sole recusant spirit? Am *I* legend? Sens-ing that something is amiss, the Domino facsimile turns towards me, a manufactured expression of sadness on her moulded face. You are troubled, she observes, and gnawed by doubt. I stare back at her, saying, Where there is a lack of understanding, there will always be doubt. What is there to understand? she asks, Are you seeking a perturbation theory explanation here? If so, there isn't one, You attended the assembly at the oasis, you were granted redemption, Accept the gift, Do not question. Looking away, towards the horizon, across the silently drifting conglomeration of lilting, putrid flesh, I say, Is it so easy to accept a gift that reeks of treachery – a gift that accords survival and death with such indiscrimination? Resuming her initial pose, gazing reflectively into the sunset, she queries, Is life itself so discriminate, then? Does life choose by sentiment or justification? Natural selection abides by the laws of dominance, allocation of ability, strength of will and aptitude, it does not bow to questionable rectitude or benevolence. You talk of evolution, I argue, something that develops over aeons, some-thing that is imperceptible to any living being or even a race. Am I? she retorts, What of the dynamics of chaos – do they take aeons? Did the Bibli-cal noyade take a million years – the sinking of Atlantis – the razing of Alexandria – the destruction of Hiroshima and Nagasaki? These events changed this world as irrevocably as an ice age, Who knows how things would have developed without them? Everything you see before you may or may not have existed – although, I doubt it, for without such culling nothing could survive, Humankind is likened to the child who has become dissatisfied with a gift and destroyed it, It has brought experience to a point of no return, You, so full of conscience and piety, stand and blame universal carnage on some deity from the Book of Revelation, but what you observe around you is not a deliberate act of genocide carried out by a higher power, it is the harvest of humankind, In its ignorance, arrogance and greed it has shifted the balance, despoiled what has been labelled, 'Mother Earth', upended the *status quo*, and tilted the dependent/interdependent scales of sustenance – in short, it has chosen negation over life, The responsibility of salvage has been passed on to an objective will, for soon the Beast shall rise to claim its eschatological domain, and all this shall cease to be, Only the 'chosen ones' will abide – only the few will carry humankind's seed to the stars, where, perhaps by means of eugenics, a new breed of humankind can accept the challenge to become superhuman, where it can become *Homo Deus*, and dispense with the futile, self-destructive barbarism that has plagued the species since time immemorial, and where, perhaps, it can obtain and sustain its true potential. A part of me desperately wants to believe and accept her specious reasoning, but some long lost, inbred sense of in/justice disallows it. Looking about me, I weigh up the cost, seeking vindication for such a vast sacrifice – and, to me, it does not tally. No one, or *thing*, has the right to choose in such a manner, to manipulate fate on such a scale – not even a god. However, personally, there remains an alternative, something unforeseen and unaccounted for by the faceless puppeteers. I still hold the freedom of choice – the freedom to choose against my status of being chosen. You may very well believe what you say, I tell her, But for one such as I, pre-programmed faith and contrived acceptance of the hypostasis breeds only antipathy and recalcitrance, You have created an itinerary, a step-by-step plan for salvation – but only for the few, Nothing changes, eh – even in 'paradise'? Why did you not simply intervene and demonstrate the error of humankind's ways? Show it the path by exemplification? Surely, such permanent devastation was avoidable, the outcome of such a catastrophe negotiable. Slowly she shakes her head. What you advocate is the confiscation of free will, she says, Such Draconian proselytization would have instilled fear, not faith, in people's hearts, The result would have been a population of robots – laws observed by inculcation and carried out by rote, Where was the achievement in that? Casting my gaze around the floating necropolis, it occurs to me that the waters are rising – already the isthmus bridging our vantage point to the mainland is submerged, forcing the white robed multitude to huddle more closely together, like sheep in a pen. I suppose, I answer her, the achievement would have been life, Life for all those poor wretches out there, and the promise of, if not salvation, then equality, for all. You make it sound like some kind of religiose communion for the proletariat, she says, and seems to have escaped your attention that there is no prospect of celestial, supernatural or eternal redemption on offer, The only thing that is eternal is eternity itself – all else is subject to the laws of thermodynamics, Those who make the journey will not become sublimated souls, they will remain beings of flesh and blood, There is no infinite heaven where they go, just a limited space, a reservoir of survival, a chance to escape what Schopenhauer was referring to when he said, 'Life here on earth is truly a bed of sorrows,' None of this resolves the enigma of absurdity, of course, it is merely a weapon to use against it – a weapon of prolongation that goes some way to validate the implementation of a Sheol, for even such a stay of execution condemns us – the survivors – to nothing more than an ontological eye flicker, Descension perpetuates the one and only promise of immortality. As a sad smile disturbs the structure of her countenance, she places a protective hand on her swollen abdomen, adding, But sometimes descension is enough. However, further comment on my part is cancelled as a unison cry arises from the mouths of the gathered 'nonpareils', their trembling fingers pointing skyward. Initially possessing no greater luminosity than Venus at its nadir, the apprehended glow swells and augments to the status of a falling star, scything an emblazoned crescent across the orange sky. As it plummets, the anticipatory exclamation turns to one of alarm, but navigational control allays any preconception of collision, the object manoeuvring towards a point north-north-east, where obvious deceleration is exhibited, allowing it to descend as gently as a paper flower. The expectant faces, raised and bathed in its effulgent glare, watch as it hovers above the sea like a gigantic golden egg. Constructed of some kind of unearthly, transparent material – through which massive and marvellous structures, conduits, orbs and futuristic transport systems can be glimpsed – it resembles a monstrous Cyclopean eye pensively surveying the reverent denizens of its kingdom. Many of them drop to their knees, stretching out their hands in supplication, while the object levitates, seeming – by some trick of the light or of perspective – to dwarf the dying solar orb of life. A symbolic eclipse that both darkens and incarcerates me in the isolation of the rebel. I am, truly, legend…

BLACKNESS MELTS TO GREY
DARKNESS FADES TO PALE
LIFE FROM DEATH
DEATH FROM LIFE

You are alone. From a rocky spine on the ever-diminishing promontory you idly watch the inexorable advance of the ocean. In the distance, obstinate diurnal antennae probe the darkening sky like the fingers of a drowning colossus, while rear-guard gulls – sole inheritors of the animal kingdom – rend the silence with plaintive squawks and cries. Caught in the throes of survival panic, their avian silhouettes swoop and dive, attacking the floating carrion with the urgency of a condemned prisoner late for a last meal. As you study them, memories of long, restless nights rise from the substratum of your mind, its flickering visions offering themselves once more for transubstantiation into oils or acrylics. Cradled in niches of nostalgia they seem to elevate you from daydreamer to acute observer, and a past image of Veronica – bathed in solar glows – materialises before you like a hologram. You remember how she used to fluff up her hair in that characteristic manner, while at the same time stretching, feline-like, good naturedly complaining of imminent fossilisation from holding such an uncomfortable pose for long periods, even as you obliviously continued transference of palpable, three-dimensional curvatures onto illusory two-dimensional board or canvas. With absence of diversion the invention of the imagination is almost cogent enough to touch, but as you realise this her facial features evanesce to blankness, only to become transformed into those of the ever-mysterious Domino facsimile from the immediate past. So, she had said, you choose to stay and perish in ignominy among the remnants of this discarded and useless world. You told me we all die, you said, ergo, as Camus promulgated, does it really matter where? It does if death is untimely and needless, she answered. Maybe, you complied, But I find the alternative less than satisfying to my moral palette, I cannot identify with such tenets or reconcile my survival with the planetary massacre of my fellow human beings, my friends, my loved ones. Observing you for what seemed like prolonged moments (thank you, Albert), an expression of contempt emanated from her artificially constructed countenance. Such conceit, she said, eventually, Why should you concern yourself with these things now, when you avoided them for so long – after living such a *noli me tangere* lifestyle? Compassion for beings whose existence you brought about, only to abandon, amounts to nothing more than fallacy. Staring at her in disbelief, absorbing the implications, you felt her words penetrate your consciousness like ice-cold arrows. Do you not consider such an attitude hypocritical, she continued, and cowardly? You now occupy a unique position from which to progress, to expostulate – perhaps to atone for a particular kind of suffering, a particular kind of death, Instead, you sit, wrapped in self-pity, conveying false probity and disclaiming all responsibility. Slowly, irrevocably, her criticism began to make sense to you, and you comprehended that the pretence had started to…splinter like…cracks in a mirror. (*With a small explosion the mirror shatters. Splinters into spiderweb cracks*). The creations were yours, she said, and yours alone, Each scene, each composition, every event orchestrated with care and precision, chosen to arrive at the now, To attempt to blame extraneous influences for the 'negation' of Domino and Veronica amounts to nothing more than self-deception, nothing more than a fictionalised travesty – and yet you persist in pointing the finger, knowing in your heart who is guilty and who should face the warranted condemnation and damnation. Lowering your gaze from the 'accusing' expression, you slowly started to fit the jigsaw pieces together in your mind, reluctantly digesting her argument while composing the obligatory counterattack – if only for the sake of mock conscience. Behind her the white garbed throng had broken up in order to form single filed lines, patiently awaiting their turn. Someway out over the now vitreous water the *coelestis urbs* – heavenly city – hovered like a brightly lit, gargantuan bauble on a Christmas tree. From the centre of its base a white beam dropped cylindrically onto the surface of the sea, illuminating the suspended figure from the oasis among the gentle eddies, hands outstretched, palms up. Simply going through the motions, you said, You're wrong, you know, someone once proposed that only those are damned who believe themselves to be so. A neat paraphrase, she said, and one that obviously provides you with spurious solace, but since I speak the truth, such words – no matter how profound – will not protect you. The burgeoning knowledge made a mockery of her proposals and you laughed out loud. Why not? you asked, If it is merely from words that my very accuser is constructed? Lowering her head slightly, she regarded you with a sustained louche stare. You are clever, she said, Perhaps too clever for your own good. How can someone be cleverer than they already are? you demanded to know. When you are clever enough to defend only the end result, she replied, What of the motivation and the initial inspiration? From where did it come – and why? The muse would not be denied, Even during the soul-searching, the doubts, the temporary abandonments and despair, it remained like a rock, like a nemesis, goading, teasing, haunting you in the small hours, attacking you at the most unlikely times, when your concentration on the elsewhere waned – even after you decided to end it, to actually destroy it, a kind of synchronisation occurred, granting sanctuary until the hiatus of anger had passed, After which you returned to it, persevered with it, worked it, reworked it until it became what it is, Determination to see it through subsumed all else, because it would not go away, because it was – and is – part of you – even if you do precipitate your own demise. And with that statement came the flash of argent oblivion, the hint of impending emptiness, bringing with it the knowledge that something had changed. A passing had taken place, and you felt the nearness of the Beast, heard it growl and saw the first glimpse of the white space that surrounded it. Nevertheless, intractability held you in check, urging you to deny the warning of the end being close. Adopting remonstration as a weapon of protraction, you said, You talk of dreams, of oneiric creations that somehow became suffused with my…reality, If such orchestrations took place, then they were the stratagems of an unconscious mind, surrealistic dramaturges that reduced me to an unwilling passenger, Each *mise en scene* was as surprising if not alarming to me as to the accompanying participants, A slave can never be in control, therefore cannot be blamed. *Qui s'excuse s'accuse*, she said, You once openly admitted the existence of the autistic fugue, of it being almost a requisite of imaginative art – but failed to recognise its role in other modes of expression, You believed in the artist's exclusive claim of refutation of preconception, on blind gifts of intrusive imagery, You now know this to be false, yet still – even after metaphorically erecting a set of conditions – you deny the acceptance of liability, and continue to refuse acknowledgement of the inalienable rights of the participating individuals – also of your own, To deny them is to deny yourself, It annuls all and condemns you to shadow. To shadow? you exclaimed, smiling bitterly, You still do not understand. Wistfully gazing across to where the faithful queued like commuters awaiting earthly transportation, you watched, as one by one they tentatively stepped on to and then across the liquid surface to offer supplication in exchange for ascension and entry into the glistening city. As each approached the seraph's welcome, they kneeled to accept his Messianic blessing, before levitating and gently rising up the cylindrical beam like oxygen bubbles in a fish tank. I understand better than you realise, she said, As one who 'thinks north' you abhor the light and cherish the dark, For you, oblivion is the blandness and emptiness of white, or even of bright sunshine, something that represents spiritual panic in the face of growing reality – or at least your perception of reality, It is not as uncommon as you might imagine, Proliferation threatens to devour your escape route to the future – and yet, when such an escape route *is* offered to you, when faced with its security, you wilfully sidestep into the white void you fear so much, You choose to remain and experience living death, to confront the noumenon of absurdity, to torment yourself with questions that can never be answered. Stretching out her hand she offered you the refuge of the antigravitational metropolis. See, there, she said, salvation awaits you, peace of mind awaits you, Inside its hermetic integument lies everything you have ever yearned for, everything you currently or will desire in the future, compressed into the microsecond of now – an Utopian abstraction, a living daydream. Also, a prison, you contradicted, A prison of blindness and disassociation, Once immured, I would be trapped in a parochial world of fugue – but a fugue based on retrospective invention, For me, there is nothing new or experimental inside that veneer, nothing undiscovered, no uncharted seas, By opting to stay here I am forced to begin again, to rebuild from more or less nothing – from a primeval foundation, As insurmountable as it may seem, I must try to fill the white space with the substance of possibility, to defy nothingness with ideas, It is the only true inheritance, To exist in permanent reverie is to abandon the responsibility you claim I rebuke – the responsibility of what you call my realism – and abrogate my true future – if there be one, To you, my sin is to abrogate my past, but this *soi-disant* past – in spite of the specious cogency of string theory – *is* gone, It is only relevant when faced with the present – something I think I've already lived up to – but the actual present exists only in the microsecond of *now*, and only from *now* can come reconstruction, In order to become reborn, one must first die – albeit metaphorically, Ergo, in order to create, one must first destroy, Soon, I shall undergo a kind of 'death', and with this 'death' will come the termination of a complete universe, Having once already been resurrected – which perhaps explains the pursual of equivocal paths and a counterfeit *felo de se* – I shall again live, but not in the way Veronica believed, The aegis, the guidance of subconscious reasoning – what Socrates identified as his *daimonion* – and the supernatural strength, were signposts on a causal road to the *now* and my understanding of it, Alternative existence must derive from alternative birth, a state of being that commits me to a confrontation with the Beast – who will attempt to relieve me of future inspiration. But since all fiction is solipsistic, the only true element of reality is the author. Wittgenstein is purported to have claimed it was difficult to write things that make blank sheets better – only the reader can either dispute or verify that. But what if the Beast succeeds? she asked, What then? Will that not bring about permanent dissolution – annul all that has gone before, grant yet more credence to the state of absurdity? You smiled at her then, a genuine gesture of affection. The Beast will not succeed, you assured her, because the incipient seeds have already been sown – some allegorically travelling within you, others flowering within me, They will float through the white nihility like metaphysical pollen, surviving under the protection of what has been created and what will be created, until taking root post-interregnum, For as long as such a seed existed, exists or is going to exist, the battle is never lost, The completeness of absurdity is kept at bay by the fact that we *are*, and will remain so for as long as consciousness defies submission to non-entity or until creative thought is neutralised. With that, you took her hand in yours and pressed it to your lips. You are free to leave, you told her, By my action is the covenant thus severed, So, go with them and accept the gift they offer you. To do so would be an admission of failure, she said, I cannot abandon you. Yes, you can, you reassured her, It was no fault of yours that you were assigned to apostatise a renegade, The blame lies elsewhere, therefore you are absolved. Lowering your hand to her swollen abdomen, you said, Loyalty to me would mean the abortion, not only of a child but of a possible future, Do you think I would deprive you of that? Do you think I would rob you of your right of descension? Lowering her face, she slowly shook her head. Across the darkened waters the last of the 'chosen ones' had ascended into the bowels of their new abode, leaving but a single figure at the base of the spectral searchlight. Its glare cast deep shadows where his eyes should have been, but you could still sense their glitter as he stared across the gulf of dying space, silently awaiting the peroration – the significance of which did not escape you. You must make haste, Domino, you said, before the oncoming insubstantiality overtakes us, The Beast is less than discriminant, and will obliterate everything in its path. Even as the words were spoken the outer containment of the golden city began to waver, as though fading slightly at the edges, becoming vaporous, like mist or as if its circumference was being airbrushed out. Such exacerbating opaqueness made vision impenetrable to the eye, shielding the inconclusive fate of its newly arrived inhabitants. Only now, she said, when it is too late, do you acknowledge the possibility of what could be. Touching her cheek with your fingers, you said, It was always nothing other than a dream, I'm afraid, and could never have been anything more. Taking your hand in hers she lowered it from her face, from which the features were beginning to fade like a pencil sketch being erased from a sheet of drawing paper. (*'There's no art to find the mind's construction in the face'.*) But now you will never know for sure, she said. Then, with a slow, fluid motion of her robe, she turned away, the movement taking her from you, across the calm surface of the sea, creating a swathe, reminding you of a gently wading swan – aloof, regal and proud. On approaching the awaiting prophet at the foot of the beam, she dropped to her knees for the benediction, before looking back at you one last time. With a sad wave of her hand she and her companion arose towards the now pulsating city, lifting their El Greco faces to the light and entering the refuge that was, to you, just a fallacious illusion of a new Jerusalem. Almost immediately the glare dimmed and flickered before extinguishing itself completely, and the great, oval ball moved slowly upward into the night sky, where it rapidly gained speed until, like an inverted comet, it blazed an ascent into the heavens. Within moments it had disappeared, abandoning you to gaze despondently at its vanishing point. And you stood where you still stand now, a lone survivor, the victor of a bittersweet rebellion – an omega man.

FREEDOM

I am alone. From the rocky spine on the ever-diminishing promontory I idly listen to the inexorable advance of the ocean. Now there is only darkness to wrap about me. As a last remnant of a created world, as a last figment of an invented universe, I feel it a duty to covet it until the final moment of nihilism. Already I can sense the coming of its enforcer, the agent of anarchy – the Great Beast...

## FREEDOM

...whose presence will first undermine and then destroy the very fabric of prose, whose force will topple the structures of creation like a house of cards. Taking a final look over my shoulder, inland, I can see that the tenebrity remains unbroken – even the last of the apocalyptic fires have gone out, the bombs diffused by my own enervation. A state of total alienation presides and the snarl of my approaching ravager becomes a snigger of victorious domination...

## I AM FREE

...echoing in what is left of blackness. Somewhere out there the waters begin to curdle and sibilate, as if intuitively perceiving nothingness – waves sucking and sliding like cornered prey. In a last grand gesture of defiance, I cast off the robe and stand naked against my enemy...

## I AM FREE

...who rises in a blaze of white light from the waters of insanity. Its glare intensifies and robs me of sight, its roar amplifies and renders me deaf, its mouth opens and I am – not unlike Ahab – swallowed by a white oblivion...which also grants me a kind of...

## FREEDOM!

*

And so, it ends, leaving lessness and nomenclatural dissolution. Fade to nothingness. Black to white. Print to blank page. Reproof of the psychological cliché that nothingness is darkness – because nothingness is whiteness. A completely white sky above a completely white landscape creates a surface from which thought slips unerringly to oblivion. A canvas desert viewed by an uninspired artist remains a shadow-less light, a shape negated brightness – blind sight. Images die in the emptiness of a glare, not against a backdrop of darkness. In darkness they are always there, but merely hidden. Inspiration is moulded within the instability of shadow, where it flickers and pulsates, demanding existence. And while it exists it represents truth, the truth of the moment, the truth of the now – a step on the stairway of forever. A stairway on which we confront the where from? – the where to? – and the why? – monosyllabic enigmas as ineffable as 'I am Alpha and Omega' and as incomprehensible as gravity. Cosmic radar blips in the vastness of time and space. From these come the what ifs? – fictionalised corollaries conceived in the dreams and memories of humankind; hypotheses of the numinous and the secular. Explorations of trifurcated beliefs – even under the personified guises of pronouns 'I', 'you' and 'we' – remain inconclusive, lost in manifold tributaries of speculation. There can only be a returning and reliving, for as long as consciousness survives – or until the great mystery is solved. There is no choice. The journey never ends. Another 'wormhole' opens and...

I am dreaming of the sea. As undulant and black as melted lead, as restless as a serpent, it convolves and reforms, replicating an endless army of waves...

## THE END-LESS-NESS

Terry Oakes was born – and still lives – in Merthyr Tydfil, a post-industrial town in South Wales. Better known, for over two decades, as a book jacket and album cover illustrator – his work adorning novels ranging from the modern horror of Stephen King to the majestic sci-fi epics of Frank Herbert, alongside artwork for music recordings by artists as diverse as prog-rockers, Hawkwind, and punk performers, The Exploited. In recent years, Terry has been writing works of fiction, from poetry and short stories (collected together for the first time in *Welcome: Poems, Prose & Prosody*), to novels such as *The Murder Men*, and the upcoming sequel; *Savage Times*. Terry is currently working on the third book in The Murder Men trilogy.

WELCOME to…

Seven thought-provoking tales of unease. Ostensibly created to produce vicarious frissons, they nevertheless carry within them valid social, moral and ethical undercurrents that await the attention of any reader interested enough to excavate them.

Plus…

Fifty-one poems that have, on the other hand, been cut from a different cloth. More eclectic and universally inspired, they examine, through humour, satire, philosophy and religion – not to mention a certain rhythmic reportage – the established perceptions of life, destiny and death; even questioning, along the way, the very concept of existence itself.

Featuring thirteen, highly-detailed illustrations by the author, this rich collection of poems, prose and prosody, is filled with inquiry and social comment relevant to an age of instability, inequality and doubt.

WELCOME: poems, prose & prosody
by Terry Oakes


Available now from Intercept Studios

*...the fall unseen through the glare of neon...the scream unheard above the sounds of the street...the impact both seen and heard...body hitting the pavement like a watermelon...*

So begins THE MURDER MEN...

...In which London's hitherto disparate underworld factions have been consolidated into a single, self-serving Organisation. But now its architect – a clever upper-class villain, called Van Marco – is mysteriously attempting to undermine his own creation: the result of which forces a cast of misbegotten characters – pimps, call-girls, drug-dealers and killers – into a deadly struggle for power and control.

Set in locations as diverse as London, the Brecon Beacons, and finally the rain-soaked jungles of Brazil, THE MURDER MEN – by renowned book-jacket illustrator, Terry Oakes – is a violent, fast moving tale of intrigue, betrayal, sexual deviance and murder.

THE MURDER MEN
by Terry Oakes

Available now from Intercept Studios

TO KEEP UPDATED ON PRODUCT INFORMATION,
AND NEW RELEASES VISIT

# WWW.INTERCEPTSTUDIOS.COM

Printed in Great Britain
by Amazon

54946483R00132